Dedicated To
My father and stepmother,
Russell and Ada Dell Ford,
and good parents everywhere.

Marsha Orwigs
(A.K.A. L.M. Nisgow)

ELPIES AMONG US

Book Two of the Elpie Trilogy

By

L. M. Nisgow

BookCover Design by Todd Hebertson

BookCoverArt.webs.com

Special thanks, as usual, to my sister, Carol Riley, for her editing, reading, love and support.

ELPIES
AMONG US

CHAPTER ONE

She heard the click as the television in the living room switched on. Simon was in his workshop, and she was almost sure that Colder and Genevieve were upstairs. Elsie had already gone to investigate the sound when Bess walked into the living room. The dog was standing directly in front of the screen, staring at the message displayed there in large capital letters.

IN APPRECIATION OF THE ROLES YOU PLAYED IN CHANGING OUR SOCIETY, YOU ARE INVITED TO ATTEND OUR PLANET'S FIRST CELEBRATION OF THE REBIRTH. WE WOULD LIKE FOR YOU, BESS AND SIMON, GISELLA, AND TWO OF YOUR ANIMALS TO COME AS OUR GUESTS OF HONOR.

WE WILL COME FOR YOU AT 11:35 PM, IN THREE DAYS. ELI, RUTH, MARTHA, DULCIE, AND ANOTHER ELPIE WHO CLAIMS TO BE CLOSE TO YOU, HAVE ACCEPTED OUR INVITATION AND WILL BE ON BOARD. WE HOPE YOU WILL ACCEPT AS WELL.

YOUR BLUEMEN FRIENDS,
SVEN, MONA, MAURICE, AND LUCA PACIOLI

"Simon!" she screamed, simultaneously with his, "Bess!" as he came flying out of his workshop, running towards the house. She threw the backdoor open and ran to meet him.

He grabbed her by the shoulders, hands filthy with soil from his garden. His eyes were wide with excitement, and a smile huge enough to be frightening covered half his face. One look at that wild expression had Bess laughing and nodding at the obvious answer to her question. "You got the message on your screen, too?"

"We're going to see our Elpies again! I never thought it would happen! Our Elpies!" Simon was so overwhelmed that he forgot about the spade in his hand, nearly skewering himself when he tried to wipe the sweat from his forehead. They both turned then, as they heard a scream from Gisella's house, a hundred yards away on the property.

"Simon, Bess!" When she saw them out in the yard together, she knew they'd gotten the same invitation. She came rushing over to them, and they ran to meet her, with Madelyn, the golden mutt, by her side, and Elsie, the brown, by theirs.

Bess held up her hand, shouting, "Careful, careful, you don't need to be running!" Gisella was almost seven and a half months pregnant, and the sight of her running with her baby-belly bouncing in her outstretched hands was extremely unnerving to the three running to meet her. She laughed at the warning, and kept running on the wide cobblestoned path between their houses. Her doctor said she could keep doing whatever she normally did, as long as she was comfortable, and she had always run.

When the group collided, they hugged and laughed, and Gisella squealed with delight---a habit that she had never quite outgrown. "So are you going?"

"Of course, aren't you? Oh--I hadn't thought about---"

"No, I don't think I'd better, not when I'm this close, but I'll still get to see my other moms and Eli! I wonder who else is coming with them?"

"My guess would be my Colder," Bess answered. "He was a wonderful friend to me, and when he helped take care of Simon, he became very protective and attached to him, too. All six of the Colders who helped us would've probably come if they could have, but it sounds as if the Bluemen only had room for a few."

"Now all I have to do is figure out how to tell Hiram the truth." Gisella gave a small laugh and shook her head.

"You know I never told him anything because it would have made me sound crazy, and if my family had vouched for me, he would have thought my insanity was hereditary."

Bess suddenly gasped. "Three days? My parents are getting here this evening for their visit! They'll still be here, and they can meet everybody and take care of the kids while we're gone. Fantastic!"

Her "fantastic" was pronounced in sync with Simon's "Oh crap!"

"And what's wrong with my parents coming then? I've never told them anything for the same reason Gisella's never told Hiram---no proof. Now they can see with their own eyes, and I won't have to lie to them anymore. What a relief that would be!"

Simon was holding his hand over his face and shaking his head. "What's wrong? Well, your mom will be fine with it. She'll probably want to have them all over for dinner. But your dad---if he doesn't want to shoot them outright, or have us tested for drugs, then he'll probably suspect me of being an alien. In the last twenty years, we've seen them what, thirty times, maybe? And *every single time* he's remarked on my accent, saying there's 'something not quite right' about it, and then giving me the evil eye."

"Oh, come on, my dad doesn't give the evil eye. My parents adore you! And we can explain everything to them ahead of time, and then introduce them to Ishmael and---"

"Oh, even better! A telepathic black cat who plays chess. So your dad will think I'm a warlock, Ishmael's my familiar, and you've been under my power all these years!"

Bess turned to Gisella, shaking her head and rolling her eyes. Then, putting one arm around her shoulders and hooking the other arm through Simon's, she started walking them towards the house. "Come on, let's continue this discussion over a cup of tea---decaf, of course."

#

The house was a magnificent oddity. Three stories high, it was a mish-mash of styles: there were turrets here, domes there, an A-frame elevation on one corner, huge medieval looking fireplaces in the living area and den, stone walkways along the turreted areas of the roof, a modern looking sun deck on the second floor, a covered porch that encircled the whole house, and balconies in different spots on the second and third floor. There was even a domed room atop the third floor to use as an observatory, with small sofas and cushions for those who just wanted to sit and enjoy the view or meditate. The whole thing was made of natural stone and wood, giving it the feel and look of blending in and belonging to the beautiful land that surrounded it.

Simon's aunt Minerva, who had left the house, land, and her fortune to him, had loved so many different styles that she decided if she was going to build a house, she wouldn't limit herself to building it in just one. The house was a typical architect's nightmare, but she had managed to find one with imagination and an open mind, and he had pulled off a small miracle by building in multiple styles that somehow, when melded together into this house, just worked. And worked spectacularly. There was a wooded area between the house and a large lake, and the third floor looked over the woods to a view of it, with the lower floors looking out on the part of the lake that stretched out to the side of the woods.

They went into the kitchen and Bess put three mugs in the microwave. Gisella sat grinning and patting Simon on the back, after he sulkily threw himself into a chair and put his head down on the huge wooden table, slowly banging his forehead up and down on it.

Laughing at the dramatics, Bess swatted him on the back of the head with the unopened newspaper from the table. "What is with you? You've never had a problem with my dad before."

He turned his head slightly and peered up at her with one eye. "Not a fighting, screaming, insult slinging type of problem. But have you *really* never noticed that he smiles and shakes my hand, but then always steps back and looks at me with this skeptical tilt of his head? I don't know what I've done to deserve his mistrust---now don't say there's not an issue---he just doesn't act the same with you around. I think he's never bought our story about how we met, and Gisella's relationship to me, and it makes him suspicious."

"Well, probably because it's all a lie, and my dad has *always* been able to sniff out a lie. Geez, when I was a kid, I couldn't get away with *anything*. Even more reason to be glad that they'll be here to see the Bluemen and the Elpies. Once we can finally level with him, he won't be suspicious of you anymore. He really does love you, because he knows that you love me, you make me happy, you're obviously a good provider, you were a partner in making healthy, beautiful babies, and you're a wonderful father to his beloved grandchildren. Those are the things that matter most to him. Even if he didn't like you, he'd love you because of those gifts you've brought to my life."

"But why does he always pick on my accent? I've explained to him over and over that I had American parents but was raised in England, so that I have, as you called it, an English accent with a 'swirl' of American. It seems like a very personal dig, and something just between the two of us, like he's 'on to me.' Faking an accent for twenty years would get pretty tiresome, I should think. And by the way, thanks for saying those nice things about me. All true, of course. You are such a lucky woman."

Smiling at him, she smoothed down the hair that she'd stood on end with her swat. "That I am, that I am."

Gisella brightened as she thought of the coming revelations. "Once they know the truth, I'll be able to tell Gramps and Grandma why I always spent so much time with 'the caretakers.' Oh, wow, my parents are going to be so excited to finally meet everybody. Especially the

Bluemen. They've talked so often about how much we all owe them, and how they'd love to be able to thank them. Wait 'til I tell them!

"Bess, I think I'll let you two hash this out in private while I head back to our house. I want to call my folks and then plan a strategy before Hiram gets home. When I call you, can you send Ishmael over?"

Bess nodded as she moved with her own mug to sit across from Simon. "Sure thing."

She kissed the both of them and headed back to her house, with Madelyn by her side.

"I can help convince Hiram, too," the dog sent.

"Thanks, Maddie. I have a feeling 'Mr. Logical' will need all the convincing he can get."

##

"We need to call Eli and see if he can drive down from college for this. After we've talked about the first Eli and the Bluemen all these years, he'd never forgive us if he missed this."

Simon had deigned to put his head up like a big boy and was sipping his tea, resigned to his fate. "I can't wait to see the kids' faces when they meet everybody. With Ishmael and the dogs the way they are, they've always believed our story, and yet---sometimes I think they have a little trouble buying the whole saga. They just accept that they have exceptional animals that they can't talk about, and that their parents, Gisella and the animals have telepathy with each other. Be nice for them to know once and for all that their folks aren't really crazy or prone to exaggerating just a wee bit.

"And I can't wait to see Eli—the Elpie Eli. Uh-oh, do you know how confusing this is going to be? Especially if, as you suspect, the other Elpie is your Colder, as you always called him. You really should have given him and the others names."

Bess looked slightly offended at this last statement. "If you recall, I was kind of busy trying to keep you alive."

Simon looked at her for a moment without speaking, then stood and walked to the other side of the table so that he could stand behind her chair. Putting his arms around her, he leaned over and nestled his cheek next to hers as he said quietly, "And you did, my love. You did."

CHAPTER TWO

Gisella hung up the phone after imparting the news to her parents, Viola and Tom. The two were thrilled, as she'd known they would be. She'd never thought of them as anything other than her parents—and only the best parents in the world, at that. They had taken her as a foster when she was only two days old, and they'd fallen in love with her almost immediately. Their hope had been to adopt and make her their daughter by law. In their hearts and minds she already was, but their feelings had no legal standing. When Gisella was five years old, her birth mother was released from prison and she'd been given custody, effectively tearing apart their family and their lives.

Besides being abusive and making plans to turn her daughter's life into even more of a living Hell as she got older, the woman had also put Gisella into a situation that likely would have ended with her murder, had not the Bluemen intervened and taken her away.

The Bluemen had temporarily left her on a planet inhabited by the Elpies, a species that looked like man-sized lizards, and communicated by telepathy. They were also empaths, which gave them an uncommon compassion for all creatures. Bess, Simon, and the Elpies---in particular, Eli and his wives, the three sisters whose names Gisella had taken on her falsified birth certificate, had been her family on the Elpies' planet. The thought of seeing that part of her "family" again was overwhelmingly emotional for her. Of course, her hormones made *everything* overwhelmingly emotional for her these days, but this time, she welcomed the experience.

The Bluemen had provided all the falsified documentation and changed computer memories all over creation in order for Gisella to be on record as an orphan, legally adopted by Bess and Simon Sayers. This in turn allowed her to actually *live* with Tom and Viola in the beautiful caretaker's house on the Sayers' estate. Bess and Simon kept a bedroom for her in the main house, for appearances and for when she wanted to spend the night with them and their family, but she had spent most of her time with her *parents,* Tom and Viola.

They had given up their old life in the U.S and come to Canada to live, for the sole purpose of having their *daughter* back with them. Before her abduction by the Bluemen, the two had even been planning to kidnap her and go on the run, in order to save their child from a situation that they knew in their hearts would destroy her.

Part of her wanted desperately to go with the group on their excursion to the Bluemen's planet, but the thought of space travel possibly affecting her pregnancy was too much of a risk. And even if there had been no danger, the idea that she could deliver early without Hiram being present at his child's birth was unthinkable. No, she would just have to satisfy herself with the little time she could spend with the Elpies when they came to pick up Simon and Bess.

Her parents had always encouraged her to develop her talents, and with Simon happy to bankroll anything she wanted to try, she'd taken dancing and singing lessons. The results of those lessons had enabled her, at the ripe old age of sixteen, to be accepted into a prestigious fine arts academy. A scout looking for a fresh young talent for a Broadway production had spotted her there, and from then on, her career had taken off.

At first, she'd loved the dancing and singing, even with all the prep involved, the long hours of rehearsal and the occasional overbearing or snitty director or choreographer. She enjoyed doing something that she was exceptionally good at, and having people admire her for it. Being in front of a huge audience and seeing the smiles, hearing the applause and "Bravo's" had been a heady experience for a teenager, but she'd been grounded enough to resist the temptation to believe all the hype. She knew who she was, and no one could persuade her to be someone else.

After two years of being a "star," Gisella realized that she wanted more out of life. She wanted her life to have more value than a couple of hours of entertainment for people out on the town. She began to think about the things that meant the most to her in life---the things that had affected her profoundly and made her understand that life was a priceless gift. It wasn't long before she knew what she wanted to do with the rest of hers.

Packing her bags, she said farewell to the lights, and went to college to train as a physical therapist. Other than seeing Simon brought back from the dead, nothing in her life had moved her as much as seeing her Elpie friend, Jonas, Eli's son, have his damaged arm and leg made whole again. He'd suffered a stroke from an injury sustained during a kidnap attempt, and was left with a partially paralyzed arm and leg as a result. She remembered how bravely he had dealt with his new infirmities, and how Eli and his wives had worked with him every day to restore what mobility they could to his affected extremities. When the Bluemen came and were made aware of the injury, for which they were partly responsible, they'd healed him.

When he'd come running out of that ship, running without a limp, and waving his arms—*both* arms at her, she'd never felt such awe and elation. Jonas had grabbed her hands and danced a hula and then did the twist--dances she'd taught him---and she had laughed for joy and danced with him. To see in his eyes what the restoration of his limbs meant to him had moved her so deeply that she knew this was something she wanted to make happen for other people, and especially other children who had been left damaged through no fault of their own.

She'd never regretted her choice. Opening her practice, and having her own clinic with state of the art equipment on the estate grounds, thanks to Simon, had been the best decision of her life. To see the faces of children when they walked on their own for the first time after an injury or illness, or when they used a previously useless arm or hand, was more fulfilling to her than anything she could have imagined. She'd cried often in her practice, and most of the tears had been happy ones.

Her career had also brought her the love of her life, her husband, Hiram. A pediatric neurologist, he had known of her first by reputation. Many of his colleagues had referred patients to her and none had any but high praise for the results of her work. After referring a few patients to her on their recommendations, he'd decided to go out himself and visit her woodland clinic, to meet her and watch her work for an afternoon.

Even if he hadn't wanted to meet her, he'd wanted to get a look at her clinic. All the patients he'd referred to her had talked about the beautiful grounds it was on, and how patient and family friendly it was inside and out.

After showing his ID to a guard at the gate to the estate, he'd followed a long, winding road flanked by huge trees, whose branches met to make a canopy overhead. He'd eventually come to a large, one story stone and wood house that exuded serenity and the promise of shelter, nestled in the woods as it was. A shaded porch with swings and rockers looked out onto a playground containing handicapped accessible equipment. Parents could relax and watch or help their children play while they waited to be seen.

Stocked with everything from toddler books to the classics, the library inside was spacious and filled with comfortable couches, tables with height adjustable seating, and had large bean bag chairs strewn about the room. Two recliners were also available for those patients who needed to rest either before or after their treatments.

But by far the most important component of the library, at least as far as most of the children were concerned, was the added delight of having Madelyn, Gisella's big, golden, therapy mutt, come in and mingle with them as they read. She always seemed to know who could use a good cuddle, or just needed a warm, soft body to lean on while reading.

It was not only the little ones that Madelyn gravitated to. On occasion, there would be a parent there who had hit the wall. Between watching their children suffer on a daily basis and often substituting themselves as the affected limb or function for them, dealing with overwhelming expenses, trying to run households that included other children, and attempting to give everyone what they needed, many parents had times when they felt that they couldn't go on. They would never voice these emotions to other adults, for fear it would seem that they begrudged the time and effort spent on behalf of their children. Yet they couldn't help but feel the strain and the drain of energy that being on constant duty invariably caused.

When one of these parents was present, Madelyn always sensed it. She would go and lay her head in the lap of the stricken adult, sometimes making eye contact, sometimes not. Simply in being singled out by the dog, the parent was made to understand that someone felt that stress and frustration, and offered compassion without judgement. Parents *and* children adored her, for she seemed to bring an aura of peace and solace to wherever she chose to wander in the clinic.

Beyond the library was an indoor pool in a sunroom that could be left open to fresh air on one side in good weather, and closed off and heated during the cold months. The room itself was decorated in greenery, white wicker chairs, and soft, coordinated colors, so that it felt more like a vacation spot than a therapy site. Beyond the sunroom was another chamber with equipment typically seen in a rehab and therapy area, but even this room had been painstakingly decorated to make it feel as if the patient was working in someone's home instead of a clinic.

Hiram was already impressed by the facility, and then he saw *her*.

One look at her, with her dark brown, silky hair put up in a no-nonsense ponytail, sky blue eyes with long, dark lashes, and full pink lips in a heart-shaped face, and he was smitten. When he introduced himself, he actually found himself stumbling for words—something that rarely happened to him. After he'd regained his composure, accepted her thanks for his referrals, and received her gracious acceptance of him as an uninvited observer for the rest of the day, he'd found himself impressed and inspired as he watched her in action.

She'd encouraged, wheedled, charmed, whined, bullied, or cheered her clients into performing whatever exercises she deemed necessary for their recovery. She could be the gentlest of coaxing angels, or the most cold-hearted monster of a taskmaster, according to what her clients needed that day to succeed. But regardless of which method or persona she had to affect with each client, they were all aware that she was working to make them whole again, would hold nothing back of herself to effect that change, and would let *them* hold nothing back, either.

What he saw as he watched her work was dedication, skill, and love for her calling and the people it served. And all this in such a beautiful package. He came *to observe* twice more before he finally drummed up the courage to ask her out.

Gisella, or "Dulcie," as he knew her, found Hiram's shyness appealing and unexpected in a doctor. Her experience with physicians had been mixed. Since most MD's were usually more intelligent than the average person and many were truly brilliant, some inevitably succumbed to the *God Complex*. Being told since they were very young that they were extraordinary, or geniuses, they eventually accepted the idea that they were superior beings, and found speaking with mere mortals tedious and beneath them---an attitude easily discerned by those spoken to. Their patients tended to respect their knowledge and loathe their arrogance.

Then there were the doctors who understood that their intellect was a gift. Yes, they had worked themselves half to death to achieve their goals, and yes, they probably had higher IQ's than seventy-five percent of the people they knew. But the physicians in this group also knew that they would not have been able to accomplish all that they had, were they not gifted with a capable mind to begin with, through no effort on their part, and that many other people had contributed to their success. These doctors tended to behave as if all human beings had value, regardless of their stations in life, and generally their patients not only admired their intelligence, but also loved them for the respect and care they received at their hands.

Hiram Guinness was of the latter persuasion. Having graduated from high school at fourteen, now at thirty-two, he was at the top of his field, admired and respected by colleagues and patients alike. He loved children, and had a way about him—a quiet confidence that could calm even the most anxious children and give courage to the most devastated parents.

Their courtship had been brief, for they both knew they'd found "the one," almost from the first date. Hiram had an insatiable curiosity about *everything*, an enthusiasm and quirky sense of humor that Gisella totally "got." Ever a gentleman, he treated her like the treasure she was. His patients and their parents loved him for his skill and for making them feel as if they truly mattered to him, which they did. And for icing, Gisella found him quite easy to look at, with blond hair, blue eyes, and a well-trimmed beard that actually accentuated his good looks.

When they were married, "Dulcie" convinced him to take up residence in her two story stone house on the Sayers estate so that she could continue to have her practice right next door. Since Hiram got along well with her parents, (whom he believed to be the caretakers), *and* the Sayers, and the house was paid for and beautiful to boot, it wasn't a hard sell.

Overjoyed at the prospect of becoming a dad, Hiram had pressed her to take off of work a full two months before the baby was due, "just to be on the safe side." Although she missed her patients, she hadn't minded getting to sleep in and then having a leisurely cup of decaf while she sat out on their deck in the mornings and looked at the woods just beyond.

She would have considered her life ideal except for the fact that she hadn't been able to share her past with Hiram. As much as he loved her, she knew he'd never believe a story like hers. She'd had to lie about why everyone in her family called her "Gisella," while he had always known her as "Dulcie." She'd had to lie about so many things concerning her past, and that was no way to start a marriage. This coming event was the answer to everything. She'd never have to lie to him again.

The tricky thing was going to be preparing him for the meeting while preventing him from sending her to the nuttery before the meeting could bear her out.

##

Three hours after she got the news, she heard his key turning in the lock. She'd put on the blue sweater that he always said accentuated her eyes, and put her hair up in a chignon, a style he loved on her—"the better to nibble your neck," he'd say. She met him at the door with a smile and a passionate kiss that he was quick to reciprocate.

He laughed and raised his eyebrows. "Hormonal surge, or just my incredible masculinity driving you wild?" Strolling to the dining room table and dumping his briefcase unceremoniously, he turned back then to give his full attention to her neck. Reaching out and enfolding her in his arms, he began to kiss and nip the nape of her neck, saying the expected, "The better to nibble your neck, said the Big Bad Wolf."

She let him finish his nibbling and then turned to look him in the eyes and uttered those words that strike fear into the heart of any man in his right mind: "Honey, we need to talk."

The look of absolute dread that came over his face was so pitiful that she had to laugh. "Oh, Hiram, don't look like that. It's nothing bad. Actually, this is wonderful news."

He looked a little relieved by those words, but apprehension was still lingering in his eyes as she dragged him by the hand to sit with her on the loveseat in the den. He hadn't said a word, but stared at her with eyes wide, awaiting her pronouncement as she settled herself to face him, sitting sideways on the cushion.

"Okay, I'm going to tell you the whole truth about my past, and that includes the past of everyone that lives on this estate. Please let me finish before you say or do anything, because you're not going to believe most of what I tell you. That's why I've never told you before, because I really couldn't prove it, and I knew you'd think I was a nut job. But in three days, I'll be able to prove everything to you.

"Before I say anything else, you have to promise me two things."

"When could I ever deny you anything?"

"Hiram, I am deadly serious about this."

"Okay, I promise."

"First, you have to swear that you will not talk to anyone about what I'm going to tell you. Ever."

"Done."

"Next, you have to promise me that you will wait the three days for my proof to arrive before you take any action."

"I swear."

"All right. To start with, Dulcie is the name on my fake birth certificate. Dulcie Martha Ruth. My real name is Gisella, and I was born in prison."

And so her story began. She told him everything. She told him about being abducted by the Bluemen only moments before she would likely have been killed by her stepfather. She told him about her life with the Elpies and Bess and Simon, and about Simon's poisoning, and his death and resurrection via the Bluemen. She told him about the telepathy she shared with Bess and Simon, and the animals on the estate, and how when Simon had generously proposed a way for her to live with her parents without the risk of them being accused of kidnapping, the Bluemen had arranged everything. And finally, she told him about all of their roles in helping the Bluemen convince The Seated to allow "The Rebirth" on their world, and the subsequent invitation to go with them to their planet to celebrate its anniversary.

All through her story, Hiram had sat in silence, concentrating on every word coming from her mouth. Now tears filled his eyes, and his voice shook as he took her hands in his.

"Dulcie, you should have told me all of this before. We can get you help. There's no shame in…. in…. having a problem. Know that I will be with you every step of the way, and that nothing in this world could make me stop loving you. Hormones can have *unbelievable* effects on the brains of some people, and chances are, after the baby is born, you'll be fine---maybe you won't even need medication."

She sighed and rolled her eyes, taking her hands out of his. "I knew you'd react like this. I don't even blame you. It's a crazy story. But you *have to* honor your promise to do nothing until the Bluemen arrive in three days and I can prove all of this to you."

"Of course. Three more days. And then you can see that this is all a delusion, and that you need to let me help you. I'll wait the three days if you agree that when the three days are over and no aliens appear, you'll come with me to a therapist. I'm sure we can find someone who specializes in this kind of thing. The 'prenatal crazies' are nothing new. In the middle ages, anemic pregnant women who craved raw meat, sometimes thought they were turning into werewolves!" He gave a desperate sounding laugh, and took her hands back into his.

She took her hands back and went to the phone. "Actually, you'll only have to wait three days to meet the *Elpies* and the *Bluemen.* I can supply you with some corroborating evidence before then."

She picked up the phone and dialed Bess. "Hey Bess, could you send Ishmael over now? Thanks. Yeah, let him know."

"Hiram, remember when we went swimming at my parents' house on the fourth of July?" He nodded. "Do you remember remarking on Simon's body---how his muscles didn't look like the muscles of a fifty-four year old man? You said his muscle tone looked like it belonged to someone in his twenties, and you wondered if he took HGH or some other weird supplement. You also mentioned that he had the most perfect teeth you'd ever seen. Well, that's because his muscles *are* only twenty years old, as are his teeth. The Bluemen replaced his muscles, internal organs, and even his teeth, because the poison had damaged everything. They *made* his teeth perfect and they also did something to them to keep them from ever having cavities."

He nodded again, but said nothing.

"You know how you love playing 'the Cat' on the 'Beat the Cat Chess Web?' Well, how would you like to finally meet 'the Cat?'"

He sighed and threw up his hands. "That would be a dream for me, of course, but what does that have to do with anything?"

In answer to a faint scratching sound, Gisella went to the front door and opened it wide. In walked Ishmael, tail and head held high as he walked straight to Hiram, and stopping directly in front of him, sat and stared into his eyes.

"Meet 'the Cat,'" she said, as she bowed slightly and gestured towards Ishmael.

CHAPTER THREE

"That is a very impressive trick, Dulcie. I don't know how you trained him to do that right on cue, but it doesn't prove anything. He's still just a cat."

Ishmael suddenly stood on his hind legs, and with one front paw on Hiram's knee, stretched out the other and slapped his face, making the man flinch back in surprise.

Gisella decided it was time to play her trump card. "Maybe his winning a game from you might help to open your eyes."

Hiram was beginning to get annoyed at this little charade. "*Sure*, that'd be *great*. Just how do we do this?"

"Well," she said, pulling a keyboard out from the back of the coat closet, "I just happen to have a specially made keyboard in my possession, for when he likes to have a game here. Fire up your lap top and I'll set him up on mine, and then I'll leave the two of you alone to duke it out."

He watched her first with annoyance and then growing trepidation when she'd finished arranging her PC and keyboard for the cat and he immediately jumped up on the chair in front of the screen. Ishmael sat, wiggled him rump a bit until he was comfortable, then looked at Hiram and bowed his head politely, in a tacit suggestion that he should begin the play.

"I'll just be out on the deck having a lemonade to cool down these pesky 'crazies.' You boys let me know when you're done." Gisella smiled sweetly and walked out onto the deck, closing the door behind her.

Two hours later, a pale and shaky Hiram came out on the deck and sat down beside her.

"He won."

"You shouldn't look surprised. He usually beats you, doesn't he? Where is he now?"

He swallowed and looked slightly ill as his eyes drifted to the door. "When we finished, he switched functions and typed that he was bored and would like to go home to supper. So I let him out. I let the cat out after he beat me at chess."

She leaned back in her chair and passed him her lemonade. He took it and drained the rest of the glass before leaning back into his own chair. "So—he has Bess' memories, and the dogs have Simon's. Where's Madelyn?"

"She was hiding out until Ishmael softened you up a bit. She's sort of timid, you know."

Gisella stood up then and went inside to sit down on the couch, looking at him and motioning to the cushion beside her, and he obediently followed her and sat as ordered. Patting his hand, she called, "Madelyn, you can come out now. He's not mad, and I swear he won't get hysterical." Then to Hiram, she said softly, "She saw someone in Simon's memory get hysterical once, and it scared her to death."

The dog peeked apprehensively around the corner and looked at Hiram and then Gisella for one last assurance before entering the room. She looked to be a mix of Rottweiler and Golden Retriever, with beautiful golden fur, a wonderfully expressive face, the powerful build of a Rottie, and ears that flopped over at the tips and looked too small for her head.

Hiram softened at the look in her eyes---he'd always been a pushover. When he saw someone distressed, he was compelled to try and soothe away the fear. He called gently, "Come here, Maddie. I swear I won't go crazy on you."

That was all it took to bring her bounding into the room, mouth open and tail wagging. She sat in front of him, waiting for something good to happen—a common pastime in well-treated dogs.

"So—she can understand me when I talk, and the two of you, and Bess and Simon and Elsie---oh, and of course, the chess master, can all speak to each other telepathically, right?"

"Correct."

"Ah, well, is there anything she wants to tell me?"

Gisella looked at Madelyn for a minute and then started laughing.

"Want to let *me* in on the joke?"

"I'm sorry, honey. Madelyn wanted you to know that the pepperoni pizza with extra garlic that you had for lunch is giving you delicious smelling breath, but she detects a bit of a problem, and thinks you should either take an antacid or eat some grass." Gisella started laughing again, Hiram looked mortified and left to go brush his teeth and find a mint, and Madelyn just looked confused.

He was back in a few minutes, and sat back down. "Okay, I did have pizza for lunch, and with everything that's happened since I came home, my stomach *is* feeling a little off. But—you could have smelled it on my breath, and you know how my stomach is. I need a little more to be convinced.

"Madelyn, will you go to the bookcase over there and bring me back the book titled 'Basketball Greats'? Please?" he added.

The dog nodded and went to the bookshelf. Turning her head to the side in order to read the titles, she found the correct book after a moment, pulled it out with her paw just far enough to grasp it in her jaws, and trotted back to him. She placed it gently into his outstretched hand, and then sat and waited for thanks, a pat, or a treat.

Hiram stoked her head and looked at Gisella with the beginnings of a smile. "Wow, this is starting to get really exciting, Dulcie---uh, do you want me to call you Gisella? It *is* a beautiful name, and it suits you."

"It would be wonderful to hear you calling me by my real name, and not to feel like I'm deceiving you all the time. I want us to share everything, and it's been so hard to always avoid the truth. So are you a believer, for sure?"

"If this is all a crazy delusion, it would make you the best animal trainer in the universe. Even though I can't really believe it yet, I can't not believe it either. I'm actually starting to get pretty psyched about meeting the aliens. I can't believe I just said that. What a woman I've got. Beautiful, sexy, smart, *and* she has intergalactic connections! All right!"

CHAPTER FOUR

Things didn't go quite as well at the main house. Even after arriving at almost midnight, the next morning Bess' parents, Sarah and Angus McPhinney, were still up at the crack of dawn. They'd already made themselves breakfast and eaten, and Bess' mom was busy making biscuits for the rest of the family by the time Bess and Simon made it to the kitchen. Bess let her take the last pan out of the oven before she herded the two into the living room and told them the whole truth and nothing but.

When she finally finished her tale, there was silence for a few minutes, and then her mother sat back, slapped her knees with her hands, and announced cheerily, "Well, I guess I'd better get to the store and pick up some supplies. Your friends may be from another planet, but I bet they won't be able to resist my double fudge caramel macaroons. Haven't met an alien yet that could! I'll make some to have with coffee for when they get here, and put the rest in bags so you'll have something to snack on during the trip."

Her husband looked at her as if she were insane. Bess smiled and nodded, and Simon went to her, hugged her and kissed her on the cheek. Angus looked at Simon, and asked bluntly, "You're an alien, aren't you?"

"Dad!"

Simon threw up his hands, gave Bess an "I told you so" look and left the room.

"Dad, how could you talk to him like that, when we just told you the whole story? I mean, I know it's unbelievable, but that's why we've waited until now to tell you—when we'll have proof. You'll *meet* proof. And believe me, he's not an alien. I just told you about what happened to him, and that he actually died. The Bluemen did some kind of resuscitation thing and then regrew his damaged organs. But I saw him suffer. I watched him die an agonizing, slow death. I was with him almost constantly, and I can tell you, he had very human symptoms and complications."

"So they took him on the ship and grew everything back all new and perky. Were you with him the whole time on the ship?"

"Of course not. If he were here on Earth, I wouldn't be standing and watching everything in an operating room, either."

"So how do you know that's really *him* you got back and not an alien? For all you know, they might have flushed his remains and sent in their own replicant."

"Oh, Dad, that's just horrible. Do you think your grandchildren are half alien, then? Because I guarantee that he and I made them together. And we used the human method, if you get my drift."

"Come on, now, I don't want to hear about that, I'm your father."

"How do I *know* you're my father? When you were in the Army, and got sent overseas, how did mom know when you came back, that you weren't some replicant that the military was experimenting on? How did she know for sure that your plane wasn't abducted by aliens, who replaced all the soldiers with their alien doubles, so that they could seed American women with alien offspring and eventually take over the government? Wow, that would explain a lot, come to think of it. Like how you *always* win at Monopoly and Gin Rummy. That's pretty other worldly."

"Hoo hoo, one to the gut, dear!" her mom cheered.

"Now there's no reason to get yourself in a snit. I'm just trying to cover all the bases."

"Dad, Simon and the kids are everything to me. I wouldn't have the kids or Gisella if not for him. I would go back to that planet a hundred times if that's what it took to have him in my life. If he's an alien and my children are aliens, then God Bless aliens, because they're the best things that ever happened to me."

"Now, Bess, you know I dote on those kids. There's nothing wrong with *them*."

"They came by way of their dad, so either they're okay and he's okay, or they're *all* aliens."

"Okay, *enough*." Simon had come back into the room after getting his temper tamped down, determined to put a stop to the arguing.

"Angus, Mom," (he couldn't bring himself to call him 'Dad' and didn't think Angus would like it anyway). "We could have continued to lie to you for the rest of our lives. But it kills Bess to keep lying to you, the parents she adores. She's had adventures that she'd love to share with you—stories that will let you experience another world with her. She can't do that with anyone but our kids, and she doesn't even talk about all of it to them. You're her parents, the most important people in the world to her, next to the kids and me. She's been so excited to finally be able to share this with you. Please don't ruin it for her with whatever it is you have against *me*, Angus."

"Here, here, Simon. I, for one, am thrilled at the opportunity to meet your friends. This is the chance of a lifetime, and if Angus is too pigheaded to admit that, then he should just go home. By himself. I'm staying and I'm *making cookies, dammit!*" Sarah walked over to Simon, gave *him* a hug and a kiss on the cheek and pronounced to Angus, "This is *my* son-in-law, and every woman should be so lucky as to have their daughter marry a man who loves her like he does, and *tries* to love her family, *like he has*. If they can replicate him, they *should*. That's all I have to say on the matter, and it's all you should too, Angus." He stared at her with his mouth hanging open as she spun on her heels and went back to the kitchen.

Simon smiled to himself as he watched her go. *I really do love that woman. No wonder I love her daughter.*

Elsie, a very large, brown, Malinois/Mastiff/Lab/? mix, had been listening to everything from behind the couch. Now she stood up and walked over to Angus, put a huge paw on his knee, and shook her head at him. He pushed her paw away, and Elsie looked at Bess to translate.

"Elsie wants me to tell you that she has Simon's memories, and they're all human."

"Oh, come on, Bess, you really expect me to believe that a stupid dog is sending me telepathic messages through you?"

Elsie put her paw back on his leg, gave a long, blood-chilling growl, followed by a snarl that exposed most of her very impressive teeth, and with her face almost level with his, locked eyes with him and nodded slowly.

"Okay, you're not stupid."

Simon sat down next to Bess and called Elsie to come to him. He stroked her back as he sent to her, once more, that she was a great dog. She leaned into him as he spoke again.

"Angus, I would really just like to know, once and for all, what it is that makes you so antagonistic towards me. You've always tried to hide it from Bess, and until tonight, she bought your act. I never dwelt on it, because I didn't want to put her in the middle. But Eli should be driving in from college this afternoon, and I don't want there to be any hostility between us to spoil this for him. He's so happy about getting to meet everyone, especially the Elpie he's named after."

"You named your son after a *lizard*?"

Bess raised her chin defiantly. "We named *all* our sons after lizards, and our daughter's named after a cat. Deal with it, Dad."

"So what is it really about, Angus? And don't tell me it's my accent."

Angus sighed, and looked at his hands for a minute or so while they all waited for his answer.

"Maybe I *have* been a horse's ass all these years. It's just that I knew you were all lying, and it was easier to take out my anger at that on you than on Bess. I loved my little girl too much to want to hold a grudge against her. Never had a problem holding one against you, though. I couldn't just call you all a bunch of liars. Sarah would've killed me."

"I still may," came from the kitchen.

"It was all just too perfect, you know? We'd never even heard about you and all of a sudden you're engaged and you're paying for this huge wedding. How everything worked out with the adoption of Dulcie just in time for you to be married, and you not having *any* relatives for us to meet---oh, and I am very sorry for your loss, by the way—I wasn't making light of that.

"All this money and the estate you just happened to inherit. It was all too perfect, and life isn't like that. Even your *teeth* are too perfect—who has teeth that straight and white? And your fancy-shmancy but not quite right accent. Plus the fact that this gal here could never lie to me worth squat. I couldn't stand the thought that Bess might be married to some big time criminal or phony. I just couldn't stand it.

"Maybe I *should* apologize to you, but the spitefulness has gotten to be a habit. I get irritated just thinking about you, and I know that's not fair. At least, I know it now."

Simon said gently, "I don't need an apology from you, Angus. I can understand how you must have felt---I have a daughter, too. I just need a change. I'll try to let it go if you'll do the same. I love your little girl too much to hold a grudge against her dad. Shall we?" He crossed the room to where Angus was sitting and held out his hand. Angus just looked at it for a few seconds before standing and taking it in his own. Bess was almost in tears at the sight, until she realized that both men were squeezing as hard as they could, while trying to out-stare the other.

"Will you two *stop it* and act like grown-ups?"

They dropped their hands and smirked at each other.

"New start, *Dad*?" Simon asked, speaking the last in a raspy voice and grabbing his throat as if choking on the word.

"New start, *Son,*" he replied and then turned to the side and stuck his finger down his throat, gagging.

Both men, Bess, and her mom, who was watching from the kitchen door, cracked up at their displays, and the laughter did wonders to brighten the room.

CHAPTER FIVE

Masses of fire red curls seemed to be bouncing across the room by themselves, until the little head beneath them presented a face from between the manic locks. Eight year old Genevieve had been skipping and running around the house, chasing her nine year old brother, Colder, for the last half hour, every so often stopping to run back to Bess or Simon for a hug and to ask one more time, "We're *really, for sure*, going to meet the Elpies and the Bluemen?"

All their lives, they'd hear stories about the lizard people and the spacemen. They had two dogs and a cat that could understand everything they said, and who could talk to their parents with their minds, and the cat could play chess, but the children had grown up knowing this and had just taken their animals for granted. They'd understood early on that they could never tell their friends any of this, and since their pets acted like regular animals when their friends were over, they would have looked like liars if they'd said anything anyway.

But this! This was something *rad!* They were going to meet aliens! Colder and Genevieve couldn't stop talking about it, and even their Grandpa was starting to get a little excited. He was even acting friendlier to their dad, which they noticed right away. One of their brothers, Jonas, who was sixteen and so barely spoke to them at all sometimes, was so hyped that he'd been joking with them and swinging them up in the air the way their dad did. He forgot to act all teenagerish with them when he was happy. The rest of the time, he kind of acted like it was his job.

To make things really perfect, their oldest brother, Eli, had come home for the event. He was nineteen and actually liked his younger siblings. It was always fun when he came home, and it seemed like he was always taller, too. He was already taller than his dad, at six-six, and the doctor said he wasn't through growing. All of them were tall, with Genevieve at five-five, Colder at five-six, and Jonas at five-eleven. The kids at school called them the "Giant Family."

Eli said that when he was in high school, in English, they'd had to read a book called "Giants In the Earth." They'd had a test on the book, and the one and only instruction for the test, which was supposed to be essay, was, "Explain what this book is about, in your own words." There was one kid in the class who hadn't read the book and knew he was going to fail anyway, so for his answer, he just wrote, "The Sayers' Family Memoirs." Even the teacher laughed at that one before she flunked him.

That was all right with Genevieve, because she knew that being tall was cool, and the kids who made fun of her probably did it just as a joke or out of jealousy, neither of which bothered her one bit. Her mom was five-eleven and her dad, six-four. Before she'd started getting her height, a friend of hers who was staying over one night was looking out the window of her bedroom, watching her mom walking down the driveway. "Wow, your mom looks like a queen when she walks," she'd said.

Genevieve had never really thought about it before—that was just her mom and that was just the way she always walked. But after that, she'd started watching her mom, and her friend had been right—she did look sort of queenly. She had black wavy hair that grew a few inches below her shoulders, a straight nose and really cool, light golden-brown eyes with black circles around the irises that made them appear even lighter. A smattering of freckles over fair skin completed the picture. She still had a comely figure at forty-eight, though she now had to work to keep her figure, to her great annoyance.

She'd asked her mom about it one night—how she did it exactly. How she managed to look like a queen. She'd laughed and then told her that *she* was going to be tall someday, too, probably even taller than her. Her mom had said that the trick to looking and feeling proud when you were tall, was to always walk with your back straight and your shoulders back, and the rest of your body would just know what to do. She'd said walking tall made a person feel confident and in control. And she'd said to never, ever, ever slouch. Slouching made you look like you were ashamed of yourself, or unhealthy, or just afraid to let people see who you really were.

On that particular day, she was of an age where she truly listened to what her mom said, and she took the whole talk to heart. From that day forward, she walked like her mom had told her to, and when she started getting tall, it really did make her feel cool. Other people noticed the way she walked then, and when they teased her about being tall, she could tell that they really didn't think it was a bad thing.

And *then* she had seen that movie, with the princess that had hair just like hers, all red and bouncy with curls. Genny's wasn't that long yet, but after the movie she'd decided to let her hair grow all the way to the floor, and then when she walked, she really would look like a queen. So far, her hair was only a few inches past her shoulders, and her mom said that if it kept growing, they might need to "discuss her options."

The kids had all drifted into the kitchen at the smell of Grandma's double-fudge caramel macaroons just coming out of the oven. She was making about a thousand of them, so she pretended not to notice when some mysteriously disappeared off the counter where she had spread them out to cool.

Standing around together, the youngsters looked like a bunch of pencils with hair. All of them were rail-thin except for Eli, who had put on a lot of muscle in the past few years. He was the spitting image of Simon, and the most like him in personality---usually patient and naturally kind, but energetic and adventurous as well, and a consummate extrovert. He treated everybody he met like an old friend, which was what his acquaintances usually became, because he was impossible to dislike. Bess' one obvious influence on him was that he was majoring in art.

Colder had honey colored hair and baby blue eyes, with smooth, olive skin and perpetually rosy cheeks, much to his dismay. With his height and looks, Bess was having to inform older teenage girls, on a more and more frequent basis, that he was only nine and way too young to have *any* girls calling him, much less fifteen year olds. She teased him about it, but she secretly worried that his appearance might influence him to try and grow up too fast.

She needn't have worried. Laid back and unconcerned about it, Colder was happy to just be a kid, and to let his mom handle the "crazy, boy-hungry girls." They could find somebody else to giggle about. He wasn't in any rush to be a slave to raging hormones, (he'd read that in a book somewhere), like Jonas. His brother would be himself until some girl spoke to him, and then all of a sudden, he was like somebody else, trying to act all cool and everything, which must be hard, because he just wasn't. Yeah, he was way ready to wait on that for a while.

Jonas had his mom's black hair, though his was straight instead of wavy, her golden-brown eyes, and scattered freckles. At sixteen, he occasionally tried the surly teenager act, but since neither parent would tolerate this and it made him unhappy anyway, he was generally even-tempered, even if occasionally aloof with his siblings. He was also extremely intelligent, and since he'd gotten his brains from his parents, he was almost *forced* to talk to them, to discuss new ideas and revelations that many kids his age were uninterested in. Which is not to say that he didn't spend hours talking on the phone about virtually nothing, with various girls who were exceptionally learned on the subject.

Bess sat at the table with a cup of coffee as she watched her children hover about her mother and her amazing macaroons, and thought for the thousandth time that she was the luckiest woman in the world. How much love could one person expect to have in a lifetime? She must have surpassed whatever the legal limit was long ago. Just looking at her children filled her heart with an overwhelming love, pride, and longing. They were all so incredible, with whole, unique worlds inside each of them---and they would be hers for such a short time. To be their mother and to have Simon by her side to see them to adulthood with her—what more could she ask?

After what had happened to Simon, both of them had become acutely aware of how fragile life was, and how easily it could be taken away or changed in an instant. She'd always held an unspoken horror, as she supposed all parents did, that something might happen to take her away before she could see her children grown; that she wouldn't be there for them when they needed her for the crises and the little things that children want to share and that only a parent would listen to and care about; she wouldn't be there to guide them with her small cache of wisdom, or to just be in existence so that they would always know there was someone in the world who loved them more than life itself. And there was that greater fear, that black terror that something might happen to one of her children---but that thought was so horrendous that her mind refused to let her even acknowledge the possibility for more than a fleeting moment.

Warm hands on her shoulders brought her out of her reverie. "A penny for your thoughts. Although, by the look on your face and the direction of your gaze, I probably wouldn't have to spend my coin. I think our thoughts are the same just now. If we could freeze this moment in time, I'd be content to stand here and watch forever." She reached up with her free hand and put it on one of his, and he leaned in to kiss the top of her head.

He sat down across from her then, and said quietly, "I just realized that we have a decision to make."

"About what?"

"Since Gisella isn't coming on the trip, that means there will be one extra space on the ship. We could take one of the kids."

She gasped at the thought. "Oh my gosh, you're right! Who should we take? With the Bluemen's permission, of course."

"I think Eli should come, with him being the oldest. Who knows, someday there might be another opportunity, but he'll be gone by then. Shall we ask him?"

##

"Oh, geez, that would be fantastic, but… I just can't."

"Why?" Bess and Simon asked in unison.

"Well, I've been meaning to tell you. See, there's this girl…"

"And you would give up the chance to go to another planet, just so you wouldn't miss a date? Think about this, son. This opportunity might never present itself again. You're just nineteen---you have lots of time ahead of you to be with your girlfriend, but not lots of chances to see another world." Simon was incredulous that Eli wasn't thrilled at the idea of space travel. And because of a girl, when there would probably be a dozen other girls in his life before he graduated from college. He was afraid the boy was going to regret this decision for the rest of his life.

"Dad, I know you think that nineteen is too young to fall in love, and I'm not saying I don't agree with you. I know I don't want to get married right now, or have a kid with somebody like some of my friends have done. I want to finish school and get established in a career before I make any major moves like that. It's just that….well, this girl is special. She makes me want to *be* somebody. She makes me feel like I *am* somebody. She's really smart and not clingy or a flirt. *She* is somebody.

"I've been wanting to bring her up some weekend to meet you, but I knew I couldn't this time. When she asked me why I had to drop everything and come home all of a sudden, and then why she couldn't come with me, since we've been talking about it, I had to lie. I hate lies. And I never want to lie to her. I've already lied, and said that I had to rush home because my eccentric, very shy and reclusive uncle was coming to see us, and I'd probably never get a chance to see him again. Do me a favor and remember that story for when you do meet her, in case she asks.

"But anyway, I just felt like a worm, lying like that. We've had to do it all our lives, and I completely understand the necessity if I don't want to see the dogs and Ishie and maybe the two of you imprisoned in a lab somewhere. But it still sucks. I just don't want to have to tell her any more lies, and if I did go, I'd be dying to tell her about everything. So I'll just be happy meeting the Bluemen and the Elpies. I guess you think that makes me pretty stupid."

Bess shook her head and put an arm around him. "I think it makes you sound like a man. What you're talking about is integrity in a relationship that's important to you, and I couldn't be more proud. This girl probably will disappear from your life sometime in the future, or maybe she *will* be 'the one.' But either way, you'll have conducted yourself as a man of honor. Until just now, I still thought of you as a boy, but I see now that I was wrong." She pulled him to her and kissed the side of his head, and he smiled and hugged her back.

Simon was still upset at his decision, but after Bess' response, he realized she was right. It was an honorable choice. So he gave him a hug too, and then pushed him back to look in his face as he spoke. "Your mom's right, as usual. You're making choices with the understanding that everything you do impacts who you are, and you want that person to 'be someone.' I'm proud of you too, son, but I hope you don't live to regret your decision."

Enormously relieved, Eli ventured, "So I guess Jonas gets the spot on the ship now, huh?"

Bess and Simon looked at each other. Neither had even considered the possibility that Eli wouldn't want to go. Jonas in space? Why not?

##

"Are you guys serious? I could really go with you?" Jonas' reaction was much more gratifying than Eli's.

"We'd have to ask the Bluemen, of course, but I don't see why they'd object. They must realize that you already know about them, and they *are* landing on our property. You weigh less than Gisella, and that would probably have been their only concern, fuel wise." Simon was loving seeing his oh-so-self-conscious son show unabashed enthusiasm about something.

"What's to think about? Yeah, I want to go! Whoa, what'll I wear, what should I pack? They'll be here tomorrow night! Oh man, I gotta make some plans. This is wild! So you're going to ask them first thing, if I can go, right?" They both nodded, smiling at his excitement.

"*This is so cool!*" he shouted, and ran upstairs to pack for space.

CHAPTER SIX

At-eleven thirty-four p.m. on the appointed night, the Allbrights, Guinesses, Sayers, McPhinneys, two dogs and a cat, all stood in silence in the clearing between the main house and the lake. Simon had surmised that this was the only place really suitable for a landing, with an open area for maneuvering the ship, and cover from the trees and the house for concealment.

No one was speaking or sending, and as the seconds ticked by, the tension and excitement in the group was almost palpable. Bess stood mulling over what she'd been wondering since learning of the visit---what she wanted to say to her friends. All these years of thinking about them, knowing she'd never see any of them again, always wishing she might see them one more time, had once more chance to tell them...what exactly? What she felt, which was---love, of course, but even more so---gratitude. That was it. She looked over at Simon, then at at Gisella and the Allbrights, and she realized that all of them needed this for the same reason. To express gratitude for what that brief period spent with these incredible beings had given them.

At exactly eleven forty-five they felt a pressure and vibration in the air that increased to the point of moderate discomfort and then suddenly vanished. Most had either put their heads down and covered their ears or closed their eyes in an instinctive reaction to the pressure, and when they raised their heads again and opened their eyes, the ship had landed. No bright lights or other fanfare--just a vessel, triangular in shape, sitting before them in the meadow.

The hatchway door slid open, and the first Eli leapt out, followed by Bess' Colder and the sisters. Suddenly, Gisella squealed, Bess screamed, "YES!" Simon yelled, "Eli!" and the three started running towards the Elpies, who'd already begun loping in their direction. The dogs reached the Elpies first, and began jumping up to bestow slobbery greetings on all of them indiscriminately. Ishmael decided to hang back until everybody calmed down.

Simon was the first human to make contact, and he grabbed Eli in a bear hug, picking him up and swinging him around, laughing. Eli was making chirping sounds, and when Simon finally put him down, he looked up into the man's face, slapped both of his shoulders, and picked *him* up to swing around.

Gisella couldn't stop squealing as she embraced Ruth, Dulcie, and Martha, first in a group hug and then individually, and the sisters were all patting her baby belly and touching her face.

Bess arrived just after Gisella, and while waiting her turn to greet the sisters, she snagged her Colder by the arm and turned him around to face her. They had been through such an ordeal together, sharing toil, hope, heartbreak and finally, joy, but she had never actually hugged a Colder. She hesitated at first when he turned to look at her, but then she felt the gladness in his mind at seeing her again, and she threw caution to the wind, giving him a huge hug and a kiss on the cheek. She felt him flinch at the unexpected embrace, but only for a moment, and then he fell into it and nearly crushed the air out of her, following through with a gentle palm to the cheek in the traditional Elpie greeting.

She thanked him once more for all the times he'd stayed with her in those dark days following Simon's poisoning. He and the other five Colders had always shown up within moments, it seemed, when she'd needed help in moving him, or holding him down in his delirium to keep him from destroying himself. When violent bouts of vomiting had spawned massive nose bleeds, they'd cleaned the blood away to keep him from choking, and watched over him at the times when she was too exhausted to keep her eyes open. They had encouraged and exhorted him as only one male can another---praising him when his strength of will and constitution caused some slight sign of improvement, and understanding with a deep compassion when his body began to fail again after a brief period of hope. They had even bullied her into eating when she was too tired or despairing to think of food. They had stayed with her to the end, and stayed again to celebrate Simon's new beginning.

They had been the truest of friends to Simon and her. She tried her best to relay those sentiments with her thanks, and asked him to send the same to the other five Colders. The stiff hairs in the mane that started on the back half of his head and ran down his spine to just before the base of his tail, raised up and pointed forward as they did with pronounced emotion. She laid her palm on his cheek again, and a moment later, Simon caught his arm and started sending to him. She assumed he was expressing the same thoughts, and when she saw that mane rise once more, she was sure of it.

Then it was her turn with the sisters, and the water works started. Of course. Overwhelming joy, sadness, or any other major sentiment often brought tears to her eyes, which *always* produced uncomfortable and truly ugly manifestations on her poor face. The first time the Bluemen had witnessed this on their ship, they'd thought she was having a medical crisis.

Oh brother, here we go, she thought, even as her heart celebrated the sight of her beloved friends. Bess and the sisters began hugging, laying palms on cheeks, sending their joy at seeing each other, and she could feel her eyes turning red, swelling, and her face going blotchy as her nose started running. Just like old times.

Then the Bluemen, and Bluewoman, Sven, Luca Pacioli, Maurice, and Mona, stepped out of the ship, and Gisella's squeals reached an even higher pitch. She launched herself at Mona, whose three arms lifted her up so that she could look into her eyes before hugging her gently.

Bess broke away from the sisters momentarily to hug Luca and then hugged each of the other Bluepeople in turn. Simon approached the Bluemen and shook hands with each, somewhat awkwardly. When shaking hands with a three handed individual, how many hands should be shaken? One, two---all three? When he got to Mona, he just threw up his hands and hugged her instead, a relief to both of them.

Simon and the Colder, before their "talk," had greeted each other with what Bess thought looked like a typical male type, love-you-but-this-feels-strange greeting: a bear hug with both of them pounding each other on the back with their fists. A little pseudo-aggression always seemed to make it okay for males to embrace. As long as they were hurting each other, it was okay.

But Bess, Gisella, and Eli the first felt no such compunctions, and squealing, chirping, tears and swelling finished the reunion.

In the meantime, the unintroduced had been standing nervously, hardly believing their eyes, and waiting their turns to interact. Luca was the first to notice this and he caught Bess' arm and sent to her. She nodded and turned to her family.

"The Bluemen want to make it possible for all of you to use telepathy for the short time they're here, so that you can communicate with them and the Elpies, and vice versa. It would be a temporary thing, only lasting until we return and say our goodbyes to them again. If you'd like to do it, come over and they'll put a device against your head for just a second. It won't hurt. It's like a computer program that amps up your brain's aptitude for communication."

All the kids ran forward, with Hiram close behind. The Allbrights came after that, a bit slower, followed by Sarah, and finally, Angus. As promised, the procedure was painless, the results immediate.

The Allbrights looked at each other and nodded, and Tom made his move. He approached the tallest Blueman, put his hand out for Sven to fret over, and started talking.

"My wife and I have been wanting to thank you for the past twenty years. You saved our daughter's life, and then you arranged for her to come back to us and helped us forge a whole new life here with her. There's no way to explain how grateful we are for everything you've done. All I can do is shake your hand---uh, hands, and say, 'God bless you.'"

Then, just to make sure he hadn't left anything undone, Tom shook all three hands of every Blueman and woman. Viola stepped forward after her husband's speech and hugged each one, something the Bluepeople were actually starting to enjoy.

Then Viola went to the sisters to express her gratitude for the love and care they'd shown Gisella when she was on their planet, and told them about her choosing all of their names to take as her own on her counterfeit birth certificate. She wanted them to know too, that the picture Bess had painted of Jonas for Gisella had hung in her room until she'd moved out and taken the painting with her. Lastly, she thanked them for having a fine son who'd been such a good friend to their little girl when she was in desperate need of one.

Then it was Sarah's turn to thank the Bluemen for saving her son-in-law, and the first Eli for saving her daughter when she was injured.

Both Elpies and Bluepeople were appropriately surprised, embarrassed, and touched by the warmth of their welcome and the outpouring of gratitude from the group. But then they had to deal with Sarah, who, when on a cookie mission, was a force of nature. She insisted that they all come to the main house for cookies and milk/coffee/tea (decaf.), and she had such a sweet way and iron will about her that they were helpless to refuse. Especially since they'd given her temporary telepathy, and couldn't even *pretend* to not understand her.

The kids were out of their minds with awe and excitement. Maurice had readily consented for Jonas to take Gisella's spot on the excursion, rendering the boy incapable of coherent speech for a bit. Bess and Simon watched him pacing and jumping around in a circle while he pumped the air with his fists and produced syllables of celebration that never quite turned into words.

The two younger kids ran on ahead, while Sarah, the double fudge tyrant, herded the rest of them into the house without mercy, even when Sven tried to back out by insisting that the ship couldn't be left alone. She countered him by saying that she *knew* there was no one in the province who knew how to fly the thing, so he had nothing to worry about. By the time he thought of a counter to her counter, he was already in the kitchen with a plate of cookies in one hand and a glass of milk in the other.

The group spread out in the expansive sunken living room, with the kids sitting on the steps leading to the couch where the first Eli sat, sending in broadcast mode to all four. When etiquette forced them to partake of Sarah's offerings, both Elpies and Bluepeople responded with shocked ecstasy to their first tastes of Sarah's cookies.

The Bluepeople were all between seven and eight feet tall, with rounded heads that appeared too large for their bodies, huge round eyes with irises from light blue to purple, oval shaped bumps in the center of their faces, with no visible nostrils, and long, almost lipless slits for mouths. Grayish-blue skin explained their title, and their three long arms ended in seven fingered hands. The ears on the sides of each head were large and wing-like in shape, cupping forward, and they moved in the direction of their focus.

Looking like large, green anoles that walked upright, the Elpies were from five-five to six feet tall. Their wilder cousin, the Colder, was as tall as Simon, at six-four, with a wider face, and deep set eyes that gave him a fierce appearance. Broader and more muscular than the other Elpies, he had black fur on his shoulders, from above his knees to his ankles, and from his wrists to just above his elbows, giving the appearance of leg warmers and mufflers. Long, webbed toes on feet covered with silky hair equipped him for treks in the snows of his home. Bess had always thought his Mohawk of stiff black hair gave him a wild look that would be a natural with piercings and tattoos.

Elpies wore no clothes other than coats used during the coldest days of winter. The one thing always seen on Eli, however, was his medicine pouch, worn on one hip and held there by a shoulder strap that went down at an angle across his chest. Taking a first aid kit consisting of herbs and such, to a planet where technology could regrow an individual's organs would seem almost farcical on anyone else. But nobody ridiculed Eli. Ever. He was considered the wisest of the wise among the Elpies, and if he thought something was a good idea, then it must be.

The sight of all of these "people" sitting together on couches, steps, and chairs, holding glasses or cups and saucers while they munched on cookies, was somehow beautiful besides being bizarre, and Simon thought that only Sarah could have managed to pull this off.

After watching them going back for multiple helpings, with his mother-in-law still acting the hostess, waiting to serve more milk/coffee/tea (decaf), Simon walked over and gave her a hug.

"Mom, you are a wonder. But I really believe you should drop all this 'double fudge, etc, and just call them 'Sarah's Marvelous Macaroons.'" She laughed and blushed, and Simon saw Bess in her face, in her happy blush, even in her easy laughter. He leaned towards her again, speaking in a quieter voice. "Sarah, I hope you know what a blessing you are to our family, in everything that you are and all that you do. And thank you most of all for making Bess." He kissed her forehead then and went back to the living room, leaving Sarah in tears, with her eyes swelling and her face going red and blotchy.

Angus was deep in mental discussions not with the Elpies or Bluemen, but with the dogs and Ishmael. Bess didn't even ask.

The Elpies were touched again when they found that Bess and Simon's sons had been named after Eli, Jonas, and the Colder. And Bess, Simon, and Gisella were humbled to learn that the eggs that were waiting to be hatched when they had left the planet twenty years ago had yielded two daughters and a son, whom Eli and his wives had named Bess, Gisella, and Simon.

The Elpies had never used names for each other before Simon came to live with them. They recognized each other's mental 'signatures,' and had neither need nor capacity for spoken language. But Simon had felt the need to have names he could identify his close friends with, and they had all readily agreed to being labeled by him and then by Bess later on.

"Elpie" was the name Simon had dubbed their species with, for when he'd first arrived on the planet and met them, he'd thought of them as the "Lizard People," shortened then to "LP's," and eventually "Elpies," with the accent on the first syllable. He thought that sounded friendlier, and suited his friends. For the humans to learn that these Elpies had named their children after them, even though they had no speech, made them feel deeply honored, for the sounds of these names would be mentally broadcast as the memories of how *their humans* had pronounced them.

In the course of the evening, or actually the wee hours of the morning, Bess showed the house to her guests, proudly pointing out her paintings of the first Eli that hung in Simon's study, and of Ruth, Dulcie, and Martha that she'd hung in her studio. The Elpies were duly impressed with her skill, and gratified by the sentiment. But in spite of all these revelations, what enthralled them most were the toilets, and they spent a good deal of time during their visit, standing and watching them flush.

Simon dragged Eli out to his workshop/apothecary and showed him his garden. Having learned how to experiment and develop remedies from Eli, he insisted on giving him a package of herbs he'd made up earlier, hoping the Elpie would find them helpful in his healing practice.

The females were hugging each other every few minutes, it seemed, and Simon and Eli paralleled them by punching each other's arms or shaking each other's shoulders, in the sheer depth of feeling that being in each other's company again brought. In spite of the years that had passed, nothing had changed between them---they would always be brothers.

Finally, Simon showed Eli the pictures of the Eli Institute for the Research and Treatment of Chronic Obstructive Lung Disease, most often referred to as "the Institute," to save even more breath. After building and staffing it, he had chaired the board for the Institute for many years, and seeing that all ran smoothly was his main occupation. In his heart, Eli was, above all things, a healer, and to have such an amazing house of medicine named in his honor was a wonderful and astounding gift that he felt he could never repay. Simon did hug him then, sending that his friendship had paid for it a thousand times over.

##

At the end of the reunion/cookie fest, the Bluepeople returned to the ship, and the Elpies stayed in spare bedrooms in the main house. Maurice had given instructions on what little could be taken in the way of luggage, and said they were scheduled to leave in six hours. They had new cloaking mechanisms for their ship, so leaving in daytime was no longer a problem. This gave the delighted Elpies a few more hours of experimentation and amazement with the many electrical appliances in their rooms, but they still considered the toilets the main attraction.

All four of the kids, even Eli, sat on the floor in the loft, a sheet covering their heads, and flashlights in every hand. This was a Sayers kids' tradition when something momentous had happened or was about to, or when one of them was going away for more than a few days. They shined the flashlights in each other's faces and mugged in the glare.

Eli sat straight up, pulling more of the sheet with him as he took command. "Okay, since I'm the oldest, I should start the meeting. First rule is, NOBODY FARTS!"

That started all of them giggling, which resulted in one of them *actually* farting, which started more giggling, and necessitated opening the sheet for a few minutes. Finally they quieted down, and Eli spoke again. He turned to Jonas and took a tone of formality as he addressed him. "Dude! This is one outrageous trip you're going on. You are hereby commanded to memorize everything you see and do so you can come back and report at the next sheet meeting. Are you seriously wild and excited?"

Jonas broke out in a huge grin, shaking his head. "Oh, man, you don't know the half of it! I can't really believe it's true though, ya know? I mean, like, I'm going to another planet? How is that possible? After everything that's happened tonight, I *should* believe it, right? I mean, we've had *lizards* talking to us in our *minds*—sending us brain videos—and *Bluemen* drinking tea and eating Grandma's cookies on *our* couch! Man, if only we could tell our friends!"

Eli shook his head. "Nah, not being able to tell them isn't that bad, 'cause like we've known all our lives, nobody would believe us anyway. But hey, guy, I'm really stoked for you."

Genevieve looked at Eli and turned her head to the side. "But how come you're not going, Eli? You should be the one to go, since you're the oldest."

He looked uncomfortable, but decided to go with the truth. "I'm not going because I've met this girl---"

He was immediately drowned out by high pitched "oooooh's" and kissing sounds from all the siblings. With his usual good nature, he laughed and shoved his two brothers, tipping them over, and gently tugged Genevieve's hair. "Geez, try and treat you kids like adults, and what do I get for it?" More ooohs and kissing sounds. "Well, true, I got all of that. So do you want to hear the rest or what?"

"Yeah, tell us the rest, big brother." Colder sat forward and cupped both ears towards Eli in exaggerated attention.

"Anyway, this girl and I---"

"What's her name?"

"Babette." More ooooh's and kisses. "You know, at this rate, we're gonna be under this sheet a long time, and if anybody farts again, we could all die." They laughed but then settled down for his story.

"Well, anyway, she's from Quebec, and she speaks French, and I tell you, this girl is so gorgeous that I didn't even know if she'd speak to me at first." The "oooh's" started again, but he stopped them with an upheld hand. "Enough. This is something I'm serious about. Where was I? Oh, yeah, she's something else. But as it turns out, she went out with me, and she's even nicer than she is pretty, and I tell ya, guys and girl, I think she may be "the one."

Colder's eyes widened. "You mean like the one you're going to marry?"

Jonas smacked him on top of the head lightly with the flat of his hand, speaking with brotherly forbearance. "No, bean brain, the one he's gonna go fishing with. Duh."

"Anyway....I don't want to have to lie to her about where I'm going, since I've already lied to her about why I came home and everything. So I told Mom and Dad to let Jonas go instead."

Genevieve's mouth flew open in a gasp. "Whoa, what did they say?"

"Oh, they were kinda surprised, but they were cool with it. They know I'm not gonna quit school or run off and get married or anything."

Colder's face took on an uncharacteristic gloom as he spoke. "Speaking of Dad....wow."

Jonas nodded his head and stared at the flashlight in his hands. "Yeah, wow is right. That was such an awesome thing to do---to hang on to Eli instead of saving himself." He looked up at the others then. "We've always known Dad was brave---you can just tell. Nothing seems to faze him. He always just does what he needs to, no matter what. But this---I am muy impressed."

"I don't know about you guys," Genevieve said, "but I wanted to hug him so bad when he was lying there dying. I just wanted to give him an aspirin or anything to make him better. It made me feel all sick and empty inside to see him like that."

They had laughed for a second at the aspirin comment, but they quieted quickly, because they all knew exactly how she felt. Colder got very serious, and said quietly, "Do you ever think about Mom and Dad dying? I mean, he's in his fifties already, and mom's forty-eight. That's pretty close to dead."

Jonas smacked his head again. "It is not, idiot. Besides, they both still look and act younger, and Dad has new insides, after all, so that's gotta be giving him some extra time."

"But what about Mom? She's got old insides."

Now it was Genevieve's turn to pop him on the head. "Don't call Mom old!"

"Will you guys stop hitting me?"

"Well stop saying dumb stuff," Genevieve retorted. "Mom and Dad are going to be around a long time."

Eli ruffled Colder's hair instead of slapping him. "Now that I'm all older and wiser, yuk yuk, I think about stuff like that sometimes, and I've come to a conclusion. Wanna hear it?" They all nodded. "Well, especially after seeing or receiving, or however you want to say it---about what happened to Dad, it makes me understand that stuff he's been spouting to us all these years. You know, when we'd been fighting or something, and he'd pull us apart and give us the lecture about how we won't always have each other around, and life is too short to waste it fighting, and we should be thanking God every day that we have a family.

"I bet you anything, that's why he says that---'cause he almost died, or actually did die, and he and Mom almost lost each other before they ever even had a family. And they probably kept thinking that they hadn't had enough time together for him to be dying like that. Then remember, too, he'd lost his mom and dad and little sister in that plane crash before he and Mom met. So he really means it---he knows what it feels like to lose someone---to lose time you really needed with someone. It's not just something adults say to make you behave.

"I think you shouldn't worry about them dying or us dying---because we could, you know---happens all the time. But we should remember that our time together is limited, so we ought to appreciate the people we love, and tell them, even when it's a bunch of little dorks like you."

They started laughing, but then saw that Eli had tears in his eyes, and they all stopped immediately. Even when he was a little boy, Eli *never* cried, not that any of them remembered.

"Seeing Dad like that just made me think that I don't tell him and Mom enough---well, how much they mean to me, and how I *never* tell you crazy imbeciles---well, I really love all of you, and I wouldn't trade one of you little farters for anything in the world. Not even Jonas. Come here, you disgusting snot breaths."

A momentous thing happened then. The four Sayers offspring had a sincere group hug, and then, being mostly male, they broke off into moderately hard punches to the arms and moderately hard hair pulling, shoving, and wrestling until they were all laughing and yelling at each other in a more normal sibling way, in order to seal up the cracks in their veneers.

##

Too excited to sleep, Bess and Simon packed the few articles allowed and then lay down to try and get some rest before morning. They knew it would be pointless to tell the kids to sleep, so they tried to mentally shut out all the talking and giggling they heard coming through the walls.

After a few minutes, Simon got up and went to his computer to check on a few things at the Institute before they left. Bess watched him from bed, and the mellow mood brought on by the evening with friends and family made her focus on her blessings once again. As she watched Simon, she found it difficult to believe that they'd been together over twenty years.

Sitting in his chair, concentrating on the screen in front of him, he looked like some fierce bird of prey, with his hawk nose, furrowed brow, light brown hair sticking up in various directions since lying down, and skin weathered from years of being outdoors in all kinds of climates. With a keen intellect, and a love of nature, Simon was a man as comfortable with an ax as he was with a flash drive. She studied him as he sat there, and thought she'd never loved him more. Their life together wasn't a romance novel. They weren't "aflame with mad passion" for each other every moment of the day, and there were times that they needed to get away from each other for a while, when one or both of them were being annoying or testy about something. Both of them had irritating habits that drove the other crazy from time to time, and neither of them was beauty personified.

Bess had never been a classic beauty, though she was striking, and hard to forget. But Simon called her beautiful. He loved her not because she was beautiful, but she was beautiful to him because he loved her, and she was always aware of that. Like any couple, they'd had their bad moments, but the years had made them closer. When she looked at his face, she saw the creases and the other imperfections, but what she saw most often was the love in those light green eyes and his big, toothy smile when he was happy or laughing, or simply welcoming someone into his presence. There was the real Simon. She would always feel herself drawn to that man---he could still make her feel glad just by walking into the room. She sent a silent prayer of thanks for the wonder of lasting love before drifting off into a comfortable haziness.

She'd almost fallen asleep when he crawled in beside her and put an arm around her waist. "Bess?"

"Hmmph?"

"Do my teeth look like dentures?"

She kept her eyes closed, and only moved her mouth, hoping not to lose her doze completely. "Of course not, your teeth are perfect."

"You heard what your dad said, that they were 'just too perfect' and that 'nobody had teeth that straight and white.'"

She could feel wakefulness coming on. "Oh, Simon--"

"At the grocery store the other day, this little checker said, 'Wow, your teeth are so perfect, they don't even look real!' She's not the first person who's said that, either. What's the good of having great teeth if everybody thinks they're dentures? Maybe I should ask the Bluemen to stain them for me, or chip one."

Now Bess sat up, fully awake. "Don't you dare! I *love* your teeth. I would *kill* to have teeth like that, and you died to get them, so just be grateful you have something that's perfect!"

He pulled her back down and snuggled close. "Are you implying that I have parts that *aren't* perfect? Should we investigate this? Is a thorough examination in order?"

She laughed and slapped his chest with the back of her hand. "They didn't replace your brain. And a *thorough* examination takes uninterrupted privacy for a protracted period of time. Privacy and time are things we can't count on right now. But we definitely need to do an in-depth follow up on this at a later time. Get some rest, Smiley."

#

Gisella was exhausted. Seeing her other "family," but knowing she had to say goodbye to them again in a few hours was an emotional roller coaster that tired her as much as the lack of sleep. Hiram, on the other hand, was still wound up like a spring and ecstatic about the whole business. He was pacing around the room with an awe-struck look on his face, while she was nodding off in bed.

"I can't believe this really happened. I actually met beings from two different planets! Two different species! Simply amazing! And…and I was given telepathy, and I can even talk to the dog without having you as an interpreter. I talked to aliens! How many people can say that? Oh—*I* can't say that either, can I? But I can talk to *you* about it. That must have been terrible for you to have to keep this from me---always having to skirt the truth. Feeling guilty when you did, but having no choice. But now you can tell me *everything*, and I have a million questions!"

She lay watching him pace and go between being sad for her and thrilled for himself. Whenever he discovered something new, no matter how small---he'd light up with excitement and practically buzz with energy, and she could almost see those wheels turning in his head. With her eyes half way open, she looked at him and smiled.

"Do you know how much I love you?" she asked.

He stopped in midstride. "No. Tell me."

"I would, but my mom always said that actions speak louder than words." She patted the side of the bed next to her.

"Ah, did she tell you, too, that beauty is as beauty does….A bird in the hand is worth two—"

"Shut up and come to bed."

"So bossy. I love that."

"Don't make me hurt you."

"Ooh, say it again."

Great dog that she was, Madelyn reached into the room and turned out the light.

CHAPTER SEVEN

Six hours later, the whole family stood next to the Elpies and Bluemen in front of the ship to say their goodbyes. She'd been excited and happy last night, but now Bess was nervous and melancholy, with an unshakeable sense of foreboding—probably just from a lack of sleep, she told herself. But she remembered the last time she'd felt this way—just before Eli's and Simon's mounts had walked into the village carrying their unconscious bodies.

This is just stupid. She'd had premonitions before that were completely groundless. Probably the idea of a spaceship had her nervous, and her gloom was due to saying goodbye to her other children and her folks.

She hugged her eldest, Eli, and then held both of his hands in hers as she spoke to him. "I'm so proud and impressed by your choice, Eli. I could wish nothing better for you than to be like your father, and especially at times like this, I see so much of him in you. Your brother and sister look up to you, so who you become, and the way you live your life will impact their lives, too. Promise me you'll always be there for them. I love you so much." Then she dropped his hands and hugged him tightly once more.

He smiled, warmed by her words but worried by them, too. "I love you too, Mom, and thanks. Thanks for understanding. And you know I'd always watch out for the munchkins. That's sort of my job, right?" He tried to laugh then, but couldn't. "Uh, Mom, is everything okay? I mean, you're just gonna be gone for a week or two, right?"

"Everything's fine. I'm just going to miss all of you." She laid her hand on his cheek and smiled, and then walked over to her other children.

She hugged her two youngest, and told them, too, how much she loved them and how proud she was of them. Then she leaned over to be at eye level with Genevieve as she added, "You can always count on Gisella and your Grandma when you need to talk to another female."

A kiss to her daughter's cheek, and she turned to Colder. "Colder, Hiram and Grandpa will always welcome you when you need advice from a man's point of view. Don't ever hesitate to reach out to either of them. They're both fine men."

Her admonishments were making the kids nervous---it sounded like she was saying goodbye forever. When she saw that in their eyes, she started joking and changed her affect to upbeat and peppy, and they responded to that with relief, the anxiety gone from their faces.

Angus grabbed her and held her tight for a minute before stepping back. "Just in case you were wondering, Simon's okay in my book now, since I know he's not the head of some cartel. Or an alien. The *lizard* Eli filled my mind with all kind of good things about him. I sorta feel like I've been brainwashed, but it didn't hurt as much as I'd have thought." Then he gave her a wink and moved back for her mom to step up.

Sarah hugged and kissed her, and brushed a hair back from her face. "Don't you worry about a thing. The kids will be fine. We're going to have a great time together. Oh, and here's a little something for the trip. You can pass these out on the ship and give some as presents on their world," she said, as she handed her twenty bags of the Marvelous Macaroons. She'd been baking all morning.

Gisella and Hiram, along with Viola and Tom, hugged everyone, and Gisella promised to take care of herself and to look in on the kids often. Madelyn was staying behind, because she felt she shouldn't leave Gisella's side until after the baby was born. Elsie was bouncing around, licking everybody, and even Ishmael had been working the crowd, winding in and out, rubbing ankles and sending goodbyes.

The Colder had made a special effort to get to know his namesake, and he said goodbye to him with a hand on his cheek and two very rough slaps on the shoulders, signifying with this semi-beating, that he respected him as an almost-man. Colder number two was thrilled, and couldn't stop himself from throwing his arms around *his* Colder and hugging him, and he was thrilled again when the startled Colder relaxed and put his arms out to answer with a hug of his own.

Genevieve hugged everybody, and after their hugs, the Bluemen and Elpies all had to run their hands through her flame-red curls, a source of endless fascination to both species.

The first Eli had come to know his namesake as well, and he sent to the young man that he was proud to have him bear his name, because he could tell that he had a fine mind and a great heart, like his father. They each gave a palm to the other's cheek, and then hugged without a beating.

Simon had given everyone bear hugs and kisses, and thrown the two younger children up into the air one last time before getting on the ship, although with their height now, the "up" in the air had become a good deal lower. He and Angus had shaken hands and punched each other's arms exceptionally hard. Bess saw both of them wince slightly. *Good, they're hurting each other. They must be starting a friendship. Men.*

When Simon had been saying goodbye to the children, they'd all said they loved him, of course, but strangely, every one of them had also said they were proud of him. With the first child, he'd been touched, but by the time the last offspring told him, he knew there must be something behind it. Too late for a heart to heart today, but there would be one on their return.

Jonas hugged the whole family---*even* his younger brother and sister, and had pronounced those words that when spoken into the ears of younger siblings by teenagers, are profoundly shocking—*I love you.* Colder and Genevieve had automatically said it back to him, which shocked them even more. Genevieve would write about it in her diary.

#

When the ship finally departed, the five Earthlings looked out of one large portal at their rapidly disappearing world and knew their adventure had started for real.

#

The trip lasted three days. Once that feeling of impending doom pressing down on Bess disappeared, she began enjoying herself immensely. It was such fun to watch Jonas enthralled by everything he saw. Fully aware that he'd probably never have this opportunity again, he was determined to absorb and memorize each detail of what he saw and experienced. The controls on the ship, the view from the portals, the "sofas" on the ship that folded around his body when he sat down, the Elpies and the Bluepeople, both of whom he was able to study at close quarters now—everything was a new discovery to be celebrated. Bess had never seen him so happy and effusive.

He was getting a huge charge out of his ability to communicate telepathically with Elsie and Ishmael, and quizzed them both extensively on what it was like to be a dog and a cat, and about their perspectives on the world. Flattered by his interest, they were both very forthcoming because of it. He did the same with the Bluemen and the Elpies, with similar reactions.

With the exception of Elsie and Ishmael, Bess had handed out a bag of cookies to everyone on the ship at the beginning of the trip, and since that time, she had yet to see a single Blueperson without a cookie in hand or mouth. She was beginning to worry if Type 2 Diabetes was ever a problem for Bluepeople. The Elpies were almost as bad, and she'd ended up passing out the rest of the bags before their arrival on the Bluemen's planet. Sven did manage to save one bag to give to The Seated, but it was very hard on him, and he was reduced to begging a few extra cookies from Bess and Simon by standing in front of them and staring pitifully at their bags. *Oh, Mom, what have you done?*

#

The one thing that Bess wanted to repeat from her first ride in a spaceship, was her hot bath in the room with a view. This was a different ship, but it had a similar room, and she took full advantage of it. She also made sure that Jonas got to experience the room---telling him he *had* to do it, but not what to expect.

When he sat down in the tub, almost up to his chin in hot water, his body's reaction was instantaneous. All the excitement of the past few days had kept him continuously wound up, and the heat in the water seemed to spiral him back down on contact, turning him practically to jelly in a matter of seconds. The water lapped back and forth against the sides of the tub with the slight vibrations of the engines, making tiny, soft, slapping sounds that proved hypnotic in his relaxed state.

Then the lights turned off and the wall in front of the tub slid back to expose a view of the universe beyond the ship. He gasped at the sight and thanked God that Gisella was pregnant and Eli was hung up on some girl so that he'd gotten to come along in his stead. Staring in awe at the grandeur before him, he gradually succumbed to the view and the water and the sense of weightlessness, and was transported from a state of bliss into the deepest sleep of his life.

He woke up two hours later to Luca shaking his shoulder and sending to him. While he was showing him the drying chamber, Luca explained that this always happened when humans used the room. The Bluemen used it for contemplation, but humans always went to sleep, and so soundly that they had to be awakened with physical measures.

He got dressed and went into the great room to hug his mom. She laughed and asked,"Well?" All he could think to reply was, "Wow. Oh yeah. Wow."

#

All of the guests had small, austere chambers where they could go for a little privacy and an attempt at sleep. There was just enough space in the rooms to deposit their luggage and to change clothes, with the bunks taking up the rest of the area. The spaces were so claustrophobic though, that most of the passengers preferred to sleep in their reclined seats in the passengers' common room.

There were portals to look out of, but otherwise, the common room was fairly dull, with all of the surfaces done in different shades of gray. Everything was functional, with little ornamentation, and the passengers hadn't seen or been invited to any areas, other than the bath chamber, that might provide a change in form or color. Looking out of the portals was an incredible experience, but after a day or so, even this ran to monotony.

The Elpies had already seen everything on the trip to Earth, so they were very happy to have the diversion of mental conversation with their friends for the last leg of their journey. The sisters caught Bess up on everything that had happened in the village in the last twenty years. Feeling suddenly lonely for the two members of her Earth family who'd chosen to stay behind, she asked the Elpies to give her love to Boris and Genevieve. Her vision blurred up for a moment when Ruth replied that the two had given them the same message for her.

They sent her that Boris and Genevieve were still making the rounds of the planet, still coveted guests at all of the villages. They'd both learned to sit on rocks in the river and use their paws like bears to snag and retrieve fish, and this had become such an obsession with Genevieve that she'd quit traveling with Boris for a while, just so she could sleep in a tree by the banks in order to start fishing first thing every morning.

But even a cat can only eat so many fish, and the Elpies frowned on killing for sport, so eventually she'd gone back to traveling and visiting with Boris. While she was fishing, though, she'd always had an audience of fascinated Elpies, and when visiting villages now, she was usually asked to fish for spectators at least once.

While rolling around in the grass one day, Boris had discovered a plant whose odor had a catnip-like effect, and he'd quickly learned to sniff out the plant anywhere he happened to wander on his new world. As a result, he was prone to wild bouts of play, frequent naps, and never seemed to have a bad day.

They sent that the gift of the CD players and CD's had given rise to regular get-togethers four or five times a year, which included feasting followed by line dancing, a skill which the sisters believed they had mastered completely.

Eli and Simon sent to each other about everything, but three things dominated their conversation: medicine---mainly herbal, and the new remedies both had been working on or tried---successfully or not, and Jonas, Eli's son, and the talent and natural bent he was showing as a healer. He saw as many patients now as did Eli, and he had taken to traveling in a regular circuit once or twice a year to hold week long clinics in villages around their small planet. Eli had never ranged that far himself, for it would have meant deserting his own village and leaving them without medical care for too extended a period. But now they could reach so many more Elpies between the two of them. Eli was very proud that his son was growing in skill, dedication, and compassion every day, it seemed

The third thing that dominated their conversation was, of course, the All-Elpie softball games that now were a weekly event, rain or shine. They'd reworked some of the gloves that Simon had sent, so that the players could wear one on the hand, and one on the tail, and the games had become much more exciting. This year, the Colders had three teams, and one of them was in the lead, but that changed frequently, and the competitions never led to acrimony between villages and individuals, as they might have on Earth. The Elpies just enjoyed the playing and the get-togethers. Once the games were done with, the feasting began, and the winning or losing was soon forgotten.

#

On their last day on the ship, having exhausted his questions for the Elpies, Bluepeople, and animals, Jonas found himself watching his parents talking together quietly, and he was struck by how they really seemed to listen to each other. A few months ago, his parents had been out to some hospital function together, and then had sat up late, talking and drinking tea in the kitchen after they'd come home. He'd been in bed for about an hour when he woke up thirsty and got up to get some ice water. He'd been walking down the hall heading to the stairs, when he'd heard some old music playing softly in the direction of the kitchen. He'd stopped at the corner of the wall where the landing looked down onto the living room and kitchen, and then he'd peeked around the edge to see where the music was coming from.

An old boom box was on the kitchen counter, and his mom and dad were dancing to its music. It was playing an old, slow song, with some silly, sentimental lyrics. His mom had her arms up and her hands clasped behind his dad's neck, with her head turned to the side and pressed against his chest. His dad had his arms wrapped around her waist, with his head tilted down so that it rested against hers. They were barely moving their feet---more like swaying to the music than dancing.

For some reason, the scene startled him. He'd seen his parents hug and kiss each other hello and goodbye, and occasionally just because. He knew they loved each other, but it was like---for the first time, he was really seeing them *in* love. They weren't in front of anybody, or being parents, or anything else. They were only with *each other*, and their closeness touched him and made him realize that they were Bess and Simon before they were Mom and Dad. What he'd never thought about was that they were still that same couple. Once in a while during that dance, his dad would say something quietly to his mom, and she would turn her head and look up at him and smile, or they would kiss slowly, gently. Not the goodbye and hello kisses he was used to seeing.

He couldn't believe that after living with them his whole life, he was only just now understanding their relationship. They were a part of each other, and right then, at that moment, nothing else mattered to them. He watched for probably a whole five minutes and then crept back down the hall and sucked up some water from the bathroom faucet. He went back to bed then, still listening to that barely audible music, and still seeing those two people in love, long after he closed his eyes.

He'd been thinking about that as he watched them now, and then he brought himself back to the present. He felt really awkward about this, but he needed to say some things to the both of them, and there would never be a better time, he figured. Rising from his seat, he hurried over to the two, anxious to catch them together before someone else started sending to them.

Stopping in front of them, he asked if they could have a private conversation. Both of looked at him with concern at his serious expression, and what might have prompted this summit.

"Mom, Dad… you told us kids your story, about when you were on the Elpies' planet---that Dad got poisoned and was really sick, and that you took care of him, Mom, until the Bluemen came back and fixed him. But man, you left out a lot of stuff."

Bess looked apologetic, and sighed. "Well, honey, there were details that were just so violent, and so ---wrenching, that we didn't think it necessary to expose you to the whole story. Believe me, there were lots of details that we would rather have skipped ourselves."

"Well, Eli told us everything. At least I think it was everything. He sent to us that he knew you so well, Dad, that he didn't believe you'd ever tell us about what you did, and that you were a hero to him and his family, and all of the Elpies, for saving their medicine man."

Squirming in his chair a bit, Simon looked vaguely uncomfortable. "Well, son, I don't know that 'hero' really fits. I only did what I had to---what anyone would have done in those circumstances."

"Eli sent that you could have fought this guy that was attacking you and beat him, no sweat, but that you wouldn't let go of his tail because the amputation would've bled him to death really fast. You *knew* you'd be poisoned and die from it, but you still held on, and you managed to destroy this guy's arm with just one hand, even with him running up on you from behind. Eli sort of sent us a movie, in a way. We even saw the guy's face, and saw it happening the way Eli did."

Bess gasped. "Oh, that was too horrible for you kids to see. I don't know that he should have done that."

"It was actually pretty exciting—kinda like watching an adventure movie, because we knew you won eventually. But the part that was hard was watching you dying. You never told us you actually died. Watching that last day had all of us tearing up, even though we could see you across the room from us."

"That was too hard a thing to show you. He shouldn't have---"

"No, Dad, he was right. We *needed* to know. And the Colder sent how, after you got poisoned, you fought to live, when most humans or Elpies would have just let go. And that when you knew it was the end, you were still trying to help Mom and Gisella. He sent that all of the Colders admired your bravery and your kindness, and that by the end, they'd felt honored to be with you on your 'last journey,' or at least that's how we interpreted it."

Jonas' voice had been cracking during the last part of his story, and Bess could see that Simon was about to minimize what Jonas had been sent, to take away some of the sting. Before he could speak, she took his hand and shook her head.

"Jonas, your father will try and downplay everything, because he's a modest man and praise embarrasses him. But Eli was right. Your dad *was* a hero and his children *should* know that. I fell in love with him when he was healthy and strong and handsome---yeah, yeah, don't you roll your eyes at me, young man---this is part of the story too.

"But after he was poisoned, I saw the other side of him. I saw him when he was completely helpless, when he was in more pain than you can ever imagine, had lost most of his hair and looked like a skeleton, and was too weak to even speak, and those were the times that I saw real bravery, and fell in love with his spirit.

"A lot of people feel sorry for themselves, and rightly so, when they're sick or hurting, and some people strike out at others in their frustration. I'd seen your dad upset before, and I fully expected that reaction when he was poisoned. But instead, he thought about me, and Gisella, and Eli and the Colders, and what *we* were going through. He fought to stay alive for Gisella and me, because he knew we loved and needed him, when letting go to escape the pain would have been so much easier on him. That was the bravery he showed every day—to fight beyond his own pain. I'm not saying it very well---but I'm glad Eli showed you, so that maybe you can understand what kind of a man your father is, and why I will love him 'til the day I die." She could feel the redness and swelling coming on. Simon squeezed her hand and smiled.

"Not to mention the fact that he saw me looking like this a lot of the time and still told me I was beautiful. Such a liar!" That made them all laugh, since she was famous for looking freaky when she cried.

"Eli and the Colder also sent us about how brave and faithful you were, Mom, and how you hardly ever left his side." Now she was really tearing up. Pretty soon she'd be unrecognizable.

"Well, anyway, Dad, I just wanted to tell you that all of us kids know now about what really happened—oh, and Eli and the Colder sent to Grandma and Grandpa, too, so that they'd know you were okay, because they sensed a little tension between you and Gramps."

Simon shook his head and laughed. "You can't keep anything from an empath."

"What I'm trying to say Dad, is…well, I always thought you were a great dad and all, but now… I'm just so proud of you, and you too, Mom, and I wanted to tell you both that. If the Elpies hadn't come, we would have never known how amazing you both really are. Kids can be tough on parents sometimes…" Bess and Simon looked at each other and chuckled.

"I know you're not perfect and chances are I'm still gonna be a pain in the butt a lot of the time, in fact, I can almost guarantee that, but geez, I love you both so much. I hardly ever say that except when we say goodbye, but with just the three of us here---it seemed like the right time, and something I wanted to do. I feel like I'm just starting to know you as people, and…well, those people are way cool. That's all I wanted to say."

Simon reached across to Jonas and pulled him over to bury the boy's head on his chest. He lay his own head on his for a few moments before planting a kiss on top of it and releasing him.

He wiped his eyes and shook his head to clear it.

"Jonas, I can't tell you how much all of this means to me. Every father wants his children's respect and love. But

I want to tell you something on the subject of bravery, if I may.

"I think real bravery is in front of us every day, and most of us just don't realize we're looking at it. Bravery means going beyond yourself and facing what seems like insurmountable odds without giving up, and acknowledging the people around you that are doing the same thing, just in different ways. When I go to the Eli Institute, I am amazed and humbled by the bravery I see in the faces of those children who are struggling to breathe and still smile when a stranger walks in the room, or when the tech who hurts them every day to draw blood, comes in and says 'Hi,' and gets a 'Hi' back.

"I see incredible bravery in the faces of those parents who would give anything to be able to trade places with their children, to save them that suffering and pain, but who do the only thing they can, instead, which is to be by their sides, hold their hands, and smile to help them keep fighting. I saw that bravery in your Mom when she was taking care of me. She hurt for my pain, but she never turned away from it. She stayed, held my hand, put cold rags on my face and prayed for me. I see that bravery every day in these parents.

"Bravery is a dad who makes minimum wage and works three jobs to put food on the table for his children whom he never gets to enjoy because he's never home. And bravery is that mom who takes care of those children alone, and only gets to see her husband for a few hours a day. She gives her life to her children and her husband, and she never gets any medals, but she's a hero just like her man is.

"Bravery is the little old lady you see in the grocery store, with the bent over back, who uses a cane and walks slowly with a limp. She's in constant pain from arthritis and the terrible toll age has taken on every part of her body, but she still goes out and gets her groceries, and speaks pleasantly to the clerks in the store, and listens when her grandchildren talk about themselves. She doesn't sit and mope about her suffering, even though her pain would knock most of us 'able bodied' folk flat on our behinds. She deals with it and lives her life with caring and dignity.

"So--- I'm touched and honored that you see me as a hero, but I want you to realize that you meet heroes every day and never know it."

Jonas nodded his head slowly, then started to get up, but stopped and looked at them both again. "There's just one other thing, and I guess it sounds stupid coming from your kid, since if it weren't for the two of you getting together, I wouldn't be here---so in the grand scheme of things, this is kind of self-serving, but---I'm really glad you two have each other."

His parents were both a little stunned, and then his mom let out a sigh and cried, "Oh sweetheart!" She folded her arms around him and kissed his cheek. After waiting his turn, his dad, with his lips clenched tightly together, grabbed him roughly around the neck with one arm and jerked his head over to slam an almost violent kiss down on top of it, followed by a back slapping hard enough to give him whiplash. Bess watched as Jonas staggered forward with a grimace/smile as he received the full force of his dad's affection, and then made his way back to his chair with a little wave over his shoulder. As moved as Simon had been, the boy was lucky to have survived.

Men.

CHAPTER EIGHT

He looked in the mirror and told himself that today was the day. All his planning, all his rage would come together today. And this was just the beginning. Looking back, he would never have believed that someday he would be a killer. But maybe if he'd found the formula earlier, he'd have started sooner.

Being a malcontent wouldn't have appealed to him before The Rebirth. He lived his life in his apartment, spoke politely to his neighbors and co-workers, went to the occasional social gathering, and lived a peaceful life of semi-solitude. He was honest and a hard worker, never shirking his responsibilities, and he found a quiet pride and satisfaction in that. And then The Rebirth began.

For a long time, he'd heard people whining about wanting more out of life. They claimed something was missing---that they needed passion, and to connect with others on a deeper level. They wanted *families* and *love.* Whiners, all of them. For generations on end, his people had lived individually, without close social ties. New offspring, when they were needed, were produced in a controlled setting, where undesirable traits were removed and talents and tastes were molded to the needs of society. The young were created and incubated in labs, and when ready, were sent to dormitories where they were taught the skills and attitude necessary to live lives devoid of irrelevant relationships and suffocating ties.

His society had relinquished family and passion in order to save its people from the constant wars that had plagued their world since the beginning of civilization, and the move had worked. Without close ties, families, or religions, there were no factions. He had been comfortable with his life, always knowing who he was and where he belonged, until the whiners started growing in numbers, and began influencing The Seated, their ruling body. For fear of going back to violent ways, The Seated had held off those who craved a different kind of life. But it was said that *they* craved The Rebirth as well, and so allowed themselves to be led by a group of traveling scholars to go and see another planet, to learn about the joys of *family,* and to see the results of *love.*

When they'd returned to the planet and announced that society was going to change, and that people should form close alliances and friendships with others, marry, and even procreate *amongst themselves*---when they had ordered The Rebirth, they had ended his life.

Many times before, and even more often after The Rebirth, he had wondered how different he might have felt if he'd had a family. When he was young, growing up in a dormitory, there were times that he'd actually pined for a mother's touch and would often dream about a gentle female who made him feel loved and important. He might have loved having a mother. But he'd been raised not to expect or need such a relationship, and even though he occasionally dreamed about a mother, in reality, he could not have stood her touch. Embracing, touching—it was all too cloying. The government had made him this way, and now they wanted him to become someone else. Just because others desired it of him, however unnecessary.

He'd tried to conform and do what he saw as his duty to the new society. He'd approached neighbors to come to his home for food and conversation, and they had accepted, but these occasions had never felt right or normal to him. He discovered that he didn't *like* the extended periods of "connecting" with other individuals, trying to act as if he thought them interesting when all he wanted was to be alone. He found himself resenting the fact that these people were in his home, even though he'd invited them. He knew that this response was irrational and unfair, but to see people sit on *his* couch, and touch *his* things, was almost more than he could bear. He would be trying to feign interest in what they were saying, but all he could think of was how they were invading his sanctum. He was usually able to maintain his mask of cordiality until the end of the visits, but afterwards, he was so distraught that he would stay up all night wiping clean anything that the interlopers had touched.

He'd tried keeping company with a female, but felt no attraction to her, and she sensed this and requested that he not contact her anymore. He didn't blame her. She was only acknowledging the truth. It was just as well, for copulation and procreation were too unsanitary and disorderly to even consider.

The idea of raising his own young appalled him. The ones he had seen in the homes of acquaintances during his attempts to interact, were messy, often smelled bad, sometimes even *soiled themselves,* and required constant attention. It was insane. There was no order to them; no logic. When he thought of having one of them in his apartment, he almost felt the need to vomit.

He'd decided to try and live his own life and ignore The Rebirth, thinking that no one would bother him if he was tolerant of those around him who chose to embark on this journey into madness. The less he interacted with others, the more at peace he became, but the more he found himself singled out by others

Instead of ostracizing him, which would have suited him well, many had made it their mission to include him in their pitiful attempts at conforming. He was shamed into going on outings, attending dinners, and once he was even badgered and coerced into holding one of their disgusting infants, as if this were some rare privilege that he should be eternally grateful for. He could barely stand to touch the creature, or have it near him, and they had bullied him into *holding it in his arms.* This last episode so enraged him that he finally knew he had to take action.

He'd found others who felt like him, though most not as strongly, and he met with them occasionally, ever aware of the irony that his dislike of groups had put him into one. They called themselves "malcontents," and talked about how much better their lives had been when they were left alone, and there were no chattering "friends" or squalling infants to shatter the silence. They talked and talked about how the government should pay for this crime against society, but no one ever acted.

He worked in the wildlife preserve, keeping count of species population and watching to see if there were any animals in need of veterinary care. Sometimes he moonlighted, taking jobs to inventory facilities that were to be demolished. While taking stock of an old science building filled with defunct equipment, he'd come across some partially burned notes with a formula still faintly legible, and a dire warning that the compound produced by this formula must never be used again. He assumed that whoever had tried to burn the notes had done so in a rush, having to flee before seeing the notes completely destroyed, and hoping the flames had finished the job and consumed them.

He'd always had a good grasp of chemistry, and this formula intrigued him. He might have gone into the sciences as a career, but lab work often meant working in close quarters with other people, something he could never tolerate.

Being a curious sort, he began doing some research and experimentation, until he'd finally come to the conclusion that this was the formula of The Six. The Six had been the scientists who had ended the years of war by assassinating the heads of families and armies with the use of a poison that killed instantly, and was untraceable. The formula was kept secret for generations, only known to those who replaced the members of The Six when they died. After many years of peace, one of The Six had decided that the existence of the formula was no longer necessary, and too dangerous to keep or trust to posterity. Hence, he had destroyed it, according to legend.

The Six were responsible for the establishment of the way of life before The Rebirth, and he dreamed of seeing the old way reinstated. Now he had the tool he needed to begin.

The Six had begun their purge by destroying the heads of the ruling families, which were the only government in the days of war. *He* would begin by destroying The Seated. There had not been a murder in their society since he could remember, and perhaps a run of violence would alert people that The Rebirth was a mistake. With no violence to speak of, there was no need for maintaining an efficient police force; no security cameras were in existence as far as he knew, as they were considered an unnecessary expense. There was no poverty in their society, and with everyone having what they needed to live a decent life, there was almost no crime. Very few even locked their doors. This would almost be too easy.

He'd worked on the formula until he felt he had the exact recipe, and then he'd had to use very precise precautions to prevent being poisoned himself. Wearing a full laboratory face mask and respirator, plus long, impenetrable gloves, he'd devised capsules which would degrade slowly when in contact with the atmosphere, and then release the poison to disperse into a room, killing anyone who came in contact with the vapors. It was out of the atmosphere within moments of the kill, and left no trace in the body. The degradation of the capsule to the point of release was stimulated by the air currents from a person's movement in the direction of the capsule. When placing them, he had to back out of the room to prevent releasing the poison. After practicing in his protective gear, he'd become quite adept at planting the poison without setting free the killing vapors.

He wasn't sure how effective the poison would be against aliens, and this group of them---lizard kind and human, might best be disposed of differently. He didn't *have* to kill them---they were simply here at the invitation of

The Seated, to be honored at the celebration of the Rebirth. They had done nothing wrong, other than *inspire* The Seated to try the Rebirth. They'd simply been living the way they had always lived.

Nothing however, would embarrass The Seated more than the loss of one of their honored guests. Their deaths would also prove that families weren't strong, weren't invincible. In fact, it would be better to kill some and leave others to mourn, showing the awful effect of love on the survivors.

After finding the location of their landing site, removing supports from underneath one section of the walkway's floor proved easier than any of the steps he'd taken thus far. If any of the tiles in this section were stepped on just right, the victim would plunge to his or her death on the street, hundreds of feet below.

Again---almost *too* easy. He'd put on a company coverall from one of the unlocked closets in the landing facility, used goggles and head protection, as would any maintenance personnel when welding or working on something above their heads, and made the "adjustments." He'd told those who'd bothered to inquire about what he was doing, that he was strengthening the supports. If there were questions later, and their police force was so incompetent that there likely would be none, he'd worn the perfect disguise.

He was ready to begin.

CHAPTER NINE

Maurice announced that the ship would be landing in approximately one hour, and that they'd all need an inoculation to help them breathe on the planet's surface. For the convenience and comfort of their passengers, the Bluemen had been inoculated to help them breathe in the ship, which was set to accommodate human and Elpie oxygenation. Both humans and Elpies had taken medication on boarding to allow their bodies to adjust to an atmosphere that differed slightly from their own. Now it was the passengers' turn to accommodate the Bluemen. The pain from the wrist infusion was minimal, and the passengers were so eager to finish their journey that the discomfort barely registered.

Immediately after, the Colder and Jonas came to where Simon and Bess were sitting, and deposited themselves in the seats facing them. The Colder was staring at Bess, but not sending. Jonas seemed unsure of how to begin, until the Colder, with obvious impatience, gave him a firm nudge in the ribs, starting a rapid-fire explosion of words from the mouth of his nervous buddy.

"Ah, well, the Colder and I have been talk---sending, and he would really like to be given a name. He says---sends, that 'Colder' is what you think his clan should be called, but geez, he wants to be thought of in a way distinct to him as an individual. I mean, you know I'm putting words in his mouth, but that's the point of what he's sending me." The Colder nodded his vigorous assent to Jonas' words.

Bess looked at Simon, and he had to bow his head quickly and avert his gaze to hide his smirk and any possible "I told you so" look that might accidentally flash from his eyes. She smiled at the Colder and nodded back.

"That's a fine idea. Simon and I were actually talking about this last week. You're part of our family, and you *should* have your own name."

The Colder sat up straighter with this, and his mane raised and tilted forward just a tad.

"Let's see, what would suit you---"

"Actually, I've already thought of one, and he likes it. Remember when I did that report in English about the origin of names?"

Both nodded.

"Well, one name that I always thought was cool was 'Barnabas,' and it means 'son of exhortation.' You told me, Dad, how when you'd been poisoned and the Colders were helping Mom take care of you, that he'd always try to encourage you, and praise you when you'd try and force yourself to eat, or drink Eli's awful tasting medicine teas. And Mom, you said that he wouldn't let you grieve when you were told about the poison and you started to lose it---how he kind of got in your face and sent to you that you needed to help Dad instead of mourning him. And you said how he'd almost forced you to eat, sending that if you let yourself get sick you'd be worthless to Dad."

Simon looked at Bess, thinking of what it must have been like for her. He'd never heard about that part of her ordeal, but since he'd spent many days unconscious or semiconscious, he knew there were huge gaps in his memories of that time. Just as well, too.

Bess reached out and took the Colder's hand, remembering all he'd done for them. "I think it's a stroke of genius, Jonas. It fits him perfectly. He'll get in your face when you need it, and do his best to support and encourage you when you don't. It's perfect."

Simon slapped him on the shoulder with a smile. "Barnabas it is." Then he held out his hand. "Welcome to the family, Barnabas."

Barnabas' mane stood up slightly, and he made happy little chortling noises in his throat as he reached out and shook Simon's offered hand. Jonas was all smiles as he and the newly named left to round up their belongings and get ready to disembark. Jonas turned around suddenly and hurried back to stand in front of them.

"And geez, both of you---*never, ever* call him 'Barney.' Never has been and never will be purple." He looked pointedly at both of them, then spun on his heels to catch up to Barnabas.

"You know, Bess, if I had never met any of our children, and they were put in a room with a thousand others, I'd be able to pick them out every time."

"And why is that?"

"Because they all say, 'geez.'"

Laughing, she leaned towards him in her seat and gave his shoulder a little shove. "I had Gisella corrupted before we even got back to Earth. 'Geeeez,' was the first word she said when we got home and she saw the main house. Am I good, or what? Remember when Jonas was a toddler, and he thought we were saying 'cheese'?"

Simon nodded and laughed. "When I told him it was just an expression, short for 'gee whiz,' he thought it was 'cheese whiz.'"

"He argued with me for years about that. I'm not telling him, but that's one of the stories I'm saving to tell his fiancée. I have hundreds of 'Wasn't he adorable?' stories to delight our sons' prospective wives with. I even have some written down so I won't forget."

"My goodness, I never realized what a cruel streak you had."

"That's not cruel. That's just a mother's love, passing on the adorable moments that will die with me unless the women who love our sons know about them and can say, 'Aww, that was so cute! You were so precious!' It's a mother's right and duty to relay a verbal history for posterity. No matter how painful it may be for her children.

"Oh, and by the way, I know how difficult that was for you not to gloat just now, about the Colder's naming. That showed a lot of strength of character, Mr. Smarty Pants, especially since I *know* you were gloating like all get out in your mind, and you *know* I know." As she spoke, Bess began digging into his ribs with the fingers of her left hand, hidden by her folded arms, in a merciless attack on his absurdly ticklish nature.

Jerking upright and looking straight ahead, he spoke through clenched teeth as he tried to capture the assailant with his right hand, hidden by *his* now folded arms. "All right, oh Vengeful One. You *can't* tickle me in public. Think of my hero image---I can't be seen squirming and giggling like a little girl. Save this for later, will you?"

He had his limits, so she stopped, but gave him a victorious eyebrow bouncing, known in their circle as "Groucho brows." Gisella had even taught Madelyn how to do them, and it was amazing in just how many circumstances Groucho brows were appropriate. Actions *did* speak louder than words.

Simon relaxed again, with the assault ended. Beaten but unbowed, he regained his composure just in time to feel the ship's engines slowing, and a barely perceptible thud as the ship touched down. Everyone sat up and looked at each other. Humans smiled, Elpies sat at attention with mouths slightly opened, and Barnabas' mane stood straight up.

Luca Pacioli walked through the hatch and sent "Are you ready?"

CHAPTER TEN

As they stepped out of the ship, with Sven leading the way, humans and Elpies alike were dumbstruck by the magnitude of the sight before them---an enormous city filled with skyscrapers of every imaginable shape and color. Everything was huge and so colorful that it flashed Bess back to her initial trip with the Bluemen, when she'd been taken into a room that had shocked her with all of the rich hues displayed. The rest of the ship had been so bland and sterile looking, with mainly grays and whites,that she'd automatically assumed this was how the Bluepeople lived their lives---in plain, boring, sterile looking abodes, in plain, boring, sterile looking clothing. Geez, was she ever wrong.

As far as the eye could see, there were massive buildings and skyscrapers, and it seemed their designers must have harbored a phobia about any two looking alike. Some of them were made in such bizarre shapes that she wasn't sure at first that they were even buildings. One had a wide base, narrowing as it rose to its center, then widening again and drooping over to one side, ending in a pod-like structure. Another started almost in a point at the ground and flared out at the top, seemingly oblivious to gravity. Not content to vary in only solid colors from one architectural feat to the next, many buildings were multicolored, with stripes, swirls, and patches of different hues, some of which caught the light and sparkled like jewels.

Overwhelmed by the city that loomed before and above them, the passengers hadn't noticed the delegation coming up the ramp to meet them. The group consisted of fourteen Bluepeople wearing beautiful, flowing robes that, though different in color and texture, were similar enough to appear official or ceremonial.

As the fourth Blueperson stepped onto one of the tiles with missing supports, rather than falling away, it clung to the neighboring tiles and shifted so slightly that the Blueman was unaware of anything amiss.

As they traversed the ramp to the landing pad, thirty-five stories above the streets below, the ever present breeze ruffled and pressed the folds of the delegation's robes against their legs. A leaf that had somehow managed to blow all the way up from its birth tree below, blew across the arch of the ramp in bouncing take-offs and landings until it finally came to rest, at least momentarily, when its stem caught in the space between the shifted tile and its stationary neighbor. A sudden gust sent the leaf up and over the void, and when the blast of air faded, the wandering pilgrim swooped and twirled towards the streets below.

#

He was watching from the next building, and seething with frustration. All but one of the group had managed to step over or onto the rigged tiles without causing the tiles to drop. The piece on the outside was connected to the hand rail, so that when the tile started falling and the victim automatically grabbed the railing, that move would only propel him or her further out into nothingness, to go plunging towards a final obliteration below. Or at least, that's how he'd planned it. How could that many people miss or manage to move freely onto the tiles he'd rigged? Struggling to remain calm, he told himself that his work might not be in vain just yet. The Delegation and their visitors had to exit the ramp, so there was still a chance for his "adjustment" to work.

##

Luca had explained to them on the ship that this was a colossal occasion for his planet. They seldom hosted delegations from other worlds, and few had seen humans in the flesh, much less Elpies. But Simon, Bess, and particularly Gisella, along with the Elpies as a whole species, were legendary as being instrumental in influencing The Seated to begin The Rebirth. Mona, Sven, Luca Pacioli, and Maurice, were also celebrated as heroes of the movement, responsible for exposing The Seated to these beings and their way of life.

There was to be a ceremony followed by an enormous celebration in honor of The Rebirth. The government had issued language pods to any citizen who requested them—no one was forced to participate---so that should any come in contact with their guests, they'd be able to speak to them mentally, in the same manner that Sven's crew did. Even as unlikely as most individuals were to meet the humans or Elpies, the majority of the Bluepeople in the city had still requested the pods. Cheaply made and temporary, they attached painlessly to the back of the skull, and could be removed for sleeping. After five days, the batteries would be spent, and the pods collected and recycled.

A list of human names to choose from for labeling themselves had also been supplied to the Bluepeople of the city, so that the humans might address them, since Bluemen names were unintelligible to them. Again, the chances were miniscule that many of the Bluepeople would actually come in contact with the humans or Elpies in the short time they would be on the planet. But it was in a celebratory, Mardi Gras-like spirit that most of the Bluepeople in the city had voluntarily chosen human names. Everyone was ready to have a good time, and the human names became a source of hilarity for the Bluepeople as they struggled gamely to articulate them audibly to each other in the week before the humans' arrival. Laughter was no longer a foreign concept on their planet.

The guests couldn't help but feel humbled and honored by this much preparation on their behalf. The most extravagant privilege the government had afforded them, however, in Bess' estimation, was that during the celebration week, everything in all of the shops and restaurants was to be free for these Bringers of The Rebirth.

Sven bowed to the delegation, and after speaking to its leader for a moment, handed him the one bag of Marvelous Macaroons that had survived the trip. Accepting the gift, he bowed to his guests, and sent, "Welcome to our home, most honored guests. We are so pleased that you accepted our invitation, though it grieves us to hear that the Gisella child could not make the journey. I am Harold, The First Chair of The Seated. Our ceremony to honor The Rebirth will be in two days, so that you may rest yourselves and become acclimated to your chambers and our city beforehand. This is Joe Bob, who will be your guide during your stay. Anything you wish, please feel free to tell Joe Bob, and he will do his best to provide it."

Simon smiled at Harold and Joe Bob and sent to Bess, "He doesn't *look* like a Joe Bob."

Looking down quickly with a fake cough to hide her reaction, she sent, "So help me, if you make me laugh…"

Most of the Bluepeople were between seven and eight feet tall, but Joe Bob was only about six feet, shorter than Simon. Bess wondered if he'd been chosen as their guide with the thought that someone closer to their size would make the humans and Elpies more comfortable. He was dressed in a loose, short sleeved shirt of solid blue, with pants of blue and neon orange stripes, tied tight at the waist with a sash, and full in the legs, but gathering again at the ankles. His shoes were of a rubbery looking material, dark blue, narrow at the heels, wide at the toes, and very long.

"I am Joe Bob and very proud to be your guide and friend here on our world. If there's anything I can do to make your stay more comfortable, please ask. For transportation to your lodgings, I have reserved two of our chambers for mass transport. The Sayers family and their furred companions will take the red car, and the Reptilian family and friend will ride in the blue. Unfortunately, there's always some congestion in the tube at this time of day , so just try and relax and be patient with us, and we'll have you in your rooms as soon as possible."

Rather than the awkward handshake that all of their guests were dreading, The Seated satisfied themselves with a bow to them as they walked down the ramp to their transportation, as directed by Joe Bob. Earthlings and Elpies returned the bows to each of The Seated as they walked past them, trying to do so without tumbling to the bottom of the ramp.

The Bluemen seemed perfectly at ease on the structure, but the humans and Elpies were trying to focus on the delegation, transportation, or *anything* to avoid looking at the dizzying height they were suspended over. The ramp had only handrails, and no walls to separate its travelers from any mishaps that might occur from a slip or fall. Looking down over or under the handrails, the visitors could see the streets thirty-five floors below. It was difficult to feel secure with only a layer of tiles and supports between their feet and those streets. When they looked straight out over the handrails on either side, they could see the nearest building rising up beside them, twenty yards away, and between them and the building, nothing except the occasional bird flying by.

The Elpies took the lead, and Dulcie was walking just ahead of Jonas, holding onto the handrail with a death grip and trying not to think about the height. As she stepped onto the tile that had failed to loosen earlier, it shifted slightly, causing one of her claws to get caught between the tiles. When she shook her foot to loosen her claw, the tile and railing fell straight down, taking Dulcie with them so fast that she had no time to react.

Behind her, Jonas saw a shift, and then the collapse, and as Dulcie began to fall, he shouted and lunged forward, grabbing her tail with one hand. Her weight threw him to the tiles, and he started sliding forward over the edge of the tile he was on---a tile that was now tilting towards the hole. He tried to grab the neighboring tile to give him a handhold, but the material was too slick, and he felt himself sliding off the edge, when suddenly, strong Elpie hands grabbed his legs and stopped his descent.

Dulcie was dangling head down, looking at the yawning chasm of buildings, with its sidewalks and people barely visible at the bottom. Only the sound of the wind and her own terrified whimpering reached her ears. Though she had wrapped some of her tail around Jonas' arm, she knew it wasn't enough to hold her weight for long, and she hung precariously over the drop, swaying in the wind. She could feel Jonas slipping at first, and when he stopped moving, she felt her tail starting to slip from his grasp. Now that he was held by the other Elpies, he shifted around and twisted so that his other hand could grasp her tail as well, but his position was still wrong for a good grip. He was screaming for her to hold on, when she heard Simon shout at her, "Dulcie, reach—grab my hand!"

Martha and Ruth were holding onto Jonas, and four yards away, Eli and Barnabas were at another hole that had opened up to the side of them, holding Simon off the edge up to his waist, so that his longer arms could reach Dulcie. She stretched towards him as far as she could, but it wasn't good enough. Simon shouted at his son, "Jonas, you've got to swing her this way! Slowly, just swing her slowly towards me!"

"Dad, she's slipping! If I swing her, she might fall!" Then Jonas picked up Dulcie's sending for him to do it, because she'd slip for sure if she stayed in this position much longer. Her weight was pulling her down.

His right arm felt like it was being wrenched out at the shoulder, his hand was getting numb, and the right side of his back was starting to spasm, so he figured she was right. He couldn't keep his grip much longer, and his left hand couldn't get as good a grip without shifting his right, which he didn't dare do. "All right! Hold on Dulcie, here goes!"

He prayed harder than he ever had in his life, praying for the strength to hold on and not drop his friend to her death. He sent to the other sisters that he needed to shift outwards to adjust the grip with his left hand, and he felt them ease him down just slightly. With his left hand in a better position now, he swayed away from his dad and then swung the terrified Elpie towards him. No good---she still couldn't reach Simon's hand.

"Come on, Jonas, you can do it! Harder! Swing your upper body when you swing your arms! Again---hurry, she's losing her grip!"

He swung again, using his whole upper body to swing away, and then threw himself in the direction of his dad with the return swing. Dulcie swung towards Simon, seeing the distant buildings fly past as she flew through the void, and Jonas could feel her slipping down further out of his grasp. She reached out frantically, and Simon grabbed her wrist. She was able to swing her other hand up then, and he grabbed that wrist as well, just as her tail slipped out of Jonas grip.

With his head down, he couldn't see that she'd been caught, and he screamed, "NO, DULCIE!" knowing that he'd lost her, that he'd let her die, then hearing those blessed words that his dad shouted out: "I've got her! Pull us up!"

In the next moment, the tile supporting Jonas' chest collapsed, and the abrupt jarring made Ruth lose her grip on the leg she was holding. He felt himself falling sideways, and knew that when his whole weight fell to the side, it would wrench his other leg from Martha's grasp. But then another hand reached down and grabbed the pocket of his jeans, stopping his sideways swing with a jerk. His mom, her legs wrapped around a railing support, had been reaching for him when the other tile collapsed. She'd lunged forward then to grab the only thing she could get a hand on, cramming one hand into his back pocket, and then a piece of denim and some thread, and Martha's tenuous grip on one ankle, were the only things between her son and the streets below.

His mom couldn't have kept him from falling by herself, but she was able to steady him enough to keep him from swinging sideways. Suddenly a long blue arm reached out and grabbed the other leg, and as Luca and Martha pulled him back up to safety, Maurice reached down and hooked an arm around Jonas' waist, to lift him up and back, so that he could light on the ramp, supporting himself on bended knees.

Dulcie was already up, trembling in Eli's arms. Simon had been watching Jonas, horrified but unable to reach him when two more tiles fell away. The ship's crew had been trying to reach them, but everyone else was already in place when they'd gotten to them. They hadn't shifted positions for fear that would cause one or both of the other sisters to lose their holds on Jonas.

Workers from the platform were frantically putting out emergency supports to bridge the area, and as soon as the first support was in place, Simon ran over to Jonas. He was already in his mom's arms, so his dad grabbed both of them, pulling them tight against his chest.

He looked over his shoulder at Joe Bob, who was standing by The Seated with a stunned look on his face. One of The Seated approached when he saw that everything was under control, and Simon sent to him angrily.

"My friend and my son came very close to being killed just now, and I'd like to know *why*. Is this area so poorly maintained that the walkways just fall apart at any given time, or was this sabotage? Any of you could have stepped on the tile that she did, so it's to your benefit to find out. We came here at your invitation, and we assumed that we would be safe. If this is from negligence, then it's criminal negligence, and if it was sabotage, then something needs to be done immediately, to prevent more 'accidents' that just might be fatal."

One of The Seated approached him, shaking his head. "We are humiliated and horrified. There's nothing we can say to make this up to you, but be assured that we will be investigating immediately into how this could have happened." He motioned to Joe Bob, who nodded his head.

"I think we'd like to go to our lodgings now and get some rest. Two in our party are very shaken, as we all are. We can continue this discussion later. Thank you."

Joe Bob motioned them to their chambers, and made sure everyone was properly settled before he closed the doors. "When we get you to your lodgings, I'll send a medic to check on your son and the---"

"Elpie."

"Yes, on the Elpie female to be sure she's unharmed. We are all so dreadfully sorry about this."

The "chambers" they were led to were in the shape of bullets, and they travelled inside what looked like giant, brightly colored hamster tubes. The cars floated on air once everyone was situated, hovering slightly until being whooshed forward at high speed. Abruptly they would slow down, then speed up, almost stop, and speed up again. For the humans, it was very reminiscent of being on the road at home during rush hour, and after a few minutes, the novelty of the ride had already worn away.

The chambers inside, in contrast to their outer coloration, were done in a soothing beige, with soft seats that had high backs to support their normal users' taller frames. With the visitors as the only passengers, their cars were quiet and cool, lit with natural light from outside that appeared and disappeared in a hypnotic rhythm as they moved in and out of the buildings' shade.

Most of the group was leaning back with their eyes closed, feeling the fatigue from the lack of sleep on the long flight, and a letdown from the terror of their near-catastrophe. A few unfortunate souls were fighting motion sickness, as well. Jonas and Dulcie had the added pleasure of being weak, shaky, and in pain from their ordeal.

Jonas sat next to Elsie and across from his parents and Ishmael. Pale and unsteady, he was grimacing slightly and holding his shoulder, and Elsie was nuzzling his arm.

Bess looked at him worriedly and reached for his hand. "Is the pain bad?"

He nodded his head, and moved his right arm gingerly, trying to give himself some relief.

"Everything on the right side of my back feels pulled or torn, and I think maybe my shoulder and elbow are dislocated." With a half-laugh he added, "And oh, geez, I'm so shaky." He gave a shudder then and sighed, shaking his head. "For one horrible moment, I thought I'd dropped her. I thought I'd let her die." He felt himself tear up with those last words, and covered his eyes with his good hand as he leaned his head back against the seat.

"Oh, Honey…" His mom reached out and put her hand on his cheek for a moment, then brushed it over his hair, and he was too tired and shaken to even be embarrassed.

His dad reached over, gently took hold of Jonas' wrist, and pushed his sleeve up with his other hand. "Judging by the medical miracles we've seen from the Bluemen so far, I'm sure the medic will be able to fix you right up." He felt the whole arm and let out a sigh as he shook his head. "Oh yeah, I can feel the swelling, from the shoulder down into the elbow, and the arm feels hot. I can just imagine how catching her whole weight with one arm must have wrenched your back, too. Here, put my bag beside you and keep your arm elevated on it until we get there---tell me when it's in a comfortable position. That won't do much, but hopefully it will keep the swelling from getting a lot worse." His mom supported the limb while he and his dad wrestled with the bag to get it situated.

With his arm finally placed as well as they could manage, Jonas sighed and leaned back in his seat again. His dad looked at how pale he was, and hovered over him. "Do you need to lie down? Let me see if I can adjust the seat." He got up and felt over the back and sides of the seat until he finally found a lever that let the back of the seat go down just slightly. The arm rests didn't fold away, so he couldn't lie across the seats. Huffing in frustration, he put one hand gently on his shoulder. "That didn't help much. Do you need to lie on the floor? I can get one of my shirts out for you to lie on and---"

"No, Dad, I'm okay. I'm not going to faint or anything. I just hurt a lot."

"Here, at least put your feet up in my lap. There---any better?"

"Actually, yeah, that did help a little. Thanks." He shook his head and closed his eyes again. "I am just so very thankful that Dulcie's okay. He opened his eyes and looked at his parents with a little smirk. "And I'm definitely happy about not ending up as a stain on the concrete myself."

"Son, we are *so* proud of you. That took fast thinking and a lot of guts to dive towards that hole."

"Well, I wasn't planning on sliding that far over. That just happened and I kinda had to go along for the ride."

"But you didn't let go of Dulcie, even when you were sliding down and your shoulder and back were wrenched. You didn't let go. You saved her life."

"No, you saved her life when you pulled her up."

"If you hadn't caught her, she'd have been dead before any of us could've reached her. You're a bona fide hero, lad. And your mom was no slouch, either."

"Oh *whoa,* yeah Mom, I haven't even thanked you. Sorry, I just---well, you know. I would've been a goner if you hadn't caught me---Martha couldn't have held on if I'd have swung completely to the side. Hey---I thought you were afraid of heights."

"I am, but when you were hanging there, my brain just automatically switched into Mom-mode, and the heights didn't matter. Once we got you back up and I knew you were safe, I sort of wanted to panic and vomit. What a way to start a vacation, huh? Are you okay, Simon?"

"Oh, I'm fine. No way Barnabas and Eli were going to drop me with Eli's wife in my hands. But I tell you, after they pulled both of us back up, I had a little spell of the shakes there, myself, and when I saw Jonas sliding down, I think my heart stopped for about a minute. I'm just thankful it's over and we're all still alive."

"But your arms? Do you need them looked at? Old guy like you doing trapeze catches---you could hurt yourself!"

"My arms are fine. I may be fifty-four, but my muscles are only twenty."

"Brag, brag, brag."

He frowned then. "I just hope they get to the bottom of this. *Never* should this have happened on a ramp that sees as much use as this one probably does."

Bess sighed and leaned back, feeling more jittery than she wanted to admit, but determined not to let this incident spoil their trip. "Well, it's over now for us. I guess there are sloppy maintenance procedures on every planet at times, or maybe just a lazy worker. It's their problem now, so let's just relax and have a nice time, after we get Jonas fixed up. We know *we're* not targets---they haven't known us long enough to dislike us."

##

In the Elpies' chamber, Dulcie was still shaking, and had a terrible headache from being upside down for so long. Her tail had been stretched and strained and was hurting badly, but *she was alive*. Eli reached into his medicine pouch and brought something out for her to chew, and then pulled her close to put his arm around her. Martha sat on the other side of her, and leaned her head against her shoulder while she rubbed her arm. Ruth sat on the other side of Martha, reaching across her lap to hold Dulcie's hand.

Sitting across from them and watching them trying to comfort Dulcie, Barnabas thought that it would destroy *all* of them if something happened to any one of them. Being triplets and empaths on top of that, the sisters' psyches were so intertwined that no one ever hurt or rejoiced alone. They all loved Eli and he loved them in return.

Clearing his mind of what *might* have been, Barnabas put his head back and tried to sleep.

#

After a prolonged silence, Bess reached for her husband's hand. "Simon, I'm scared."

He opened his eyes and turned his head to look at her. "I know, this was really ho---"

"No, I mean about the ceremony. You know—they'll probably be giving speeches."

"Oh no, I'd forgotten about that. It's been so long."

Jonas opened his eyes and looked over at them, his curiosity tweaked. "Forgot about what? What's she afraid of?"

Simon sat up and looked at Bess pointedly while addressing Jonas. "Son, there's something you need to know about your mother."

"What?"

He turned his gaze back to his son, and his voice took on a tone of annoyance. "Your mother has an almost *pathological* inability to stay awake if she sits for over five minutes in any gathering where some poor soul is speaking. Not only does she fall asleep, but her head nods down, then jerks back up when she tries to wake up, then nods down again, back and forth, back and forth, like a sloth with hiccups. *So* inconspicuous. *And* she snores."

Bess looked appalled. "I do not!"

"Yeah, you do, Mom," Jonas said authoritatively.

"Well, certainly not like your father."

"Of course not. *Nobody* snores like Dad." He smiled proudly at his father. "He's my inspiration."

"No, Bess, not like me, although really, how would you know since you're asleep when you do it? No, instead of a nice big, robust snore, you make these weird little animal noises----squeaks and grunts, and sometimes you whistle through your nose, and twitch and sort of whine."

"Yeah, Mom, he's not kidding. You know what Saint Eli used to do when we were little kids? I know you think he's so nice and all, and I gotta admit, he is pretty cool now, but he used to really put stuff over on us younger kids when we were little. Whenever you'd fall asleep on the couch, watching TV or reading, and you'd start making those noises, Eli would tell us you were possessed and for us to run to our rooms and hide so he could pray over you."

Bess and Simon both gasped.

"Yeah, so while we were hiding in our rooms, scared out of our minds, he'd raid the cookie jar, hog the TV, and do whatever he wanted without little kids around to bug him or tattle. As soon as you started to wake up, he'd come and tell us that he'd cured you, and it was safe to come out. That was so we wouldn't scream and get hysterical when you stuck your heads in our rooms to see where we were. That could've given him away."

"Oh my gosh! To think of you poor little things being so terrified, and of your own mother---how horrible! Just *wait* 'til I get hold of him."

"Mom, it's alright---that was years ago, and we all found out he was lying and that you were okay when he accidentally broke the cookie jar. When we came in to see what happened, he had his mouth full of cookies instead of prayers. He fessed up and shared the cookies, to get us to promise not to tell you."

"Well, back to the subject. Did you never wonder, Jonas, why *I* went to your PTA meetings instead of your mom, or why we always sat on the back row for awards ceremonies they had at your school? That's why. You really think that could happen here, Bess? You don't think that being on *another planet* is enough to keep you awake?"

"Maybe I could get Eli or Joe Bob to give me some kind of stimulant."

"Are you *out of your mind*?" he half shouted.

"Dad! Geez, what's so awful about that?"

"Oh, Simon, I was just kidding."

"Well, it wasn't funny. There was nothing funny about that night. It left me with a *very bad* taste in my mouth that comes back whenever I think about it," he retorted angrily.

"Okay, if you're going to talk about stuff in front of me, then you have to explain yourself, Dad."

"Well…you've seen your mother when she's had a second cup of coffee, right? Can't stop talking for two hours, wants to rearrange all the furniture, and then goes into her manicky painting mode."

"Oh, come on, I haven't done that in years. I almost always drink decaf or just one cup of the real thing."

"I'm not talking about *now*. I'm telling our son a story, if you don't mind."

Bess sighed, rolled her eyes and slumped back in her seat.

"When you were just a baby, Jonas, I was given an award by the Herbal Medicine Scholars' Society. May not sound like much to you, but it was huge for me, since they were honoring a book I'd just had published on the subject. Your mother insisted on going with me, to *be there for me,* even though I discouraged her due to her little problem. She swore she had it under control, and against my better judgement, I took her with me to the affair.

"Little did I know---your mother had bought a pack of these energy tablets you buy at the convenience store---"

"Oh Mom, you didn't---"

"And she takes them without telling me, right before we leave for the dinner.

"We get through part of the dinner okay, but then the first speaker begins talking, and all of a sudden, your mother starts humming. Very quietly, but still loud enough for everybody at our own and the surrounding tables to hear. So I reach out to take her hand and send to her to stop, and she does. But *then* she starts trying to thumb wrestle with me. I'm trying to put my hand over hers and hold it down without attracting any more attention than she already has, and she starts giggling, and you know what she's like once she starts giggling.

"Now, your mother is usually very well-mannered in public, so I'm starting to get the idea that maybe she's taken something. You know your mom and I can send to each other, but what you don't know is that we can *reach* for each other's thoughts or experiences, in a very limited way, if we really have to. It's a big breach of privacy, so we rarely do it. But in this instance, I felt it was warranted. And sure enough, when I felt her mind I could tell there was some outside influence affecting her inhibitions and reasoning.

"So I figure the best thing I can do is to get her to drink lots of water to try and dilute whatever's in her system. I send to her that I need for her to drink, and she sends back, "Okey Dokey," which she's probably never said in her entire life. She's stifled her giggling, to my great relief, but then she starts humming while her lips are in the water, making these gurgling, blubbering sounds that have half the tables around us staring. So I get the water away from her, and by then I'm just wanting to get out of there, but *I* have to speak next.

"She's dabbed her mouth dry, and put this composed look on her face, so I'm thinking *maybe* we're out of the woods. *But now* she arranges her fork and spoon and leftover meat into a sort of ski jump, gets some of her peas, and starts rolling them down the ramp and off the spoon to send them flying a whole inch or two through the air. And each time a pea goes flying, your mother, in this little mouse voice, very quiet, but still audible, is saying, 'Wheee, wheeee.' And since at five-eleven, she's taller than most of the women and half the men seated, she's visible to almost everyone in the room, and the speaker in particular, who by now, no one is listening to, with all eyes riveted on her."

Jonas was laughing, but Simon was getting angrier with every remembered trespass, which he seemed to have memorized in startling detail.

"Well, at this point, I had to do something to keep her from disrupting the *whole affair*, so I take her arm and escort her to the car. The parking lot was guarded and perfectly safe, so I tell her to lock the door and stay there until I finish. She says, 'No Problem!' and that she'd be happier sitting and reading the newspaper anyway, so I went back in."

"You left your children's drugged up mother *alone* in a locked car? Not cool, Dad, very not cool."

Simon looked a little sheepish. "On retrospect, I have to admit that *was* a bit irresponsible of me, but I was desperate. The whole banquet hall was full and waiting for me to speak. I couldn't just disappear, and I couldn't keep her in the room.

"So finally, I finish my speech, get my award, and rush out to the car. Fortunately, no one asked what was wrong with your mother. I mean, which would be more humiliating, saying, 'Oh, sorry, excuse my wife, she's a bit mental,' or 'Oh, sorry, excuse my wife, she's on drugs?' Everybody tried to act like it didn't happen, which was wonderfully civilized, I thought.

"So when I get to the car, *of course,* your mother isn't there. I'm looking around for her, when at this park across the street I see a bunch of people gathered around something." He stretched his hand across his eyes and forehead for a moment, clenching his teeth, then took a deep breath, looked at Jonas and shook his head. "Jonas, you cannot *imagine* the feeling of dread I had crossing that street and working my way to the front of the crowd.

"There's your mother, dancing by herself in front of a street musician. And when I say dancing, I mean *dancing.* You've never seen your mother when she completely lets go and *dances*, and you *shouldn't*, but she was doing it then. You know how in the movies, when something like that happens, how the whole crowd smiles and starts dancing along? Just so you know, that's *rubbish.* People were staring at her, some with pity, some in obvious distaste, and some laughing, but *not* in a nice way. I almost felt compelled to punch a few faces to defend her honor."

"Dad, I don't see what the big deal was. Lots of people dance to street musicians' music."

"Yes, well, it wouldn't have been *quite* as embarrassing if there had *been* any music, but the guy was taking a tobacco break. He's standing there, leaning against a tree, sucking smoke into his lungs while he watches your mom dancing in front of his guitar case.

"So I grab her arm and start pulling her with me through the crowd, and people are saying things like, 'Get that woman under control or don't let her out of the house,' and 'You should get her some help, Buddy!' and 'Whatsa matter, didn't take her meds this morning?'"

"Mom, did all that really happen?"

"Ummm….I don't have very clear memories of most of that night. Just the vague impression that I really had fun."

Simon jutted his jaw out and turned to her angrily. "Sure, *you* had fun, *you* were *stoned!* But it was a horrible, humiliating night for me. And then I had to carry you into the house and *up the stairs* because you conked out about a block from home, after giggling and hanging out the window and waving at everyone like an idiot the whole time before then. Yeah, it was a *great* time!

"Oh, and *then*, just to put the shine on the diamond, when I set your mother down on the bed, she sits up, looks at me sweetly, says, "I love you," and throws up all over my tux. And since she was too trashed to help me, cleaning up *after her* and then cleaning *her up*, was just icing. I probably could never have slept after all that anyway, but with her having such a pronounced reaction to the stuff, I ended up staying awake all night just to be sure she was breathing okay and not vomiting in her sleep. Yes, it was a *glorious* evening, just as I'd hoped it would be."

"Wow, Mom's a stoner!" Jonas was cracking up at that last scene in his mind. It was too gross not to be funny.

Bess reached over and swatted the boy's leg. "See what you started, Simon?"

"*I* didn't start it!"

"All these years, and you've never forgiven me. I said I was sorry about a thousand times. I did what I thought would help me to attend something in your honor. I had no idea those pills would affect me that way."

"You're an intelligent woman. You should have assumed they could."

"It's been fifteen years, and I can't apologize any more than I already have. You need to *let it go*. Cleanse your soul, *renew* your spirit, and all that. You'll feel so much better letting all that anger just float away out of your head." She was having trouble keeping a straight face, but she knew that laughing just then would be the worst thing she could possibly do. Then Jonas jumped in.

"Yeah, Dad, come on, get over it and be a man!" He was biting his bottom lip to keep from laughing.

Simon looked at Jonas in disbelief and then at Bess in annoyance. "Did he come with you? Who *is* this kid?"

"Come on, Dad, what do you always tell us kids whenever we get into it? About misunderstandings, and how everybody makes mistakes, and we'll regret it someday if we don't settle our differences and learn to love each other, and on and on and on. So can't you follow your own advice?"

He felt as if steam must surely be pouring out of his ears. Especially since Jonas was right, which only made everything worse. If he ever wanted credibility with his son again, he knew he'd better straighten up and eat crow. But how to do that eluded him just then. Looking out the window at the multicolored buildings whizzing by, he tried to think of something he could say with sincerity.

Then Bess leaned against him and took his hand. "I'm sorry, honey. I should never have made light of that night. I know I spoiled a really special occasion for you, even if it *was* unintentional. But you've stayed married to me another fifteen years in spite of it, so can't we please just leave it behind? You and I know more than most--- life is too short and uncertain to let anything come between us. I don't want us to have even *little* hostilities lingering beneath the surface, waiting to fester. You can stick me with pins or pull up my fingernails during the ceremony to keep me awake, and I swear to never take anything stronger than one cup of coffee again. Deal?"

It took him a minute to switch off his resentment. Still not completely pacified, but knowing he should be, he gave her a forced smile, squeezed her hand back, and said, "Deal."

The cars came to a stop in front of a green and blue swirled high rise, and Joe Bob opened their car's door. "We're here!"

As they stood up to disembark, Jonas gasped and winced, holding his right arm tightly against his chest with his left. His parents both reached for him, but he shook his head, stood up straight, and laughed. "Whoa Dad, I think you were in more pain than me just now. It looked like your teeth were about to break when you gave Mom that smile."

Simon pulled his fist back and punched it into his palm, as he looked threateningly at his son.

Jonas just smiled. "Geez, the things you learn in outer space---"

#

He'd stood and watched the whole episode on the bridge from the next building. How could everything have gone that wrong? It would have been perfect if that cursed boy hadn't grabbed for the lizard when it fell. At least the incident had caused The Seated some embarrassment, but it was nothing he could show to the public as proof of anything.

He reminded himself that he was resourceful, and he was just beginning, after all.

CHAPTER ELEVEN

Their lodgings on the third floor were beautiful and luxurious. Identical apartments with adjoining rooms within each were given to both the Sayers and the Elpies. They were carpeted in deep, velvety, dark green material, with large living areas that had overstuffed, mauve and green swirled couches and loungers, and cushions around the floor for those who preferred lower seating. Each apartment had a spacious bathroom done in deep red, marble-like material, with sunken tubs in dark blue stone. Bess judged the beds to be at least nine feet long, and both of the apartments boasted beautifully appointed colors throughout, with curtains and beading that brought to mind a scene from The Arabian Nights.

A long, ornate table in a burgundy colored wood dominated the dining room in the Sayers' apartment, with seating and space to accommodate eight comfortably. Next to this was a kitchen in pearl gray with a plethora of appliances that were a complete mystery to the Earthlings. The best thing about the rooms, as far as Bess was concerned, was a balcony that ran the length of the apartment and looked out onto a wooded area. The best thing as far as Jonas was concerned, was that he had his own adjoining rooms.

His rooms were identical to his parents,' and when he walked into his suite, he couldn't believe it was all his---at least for a few days. The bedroom had an enormous cabinet that stood chest high on a human and ran the length of one wall. It was curved on the edges and had long, shallow dips and bulges in it, and the colors---a deep, rich blue with dark purple swirled in---followed the curves of the cabinet---a flow of color from one end to the other. There were drawers, separately doored compartments small and large, and a few cubbyholes hidden behind sliding doors, all within this one beautiful piece. It was made from a material that felt like a cross between wood and rubber, with a satiny finish giving it such a soft look that Jonas wanted to climb on top of it and lie down.

The walls were almost completely soundproof, so they could play music, talk, laugh, or even shout without fear of disturbing their neighbors. Although in this case, their only neighbors were the Elpies, staying in their identical suite down the hall, for the visitors had been given the whole floor for their stay. The Elpies loved the rooms, but were disappointed that the toilets didn't swirl the water.

Bess sent to them to avoid using any of the appliances in the kitchen, for fear of starting a fire or something worse, and the sisters were more than fine with not cooking. Joe Bob had informed them that the first floor dining room would be supplying them with meals twice a day, and the Elpies were ecstatic with this news. On the way to their rooms, the five of them had stopped at a shop on the first floor where Blueman delicacies were complimentary to them, and one orange colored, slimy treat that had caught their attention had made them chitter with pleasure at the taste. Now they were making plans to taste *everything.*

They were all glad to see Dulcie recovered enough to share in the excitement, but with the amount of pain she was having, she couldn't maintain her enthusiasm for long, and Eli had hurried her up to their apartment for a rest.

Shortly after their arrival, a medic came to see her, and after scanning her tail, ran another device over and around it. When he'd finished, the pain was gone. Then he ran the same devices over her head, with the same results. The Elpies stared at "Bart," with disbelief.

Uncomfortable with the foreign experience of their lavish praise, he stepped away from their palms gently, so as not to offend. "I did nothing extraordinary. These are very simple machines and I use them all the time. I'm, uh, happy to have helped." He bowed slightly then, and rushed out of the room.

Simon ushered Bart in hurriedly when music signaled his arrival at the Sayers' door. After the thrill of seeing his own set of rooms began to die down, Jonas' pain pushed itself back to the forefront of his senses, and it was starting to make him nauseous and a little dizzy. He was lying back on his bed, propped up with cushions Bess had shoved behind him, and his pasty color had both of his parents worried.

As he'd suspected, he had several small muscle tears in his arm, his shoulder was almost completely dislocated, his back was spasming enough that he was having difficulty standing or sitting, and it was painful to breathe. When Bart introduced himself and brought three handheld machines out of his bag, as much as he wanted to believe, Jonas was skeptical that these puny things could really take care of his injuries. But after using the first two to diagnose and stop most of the pain, Bart ran the third device over his shoulder with a slight pressure. Jonas felt a shift in the joint, and an immediate relief from the strain and tension in the shoulder. He swung his arm in a circle and laughed. "Whoa, that's incredible! It feels fine, like nothing ever happened! And my back doesn't hurt at all. How the heck do they do that?"

Bart nodded, gratified by the response to his ministrations once more. "I'm not a scientist," he sent. "I merely use the devices developed by someone else, and enjoy their effects on the injured. It gives me great satisfaction to see someone's pain disappear."

Jonas grabbed one of his arms and then held his index finger up in front of his face. "Wait, please, I have something I'd like to give you." He rushed to the other side of his room, and digging into his bag, brought out his last two macaroons and held them out to Bart.

"This isn't much to offer, compared to the amazing things you just did for me, but you can't get these on your world, and I can guarantee you'll like them."

Bart bowed his head in thanks, and out of politeness, took a tentative bite when Jonas explained what they were. The look in his eyes on that first bite said it all.

After Bart had finished packing up and saying his good byes, they were left alone to try and get a few hours' sleep, something they all needed badly. Elsie was bunking down in a special bed made for her in Simon and Bess' rooms, and Ishmael had his own bed in Jonas' rooms. Before his nap, Ishmael sent that he was going to check out the woods as soon as he spoke to the Bluemen to be sure it was safe. Elsie was content to simply hang out for a while in a place that wasn't moving.

Three hours later, after sleeping like the dead, Simon roused himself when he heard the entry music playing. As he opened the door, Joe Bob rushed in uninvited and sat on the couch, obviously upset. Simon followed him in and sat on the opposite couch to receive the tidings that had the Blueman so disturbed.

"Terrible news! One of The Seated was found dead in his apartment a few minutes ago. He was there to greet you this morning, and seemed fine---in good spirits and strong in body. We don't *have* deaths like this here. Disease has been conquered, and all of our people live to old age. There was no reason for him to die!"

"Was there any sign of foul play?"

"You mean---did someone kill him?"

"Yes, any sign of forced entry, signs of trauma on the body?"

"We haven't had such a thing in… in as long as I can remember, and I am close to two hundred of your earth years."

"That's very impressive, but don't you think it's a possibility?"

"No."

"Did anyone check the security cameras?"

"Why would we need those when we have no crime?"

"Why indeed? May I express our condolences to all of you, then. Where did The Seated one live?"

"One floor above you."

Elsie rose from her bed, stood in front of Joe Bob and sent, "I'd like to see his apartment and sniff around inside. I might be able to tell you something about what happened."

Joe Bob looked horrified at this desecration until Simon explained that Elsie was a Search and Rescue dog and an excellent tracker, and had worked with the police back on Earth. "I can't tell you what to do. It's your planet. But if it were someone I cared about, I'd want the dog to have a look and a sniff."

Reluctantly, Joe Bob took a red disc from his pocket, manipulated it, and a picture appeared in the air before him. He began speaking to the image in his own language, and the Bluewoman in the image spoke back. After several minutes of debate, he turned off the picture. He looked irritated, and didn't try to keep the annoyance out of his sendings as he responded to Simon's questioning look.

"I have permission to take you there." By his tone, he obviously had expected and hoped for an immediate refusal to Elsie's request. "Oh, one other thing before we leave." He brought out two identical red disks and handed them to Simon. "These are like your cell phones. They are only programmed to reach me directly, however, so that should you need anything, you can reach me instantly. You simply run your finger along the pattern engraved on the surface, and then press the button on the end. I'm leaving one for you and one for your wife. Please inform the Reptilians that if they need anything, they can send to you, and you may call me on their behalf." Simon thanked him, stopped to tell Bess where he was going, gave her a disk, and ten minutes later, Elsie, Simon, and Joe Bob walked into the deceased Seated's apartment.

##

The door to the apartment was open, and several officials were there, looking down at the body, seemingly at a loss as to what to do next. The body was lying in the beautiful ceremonial robe that The Seated had greeted his visitors in. There was no blood or injury apparent, and only a blank, almost peaceful expression on the Blueman's face---he didn't appear to have suffered or been in pain. An overwhelming sadness gripped Simon, at the thought of this kind Blueman, so full of life, so welcoming only hours before, turned now into an empty husk, and possibly because someone wanted it that way.

A vehicle was on the way to pick up the body, and next of kin had been notified, but when Simon inquired of Joe Bob, he was told that no police or investigating personnel were expected. Forensics were viewed as unnecessary, and security for The Seated had been deemed the same. The Bluemen's faith in the supposed lack of crime on their world was absolute, it would seem.

Elsie walked first to Joe Bob, with a polite sending of, "Excuse me, but this is necessary. I need to know what a normal Blueman smells like." Joe Bob stood stock still, extremely uncomfortable and embarrassed but cooperative, as the dog sniffed him thoroughly--- *everywhere.* "Thanks," she sent, when she had finished being way too personal.

Then she went to the body on the floor, and sniffed it in the same, slow, meticulous and intrusive manner. She went back to the mouth and nose several times, and finally settled there, sniffing intently for several minutes. When she finished, she looked at Joe Bob, and sent, "He died from something he breathed in. If it was still in the air, all of you would be dead, too. I don't know what it is, but I know what it smells like, and I know it kills Bluemen."

The Bluemen in the apartment appeared startled, looking at each other and back at Elsie nervously, but to their credit, they all stayed.

She began sniffing the floor, starting at the door of the apartment, and stopping about three feet from the body, at a spot next to the wall. "It was right here. Whatever killed him was placed here, but there's nothing there now except a very faint odor. I can smell everyone that was in the apartment, but there's been so many, I don't know which one was responsible."

She sent, "Sorry," to the other officials in the room, and proceeded to sniff them. "I need to know all of your scents, so I'll remember everyone I smelled in this room. I'm just a dog, but I think he was poisoned. Well, actually, I'm just a dog, but I *know* he was poisoned."

Gasps and exclamations sounded throughout the room. "That's insane!" Joe Bob sent indignantly. "The last time poison was used on this planet was when..." Another collective gasp rose from the Bluemen.

One of the officials stepped forward and began to send. "The Six used a poison that was said to be instant and untraceable, but it was destroyed, along with the formula for it, many, many years ago."

"Why would anyone want to kill The Seated?" Simon asked.

Joe Bob was incensed.

"There *is* no reason for anyone to kill another! There have been the occasional malcontents---those who never wanted The Rebirth, and have petitioned to return to the old ways---but they are so few that no actions were ever taken about their complaints. And regardless of their feelings, no Bluepeople would ever take their anger this far."

Simon turned towards the officials and spoke. "I know she's 'just a dog,' but I'd trust Elsie's nose over any suppositions you might have about your lack of crime here. If I were you, I'd certainly want to launch some kind of investigation, *and* establish some sort of security for the other Seated. If you say this poison was untraceable, that means the only thing you'd have to go on is motive and witnesses. That's where you need to start."

Simon was about to ask Joe Bob to take Elsie and him back to their apartment, when two of the Bluemen asked to speak with him alone. Joe Bob was approaching Simon, and when he saw who he was speaking with, his annoyance was evident. Seeing Joe Bob coming towards him, Simon held up his hand to hold him off, saying, "I'm sorry. These gentlemen asked to speak with me for a moment. I'll be with you in just a minute." Anything that annoyed Joe Bob that much might be interesting.

The Blueman looked daggers at him, but bowed politely and turned away.

"Hello, Mr. Simon. My name for your visit is Elliott, (for Elliott Ness), and this is my associate, Watson."

Elliott wore a dark brown vest, with brown and black striped pants, tied at the waist with a black sash. The pants were of the same type that most of the Bluepeople seemed to favor when not in the brightly colored robes---full in the legs and gathered at the ankles, except that Elliott's pant legs were tucked into light brown boots of a soft looking material for the uppers, and a hard sole. Very sober looking compared to what the visitors had seen so far.

Watson, on the other hand, wore a bright, Kelly green, long sleeved shirt, and the same type of pants as Elliott, except that Watson's had bright green and red stripes and swirls. His pants were also tucked into boots---bright red ones. The two looked as if their personalities were complete opposites, and yet something about the way they moved and spoke together told Simon that they were good friends.

If it weren't such an ugly and sad occasion, Simon wouldn't have been able to keep a straight face at the names they'd chosen for themselves. "May I hazard a guess, that you, Mr. Ness are in law enforcement, and Watson is in forensic medicine?" They both nodded, pleased that he understood the significance of their choices.

"But I've just been told that there *is* no forensic medicine department because it isn't deemed necessary, and that no police investigation was thought necessary either. And just call me 'Simon.'"

They all shook hands—six times, total, and then Elliott explained, "That's why we wanted to speak with you in private. We came here on our own today, as our presence was not requested. Our immediate superior has never been interested in pursuing matters involving possible violence. It's true that we don't have many, but when we do, he wants to find a plausible alternative explanation.

"I am what you would call a police official, but seldom allowed to try and function in that capacity. I, like you, *believe* your dog and feel that precautions should be taken to safeguard the remaining Seated. I *will* see that this is done. I appreciate your suggestions in this matter, because since you said all of this in front of the other officials, our superior can't ignore the suggestions as he would if just Watson or I made them."

"Who's your superior?"

"Joe Bob."

"You're kidding me."

"I have never found our situation at all amusing."

"I apologize. I didn't mean that I found it funny. It's just an English expression of---surprised consternation."

"Oh. Well then yes, I was kidding you."

"No, I mean, well… Anyway, I hope you can find something out soon. So Watson, what do you do, exactly?"

"Actually, I'm a chemist, but I've also been trained in anatomy, physiology, and medicine. Unfortunately, I mainly collect and tag bodies for the morgue. I'm also allowed to do minor chemical analyses and experimentation. But since The Rebirth, our populace has been given access and permission to watch entertainment programs from different worlds and read books from other civilizations, as well. I've read dozens of your books on forensics, and have watched all the episodes of every forensics program that your television offers, and I think by now I would do quite well in that field. We *should* have a forensic medicine department.

"Joe Bob is always saying that we need no security because we have no crime, though I think saying we don't have *much* crime is more accurate. But how can he say that we have no murders, when no one is ever allowed to examine any bodies, and no investigation is ever made?

"Over the years, we've had many bodies come into the morgue whose causes of death, or at least the explanations of them were very suspicious, in my opinion, but no questions or doubts are ever allowed. Elliot and I believe it's because Joe Bob feels that crime is a smudge on his management record, and since *he* doesn't feel threatened by anyone, a few murders here and there aren't a concern for him."

"That's terrible. Have you ever complained to his superiors?"

"Oh, Elliot tried once, and I tried in another instance, but in both cases, Joe Bob had the ear of The Seated that we spoke with, and our concerns were viewed as paranoia, induced by enthusiasm for our jobs. Neither of us was ever penalized for complaining, but we were viewed by some as alarmists, which made anything we complained of afterwards, that much easier to ignore. That's why we're so grateful that you said something in front of the other officials. If there *is* a possible danger to the remaining Seated, Joe Bob and the others here cannot ignore this, and we'll have reason to officially start an investigation. Anything else you can suggest, please do so, and when at all possible, do so in front of witnesses."

"What I don't understand, is that if Joe Bob is so high up, why was he assigned as our guide and helper? He doesn't seem too happy with that job."

"He was appointed as your aide because it's considered a great privilege to be able to help and interact with the Bringers from another world. Anyone else, ourselves included, would have been thrilled and deeply honored to be given this opportunity, but we've noticed his attitude as well. He hides it, but not completely. You're probably meant to notice his slight distaste so that you won't ask much of him. I think he simply dislikes having *anyone* telling him what to do, or asking him for help. He sees it as beneath him, I believe."

"Yes, I get that same impression. Anyway, I'll be happy to talk with you whenever you wish, and good luck on getting official sanction for your case."

Elliot stopped him as he was about to turn around. "Oh, Simon, one more thing, if you don't mind."

"Yes?"

"No one has introduced us to your brilliant canine."

Elsie stood up and took a step towards the Bluemen, flattered and gratified by the request. It was *about time.*

"You're absolutely right. I beg your pardon for the oversight, and yours too, Elsie. Elliot, Watson, this is one of my best friends, an amazing scent hound, outstanding guardian, coveted search and rescue partner who has helped our own police force many times, and all-around great dog, Elsie."

Elsie stepped forward and proffered her paw, shaking hands six times, and making fast friends of the two Bluemen.

After a few polite sendings between the four, Simon turned to Joe Bob and sent with an only partially hidden smugness, "Joe Bob, we're ready to leave now."

CHAPTER TWELVE

Within the hour, news arrived that another of The Seated had been found dead in his apartment. Elliott came to Simon and asked if he and Elsie would accompany him to the scene to have Elsie sniff there, too. With a second death, Joe Bob was finding it more difficult to deny Elsie's claims of foul play.

When they arrived at the site, everything was much the same as at the first. Viewing the body, Simon once again was filled with sadness and felt his anger rising as well, at the pointless loss of life---especially since this victim was Harold, The Seated who had first welcomed them so graciously to the planet.

Elsie sniffed the body and the apartment until she found the spot where she felt the poison had been deposited. It was on the floor next to a wall, just as the first had been. Many of the multiple Bluemen scents in this abode were recognizable to Elsie as having been present in the first apartment, since The Seated often met together in their homes, and tended to share the same circle of friends.

When she'd made her pronouncement of poison again, Simon told Elliott, loud enough to make sure all the other officials heard, "It's *urgent* that you contact the rest of The Seated, and tell them not to return to their homes. Put guards on them and have their locations remain secret from the public until this is solved. It will mean a long day, but if you'll take Elsie and me to the others' apartments, she could search for poison in all of them. She insists that it's harmless to humans and any other Earth species, so she and I could do the search and prevent further casualties to your people."

These suggestions made perfect sense to Elliott, who'd been put in charge of investigating, once the second death had been discovered. The other officials had reported

Simon's recommendations and Elsie's findings to the remaining Seated, who had simply bypassed Joe Bob's authority and assigned Elliott and Watson to the case. "That's very generous of you both, Simon. Any measures that could prevent more deaths should be put in place immediately. I'll notify a few people who can expedite informing and rounding up the rest of The Seated, and then we'll get started with the new searches, if that suits you and Elsie."

Six hours later, they'd searched each of The Seated's dwellings, and Elsie had found poison in all of them. She and Simon had gone in together in each case, with the Bluemen waiting outside of closed doors. In every home, small capsules were found against a wall that was close to the front entrance. Frantic calls were made by the other officials, as directed by Elliott, and the apartments were sealed off. Throughout the day, Joe Bob stood watching the procedures sullenly, and whenever Simon happened to glance in his direction, the Blueman would give him a look of undisguised hostility.

Now directed by Watson, Bluemen in full protective clothing arrived to collect the capsules, but each time they approached the hidden poison, the capsules would disintegrate, with their payloads dispersing into the air. Elsie and Simon went in with the first protected Bluemen when they attempted to retrieve the specimens, and when the gas was dispersed, he smelled a pleasant, floral-like odor that dissipated quickly and caused no discomfort to either human or canine.

After the fourth apartment, Elsie instructed the Bluemen to give the specimen container to Simon, and to let the two of them go in to collect one, since the capsules hadn't disintegrated at their previous approaches, as they had in response to the Bluemen. All they could surmise was that Bluemen gave off a chemical in the air that the capsules reacted to, and apparently it was given off in their respirations, since even in hazard protection suits, the

Bluemen still set off the disintegration. Simon was able to pick up a specimen without difficulty and place it in a container. He was starting to put the lid on, when Elsie sent to him to wait.

"I want to try something. Bring it into the tub."

Simon obeyed without question, since she'd been right about everything so far. After instructing him to place the capsule in the stone tub, she jumped in and urinated on it. The capsule instantly solidified into a dark grey mass. Simon was incredulous.

"What happened? Why did you do that?"

Her tail was wagging now, as she sent, "I did it because my nose told me to. I could tell by the smell that my pee would kill the poison."

"But how could the smell tell you that?"

"I don't know, I'm just a dog."

The news of this development was intriguing as well as encouraging to Watson. He gratefully collected the solidified specimen from Simon, and requested multiple jars of Elsie's urine.

"I need to drink some water first. Give me a few minutes."

#

The rest of the day was a little labor intensive for Elsie and her bladder: drink water, find poison, pee on poison. Repeat. By peeing on the capsules already in the specimen containers, she didn't have to foul the apartment tubs, something she'd felt very guilty about, being a good dog. By the time they finished with the last abode, Simon, too, was getting a bit tired of having to hold the specimen cups over Elsie's pee producer, and he doubted he'd ever washed his hands so many times in one day. Watson had them retrieve about a third of the capsules in containers minus Elsie's renal contribution, so that he could experiment with them later.

Canceling the ceremony seemed the only logical and honorable action for the officials to take, because of the possible danger to the remaining Seated, and also out of respect for the deceased. But due to the expense already put out, the celebration for the citizenry was to take place as planned. Although saddened by the tragedies, Simon was grateful and relieved that he wouldn't have to keep Bess awake through any Bluemen speeches.

#

Watson had been working on a chemical analysis of Elsie's urine, attempting to synthesize it for a whole day, and now he went running down the hall to Elliott's office, charging in without knocking.

"I did it!" he shouted.

Elliott looked up in surprise. "Congratulations! What did you do?"

"I broke down the dog's urine into different chemicals, and now I have successfully reproduced it! Synthetically, of course." Leaning over Elliott's desk in excitement, Watson was talking almost in his face. On the chance that his friend's excitement continued to escalate, Elliott subtly pushed his chair back.

"Glad to hear you haven't resorted to peeing in a cup. Is there a big market for synthetic dog pee?"

"There will be if there are many more poisonings. Don't you see, not only can we now neutralize the poison when we find it, but I can make a preventative to protect the remaining seated!"

Elliott stopped his report to give Watson his complete attention, because even if he didn't, he wouldn't be able to get anything else done until he left his office. Watson's enthusiasms were never easily quashed. Besides, this was intriguing.

"Don't tell me they'd have to drink it. Even *synthetic* dog pee is---"

"No, no. When the poison comes in contact with the urine, it solidifies, and its attraction to the urine is so strong, that it reacted even through the capsules it was in, when Elsie peed on them in the apartments. When I was experimenting, I put the urine in a container with holes at the top to let some of the vapors escape, punctured a capsule of the poison to release those vapors, and as soon as the two met, the poison solidified into tiny black particles and fell out of the air, dropping harmlessly to the floor. The urine is in liquid form, but something in the poison causes a chemical reaction so violent that the pee vaporizes and seeks it out."

"That's incredible! But how do we protect The Seated with your concoction?"

"I've thought about that. Since the poison must be inhaled, we need to have the pee next to the nose and mouth.

"That's a disgusting prospect."

"Be serious. What about a vial on a chain, as a necklace?"

"Would something around the neck be close enough to react to the poison if it reached the nose or mouth?"

"Oh, yes. Just as the way the poison seems drawn to the chemicals in our bodies, it's drawn to the chemicals in the dog pee even more so, and the pee is drawn to it. They seek each other out in the air. Come watch!"

He'd always been impressed with Watson's energy and facile mind, and to see him working this enthusiastically and successfully proved, to his way of thinking, that his esteem had been well placed. Elliott thought him sure to make an impact on the credibility of their investigation. It had always surprised him that so few people recognized the genius in this man. All he needed was the chance to use it.

His office was a round room, with walls of a rich, vibrant blue, with lighter blue and green shades over the windows. The blues were accented with the ever present Blueman pillows of deep purples and browns placed precisely on the small blue couch, with larger sitting pillows in the same material positioned on the floor, on either side of the couch---everything tidy and balanced. There was nothing to show that this was the office of a police official, other than Elliott himself. Of average height for a Blueman, around seven and a half feet, he always carried himself tall, attempting an air of authority and steadiness, the way he felt a law person should.

He walked down the hall, following the animated Watson, who was talking more to himself than to Elliott. "It's amazing how the chemicals are drawn to each other. Once one is in the air, it immediately seeks out the other, and dog pee has a much greater attraction for the poison than does our mucosa. I've checked it out several times, and I need a witness for the final test."

Watson's lab/office was the complete opposite in character from Elliott's. Bright colors everywhere, in no particular scheme, and though chaotic, the room transmitted a sense of energy, passion, and intelligence, much as Watson did. At just seven feet, he was a dark grayish-blue, with light blue eyes that seemed to be forever moving, and missed nothing. He always wore the brightest of colors, which as well as blending him in with his office, seemed to exude his personality. Looking around the room, Elliott thought it looked as if his office had birthed him. All this color and chaos left in a heap overnight, and POOF---a Watson was born.

There were notebooks filled with writing only intelligible to him, strewn in a seemingly haphazard manner all over the room, and yet he knew where every piece of information was at any given time, and could lay hands on it immediately, when needed. With only the minor experimentation that he'd been allowed at his job, he'd still managed to develop a few exciting compounds over the years, though none extraordinary enough to make him a star in the chemistry circles of the planet.

He hurried Elliott over to a five by ten feet sealed chamber walled on one side in a transparent material from waist level to ceiling. Within the chamber, a vial of synthetic dog urine was set up, sealed on the top except for a few small holes for the escape of vapor, and approximately four feet away, was a capsule of poison with a blade poised over it.

In his excitement, Watson was hurling his rapid-fire explanation so fast that Elliot could barely keep up. "All right, the first thing is, don't let the poison frighten you. It's sealed into the room. Also, it decays rather quickly in the air. If a person walked in even one or two minutes after the poison was released, probably no harm would come to him."

"Probably?"

"That's not the issue right now. Focus on the capsule of poison. The vial is full of my synthetic compound, which is not warmed or otherwise stimulated to vaporize. Watch what happens when I cut open the capsule."

He flipped a switch, the blade fell, the liquid in the capsule vaporized, and instantly, there was activity in the vial of synthetic urine. It was as if the liquid was being sucked out by the poison. A yellowish gas blew out of the vial with such force that the vial itself shook. The yellow vapor and invisible poisonous gas met midair, and when they met, tiny black crystals took shape and fell to the counter below.

"*You see*?" Watson shouted. "Did you see that? Is that not fantastic?"

Elliott *was* impressed, but as a "law man," he felt that whooping didn't fit the image he wanted to impart. "Watson, you astound me. I can't believe they haven't mounted your brain and put in on display somewhere yet. Congratulations! Well done!"

"Now, my friend, I have a great favor to ask of you."

"No, I'm not going to swallow any poison. Or breathe it in, either."

"I'd *never* ask you to do something like that! I want you to watch as I try out using the vial as a necklace."

"Does your wife know you're doing this?"

"Of course not. She'd be afraid I might die, so she'd have to kill me first, to save me."

"That's what I thought. What if something happens to you? What am I supposed to tell her? How could I face her? You know Joe Bob won't let me carry a weapon."

"Oh, come on, Elliott. She's a chemist too, so in the long run, she'd understand. Besides, there's no way to stop me, other than pulling your weapon on me, and since you don't have one…"

"You know, as often as we argue, you're still my best friend, and I really don't want to see you kill yourself. Maybe I should wrestle you to the ground and keep you there until you give up on this suicide mission."

"Elliott, I'm touched, really. I consider you my best friend, too. But I'm in better shape than you, so the wrestling thing probably wouldn't work. Besides, if you won't stay and watch, you know I'll just do this when you're not here. The whole reason for you being here for this is that I need a witness to prove that I did test this before giving any of these necklaces to The Seated. Also, in case I'm wrong, someone will know, so that my body doesn't just rot in here, and you could tell my wife that I died for something I believed in. That's better than saying I died because I was stupid. Puts a whole different slant on it, don't you think?"

Elliott sighed. "All right, go ahead. Hey, if you're wrong about this, can I have your file organizer? I always did admire that."

"Sure."

"Could I have that in writing?"

Watson scribbled out a note, dated and signed it. "Here---take it. It's nice to know you have so much faith in me."

"You should appreciate that I admire your taste in file organizers. Most people---I wouldn't take their organizers if they paid me. Thanks. I hope I end up having to buy my own."

"Thank *you.* That means a lot, coming from someone as cheap as you."

Watson stepped into the room and sealed it, then around his neck, put an amulet he'd made and strung on a cord. Once his protection was in place, he manipulated a small robotic arm to place another capsule of poison onto the cutting plate, and stood directly beside it. Despite having complete confidence in his findings, he could still feel his heart pounding, and his hand shook a little bit as he held the button to release the blade.

Elliott was having the same reaction as he watched his friend. Watson took a deep breath and pushed the button. When the blade came down and the gas hit the air, he could feel the movement of the amulet on his neck as the synthetic pee shot out to meet the poison, and he heard the tiny patter of solidified poison pellets hitting the counter top. He smiled exultantly at his friend through the glass, and then passed out.

#

He heard his Blueman name being screamed, and felt hands turning him over. Opening his eyes, he looked up into Elliott's frightened face. "Can you hear me? Are you poisoned? Should I call a med-transport?"

He sat up slowly, a little dizzy and headachey. "Help me up, would you?" He got to his feet sluggishly with the help of his friend, and then when the dizziness passed, he started laughing. "I did it! I actually did it!" He started dancing, holding onto Elliott's arms in an attempt to get him to dance with him, but he jerked his arms away, stormed out of the room, and slammed the door.

Watson stopped dancing mid-step, having to lean against the wall when a moment of vertigo hit again, but then ran after his friend as soon as he could stand. Catching him halfway down the hall, he grabbed his arm and demanded, "What's wrong? If you really want the organizer that bad, I'll give it to you!"

Elliott jerked his arm away, and almost shouted, "I thought you were dead! That wasn't amusing at all! Find somebody else to play your practical jokes on. You don't do that to a friend!" He turned away and started walking again.

Watson ran after him and grabbed his arm a second time. "Elliott, wait! That wasn't a joke---I wouldn't do that to you. I was just so nervous and scared that I fainted when it was all over. I fainted at my wedding, too, so I have experience. I'm sorry if you were frightened for me."

Elliott looked at him suspiciously. "You swear that wasn't some kind of stupid joke?"

"I swear on my test tube's rack. Friends?"

"Well…of course. Sorry I reacted that way. It's just that I was scared to death for you, and then when I saw you fall… It's a good thing I *don't* have a weapon."

They both started walking back to the lab. "So what now?"

"I think the best thing to do would be to make more of these amulets, and give one to each of The Seated to wear until we find out who's been doing the poisonings. I never could break the poison down completely. After I do tests with the last two capsules that weren't peed on, I plan on destroying the rest of the others. Why should we even have a poison like that? And what if it got into the wrong hands---well, I guess it did already, but you know what I mean. It should have been destroyed, like it was in the stories."

"While you're making the amulets, I'll notify Joe Bob. He'll probably be angry that you were able to accomplish anything, but he doesn't dare refuse us the chance to help The Seated now that other people know about this. We don't tell anyone about this besides him and The Seated, and Simon and Elsie, of course. We don't want this maniac resorting to other means of murder that we might not be prepared for."

Elliott was turning to go back to his office, and Watson to the lab, when Watson turned back around. "Have you had any luck getting that fingerprinting info from the FBI, or was it the CIA?"

"I started with the FBI computer programs, and integrated the CIA's. I can make them work together and I've changed them enough to use Blueman prints instead of human. It's not as easy to lift programs and transfer material from those sources as I'd thought it would be. Earth safeguards are usually pretty simple to overcome, but theirs were a bit trickier. I've been working on this for years now---it hasn't been because I didn't have it ready, that I haven't tried it out. I just never thought Joe Bob would give me a chance to use it. That's all I've been waiting for."

"I know that it's a shame to feel this way about terrible circumstances, but as far as our careers go, I haven't been this excited in a long, long time. I actually feel like we may be saving lives with what we're doing."

"Let's hope that's true."

"And Elliott---"

"Yes?"

"Not to be an alarmist like they say we are, but---well, now that you're going to be following up on leads, and interviewing suspects, you really should be carrying a weapon. You should speak to Joe Bob about it again, or maybe try to get word to one of The Seated about it.

"What if you find the poisoner? What if he doesn't *want* to come with you to be incarcerated? What are you supposed to do? Say 'Come along now, or I'll thrash you with my credentials?'

"I know you have a staff now, but they won't always be with you. You're going to do a great job on this case, I know it, but by doing a great job, you'll also be making yourself a target. I worry about you, my friend."

"Your concern is appreciated, and I've had that same concern myself, believe me. I'm just trying to find the right opportunity to broach it with him, because I doubt that I could get through to The Seated. But you're right. I can't put it off much longer."

##

"This is the chance I've been waiting for all these years."

Elliot was sitting at the table, looking down into the baby pit, watching his five month old feed himself. All of the newer homes on the Bluemen's planet had built in baby pits, with sliding panels to cover and blend them in with the rest of the floor when not in use. Baby pits were usually round, about four feet in diameter, and padded with soft, waterproof material decorated in bright colors and patterns. They came with hoses built in and drains at the bottom. Bluebabies were much more advanced at an earlier age than human babies, and with three hands, they were adept at feeding themselves as well as covering the entire area with food.

Babies were put into the pits naked at mealtime, and the food handed down to them. When the meal was over, parents simply hosed the baby and the whole pit clean, with everything going down the drain except for the baby. Elliott, and his wife, "Charlotte" for the week, thought the pits were the best invention ever. The baby was able to feed himself without having to be cautioned constantly about not throwing food around or making a mess, and he adored being hosed off. Charlotte loved ending the meal with the baby laughing in delight as he was doused clean.

"Well, I hope it makes all these years worthwhile. You've been given so little credit for your ideas, and had everything shot down that you tried to establish---I don't know how you've put up with it. I admire you for sticking to it, and I know that you really love the idea of police work, but there have been so many times that I've wanted to *demand* that you tell Joe Bob that he could take that job and---"

"Thank you, dear, for *not* demanding it of me. I know it's been hard on you, with me always frustrated and angry about everything. But I feel like this is a beginning for us, now that Watson and I have been handed this investigation. For the first time, I feel like I'm doing real police work. That I'm not just some token official that Joe Bob has appointed so that he can prove he has everything covered."

"The only thing that's been hard on me, Elliott, is seeing you treated with disrespect. With all that you've studied and researched, you know more about security than that pompous little sycophant ever knew existed. All he cares about is that The Seated *think* he's on top of everything, and that there's no problem, even though there is." She was drying off the baby while she complained, and was voicing her anger in a happy, cooing voice so that the baby wouldn't get upset.

"Well, bluest, if you said all of that to Joe Bob in the same tone you've just told me, perhaps he would listen. Or at least he might feel all happy and cuddly, and ready for his jammies while he was writing my termination notice."

She laughed and threw the towel at him. "Honestly, I don't know why you've stayed all this time, and Watson, too, when you've had other offers of employment. Anyone who knows either of you knows that you're both brilliant and driven to be the best at whatever you do. Your inferior superior doesn't deserve to even share breathing space with you."

He looked at her and thought what a lucky Blueman he was, to have someone like her think so well of him, and be willing to stand by him for so many years---even giving him a son. He went to her chair and caressed her ears with two hands, while he played with the baby's ears with his third.

She tilted her head back to look up at him, and spared one hand to touch *his* ears, which he flicked forwards and back several times, making her laugh again. "Not in front of the baby!"

She was wearing a loose, solid purple, sleeveless shift that came to just past her knees. The color accentuated her lovely light blue skin, the fit showed off her bony arms and straight back, and the clingy material molded itself around her large, knobby knees. When she dressed like that, she drove him wild. And well she knew it.

He walked to the cold cave in the stone wall of the kitchen and took out a drink, serious again. "Watson and I have stayed for the same reason. In the hopes that someday, we could find justice for the people that we know may have been murdered, and maybe set in place a type of system that could track down murderers and prevent them from ever doing harm again. There is so much technology about this kind of thing on Earth, and we could extract it, duplicate and improve it easily. But nobody has ever been allowed to, because Joe Bob has held his position for over a hundred years, and he's so firmly established in The Seated's eyes as the authority on everything to do with security.

"But now, with a danger to The Seated themselves, and someone from the outside that they can't ignore, stating the blaring incompetence and negligence in *not* investigating these deaths, we have a real chance. And we're going to use it."

##

"You did *what?*" she asked angrily.

"I tested it out. Somebody had to, and I couldn't very well ask someone else to do it."

Watson's wife, "Lucretia" for the week, stared at him in disbelief, and then threw down the satchel she'd been carrying. Just home from work, she was in her business attire, of a flaming orange, very fitted, long sleeved shirt, and skin tight yellow pants, swirled with green. She'd kicked off her green shoes the moment she walked through the door.

"How can you risk your life for that job? Aarrgg---I could *kill* you for this!" she said, shaking three fists in the air.

"That's exactly what I told Elliott. Which is why I didn't tell you ahead of time. Look, sweet ears, you can't tell me that you haven't done anything dangerous in your experimentation. But you're careful, you take all the necessary precautions first, and then you act on what you know. I did the same thing." He finished taking a slab of meat out of the cooker, smelled it, seasoned it some more, added some sauce, and put it back to cook a little longer before he turned around to face her again. She was standing and fuming at him, with two arms crossed and one holding onto the back of the chair.

"And, as an added precaution, I had Elliott as a witness."

"Which would have done you no good if you'd been wrong, and ended up getting poisoned. You'd have just given him nightmares for the rest of his life, and *you'd* still be dead."

"Oh, I hadn't thought about nightmares. Well, he'd have forgiven me eventually. He never could hold a grudge." He walked over and embraced her with all three arms, bending his knees a little, trying to get her to look into his eyes. She turned her head away and kept two arms folded, while the third reached out for the cooking glove he'd tossed onto the table. While he was trying to nuzzle her ear, she thwacked him repeatedly on the back of the head with the glove.

"Ah, I knew you'd come around. Wait until you taste this dish I've been making."

"You are *not* getting out of this that easily! You think you can risk your life and then come home and make dinner and have everything be okay?"

"Everything *is* okay. More okay than it's been in years." She was still thwacking him on the head, but the blows were coming slower now and more rhythmical---more like a metronome than a jackhammer.

Finally she unfolded her arms, and letting the glove drop, she returned his embrace. "Oh, I don't know why I get so angry with you about things like this. I knew what you were like when I married you." Then she grabbed both of his ears and pulled his head back so she could look him in the eye. "But you know I love you, and the idea that you could die for some advancement in forensics that your *superior*, won't even appreciate, just makes me so angry. And I call him your *superior*, only facetiously. It's not worth it. Your life means so much more than that stupid job does. So much more to me." Then she let his ears go and laid her head against his chest.

"Sweet ears, do you really think I would do anything haphazardly and risk my life, when I have you to come home to? Not a chance. And the job isn't stupid---or at least it doesn't *have* to be. The constraints that Joe Bob puts on it make it appear stupid. But everything is changing with these poisonings. He can't pretend there's not a problem. That tack doesn't appeal to The Seated when they know it may be *their own* murderer who's running around loose out there. Things are going to change. You'll see."

CHAPTER THIRTEEN

Since Simon and he were still tied up, Joe Bob had arranged for another Blueman to go ahead and take Bess, Jonas, and the Elpies on the tour of the city that had been planned for all of them. When music signaled someone at the door, Bess flipped the switch for the view screen and saw the Elpies standing in the hall.

She opened the door, bade them come in and took Dulcie's hand. "How are you feeling?" Nodding vigorously, she sent of her miraculous healing by the Blue medicine man, and twirled her tail in her hand as proof. Bess hugged her and laughed, and then stood back to look into her face. "I am so very glad to still have my sister."

The Elpie chittered softly and gave palm to her face. Then she sent that the real reason they'd come over early was to see Jonas and thank him. They'd already thanked Simon, but it was Jonas who'd kept her from falling to her death in that first horrible instant.

Bess called to him and led the group into the living room. When he came out of his rooms and joined them, the three sisters and their husband stood in a circle around him, laid their hands on him, and began sending. They sent of how much their sister and his wife meant to them, and about her children and grandchildren who waited at home for her return. They showed him what her loss would have meant to each of them, and then they showed him their celebration of her life given back to them *by him.* His was the hand that had held her over the abyss, and continued to hold, even when his own body was sliding towards the edge. Waves of gratitude and affection washed over his mind, so intense that he finally was brought to tears and had to sit down. They sent that they owed him a life, and that he would ever be remembered by them with love and gratitude for what he had done.

Bess watched as her son received the sendings, and saw in his face how humbled and honored he felt. Her heart bursting with love and pride for what he'd done and was experiencing now, she sighed in resignation as the onslaught of blurred vision, nose dripping, and face puffing began once again.

##

They would have been having a perfect day, if only Simon had been with them.

There were dozens of small bakeries, sweet shops, and fast food-type establishments along the route they walked as their guide expounded on the sights of the city. The buildings themselves, with their fantastic shapes and colors, were a marvel to the group, and the city was arrayed with bright, twirling streamers hung along the walkways, and sparkling lights that were strung back and forth across the streets. The going was very slow, since the city had been waiting for them and free food was being offered from all directions.

The Elpies had dedicated themselves to tasting every delicacy possible, so they were in a gluttonous bliss. Bess and Jonas had tried what didn't look suspicious or frightening, but even with being selective, they were stuffed to the gills. The two of them and even their guide were becoming more and more astounded at the amount of food these skinny reptilians were capable of downing without actually exploding.

Another reason for their slow progress was the many Bluepeople who'd opted to take the translators to wear, chosen human names, and were now dying to make contact with the Earthlings and Elpies. Some were too shy to actually address them, but others would politely introduce themselves and make mental conversation, just for the thrill of speaking to an alien. Their guide, Samson, allowed these conversations to last only a minute or so, and then would hurry them along. The Earthlings and Elpies, though a bit overwhelmed, were happy that so many were friendly and pleased at their presence.

Just seeing the clothes worn would have been worth the tour for the visitors. Bluepeople of both sexes donned the beautiful flowing robes, made in every color and design imaginable, from above the knee to ankle length, and from sleeveless to long sleeved. Others favored shirts and pants: skin tight or loose tops with the pants sashed or sewn fitted at the waist, loose around the legs and often drawn close at the ankles, making them look like alien gypsies or Bluemen pirates. A few preferred their trousers tight but belled at the bottom, and with the bright colors, Bess felt like she was seeing sixties' refugees in blue. The shoes ranged from sandals to boots, in the same wild array of colors. Shiny seemed to be in vogue at present, and the metallic-looking materials were particularly eye catching. The Blue people and their city blended perfectly.

##

Following through the city was becoming more and more difficult with the crowds that kept gathering around the aliens. He'd hoped to kill one of the lizard females today. When he saw how the four reptiles reacted to the distress of one of their females when she fell through the loosened tile, and that even the humans reacted strongly, this seemed the perfect choice. If one of the females were to die, this group would be a prime example of the devastation caused by grief when a family member or close friend was taken by death---just one more obvious drawback of families and close ties.

His knife was in the sleeve of the vibrantly colored long robe he had worn to fit in with the happy crowds. Even protected by the voluminous material, however, the touch of so many people as they brushed by him, or bumped him and excused themselves, was making him nauseous and nervous. Why did people want to be in places like this, where they were moving together like animals, and had to interact constantly just to prove they had manners? So many people breathing in his face---frequently, he found himself frantically blowing out air when he accidentally inhaled the foul smell of another's breath. The specially crafted lights and ornaments strung along the streets and above the walkways only made it more claustrophobic.

He'd thought the crowds would be helpful---that he could slip the knife into one of those leathery bodies and then stop moving as the crowd kept surging forward with the dying creature in tow. By the time the situation was understood, he would be gone. But there were *too many* people.

##

The music coming from many of the store fronts held a strange appeal for Jonas, and when they were about to pass what looked to be a dance club, he begged for their group to stop and go in. Since there was no age limit for humans and Elpies, and the idea intrigued all of them, they stepped through the door.

The frames of the walls were black, but within each were panels that looked like stained glass, and these covered most of the wall. The panels were lit from behind, and the colors of the "glass" changed as the hues and intensity of the lights altered to the beat of the music. The room was an octagon, and instead of stained glass, two of the walls, while still lit from behind, were filled with water that bubbled up to their tops, in synch with the current rhythm being played. When the water was within a few inches of the ceiling, it spilled over and turned into small rapids that curved through and over glistening mounds of multicolored glass until they finally reached the bright blue pools at the bottom of the walls. The dance floor was black and shiny, and reflected the colors of the glass and the patterns made by the water.

The appearance of the group started a high spirited commotion, with Bluepeople crowding around the table they'd been seated at by the owner of the club. All of the visitors had Bluepeople pulling at their hands, begging for them to get up and dance.

Jonas, normally very much on the shy side when it came to dancing in front of people, felt no such compunctions here, knowing that he'd never see any of these beings again. Freed of his normal inhibitions, he threw himself into trying to learn Blueman dancing. And when the Bluepeople asked him to teach them to dance like Earthlings, he obliged them. Dozens came out on the floor to try and imitate him. Not only was he not ridiculed for his skills, but he was the one *everyone* wanted to dance like. Even his mom and Sampson followed his lead, dancing and laughing at their own blunders.

The Elpies, not just freed, but *void* of inhibitions, as always, were into some serious gyrations. Reptilian bodies were not created for dancing, which only made the sight of their frenzied efforts more wildly compelling. Even in the midst of her own dancing, Bess kept feeling her eyes drawn to them. Elpies saw life as a grand adventure, and savored every single experience, every moment. To feel the abandon with which they plunged into each new thing was to understand joy and celebration. Having her son here to experience them too, just made everything sweeter.

##

He abhorred dancing, but it was perfect for his needs. With all the ridiculous convolutions and jerking movements going on, someone could be in the throes of agony and everyone would just assume it was part of the dance.

He set his sights on Martha as she bounced and wiggled to the music with a Blueman. The music was loud, and the floor was crowded, with lots of flowing sleeves to disguise the movement of his own. He edged the blade out slightly and grasped it in a killing grip as he danced his way towards her. Oblivious to his presence and the threat he represented, she and her partner twirled and moved in his direction.

Closer and closer---only two more couples between them as he followed the music towards his prey. One more couple, and then he was beside her. As he tensed to shove the knife into her side, her large dance partner put his arm around her waist and whirled her around. He almost screamed at him to get out of the way, but calmed himself and danced towards her back until the knife was only a few inches away from her green skin. He shoved the knife forwards as two other dancers bumped into him, hitting his arm from the side, and causing the knife to clatter harmlessly to the floor. It was all he could do not to throttle the Blueman that had bumped him, but the other was apologizing and wanted to help him find what was dropped when he'd so carelessly collided with him.

He stood up and rushed out the door. If the other saw that what he'd dropped was a knife, it might set off a panic, and he could be captured, or at the very least, trapped with the hoard of dancers, and he had reached the limit of his tolerance for the closeness of others. As he rushed down the street, jostling a few surprised citizens out of his way, he decided that destiny must have some other means of success in store for him. And he would find it.

##

Many feet were stepped on, no apologies were made, and all attending species had a remarkable experience. Before they were finished, a crew from the City Information Authority arrived to record Earthlings and Elpies celebrating with Bluepeople.

By the time they left the club, they were all exhausted, so a tube car was taken back to their apartments. Jonas flopped back in his seat, not even aware that he was smiling dreamily. *I've been dancing in a club on another planet, when I can't even get into a club on Earth, and I had aliens trying to dance like me! I'm sort of a hero---I saved somebody's life, I'm seeing an alien city, I've had Bluewomen flirting with me, have eaten and actually enjoyed stuff I've never seen before, and now I'm going back to my own luxury apartment. We're celebrities and everybody loves us. Life is so way good.*

The Elpies were chittering and sending to each other frenetically, tired and filled almost to bursting with all the free food, but still excited about all they'd done, seen, and eaten. Barnabas sent to Bess, for fear that Samson might have difficulty understanding his way of sending, that the Elpies thought this a wonderful place, and they wanted Samson to thank the city for their generous welcome. They also wanted the city to know that they hadn't tasted a single item of food so far that wasn't delicious, and that they'd loved dancing with Bluepeople.

When Bess relayed this to Samson, his mind radiated happiness, and she believed she could actually detect a smile on the lipless Blueman's mouth. He bowed graciously to the Elpies, and they all chittered happily and bowed back. Everything was a hoot to an Elpie.

CHAPTER FOURTEEN

Ishmael was watching a bird while he sat on the branch of a huge tree in the woods behind their building. Joe Bob had sent to him that these woods were part of a wildlife preserve, and though it did have a few large predators, he should be safe if he stayed in the trees. Citizens were free to visit, but they were required to carry fire sticks while on the premises. These were six feet long batons that could transmit a shock to even a huge animal and temporarily incapacitate it. Kept in a chest outside of the reserve's gate, a kiosk there showed recorded demonstrations on their use. Most of the larger predators had come into contact with fire sticks at one time or another, and because of the remembered pain of those contacts, usually left alone any visiting Blueman who carried one.

Ishmael had been invited to go to the city on the tour with the others, but he hated crowds, and he had been to cities. It didn't matter if the city was full of humans or aliens---the beings on the streets would be hawking their wares. He'd heard about everything in the shops being free to them, and not only did he doubt that, but he still wouldn't have wanted to go with them. Without hands, what would he really covet? To him, cities represented only boredom and a waste of time.

The woods---ah, *they* were worth exploring. With the size of these trees, he could travel from one to another without ever having to descend. Up above the world, hidden in the leaves but able to see everything below, life took on a different perspective. In the trees, he felt invisible and invincible. He was *master* of the treetops. Except for snakes. And the occasional monkey. And hawks and owls. Okay, maybe not the master, but at least high up on the food chain.

He'd seen some very interesting large animals: a cat-like creature with stripes on the top half and spots on the bottom, standing probably a little taller than a lion and possessing huge fangs, and then there had been something like a bear, with turquoise colored fur and a head that was pointed like an anteater's. It apparently shared a mutual dislike with the cat thing, and they'd had a hissing and growling stand-off directly under the branch that Ishmael was sitting on that morning. Try to find *that* in the city.

About half way through with his planned exploration of the woods, he started getting hungry and decided to sample the local fare. This red speckled bird thing looked promising, as it seemed very slow on take-off. He'd been following it from limb to limb, just observing its pattern of locomotion, and was about ready to make his move, when he felt the tree shudder a little, and looked up to see a giant version of the bird he was watching. It was three times his size, and *it* was watching *him*.

He slowly turned to face away from the smaller bird and began slinking off, keeping his body as low and close to the branch as possible. The larger creature's head turned, following his movement. He began moving faster. A loud squawk and a crashing of branches sounded as the thing plummeted down through the tree towards him.

He lit out at a dead run through the branches, with the eagle-thing straining to catch up. Unable to spread its wings to fly, it was much slower at maneuvering through the branches. Looking over his shoulder, panting hard, his heart pounding, he didn't see the creature, but he knew he wasn't free and clear yet---that thing didn't strike him as a quitter.

Crawling into an area of branches with thicker foliage, he held perfectly still and watched. At first there was no sound. Then he heard a slight rustling directly behind him that changed into a thrashing as the creature tore through the branches in an attempt to reach him. The only escape was below, so he jumped---a good twenty feet straight down. All four legs were spread wide as he fell, and he landed upright to speed off into the undergrowth.

The eagle-thing was screaming in rage now, as it dove to the ground and began to run through the brush after him. Ishmael was terrified but having fun, as well. Due to the Bluemen allowing him to retain Bess' memories, telepathy, and the lovely side effect of a human life expectancy, his attitude was not that of your typical cat. The added time was great, of course, but boredom could set in from time to time. The last twenty years away from any kind of danger had whetted his appetite for a little Adrenalin rush. And no bird, especially a large one, could corner like a frenzied cat.

He ran through the brush, trying to look upward as he did, to spy the balcony and the tree he'd leapt to from there. The tree was inside the reserve, but its huge branches stretched out high above and over the fence, making a perfect walkway for him to cross over. As he was running, his foot touched something thick and rubbery, and he jumped two feet straight up, every hair puffed out away from his body. The huge snake started moving with a shudder the moment his feet disturbed it, but his jump had ended with him clinging to the side of a tree, much faster than the enormous reptile could maneuver. He *hated* snakes.

Running through the brush in the direction he'd taken, the eagle-thing was in a direct path with the snake, so Ishmael climbed higher into the tree and turned around to watch the collision. He was sure that in a few moments he was going to see that beasty-bird being crushed in the coils of the constrictor. Harsh, but interesting.

The snake felt the vibrations coming towards it, so it turned towards them, waiting to strike. As soon as the creature came charging through, the head and first three feet of the snake went flying towards it, mouth open to grasp its prey. To the unhappy surprise of reptile *and* cat, the bird leapt straight up over the head of the striking snake, to come down with its claws and beak ripping at the base of its skull. Still writhing, it was dead within a minute.

Ishmael scurried up the tree when he saw the results of that contest. When it caught his movement, the bird jerked away from its grisly feast and flew at the tree. Ishmael had tried countless times to catch squirrels at home, but the fluffy tailed rats were invariably too fast for him. One thing he'd always grudgingly admired about them was the way they ran around the trunk on the way up a tree, always staying on the other side and so completely out of sight that at times he wasn't sure if they were even still on the tree with him. Using the same strategy now, he found the trick worked just as well *for* him as *on* him.

The eagle-thing would scream and swoop at him with its claws out, ready to rip him to shreds, and he'd quickly switch to the other side of the trunk. After multiple repeats of his squirrel maneuver, he finally reached his bridging branch, zipped across it, and made his leap for the apartment. His claws were already on the balcony railing when he felt a tug and a pain on the end of his tail. That fired up his engines, and he launched himself across the balcony and tore through the open door, whipping around in mid-leap to hit the button that closed it. A split second later, he saw his pursuer flip around to come in feet first for the killing blow, as he stood unmoving behind the glass.

The bird's feet hit with a thunderclap sound, and it ricocheted off the transparent door, falling stunned to the floor of the balcony. Ishmael thought its legs might be shattered, or shoved up into its abdomen enough to cause mortal injury, but after a few moments, it stood up, shook its head, and stalked over to the glass, staring death at him.

Ah, but this was his forte. He sat as close to the glass as he could and stared back at the thing. Their optical duel lasted a good five minutes before the creature let out a shriek and flew away. Staring was Ishmael's specialty and he could do it for hours with hardly a blink. Didn't do him much good against large teeth or beaks, but he could knock 'em dead from behind a glass door.

Turning to look at his tail for the first time, he saw that the very tip was taken off. He hadn't lost much blood, but decided to go downstairs and present his tail to the guy at the front desk and see if he could scrounge up some first aid for one of their honored guests. He licked the wound a couple of times and decided the day had been worth it.

##

Dusting all of the apartments for prints had seemed like fun at first, since it was a new experience, and something he'd been wanting to try for years, but the job quickly became tedious and overwhelming. Deciding his talents would be better put to use elsewhere, Elliott directed his staff in the procedure, then left to start interviewing people in the buildings where the poison had been found.

His staff. How strange and lovely that sounded. He'd never had a staff, never been allowed to truly investigate anything. He didn't know how all of this was going to play out, though. Joe Bob was not someone to take a slight graciously, and his authority had been bypassed quite a bit in the last few days. Elliott hoped he wasn't planning to take revenge against Watson and himself when this was over and they no longer held the attention of The Seated.

The problem with fingerprinting on this planet was that there was no database. No one had ever been fingerprinted, so there were no prints to compare to the prints they found. With all the amazing scientific advancements made in medicine, space travel, architecture, and the other wonders on this world, it was absurd that anything to do with crime or criminal investigation had been completely ignored. There *was* a wonderful dearth of crime on this world, stemming mainly from the fact that it had been engineered out of most people when they were being produced in the laboratory. But they were still individuals, they still made choices, and not all of the choices were good. People still had petty quarrels that occasionally erupted into something more.

How ironic that the individual responsible for curtailing the more serious spats that had grown from greed, jealousy, or pride, was a prime example of what these emotions could wreak if allowed to grow. How many possible murders had gone unavenged by the law because of the pride of this one man, "Joe Bob," and his desire to appear completely in control? How many more murders had occurred because the perpetrators knew that they had nothing to fear from the law? Joe Bob may not have started off evil, but he'd allowed himself to give in to his pettiness and jealousy until he'd become a danger to the society he was sworn to protect.

The dilemma for those trying to do their jobs despite the antagonism of their superior, was of course multiplied by the fact that Joe Bob had been in his position for so long that The Seated automatically deferred to him as the authority in Security measures. They believed him out of habit, and when anyone questioned his actions, he managed to twist the facts enough to make his detractors appear petty and jealous.

But at least now that it was The Seated themselves who were in danger, they had begun to ask questions for which he had no answers. This danger to The Seated had allowed Elliott and Watson to make a stand for police work and all that it entailed, including medical forensics. Both Bluemen were aware that the future of police work on this planet might well lie in their hands, depending on how skillfully or poorly they managed this crisis.

The best way to start, Simon had said, was to look for motive and witnesses. Elliott had questioned people at all of the buildings where poison was found, and the one common thread found in a few of these interviews, was that on the day in question, several people remembered seeing a tall man in the building. Nothing more specific than that.

He'd also interviewed a few people who had been identified as malcontents by others who lived in these buildings. He'd not been impressed by any of these as being angry or volatile enough to commit murder, and all of them had, naturally, professed an abhorrence to the idea of violence to further their cause. None that he'd spoken with were tall.

His idea with fingerprinting was to try and go through the fingerprints in each apartment, and try to find one that was present in all the apartments. The problem with this tactic was that The Seated had many friends in common. Fingerprints needed to be taken from all of The Seated, including the dead ones, and from as many of their friends as could be reached. This would take time, and time was something they might not have if they were to prevent a murder by means other than poison.

Watson had shown up at one of the apartments today looking for him, all aglow with his recent accomplishment. Elliott had been walking through one of the rooms, hoping to find other clues, when his friend had stuck his head in and motioned for him to come outside to talk.

"Hey, how's it going on your end?"

"Terrific! I fingerprinted The Seated we have in the morgue, which was really a sad business, but that's one more thing done. What I came to show you were these!" He reached into a box he was carrying and pulled out an amulet he'd made. Instead of an opaque, grayish locket on a string, the amulet had been painted a periwinkle blue, with red geometric designs and purple swirls throughout, and it was on a Shurcisian chain.

"Beautiful! These designs look ceremonial---everyone will think they're just part of The Seated's official garb. But where did you get the money for the chains? They must have cost a fortune!"

"Hopefully, if we're successful with everything, by next year I'll have a better budget. I'd better, because these *are* next year's budget."

Elliott covered his face and shook his head. "Tell me you didn't."

"I can't, because I did. Look, the way I figure it is, if we don't do well in this, Joe Bob's going to find a way to have our jobs, anyway. If we *are* successful and can prove that our methods matter to this society, then everything's going to change. To get The Seated to wear these and have them blend in to avoid questions, I had to make them look good. And my cousin did the painting for free. He owed me. Now I owe him."

"Do The Seated know they're going to be wearing amulets of synthetic dog pee?"

"I didn't feel it necessary to go into all the unpleasant details. I told them that they're poison preventatives, and all of them said they'd wear one. I just have to deliver them---I don't trust anybody else to, especially since we don't know who the killer is. Well, I need to get moving, but I just had to show you. I'm having so much fun! *Of course*, I'm sad, too. But I'm having so much fun!"

CHAPTER FIFTEEN

A cold, wet nose thrust against her bulging abdomen woke Gisella from a sound sleep. It was two a.m. and she'd been in the middle of a lovely dream. Madelyn had her nose pushing hard against her belly, and she was sniffing obnoxiously all around it, making loud chuffing noises in between her hyper sniffing.

"What is it Maddie? Doggie door stuck again? You need to go out?" Gisella heard herself muttering without moving the rest of her body. "I'd really rather you just bark. The wet nose is pretty nasty. You even got my gown wet---eew."

The dog was trembling with agitation as she sent. "Gisella, wake up. You need to go to the hospital right now. Something's wrong. I can smell blood high up in your belly." Gisella sat straight up, jumped out of bed and rushed to the bathroom. She returned in a few moments, sighing and shaking her head in relief. "Maddie, I didn't see any blood when I checked. I feel fine. Haven't even had any Braxton-Hicks." She'd been plagued with these "false labor" contractions ever since the beginning of her seventh month. Uncomfortable, but not unbearable, these had petered out in the last couple of days. "Go back to sleep," she said, as she lay back down and rolled onto her side, facing away from the dog.

A large paw on her shoulder told her this was going to be a long night. "You need to wake up and go to the hospital NOW," she sent again.

Gisella rolled back towards the dog, trying to keep the irritation out of her voice. "Madelyn, I told you I'm fine, other than needing to go back to sleep. There was no blood, I'm in no pain."

"You're not *listening*. I sent that the blood is high up. It's only a tiny bit, so you wouldn't see it all the way at the bottom yet. But something is really wrong and you have to do something now! Never argue with a dog's nose!"

Gisella stared off the side of the bed at Madelyn's sincere, worried looking face. She started thinking about service dogs who could warn their masters when seizures were about to strike, or when their blood sugars were too low or too high, and dogs that had alerted their owners to melanomas and other types of cancer. She thought about cadaver dogs that could smell bodies from fifty feet under water, and dogs at the airport who could sniff out bugs or snakes or drugs—whatever their noses were attuned to, they could find.

All during her pregnancy, Madelyn had been almost constantly by her side, and she would carefully sniff over her abdomen several times a day to be sure everything was fine. Gisella had thought her concern sweet—she'd never even considered that Maddie might actually smell something she needed to know about. Suddenly she was frightened.

She rolled over and shook Hiram's shoulder. "Hiram, wake up, we have to go to the hospital!" She was already getting dressed before he became coherent.

He sat up groggily, and then what she'd said registered in his brain. "What's wrong? Did your water break? Are you having contractions?"

"No, I feel fine. But Madelyn says she smells blood up high inside my abdomen. Come on, get up, we have to go!"

He groaned loudly, sighed, and fell back onto his pillow. "No bleeding?"

"No."

"No pain, unusual discharge?"

"No."

"So, we're getting up at two in the morning to go to the hospital because the dog said to."

"Yes."

"Gisella, good grief, I know you love the dog and all, but this is ridiculous."

"Hiram, I'm telling you, she knows something is wrong. Think about those dogs that can sniff out cancer. People said that was crazy at first, too, and now they're training dogs to do it."

Still not sitting up, he raised his voice to carry to the other side of the bed. "Oh, Madelyn, congratulations! I had no idea you'd gotten your license in obstetrics already! You must be a whiz to finish so fast. Seems like only yesterday you were drinking out of the toilet. How far you've come!"

"Hiram, get up, or I'll drive myself."

"No, you can't, it could be dangerous," Madelyn sent.

"Oh, for pity's sake---"

Suddenly, seventy-five pounds of angry dog was standing over him in bed, staring down at his face with a snarl on hers. "Do I have to bite him?"

After his initial shock at her appearance, Hiram shoved the dog off the bed, his voice gruff with annoyance. "*All right, all right*, we'll go, but we'll feel like idiots when they ask us why we're there."

"I don't care," she called over her shoulder to him, as she let Madelyn into the back seat of the car and then climbed into the front. Hiram had thrown on a T-shirt and pair of old jeans, and slid into the car just as she finished adjusting her seatbelt.

"So when we get to the hospital, what should I tell them? Hi, she feels fine, but the dog told her to come in, and since we've been to obedience classes---"

"Hiram, let me ask you. If there was only a snowball's chance in Hell that there was something wrong that might harm the baby or me, don't you think it would be worth an early morning drive just to be sure we're both safe?"

He was silent as the garage door opened and the car rolled out onto the drive. Finally, he sighed, reached over and squeezed her knee. "You're right, my love. I wouldn't want to take that chance. It just seems so absurd when you say it out loud--- 'because the dog said to.'"

Fifteen minutes from the hospital, Gisella gave a gasp.

"What's wrong?"
"I'm starting to have pain. High up in my abdomen."

CHAPTER SIXTEEN

When they arrived back at their building, the Elpies headed to their rooms for a quick nap, and Bess and Jonas hoped to do the same. Walking into her room, Bess was greeted by the sight of Simon stretched out crossways on the huge bed, fully clothed, Elsie sprawled on her own bed, and both species snoring loudly.

She kicked off her shoes and crawled in beside Simon, snuggled close to his back, out of the path of his snores, and slipped an arm around his waist. He made an incomprehensible snuffling groan, which she chose to interpret as, "love you, too," reached one arm behind him, patted her hip, and was instantly asleep again. He was more touchable and just as effective as a space heater, radiating heat several inches out from his body, and as his warmth and nearness relaxed her, she drifted easily into sleep.

##

The door chimes brought Jonas awake first. He'd been wiped out, but too pumped after all the dancing to sleep soundly. Sort of half-dozing, he'd been in a pleasant haze when he heard the chimes. His dad's snoring was audible through their connecting doorway, and since his mom hadn't closed it, he thought it would be okay if he ran through to answer the door so they could sleep a little longer.

Running through the thick carpet in his bare feet, he saw his parents fast asleep, with his mom's arm around his dad's waist, and her head tilted forwards against the back of his shoulder.. He thought they looked kind of cute that way and then wondered if he would have thought that a week ago. Since all of this had first started, he'd been seeing them more as people, instead of just his parents, and it had changed his perspective on a lot of things.

He flipped the lever that activated the small one-way glass screen. There was a Bluewoman outside that he thought was Mona, so he opened the door. When he saw the whole person, he was sure of it, though she looked very different in a scarlet and blue robe instead of her ship's uniform.

He raised one hand in greeting, and stepped out into the hall with her. "Hey Mona. My folks are asleep. We're all still a little jet-lagged. What's up?"

She patted his head, something she'd seen humans do with children. Jonas wasn't exactly a child, but not grown either, so it seemed appropriate. "Since the ceremony has been called off, it frees your time. Maurice and I would like to invite you, Sven, and Luca and his wife to our house tomorrow night for dinner, and to meet our families. We could pick you up at the tenth chime. I've already seen the Reptilians, and Eli has accepted for his family."

Jonas looked back towards the door, hesitated a moment, and then said, "Sure. I know my folks would like that, especially if the Elpies are going."

"Elpies?".

"Oh, yeah, I forget that's not their real name. My dad started calling them that. 'LP' are the initials for 'Lizard People," in English and that's how he first thought of them. But when he got closer to them, and really became friends, he changed 'LP' to 'Elpies,' because he thought it sounded friendlier. And they like having names, even if they can't say them."

Mona nodded, as she'd seen humans do. "I see. It does suit them. Well, we will see you and the Elpies tomorrow at the tenth chime. Good." She patted his head again, which he accepted stoically, and walked back to the elevator.

Closing the door, he heard his dad ask, his voice half muffled in his pillow, "Who was that?"

He tip-toed to the bed and said quietly, "It was Mona. She---"

His mom spoke from somewhere behind his dad's shoulder. "It's okay, hon, I'm awake. You don't need to whisper."

"Mona came by to invite us and the Elpies to her and Maurice's house tomorrow night with the rest of the Bluemen from the ship, so we can meet their families. I accepted for us. Why don't the two of you get some more sleep?"

Simon was watching him as he delivered the message, thinking about that little boy that Jonas used to be, only yesterday, it seemed, and how he was turning into a man right in front of them.

Bess raised one hand in a wave above Simon's waist. "That's fine. Thanks for getting the door and handling that."

"No sweat."

He saw that look in his dad's eyes and knew a "dad" moment was about to materialize with something sentimental. His practiced impulse was to get out of there fast, before his dad had a chance to say anything. But then that picture Eli had shown them of his dad dying, unexpectedly came to mind, and suddenly he thought how lucky he was to have a dad like him. Then he thought about those murdered Seated, and that their kids, if they had any, would never get to hear their dads' voices again. So he stayed and looked back at his father, and found himself *wanting* to hear his voice.

"Hey Jonas---I just want you to know I'm proud to be your dad. You really have become a man in so many ways, and it's happened so fast. Love you." He reached out with one long arm and grabbed him around the neck to plant a kiss on top of his head.

Rather than rolling his eyes and saying "*Geez*, Dad," like he usually did at these moments, he found himself almost tearing up instead. "Thanks, Dad. Love you, too."

He could see the pleased surprise in his dad's eyes at that response, and when he stood up to go back to his room, he felt happy and moved, with a sense of fulfillment rather than embarrassment. *Maybe this is what happens when you start becoming a man.*

##

After another hour's sleep, Bess and Simon felt much better, and they were just going into the bath to freshen up when the door chimes sounded again. Bess went to the door with an "I'll get it," and flipped the lever to activate the window in the door. She looked out and saw no one. The chimes rang again, and she called, "Who's there?" through the door. An annoyed sounding meow answered her question, followed by a sending of "Who do you think?"

When she opened the door, in strolled Ishmael, tail held high, but with a bright blue bandage on the end. "Ish, I thought you were still in the park. Oh my gosh, you're hurt! What happened?"

Simon came out of the bath, and Jonas from his room when they heard Bess' exclamation. The cat waited for both to arrive so he'd have a complete audience for his story. When the four of them, including the dog, were standing in front of him, he nodded towards the balcony and sent, "*That* happened."

They all turned to look in the direction of his nod, and there on the railing of the balcony, sat the giant version of the red speckled bird. Bright red, with white and black speckles on its chest, and a white strip running the length of both wings, it was larger than a golden eagle and looked as if it must weigh at least thirty pounds. It had a quasi-bird-like face, a huge beak, little black eyes, and was staring directly at Ishmael.

All three humans instinctively jerked back with a start when they saw the size of the creature in possession of their balcony. "Whoa, what the heck did you do to make *him* mad?" Jonas asked, never taking his eyes off the eagle-thing.

"I didn't get *to do* anything. But I was considering eating one of his smaller relatives when he took exception to the idea."

"He could read your mind?"

"No, but I was in stalking mode and aimed at the thing when this brute came up behind me. Chased me all the way here, and I barely made it. Had to run in and hit the close button for the balcony door to keep the thing from flying in after me. It slammed into the glass and then sat on the floor of the balcony and tried to stare me down. Of course, I won the stare-off. But he did do this," he sent, and held up his tail for inspection.

Simon took his tail in his hand and surveyed the bandage. "Is it bad?"

"No, he just took the tip off. I went downstairs to the front desk, and they whisked me in to see this guy down the street. He put some kind of spray on it and then did something with a hair dryer looking thing, and sent that the bandage will fall off in a week, and the missing part will have grown back. Cool, huh?"

Bess picked him up and rubbed him under the chin. "It's cool that you're still alive. Maybe you'd better forego the woods for the rest of the trip."

"Yeah, I might do that, since I think I've probably checked out everything of interest anyway. That is, if you people are all through shopping. I'd gladly risk my life to avoid a shopping excursion."

"I think we're done with the city for now. Wait until we tell you what's been going on."

Suddenly Elsie made a mad dash for the balcony door and hit the button to open it. The eagle-thing was big, but not stupid. It whirled around and threw itself into the air, but not before the dog managed to snag a tail feather in her teeth.

They stood in stunned silence, looking at Elsie standing there with a feather hanging from her lips. Ishmael shook his head and sent, "I love that mutt."

##

The next morning, Samson arrived at their door, and sent that since Joe Bob was still unfortunately detained, he had been given the honor and privilege of escorting them on another planned outing---this time to the wildlife preserve behind their apartments.

Adult visitors were not required to have an escort, but as Ishmael had been informed, they *were* required to carry fire sticks, which were kept in a chest by the gate for visitors to pick up before they entered. These sent a shock that could be dialed up or down, according to the size of the animal encountered. The average Blueperson was much more trustworthy and less prone to cruelty than the average human, so the chest was never locked, and the only animals who had ever experienced the discomfort of the business end of a fire stick were those who had experienced it in the act of attacking a visitor or staff member.

The preserve would be closed for visitors during these celebratory days, so Samson had arranged for a private picnic on the grounds. There was a force field around the main path and it encircled an area in the center where visitors could eat and watch the animals at close quarters. A sumptuous "natural" meal had been prepared for them and would be laid out as soon as they arrived at the eating area.

Bess was relieved and happy that Simon was coming on this excursion. So far, he'd missed all the fun and he'd had to look at dead bodies, as well. What a treat. Not to mention that she'd missed his company, though she *had* enjoyed having Jonas to herself yesterday. It wasn't often that a mom of a teenaged son got to see him in action on the dance floor.

Though he felt a little subdued, Simon was looking forward to the trip into the reserve. He *had* felt that he was missing everything, but thought it only right to step in on the investigation when he realized how unprepared the Bluemen were to handle any type of violent crime. Good grief, he was just a *biologist*, but he'd watched enough police shows, and had enough practical experience to tell that certain things needed to be done. They hadn't even used fingerprinting before this.

Even though Simon's help had been accepted, he could feel a smoldering resentment in Joe Bob for his interference. Simon knew he was aware that his statements at the crime scene had influenced The Seated to allow Elliott and Watson to take over the investigation. He hated to start a holiday with ill feelings anywhere, but it wasn't *his* idea to have someone murdered.

Today though, he was done with it. He was a tourist, and he was going to tour. Good deal. Ishmael came over and sat on the floor in front of the bed where Simon was sitting to tie his sneakers, and started sending. "For obvious reasons, it would be a good idea if you'd put me in a bag or inside a coat or something to hide me until we get to the protected area in the woods."

The three humans laughed, as Jonas walked into the bedroom to talk to his mom. "What's a matter, Ishmael, afraid of being snatched up into the sky?"

"Or dismembered on the ground. I like a challenge, not an execution. I can't torment the thing if I'm in several pieces."

"Okay, I can dump everything out of my bag and carry you in that, but you'd better duck your head. I won't fight a bird that size for you, especially when you've been teasing him."

"Oh, Ma, you know you would."

Bess laughed, but shook her head. "No sir---I see that thing and I'm dropping this bag and heading on down the road."

Jonas interrupted before the cat could think of a good come back.

"Mom, do you think we need to use sunscreen? I don't know anything about what their sun can do to human skin."

"I don't know either, but you don't have to worry about it. Sven said the inoculations they gave us on the ship took care of that---it adapts us to everything on this planet, including their sun."

"All right! I'm liking this place more by the minute. Hey, come here, Ishie, and I'll load you into Mom's bag. I'll carry the bag for you, Mom, since Ishie's getting a chess bottom. Wouldn't want you to get a hernia carrying 'Leo the Lard.'"

"What? I'm as sleek and fit as I ever was. You should have seen me running and jumping from tree to tree to escape my feathered assassin!" He surreptitiously glanced at his rear end from over his shoulder---geez, he did look a little bottom heavy. Did he just think "geez"?

"Well, maybe you should take that run every day." Ishmael glared at him and Jonas took a step back, held his hands up in front of his chest, and shrugged his shoulders. "I'm just saying."

"Didn't your mother teach you any manners, young man?" he sent indignantly, as he ducked his head down and settled into the bag.

"Only your friends will tell you. You should thank me for my honesty."

"Maybe in gratitude, I'll cough up a hairball in your shoe. Or your underwear."

"Hey, you do that, and I'll feed you to the bird myself."

Simon stood up and clapped his hands. "All right, children, no more fighting or we'll have to leave you at home with the nanny." Elsie looked up at them, mouth open wide and tongue hanging out, and wagged her tail.

"Let's go have a good time with the local fauna."

Elsie sent to them to enjoy themselves, while she settled back down for a nap. When she'd heard about the excursion and how some animals might occasionally charge the force field, she'd excused herself from the trip for the sake of everyone else. She'd explained that she might have Simon's memories, but she was still a dog, and she knew that she'd be barking the whole time, and might even charge the force field herself, and who knew what chaos that might cause. Her humans saw the wisdom of her decision, and appreciated her courtesy.

When they headed out of their apartment, the Elpies were already waiting in the hall for them, sending with Samson. Eli sent to Simon that he liked this one better than the testy short one, and Simon nodded in agreement. Samson had seemed more genuine than Joe Bob from the very beginning. Bess had thought Joe Bob charming, but she hadn't crossed him yet, like he had.

They went out the back entrance of the building, since a path starting there led straight to the preserve. Sunny, but a little on the cool side, with a very slight breeze, it was perfect weather for an outing, and Simon could feel his melancholy lift as Bess reached out for his hand.

At the gate, Samson turned to them to send. "You don't need to worry about carrying fire sticks. The kitchen staff will have them and I'll pick one up. The large predators know what they are, so they'll rarely bother anyone carrying one. The only reason we'd need them anyway, is if the force field went off unexpectedly, which has never happened, to my knowledge." He opened the chest and took one out, but before he could close it again, Simon put his hand out to hold it open. "I'd like to take one, if you don't mind, just to see how it works."

Samson tossed him one. "Be my guest. Let me show you how to operate it."

"Wait just a moment, if you don't mind. I'd like for all of us to get the chance to learn."

With a look of surprise, Samson nodded, and Simon went back to the chest of fire sticks and tossed one to Jonas, Bess, Barnabas, Ruth, and Dulcie. Eli and Martha politely refused the offer. Jonas tried to be cool about it, but he was flattered and proud that his dad thought him adult enough to be included. Barnabas didn't try to be cool. Cool wasn't an Elpie thing. He was looking the stick up and down and chittering excitedly, his stiff mane standing up and forward on his head with pleasure at handling this new toy.

"All right, Samson, our brains are ready, if you want to go ahead and explain."

Simon and the others looked at Samson expectantly, so he swallowed his questions and began the class, looking at each of them as he sent. He explained the different settings to be used, according to the size of the animal. "None of these would kill our largest predators, but they would incapacitate them temporarily, and I can guarantee they wouldn't be coming back for a second dose after being knocked out by the first. I understand it's very painful, which is the point. Aversion training."

They began walking through the shielded pathway, and the wild, exotic beauty of the place was overwhelming. All the colors of the spectrum, at their brightest and most subtle hues were visible within just a few feet of the entrance. There were turquoise trees, with red fungi clinging to them like babies to their mothers; green and blue flowers as big as human heads; orange and yellow creatures that flitted from flower to flower like hummingbirds, except that these had no visible wings and were as big as guinea pigs, with huge eyes and glowing blue noses that shot forth multiple purple appendages into each enormous blossom.

They hadn't gone far when Ishmael sent to Jonas to "let the cat out of the bag." He jumped down and began walking with the group, mesmerized, as were the others, by the wonders they were seeing. The forest was actually more of a jungle, and the trees and other plant life were so thick that the sunlight was kept out for a good fifteen minutes of walking before they emerged into areas of grasslands and watering holes.

Here the wildlife was easily visible, and there was movement and action going on everywhere they looked. A large gray animal, with a huge mouth in a squat head that resembled a frog, resting on a body similar to a Komodo dragon's, waited motionless in an area with grey and green grass. The visitors wouldn't have seen it, had not Samson pointed it out. They stopped for a few moments to watch, and it wasn't long before a hapless herbivore, the size of a pig, with a bluish hide and small rounded ears, ambled past the creature. It moved so fast that the watchers' brains barely registered what they'd seen. One moment, the blue pig-thing was there, and the next it wasn't. They only remembered seeing a blur over the other creature, and then it appeared to be sitting right where it had been, but with a new, huge bump bulging out on both sides of its abdomen, and the bump was jerking and making squealing noises.

Bess turned away, slightly nauseated, and overcome with pity for the victim. She knew it was nature's way, but she didn't have to watch it.

They saw large, turquoise furred, bear-like animals trying to swipe creatures they supposed were snakes out of the water, and the occasional huge blue-striped cat, with red, or sometimes white dots on the lower half of the body. These would slink as low to the ground as possible when traversing the grassy areas, and then stand and stalk their prey when they reached the trees again.

Something akin to a boa constrictor had been travelling parallel to the shielded path, and Ishmael was peering at it intently when the whole party yelped and jumped in surprise as a huge eagle-thing came plummeting out of the sky to land in a flurry of claws and beak upon the snake. Death came swiftly with the first blow from above, and the eagle-thing began ripping off chunks of flesh and devouring them whole. It was throwing its head back to facilitate swallowing, when its eyes caught sight of Ishmael.

All hunger forgotten, it screamed and puffed out its feathers, stretched out its wings and rushed to the edges of the force field, as if it could pull the cat out to itself by sheer will.

Samson watched the confrontation in surprise. "Do they know each other?"

Jonas laughed and shook his head. "Not as well as that thing wishes they did. He's been wanting to eat Ishie from the get go, and unfortunately, this is one cat that gets off on tormenting his opponents. He sits inside the glass door of the balcony and just dares it to kill him."

Samson gave a worried look at the cat and then focused on Jonas again. "It's good that you're leaving the planet soon, then, for these creatures have very long memories, hold a grudge, and have been known to fly out of the preserve to pursue prey for many miles. He looked pointedly at the cat. "You were wise to hide yourself on the way in." Everyone else turned to him and added their own meaningful looks, which he chose to ignore.

Twenty minutes of walking brought them to a clearing that had tables set up with glasses of fresh, cold water and juices, and plates full of a sumptuous variety of raw fruits and nuts, with soft balls of a bread-like substance baked in a crunchy outer shell. Slabs of something resembling cheese, with a tangy-salty taste, set off the fruits perfectly. Bright orange, soft fruits tasting like a cross between cherries and mangoes were by far the favorite, with a green, crunchy, tart-sweet fruit coming in second.

The group sat down and dug in without ceremony. While cutting the worst glare from their sun, the force field still allowed a clear view of the sky, which today was a bluish-green, with wispy white clouds scattered about. Still awed by the sights surrounding them, the tourists nevertheless managed to focus on the food as well.

Everything was delicious, and the Elpies, especially, made sure that each morsel was tasted and savored.

In the middle of the meal, a lion-like beast suddenly lunged towards the group. When it was almost to the force field, all of the Elpies turned towards the beast and hissed, and the Colder stood, with his black hairs standing up and forwards on his head and back. He opened his mouth wide to show his long, dangerous teeth, and jutted his head out towards the beast. Confronted with unified Elpie ire, it skidded to a stop and then, back pedaling with all four feet until it felt safe to turn and run, the creature bolted. The attitude and appearance of these strange creatures completely undid the cat's prey drive, especially when it saw the face and felt the sendings of the Colder. He'd sent that he was a hunter too, and he was not afraid.

##

They had been paced for the duration of their walk, and were now being watched. He held his fire stick in front of him and made it crackle now and then, to remind any hungry beast just what the thing was capable of. They knew him, and knowing what *he* was capable of, they stayed out of his way as he silently walked the caretakers' path that ran parallel to the shielded walkway. The path was densely camouflaged to prevent visitors from seeing staff at work, but he could still make out the movement of his targets through the leaves. He carried the type of fire stick given only to staff who routinely travelled the most dangerous areas of the preserve. These had a voltage deliverable that was not only strong enough to kill animals much bigger than elephants, but could blow a hole straight through a smaller creature.

Had Elsie been with them, his scent would have been recognizable as the one she'd found at every dwelling where poison had been planted. She would have known.

It was a temptation to just turn off the force field and let the group be eaten, but that would prove nothing to his people. And with the number of fire sticks being carried by the group, many of the predators would be hesitant to attack. Besides, there were too many Bluepeople working in the area, and if he was responsible for *their* deaths, public opinion would turn against him before he'd had a chance to make his speech.

As he watched the group, he couldn't help but notice the man's protective attitude towards the youth and the woman. When she'd turned away from the sight of the kill, his arm had immediately come up to rest on her shoulders in a gesture of comfort. And when a large animal had run towards the group, he'd stepped in front of the youth, trying to make it appear that he'd stepped up for a better look, apologizing to the boy afterwards for obstructing his view. Later, as the boy had leaned forward to look closer at a constriction killer, the father's hand had shot up in front of his chest for a brief moment, in an automatic protective restraint. The man and boy had both laughed then, realizing this was foolish with the shield there to protect them. Even when they sat to eat, the man seemed to be on guard, watching the other two and the area around them nervously, as if he might need to take action if something went wrong with the shield.

With the meal finished, workers cleared everything away and then left the reserve. Samson stayed on with the visitors, answering all their questions and pointing out different examples of wildlife until everyone's curiosity was satisfied and they were ready to head back.

#

He'd made a decision. He hadn't the time to take out any of the lizards himself, but now that all but one of the Bluemen was out of the reserve... He would wait until the group was only a hundred yards or so from the entrance before shutting off the force field. If he turned the entire field off now, it would be too suspicious of intentional sabotage. If there was only a partial failure, it could still be considered a possible malfunction. With that many fire sticks on board with the group, probably not many predators would attack, but there were usually a few around who had never experienced the pain of a shock. If he could take out one or two more of the group before tomorrow, things would be that much easier, and decidedly more interesting.

#

The visitors and their guide were feeling mellow after a good meal and the leisurely walk in beautiful weather. The entrance up ahead had just come into sight, when suddenly there was a palpable change in the atmosphere around them. The whole group had felt it and stopped on reflex to look at Samson, who immediately took the safety off his fire stick and peered in all directions.

He tried to keep the fear out of his thoughts as he sent to them. "That was the force field shutting off."

They stared at him in shock, but he shook his head in reassurance. "Don't worry, we're almost out, and just the sight of fire sticks is enough to deter most predators, or---at least the ones who have come in contact with one before."

"And what about the ones who haven't?" Simon asked, furious at yet one more unforeseen danger to his family.

"Well, just in case, it would be good if you'd all take the safeties off your fire sticks and adjust them to the highest level. I'll take the rear, and watch behind us, and the rest of you make a barrier around those that are unarmed. Oh, and one of you should watch the sky. Don't run---that would just attract predators. Just walk calmly. We're almost out."

As they walked towards the gate, the pathway with its covering arch full of flowers and vines seemed sinister now, rather than beautiful, as it had before. The animals hiding in the trees and bushes seemed to be aware that something had changed, and the group could feel eyes on them. Hungry eyes. Bess moved to walk beside Jonas, and when Simon looked at her face, he was startled by what he saw.

Bess had always been a softie where any animal was concerned, and he assumed she would be fretting now about perhaps having to hurt something. But he had never seen such ferocity in her eyes and aggressiveness in the set of her shoulders. Then he realized---she was beside *her son.* She was not an animal lover or pacifist at this moment. She was a *mother,* and woe to any creature foolish enough to try and touch her child. This fierce, battle-ready female was a side of her that Simon had never seen. Hmmm--he rather liked it.

They were almost to the gate, when a wolf-sized, bright green canid, with mouth wide open and going in for the kill, burst out of the bushes to the side of Samson, too fast for him to react. Before anyone could get their fire sticks trained on the creature, Barnabas, in one smooth leap, stretched out an arm and caught the creature by the throat with one hand and then shifted direction midair to slam the beast down onto its back. He landed in a kneeling position beside it, still holding it by the throat, and as soon as the animal hit the ground, the Colder leaned towards its face, opened his jaws wide and hissed, with his mane standing up and forward. He held eye contact with the canid until it went completely still and limp. The rest of the group was frozen in place at the sight, and after a communal gasp, the only sounds were the breathing of the Colder and the canid.

Very slowly, Barnabas released his grip and stood up, never losing eye contact with the animal. It lay without moving for a few seconds after its release, then flipped over and took off at a run. Barnabas turned to the group and shrugged, sending that he didn't want to hurt any of the animals unless they really had to, and then he picked up his fire stick and started walking again.

Bess made eye contact with Simon, and both mouthed "WOW." Rushing forward to come parallel with Barnabas, Jonas held up his hand, which the Colder high fived with a little tilt of his mane for emphasis. Having known this Colder for many years, none of the other Elpies seemed surprised.

When they reached the gate and exited, putting away their firesticks, Samson, a much lighter blue than usual, put two of his shaking hands on Barnabas' shoulders and thanked him for saving his life. Barnabas nodded and gave a "no big deal" shrug.

#

As he watched the aliens walk out of the gate, amazement and fury filled him. *Once again*, the entire group had survived. Gripping his fire stick tightly, he reasoned with himself that today was just an experiment, and not at all necessary for the culmination of his plan for tomorrow. Everything was still falling into place.

When he thought about it, he couldn't have asked for a more ideal situation. After what he'd seen in the picnic area, he knew that if he killed the boy and woman, it would destroy the man. And *he* would record and explain to his people, as he showed the deaths of the two, that this was the evil of families---it bound beings together so tightly that they couldn't live independently. They fed off of each other, and so when one died, the survivors were helpless to lead normal lives afterwards, with the pain of grief overwhelming their minds. Loathing himself for failing to protect his family, the man might possibly lash out at The Seated. Or even better---they might see a suicide. Ideal. Tomorrow.

CHAPTER SEVENTEEN

Hiram stepped on the gas and they made it to the hospital in record time. He sped up to the front of the Labor and Delivery entrance, jumped out, grabbed a wheelchair, and rushed back to the car. He had Gisella through the doors, past the waiting room, and into the back area, accompanied by Madelyn, before anyone could stop him.

An angry nurse and security guard were running towards him, when he flashed his ID badge. "I'm Dr. Guiness and I want a STAT ultrasound and CBC done on this woman, and whoever is on call for obstetrics, I need called immediately. Tell him we need to rule out an early placenta abruptio on a thirty-five week primip. And that dog is a trained service dog, so she can be in the hospital legally."

Then he looked at Madelyn and said, "OK, Maddie, you've done your bit, and very well, but this is my territory. Why don't you have a seat in the waiting room so you don't get in the way back here and trip somebody up? I'll come out and talk to you as soon as I know anything."

Madelyn wasn't happy about that request, but she could see the wisdom in it, so she nodded and walked back through the double doors, pushing them open with her nose, and then hopping up onto one of the chairs in the waiting room. She sat straight up on the seat, making eye contact with no one, and stared at the double doors in total concentration.

The nurses and security guard who'd witnessed Hiram's conversation with Madelyn, and her reaction to his words, were now staring at *him*. He looked back at them, and said the only thing he could think of. "She's a very well-trained---obstetrics dog."

Staff members were bustling around, trying to carry out Hiram's orders as fast as possible. They'd given Gisella a gown, and she whispered to Hiram as he held it up for her to slip her arms into, "I thought you weren't supposed to give orders in the OB department unless it involved neurology."

He whispered back, "They haven't thought of that yet. The doctor on call will, but he probably has a wife too, so he'll let it slide."

A trim man with curly salt and pepper hair, glasses, and a lab coat, stormed over to them, but stopped when he recognized Gisella. He looked up then and demanded, "Hiram, what's going on?"

Fortunately, Dr. Jorge Rivera was Gisella's doctor, and he'd just finished checking a patient who was having some post-partum complications. When Hiram was done with his explanation, even telling the part about the dog not leaving Gisella's upper abdomen alone, the good Dr. Rivera, being a thorough physician, decided to overlook the dog part and examine his patient, once she'd told him about the pain. When he palpated her abdomen, the skeptical look on his face turned to concern.

"How are we coming on that ultrasound and CBC? We need those STAT!" Gisella was on a stretcher by now, and he pulled the sheet down and raised her gown to use a doppler on her abdomen. "Well, the baby's heart rate is down just a little, but not too bad. Your abdomen feels a little different at the top, so we'll just see what the ultrasound shows. If this is an abruptio, as your husband is concerned about, it's a very early one, and that's what counts. Since your pain is increasing, we need to rule that out. In an abruptio, the placenta pulls away from the wall of the uterus, and you start bleeding there. If the area pulling away is in the center of the placenta, there may be no obvious bleeding from the vagina."

Her composure was starting to wear thin. "So what happens if it *is* an abruptio?"

"At thirty-five weeks, we can go in and do a quick C-section without too much danger to the baby or you. Without a C-section, both of you could be in serious trouble, and very quickly."

Gisella lay there, nodding her head, trying not to tear up. She was in the hospital, her own doctor was here, Hiram was here, Madelyn was here, and a C-section was no big deal, she told herself. Everything was under control, she told herself again, as they wheeled her in for the ultrasound, with Hiram holding her hand. One of the nurses came in with a nasal cannula to start her on oxygen, "Just to give the baby a little boost," she said with a smile.

Dr. Rivera turned back to Hiram. "When we're all done, I need to talk to you about that dog."

CHAPTER EIGHTEEN

Even though they'd gotten out of the reserve in one piece, Simon was still livid about the failure of the force field. Too many things had been happening to put his friends and family in danger. But Bess convinced him to let it go for now, so that they could have at least one nice day together---something they hadn't had on this planet as of yet. The rest of the group voted to do a little window shopping, so Simon sucked it up and put on a happy face to keep from ruining everyone else's day.

Ishmael was dismayed to find himself being toted along on a shopping trip, especially since after what Samson had said about the eagle-things, he'd felt it only prudent to remain hidden whenever they were out in the open. The only sight *he* was seeing was the inside of a canvas bag. Not his idea of a fun outing.

However, as soon as the group went inside the first shop, his head popped up, and he became the instant center of attention, something not objectionable to him at all. Every Blueperson there wanted to stroke his fur, and why wouldn't they? He was a gorgeous black, with thick, glossy fur that begged to be touched. As long as the attention givers were gentle, he was happy with that. The Bluepeople were exceedingly careful when touching him, not only because he was so fragile looking and small compared to them, but also because they didn't know if he might bite if provoked, which showed they had smarts as well as manners.

Jonas couldn't focus on the shop. When he'd been sending with Barnabas on the flight to the Bluemen's planet, Barnabas had sent to him that all intelligent beings possessed some form of empathy for other creatures, but most never developed it. He tried to teach Jonas how to touch another's mind, to taste the pain or mood of someone else, or even the "essence" of that person. He'd tried it on the ship, and was able to do it a bit with the other Elpies, who would look up and send a mental smile when they sensed his attempts. Since they felt Barnabas' touch along with his, they understood that he was teaching him, and therefore didn't see his efforts as an intrusion.

He hadn't even thought about reaching for the minds of his own parents, because stupidly, he'd thought he understood them. They were his parents, after all, and he'd spent his whole life with them.

But today, seeing them in the reserve.... Seeing his mom edge closer to him, with her fire stick in hand, he could *feel* the ferocity in her. All of a sudden, she wasn't just his mom---she was a *warrior, a she-bear.* Geez, that sounded dumb when he said it out loud, but it was true.

With all the alien items in the shop, he knew he probably ought to be taking advantage of the opportunity and really look at everything. Every *thing. Things* just didn't seem important to him right now. Right here, right now, he felt like he could maybe do it. He could maybe reach into his parents' souls and understand who they were as people. A week ago, he wouldn't have cared that much, but now---it seemed important.

He watched his mom for a while as she sent with the Bluepeople who approached her and wanted to see Ishmael. She'd taken the bag from him after she'd heard Samson's warning, and he knew it was to protect him. He focused on her face and tried feeling for her essence without making her aware of his search. It was like mentally walking through a waterfall at first, but then his mind broke through to hers in a rush.

He saw her stop and look around questioningly, and he quickly picked up a vase and pretended to examine it. Seeing nothing unusual, she gave her head a little shake and went back to sending to the Bluewoman petting Ishmael. He'd frozen his efforts when she'd looked up, but now he carefully slipped back in and found the part of her that he knew but didn't really understand. It was a warm softness, almost like a worn, homemade quilt, that wrapped itself around thoughts of her children, his dad, and her parents. There was so much gentleness, love, and passion in that warmth, that he wanted to stay there and let himself sink into it, resting in its welcoming comfort. He almost had to *tear* himself away, remembering that he was in a store, around lots of Bluepeople. He started walking, trying to look like he was browsing, and reached out to touch that essence again.

This time he found that ferocity---an urgent need and determination to protect her children, husband and everyone she loved, at all costs, and he was stunned at the strength of it---at the strength in her. He knew she loved him, of course, but he'd never truly seen the two sides of that love, there at her center.

In that tunnel of forest today, when the force field *had* been working, he'd seen his dad's transparent attempts to hide his protectiveness, with his casual, accidental stepping in front of him whenever there was some kind of even remotely dangerous looking creature close by; he could see him checking around constantly for any kind of threat, and it wasn't because he was afraid for himself---he was afraid for him and his mom.

He decided to try and touch his dad's essence while he was busy fuming over their situation, hoping his anger would keep him from noticing that his son was snooping in his brain. Compared to the Elpies, he knew his attempts were pretty much wimp city, but he still managed to breach the wall. As with his mom, what he found was something that he already knew, and yet came as a revelation.

Will. Sheer, indomitable will. His dad had a force of will in him that was almost scary. He saw in a flash that whatever his dad felt he needed to do *would* be done, without thought or concern about how he might be affected by it, and that will was centered around his love for their family and friends.

The other thing he found in his dad's essence was goodness. Yeah, he knew his dad was a good guy, but this… He thought of all the times he'd seen little examples of his kindness to strangers, acquaintances, and especially to his family. But he'd never understood how deep it ran. It was like something shining inside of him---it made him want to touch it. He wished he could take a clipping of it, like he'd seen his dad do so carefully with his plants, and put that piece inside of himself so that it would grow in him. That was the reason the Elpies loved him so much. It wasn't just what he'd done for Eli. When he'd touched their minds gently on the ship, he'd felt that goodness in *all* of them. It was different with them, but it was still recognizable. And they recognized it in his dad. He drew his mind away then, and back to the store, when he saw his dad looking back at him.

Walking up to him with a concerned look, he put one hand on his shoulder, and bent his head to be at his level, searching his face. "Son, are you okay? Still rattled by that incident in the reserve? Don't be embarrassed to talk about it---that was a scary thing. I was worried about something like that happening, with everything else that's been going on. That's why I tossed out the sticks to everybody, and I knew from the way you've handled yourself on this trip that you could handle one of those if you needed to."

Then with a strong arm that brooked no resistance, his dad reached around his neck and pulled Jonas to him, planting a kiss on his forehead, right there in the shop, in front of everybody in the store and all the gawkers and well-wishers staring at them through the store windows, and he didn't care, because he knew where the kiss came from---could almost see the shine.

##

At first everyone seemed to be enjoying the sights, but try as they might, neither humans nor Elpies could overcome the effects of a huge noon meal. With the exception of Ishmael, of course, they all wanted to take advantage of this incredible chance to see an alien city and all its charms, yet they found their torpor overcoming that desire. When the group members finally realized that *all of them* were miserably sleepy, they gave in and headed back to their lodgings for a quick nap before dinner with the ship's crew.

##

While everyone else was still asleep, Simon slipped down to the front desk, and handed a card to the Bluewoman behind it. He had only the disk that Joe Bob had given him to contact anyone, and since the only Blueperson it would reach was Joe Bob, the only way he had to reach Elliott or Watson was through someone else. He knew if he asked Joe Bob to contact Elliott, the message would never get through.

"Excuse me, but could you contact the Blueman on this card for me?"

"Certainly sir, would you like to have a seat here and wait?"

"That'd be great, thanks."

In less than thirty seconds, she had Elliott on a disk for him, and asked if he'd like a visual in the air in front of him. He declined, since he needed to protect his friend from the possible wrath of Joe Bob. He didn't want him or anyone else knowing about this conversation.

A small screen on the disk brought Elliott into view. "Hey Elliott. Listen, something happened today that I'm really suspicious about, and I wondered if you might be able to look into it right away, in case there's any evidence that might be gone by tomorrow." When Elliott expressed concern and assured him that he would help, Simon proceeded to tell him about the incident at the reserve.

Bess had thought it was just an electrical problem, her reasoning being that if someone had wanted them eaten, the force field would have been turned off when they were the farthest away from the gate, instead of within sight of it. But Simon thought just the opposite.

Close to the gate, their guards would be down, with their thinking that they were almost out of the reserve, *and* it wouldn't look as suspicious. Maybe the goal hadn't been to kill all of them. Maybe the plan was to pick off one or two at a time. Like on the ramp at the landing area. And while he was asking Elliott for favors, he asked him if there was any way he could find out if Joe Bob had ever checked into that "accident" with the ramp. There might be clues there that they hadn't thought of looking for before.

The Blueman was very uneasy when told about what had happened at the reserve, sending he didn't think it likely that either episode was an accident. Even though the Bluemen didn't have an adequate police force, they still had very sound workmanship in almost all other areas, and there were always backup mechanisms in place wherever a mechanical failure could prove dangerous.

"Where are you going to be this evening, Simon?"

"We're just going to some friends' apartment. We'll be in a group."

"Be careful. I'll head out of here in a few minutes. There's just one thing I have to take care of first. I'll give you a call at the front desk tonight about what I found out."

"You don't know how much I appreciate this, Elliott. It's really good to feel that there's *someone* in authority that I can trust on this planet. Talk to you later."

##

"*Certainly not.* I've stood back and let you have your little investigation, and tried not to laugh at your pitiful fingerprinting frenzies. You act as if you're some excited child with a new toy, trying to look like a grown-up. But now you've gone too far. I will not sanction any type of weapon for you. They're dangerous, unnecessary, and they set a precedent. If you start carrying a weapon, all the other officials will want one."

"How can you say a weapon for *me* is unnecessary, when I'm going to investigate a possible killer? I might actually find him, and if I do, I don't know what kind of weapon he might have. And as for the other officials, they don't need to carry a weapon, because they're not *doing my job*! What is wrong with you, man? Do you really *want* people to die---and me in particular?"

Joe Bob slammed the folders he was carrying down on his desk and screamed, "GET OUT! And when all of this is over, and The Seated aren't running scared anymore, don't expect to have a job here. You've insulted the wrong man, my friend. Get out---*now*."

Elliott stormed out of the room and slammed the door as hard as he could, gratified to hear something fall off the wall and shatter. He needed to go to the reserve *now*, and all of his staff was out working on fingerprinting. It was insane for him not to have a weapon. At least he could pick up a fire stick outside of the preserve. He stopped by Watson's office to let him know what was up, and then headed out alone.

##

An hour later, after grabbing a fire stick from the chest, and reviewing its use at the kiosk, Elliott climbed over the fence and headed down the main path. The tunnel-like atmosphere made by the vines and branches overhead was oppressive, and he felt himself sweating with nerves more than from the heat. He'd never been any place like this by himself, and especially not while looking for a murderer.

The leaves and trees on both sides and overhead creaked and rustled with every breeze, and he could hear the scuttling sound of small animals making their way unseen in all directions. He was trying to stay alert to any suspicious noise, but there were *so many* noises that he didn't know which way to look.

Hearing a sound to his left, he almost stopped breathing when he saw a striped, lion-sized cat staring at him, unmoving in the bushes. He grabbed his fire stick and shot over the cat's head, making it yowl and run. He had to sit down for a minute after that, to collect himself and to wait for his hands to stop shaking.

"I'm sorry, but the reserve is closed today. How did you get in here?" came a voice from directly behind him.

He jumped at the sound and whirled around to see a tall Blueman in a reserve uniform standing behind him with a polite expression on his face. When his heart started beating again, he answered him. "Oh, sorry---you surprised me. Here's my ID. I'm a police investigator, and I'd like to check out a supposedly accidental power failure of the force field earlier today. And in answer to your last question, I climbed the fence."

After looking carefully at Elliott's ID, the Blueman spoke in a friendly manner. "Well, you came at exactly the right time. I'm one of the technicians, and they called me about it after the fact. I was just going to check the control panel. You're welcome to come along."

"Thank you so much. That will probably save me a lot of time. Are there many workers on duty?"

"No. The reserve is closed today. I was told they had a private party in here earlier, and some staff people were here for that, and to check on some of the animals, but everybody's gone home now. I'd be home myself, with the wife and kids, if I hadn't gotten this call."

"You've got kids? How many?" As he walked behind him, he was noticing how very tall his guide was. He began to bring his fire stick to the front of his body, where he could maneuver it more easily, but the thing was awkward to handle, at best.

"Four."

"What ages?"

There was an extended silence, and then he said, "Six, five," and then he turned and shot him in the chest with his fire stick on full. Elliott crumpled to the ground without making a sound, and there was a ragged hole going all the way through the upper right side of his chest. He debated whether to blow off his head, just to be on the safe side, but it would make the body too messy to handle. He needed to hide it until he was finished. After tomorrow, it wouldn't matter.

He dragged him the short distance to the gate, and then left him in the bushes while he went out to open the gate and throw the lid to the fire stick chest open. Nobody else should be coming for a couple of days, and the body wouldn't start smelling until tomorrow night. By then it would all be over.

Standing in the entrance, acting as if he was checking the hinge on the gate, he looked in all directions to be sure no one was around, then hurriedly grabbed the body, carrying it out the gate and tossing it into the chest. He slammed the lid closed, wiped away the blood smears on the outside of the chest, went back inside the reserve, and locked the gate.

##

There had been an unforeseen problem with Mona's preparation unit, so the meal that evening was rerouted to a nearby restaurant that was a favorite of the Bluepeople in the group. Reservations were waived due to the celebrity of the guests, and this being the week of celebration for The Rebirth, everything was on the house.

The restaurant was on the first floor of a brightly lit, magenta colored building that was formed in the shape of crystal cut glass on one side. The crystal cut produced a prism effect that showered the room with color as the windows caught the light from the thousands of multi-hued bulbs strung across the streets and sidewalks in honor of the celebration. Tables were set elegantly, with lavishly carved wooden utensils, multicolored metal plates, and goblets of the same material. A massive chandelier hung in the center of the room, with hundreds of tiny, sparkling white lights that accented the area rather than lighting it. Each table had a translucent flame bowl, and the atmosphere of the whole establishment was cool and inviting.

There were no city ordinances restricting companion animals from restaurants, so Ishmael sat in a baby seat to elevate him to table level, and Elsie sat on the floor, per her suggestion, since she knew she was a messy eater. She'd always been a considerate dog and she did, after all, have Simon's manners.

Maurice and Mona had three children, and all but the youngest were grown already, and living in other cities. The youngest was only four years old, and Mona informed Bess that even Bluepeople had surprises now and then. Luca Pacioli and his wife, who was "Lola" for the celebration, had three children as well: three and seven years of age, and one sixteen year old who had chosen to be "Heidi," and insisted on sitting next to Jonas.

Since there were children in the party, Elsie was in the best of moods. She adored little ones, and the species didn't affect her enthusiasm. They'd been offered a private dining room, so she was free to romp with the children while they waited for their food, even giving the smallest child a ride on her back. A thin, petite little thing, she threw her arms around the dog's neck and laughed in delight as Elsie slowly made her way around the room.

Heidi's constant, unwavering, and somewhat intrusive attention flattered Jonas, but was also a bit suffocating. She wanted to know everything about him, and especially everything about his love life: if he had one, if he had a girlfriend, did he call girls, etc., etc. He wouldn't have been able to eat much of anything if he hadn't been able to send instead of talk, and Heidi might as well not have been served at all. She only stopped sending long enough for Jonas to give brief answers to her questions.

By the time she'd finished grilling him and he'd thought about his answers, he decided he really wasn't all that interesting. Apparently Heidi disagreed, because she kept making noises that sounded suspiciously close to giggling, and slipped one of her three arms through his, a move which earned her disapproving stares from her parents.

With the exception of the cat, everyone was enchanted with the Blue children. They reminded Bess of the Elpie young, in their complete lack of shyness. The two youngest would climb onto the laps of different adults, and the three year old, especially, was fascinated with Barnabas' long, sharp teeth. She would sit in his lap, boldly pull his jaws open, (with his amused cooperation), look at his teeth, touch the points, and then slam his jaws closed with her little hands. She repeated this over and over, and each time would make huffing little sounds that were obviously laughter. Laughter---Bess knew Luca must be so proud. All those years of trying to understand humor and laughter, and here it was, genuine, and effortless. It came naturally when one was raised with love.

Sven was seated next to Bess, and she couldn't help but notice that he had no wife or children with him. Though the three year old had climbed onto his lap, played with his face, and spoken to him affectionately for a few moments, he still seemed left out, and it saddened Bess to see that.

She leaned towards him and spoke quietly. "Sven, how have you been doing? How has your life been since The Rebirth?"

He looked back at her, a little sadly, she thought. "Oh, I still go out in the ships to study, as before. We've discovered a few new species, enriched our knowledge."

"Has The Rebirth enriched your life as you'd hoped?"

He looked at her knowingly. "You mean, have I 'connected' with anyone?"

Bess looked down, embarrassed at her intrusion. "Well, yes, but only if you want to talk about it. I just wanted to see how you've been---I don't want to be rude or try and pry into something if you feel it's too private to speak of. I apologize."

Seeing her embarrassment and contrition for making him uncomfortable, he reached out and patted her hand gently. "No, it is I who am sorry for reacting that way. I know that you care about me, and I can sense your concern in your sendings. It's just that---the way my life has been was not what I had in mind when we were working for The Rebirth to come about."

"Would you like to send to me about it? If not, I understand."

"There's not so much to send. I had always longed for a family. When we met Gisella as she was at the time we took her from her evil mother---holding her when she would climb into my lap and curl up to go to sleep---that stirred such a longing in me to have my own young to nurture and love. I *knew* that I was meant to be a father. But it was not to be, after all."

"But why?"

"When I found a female that I was attracted to, and who reciprocated my feelings, I was ecstatic. We began seeing each other, and then living together, but apparently, I'm too difficult to live with."

"What happened?"

"She said that I was too domineering and set in my ways. That I didn't know how to compromise. I suppose she was right. But that is who I am. I know no other way to be."

"So she was the only female that you ever tried to have a relationship with?"

"Oh, no. I've tried three times over the years, with much the same results. I finally resigned myself to the fact that I will never have a wife, and never be a father. Luca and his wife, and Mona and Maurice, have been very kind. They've included me in their families over the years, and I'm close to all of their children. But it's not the same as having my own. I am still alone."

Now Bess reached for his hand, and squeezed it. "Oh, Sven, I'm so sorry." She hesitated a few seconds, uncertain of whether she should say anything, but then decided that if this was her only chance to possibly help him… "Would you mind if I gave you some advice?"

"Not at all. You and Simon have been married these many years. You must have learned something about how to live with another person, for your bond to have lasted."

"Oh, yes, marriage is definitely a learning experience. And that experience is why I'm telling you that you shouldn't give up hope. Anyone can change, Sven. But you have to want to. You can't just throw up your hands and say that's 'just the way you are.' You don't have to be someone that you're not, but you can become *more* than you are. You can add to that person by learning to compromise.

"You're at an obvious disadvantage, from my point of view. First, you were raised to be on your own, so you never had compromise drilled into you. Second, you have been the captain—that's what we call the leader on a ship---for most of your adult life. You're used to giving orders and having them obeyed. You're used to having a *crew,* when what you need now, is a *partner.*

"If you were going into business with someone, you wouldn't expect him or her to say 'yes' to every single idea you had, would you?"

He thought about it and then shook his head.

"No, because you need that partner's ideas to help you manage your business---to present a new outlook on how to make your business better, and to support you by becoming half of what you represent as a business. A partner *is* the other half of your business.

"Marriage is the same way. I'll think I know best about something, and then Simon will come up with a completely different opinion. Of course, my first thought on hearing his opinion, is, 'Well that's stupid.'"

Sven nodded his understanding.

"But if I don't want a quick divorce, I won't say everything that comes to me off the top of my head. If I can look at something from an objective point of view, then maybe I can see a way to compromise so that both of us will feel satisfied, or I may see that his really *was* a better idea.

"Of course, there are those times when no matter what, I still feel I'm right and the situation is important enough for us to hash it out. By that, I mean to 'discuss' it, and maybe argue, but never in an ugly way, because the worst thing you can do in any relationship is to insult one another, or call names. You can't take back words.

"Occasionally, when we're both absolutely sure that we're right, I have to ask myself what the disagreement is really about in the first place. Does it really matter if I get my way? That I hear him say, 'Yeah, you're right'? Is the thing being discussed, that important?

"Sometimes, giving in, just saying 'OK, we'll do it your way,' or just letting my point not be made this time, is the best thing. In the grand scheme of things, my being right didn't really make a difference, but having peace and harmony in our relationship did. And I know Simon does the same thing. In fact, he probably does it more than me, because the little things aren't so important to him.

"Can you see what I'm trying to say? You can do the same. It's hard not to have your way, not to be seen as the authority on something, when you feel that you are. But you can do that, Sven, if a relationship is important to you. Simon and I have had twenty years together, and our marriage and family mean everything to us. Nothing would be worth harming that relationship. And if you have children, oh my gosh, you *have* to be able to compromise with each other. Raising kids is always going to trigger differences between you, but you have to show a united front when you deal with children.

"Is any of this making sense to you, or are you just sitting politely and vegging out while I'm talking?"

"I'm not sure I know how to 'veg out,' but the things you're talking about---I can look back and see how a change might have made a difference."

"Okay, so now I'm really getting pushy, but I think I know the kind of female you need in order to make it work. Are there any female captains?"

"Of course."

"How do you become a captain?"

"You have to attend a school that trains for flight, and then those who are deemed suited for leadership are enrolled in a flight leader's academy."

"I could be wrong, but Sven, I think you need to find yourself a female captain, or one in training. You're very authoritative and forceful---necessary qualities in captains, I'm sure. But those traits probably make you intimidating to most females. They either feel like they have to argue all the time, or be totally submissive, and I can't imagine wanting to live with either situation.

"But a female who was born with those same traits in her character, and who's gone through training to accentuate them---she'd be a match for you. You'd be dealing with a partner who, from the beginning, you'd know you had to listen to and work with, and she would know the same, because of your background. Don't you find that your conversations with other captains are a little different than those with your crew, at least when you're flying?"

"Well, yes."

"Of course they are, because knowing another person is a captain automatically makes you respect that person as an equal. You don't talk as if you and only you have a worthwhile opinion. Find yourself a female captain, and I would bet money that the right one will work for you. But there has to be that chemistry between you, too. Don't just go with any female captain that can have a polite conversation with you. Have lots of conversations with lots of captains, until you find that one captain that makes your heart go pitty-pat."

"Pitty-pat?"

"Sorry. That's just an expression. It means the feeling that you get when you meet someone and suddenly you're excited. She's special, and she makes you feel as if there's only the two of you in the room when you're talking. One that makes you look at her when she walks through a door, and brightens your day when you think about her. That's what we call 'chemistry,' and there's no substitute for it. Everything else can be right about another person, but if there's no chemistry there, it won't work---you'll never be satisfied in the relationship. Something will always be missing.

"Well geez, I have certainly been shooting off my mouth, as if I'm the great all-knowing wizard of relationships. I'm sorry. Once I get going, I can't stop myself. Maybe the food will come soon, and that will shut me up."

Sven was looking at her pensively, but she thought he looked a little less depressed. He didn't speak for a minute, but played with his eating utensils, and then took a drink. Finally, he sent, "What you're saying actually sounds logical. I think this is sound advice that I may try. Tomorrow. Thank you for caring enough to speak with me about it, Bess. I understand what you mean by 'chemistry,' and I can see that you and Simon have it still, by the way you talk together and look at each other. That's something I would very much like to have---perhaps with another captain as my partner."

Bess smiled at him, squeezed his hand, and prayed that she hadn't steered him wrong.

Ruth sent to Bess that the Bluechildren made her miss her grandchildren. She smiled at Ruth and nodded, and wondered how Gisella was faring. That baby was going to have lots of grandparents around. Legally, or at least, legally on her forged papers, Gisella was their daughter, but in spirit, she would always be Viola and Tom's. That didn't mean that Gisella didn't love Simon and Bess. They'd just have to think up some special grandparent type names for themselves, and save "Grandma" and "Grandpa" for the Allbrights. Viola and Tom were fully aware that they were going to have to share this little one, and were just fine with that. No child could have too much love, as far as they were concerned.

Simon nudged her knee with his and tilted his head. "Are you still with us? The food's coming, and you're staring off into space. Thinking about the kids?"

"No, about Gisella and our new sort-of grandbaby. I can't wait to hold it." They were still saying "it" because Gisella and Hiram had opted not to be told the sex of the baby before the delivery. Gisella said knowing ahead of time would be like opening your Christmas presents early.

Simon stretched out his thumbs to touch each other and held up his index fingers to frame her face. "I can just see you in that old rocker you insisted on using for all of our kids. If Eli is as serious about this girl as he sounded, it may not be long before we have grandbabies of our own. I hope he means what he says about not rushing anything."

"I'm not worried about that. I think he's a lot more thoughtful about these things than we ever gave him credit for." She smiled and nodded her thanks as a plate of something was set before her. "At this point, there's no sense in worrying about it. He will do what he will do." Simon grimaced in affirmation.

The food was completely unidentifiable to the Elpies and Earthlings, but surprisingly tasty. They asked a few times what this or that was, but after a while, they realized the answers were inconsequential. The Elpies, thrilled with every dish, were shoveling it all into their mouths with astonishing gusto.

When they finally finished, thanks were sent all around, especially to the proprietor, who besides saying that he was honored, noted that a huge crowd had gathered to watch the aliens eating, and many among those watching had made reservations. He sent that they had only made his business more profitable and celebrated than it already was.

##

Before ending the evening, they headed back to Mona and Maurice's apartment for a visit. The high rise they lived in was only slightly less luxurious looking than where the visitors were staying. The foyer itself was resplendent in its majestic stone walls, with some areas polished and some left rough and natural, and everything was set off by gold and black reflective chandeliers. When they reached the apartment door and Maurice opened it, Elsie uncharacteristically shoved him to the side and barged ahead into the room, then rushed back out, almost knocking Mona down as she tried to enter.

"No Bluepeople in this room! Stand back, there's poison!" she was sending to the group as forcefully as she could. They all stood back in dumb horror, parents clutching their children close, as Simon rushed back into the apartment with Elsie. The door was kept slightly ajar, and the group in the hall could just make out the two in the apartment looking at something on the floor by the wall in the living area. Then Simon picked the object up, and he and the dog went into the bathroom.

When they came out, Simon walked out of the apartment and addressed Mona. "Sorry about this, but Elsie had to pee in your tub."

Bess gasped, completely mortified. She grabbed Mona's arm, poison completely forgotten, and said, "Oh, I am *so* sorry! She *never* does anything like this!" Then she turned towards the dog in disbelief. "Elsie, what in the world has gotten into you?"

Simon looked exasperated and took her arm. "Bess! Remember? Elsie's urine neutralizes the poison. I took the poison into the tub so that her mess would be easier to clean up, but she just saved the lives of all the Bluepeople here by performing her little miracle."

The fog of mortification vanished instantly, and Bess turned to Elsie, slapping herself on the forehead. "How could I forget? Oh, I'm so sorry, girl. You're such a great dog!" She scratched Elsie's head and all was forgiven.

The shock of the idea reverberating in her thoughts, Mona put her hands on Simon's shoulders as she sent. "You mean someone just tried to murder my family?" Maurice put his arm around her protectively after scooping their child up into his arms.

"Whoever did this must have been watching you, to know when you'd be out. If he's been watching all of you, his intent may have been to poison everyone here. I don't think he knows yet that humans and Elpies aren't susceptible to it. Let's go down to the foyer, and I'll contact Joe Bob. He can find some place safe for you to stay until they catch this maniac. He needs to place guards on all of you, and on us, too, for that matter. When the authorities get here, Elsie and I need to go to your apartment, Luca, and yours too, Sven, to sweep it for poison."

Luca and Lola were holding their little ones, and Heidi was conveniently clinging to Jonas' arm for comfort. They decided that if someone was after them, it would be wiser not to wait here, in case the poisoner was still lurking in the building. Just down the street was a large but fairly quiet lounge, so they headed there to wait.

Joe Bob and Watson, with his team and Elliott's, showed up in record time, with several people in full protective gear again. Half of the unit took Sven, Luca, Elsie, and Simon to the Bluemen's apartments, where Elsie found the poison in both places without difficulty, and neutralized both capsules after drinking a bowl of water.

The Elpies and Humans were taken back to their apartments, and the Bluepeople to a safe, temporary living area, but not before Heidi grabbed Jonas by the head, roughly pulled him to her, and planted a very wet kiss on his lips in front of the whole group, too fast for her parents to intervene. Luca and Lola were speechless with humiliation and shock, and as they grabbed her arm and dragged her away with them, they held up their free hands, shaking their heads and looking at Bess and Jonas with eyes full of apology and pleading for forgiveness. Bess couldn't help herself---she started laughing, and the Elpies appeared to be doing the same. Jonas had a bizarre expression on his face---a mixture of embarrassment, surprise, and a little bit of a smile and frown mixed together.

Heidi's family was pulling her along by two of her arms to follow the authorities to their lodgings, and she was looking back and waving as she sent to Jonas. "Sorry to surprise you, but I've seen so many pictures of humans doing that and well---I've just always wanted to try it, and it looked like our evening was being cut short, so---I had to go for it. I *liked it.* Maybe we could try it again before you go home, if I can convince my parents to let me see you. I had a wonderful time tonight! Bye!" He laughed and waved back, waiting politely until she was out of sight to wipe his mouth and face off, and then shook his head and rolled his eyes at Bess.

When they reached their apartments, Simon had Elsie check the Elpies' and their own for poison, but there was none. Joe Bob came back with Simon to the Sayers' rooms, and Simon asked him to sit. He stood up in front of him as he spoke. "Joe Bob, I want you to arrange for us to be taken home immediately. I will not have my friends and family put in danger. At first, I'd thought that this was some kind of personal vendetta against the Seated, but now I think it's a vendetta against anyone who had something to do with bringing about The Rebirth, and with all the publicity, my family and friends would be easy to target. I want armed guards outside of our apartments until that can be arranged. Security cameras, too."

Joe Bob looked abashed. "I'm so sorry about everything. I'd gladly do what you ask, but no ship will be available for three days at the earliest. Fuel constraints have limited our off-planet vessels, and none will be back until then, even if we call for emergency acceleration. The distance couldn't be traversed any faster."

Simon began pacing and running his hand through his hair in frustration. "My best friends, my wife, and my son came here with me in good faith, never doubting that we would be in safe hands. So far, one of my friends and my son have almost fallen to their deaths, a force field mysteriously turned off, which could have led to any of us being mauled or killed, and now there's an attempted poisoning. If something were to happen to any of them---"

"Please---don't worry. Since the incident with The Seated that lived in this building, and due to your presence, along with that of a few other dignitaries who reside here, a watch has been kept on this building, and we *will* put guards and cameras outside your door. The presence of the watch is probably why no one planted poison here. As soon as we have the vessels available, we'll send you home."

"Where was Elliott tonight?"

Joe Bob shrugged his shoulders. "He didn't answer his call, so I came instead. Just as well. His work can be a little sloppy at times. Like his not being available for this call tonight."

"He never seemed like the unreliable type to me. Just the opposite."

"Yes, I know, you think he's taking care of everything, and he's a 'buddy' by now, but that's because you really don't know my people as well as you think you do."

Simon bristled at the slight, but said nothing to fuel the fire. He thought that probably Elliott had gone to the reserve without telling Joe Bob, and was still checking things out. Better for Elliott if he said nothing, so he simply thanked Joe Bob for coming, and ushered him out the door.

Once he was gone, Simon told Jonas that he wanted him to leave the adjoining door to their suites open at all times, and he was not to set foot out of the apartment without Bess or himself. Then he hugged him roughly, planted a kiss on the top of his head, and started to go back to his own rooms, but stopped and turned back.

"So....how was it?"

"What---oh, *The Kiss?* Well, it totally took me by surprise, and in a way, it was sort of horrible---Bluegirl spit is pretty nasty tasting and gross----but in another way, it was kind of *compelling.* Don't think I'd ever want her to do it again, but it was one more item to chalk off my 'things I've never experienced but might like to try' list."

Simon laughed and slapped his back loudly. "That's my boy!"

Bess saw him coming through the door with a semi-smile on his face. "I heard slapping sounds---that means male bonding going on?"

"Yeah. Have I ever said how much I love that kid?"

"Yes, you have."

Later, as they lay in bed, too tense to sleep, Simon reached over and put his hand on her waist. She was already facing him, watching him in the dark. "You awake, Bess?"

"Mmm-hm."

"You remember our little 'cathartic moment' about the scene at the awards dinner? I always knew the whole business was about good intentions gone awry, but somehow I could never let go of the disappointment and resentment until that day on the ship. Since then, I've kept thinking about how incredibly stupid it was, with the wonderful life we've been given, and all the happiness and love we've had with each other, to hold on to something like that for all these years. What a petty, small thing it seems in comparison to the whole of our lives together.

"We'll be fine, of course, but what with Bluemen dying, and knowing that someone might be after us, it just makes me want to cherish what we have in each other. You were right---life *is* too short and uncertain to push away the people we love."

She smiled in the dark, shifted into his arms, and said, "Amen."

Her smile only lasted for a moment, as the reality of the attempted poisoning came back to her, and that sense of foreboding overwhelmed her once more.

CHAPTER NINETEEN

Burning, so much burning. He flushed his eyes with water for an eternity, it seemed, until finally some of the burning abated. Then running to the kitchen, he grabbed an icy container of leftover food from the cold cave and held it to his eyes. Gradually the pain began to dissipate, and after daring to take the cold pack down, he went to the mirror to look at his eyes.

He could see they were red, but couldn't see them that well. If he strained, squinted, and blinked, he could get a fairly clear picture, but his peripheral vision in both eyes was very fuzzy. *STUPID, STUPID, STUPID!* Of all the times to do something stupid, it had to be now, when he was so close to the culmination of his plans.

Making a last batch of capsules, he had left off his eye shields---the *only* time he had been so careless---and one of the chemicals he was pouring had splashed up into his eyes. He couldn't go for medical care because the physicians would require him to say *what* he'd gotten into his eyes, and *how* he'd ended up with it there. Now his vision was affected, and he'd never be able to manage the delicate task of putting the poison into the capsule developer. He could buy a magnifier, but his vision was blurring on and off, and he couldn't risk a mistake when handling the poison.

But what had happened to his victims? It should have been broadcast, with this many deaths---the public should have been informed. He hadn't seen anything about more poisonings though, and this morning he'd seen the humans and reptiles again, and they seemed unaffected. Could they possibly be immune to the poison? After planting the capsules in the remaining apartments, he'd gone to the restaurant he'd seen on the broadcast, followed them to one of the apartment buildings, and watched through the transparent foyer doors. When they'd stepped onto the elevator, he'd come home to wait for the broadcast of new deaths in the city. But nothing.

He hadn't meant for the visitors to be poisoned---he had other plans for them. It had come as a surprise to him, after watching the first Blueman's apartment and planting the poison, to see him later in the foyer, obviously waiting on someone. When he saw the rented multi-transporter stop to pick him up, and recognized the other Bluepeople within, it seemed too good to be true. With all of them leaving together, he could plant poison in all of their apartments with ease, having gathered their addresses months ago.

He'd had no idea that the alien Bringers would be with them until he'd seen a piece on the broadcaster when he'd arrived back home after visiting the other apartments. At first, he'd been upset that the drama he'd planned would be ruined if they all returned to one of the poison sites, but chances were that the Bluepeople would enter their homes first, and seeing them die, the others would step back before all were killed. He'd gone straight to the restaurant to monitor their movements. His hope was that the aliens would return to their apartments where there *was* no poison, and the surviving Bluepeople would return to their own homes eventually, where they would meet the same fate as the rest of the crew and their families.

If they'd found his poison and somehow managed to neutralize it, they must have guessed who his intended victims were, to be prepared enough to prevent new poisonings. And that meant there would be more precautions---guards, locks, cameras, things he hadn't had to worry about or deal with before. Well, poison wasn't the only way to make a statement. Maybe it was time to get rid of the poison, and start on the next phase of his plan. But he needed to make them drop their guards, and he needed to separate and isolate the lizards and humans. He couldn't handle that many creatures at one time, and hadn't been able to obtain or make explosives without exposing himself for arrest. He needed help.

##

Chiming from the entry way brought him to the door. He flipped on the screen and saw his friend from the malcontent gatherings holding a box of something in his arms, so he opened the door and invited him in.

The other Blueman, "Cecil" for the week, to make himself blend in, deposited the box on a table in the kitchen. "Alan" followed him into the room and looked inside the box.

"What's all this?"

"Haven't you seen the broadcasts about the dead Seated? That they couldn't find the means of death, but suspected poison?" He smirked and pointed towards the box.

Looking at the box again in confusion, the meaning of the man's gesture suddenly became clear, and he jerked back from the box to stare at Cecil, aghast. "You? With this?"

"Yes. I got sick of all the talk with no action. Now, perhaps they'll listen to reason."

Alan couldn't believe it. This one had always seemed more intense than the others in the group, but *murder*.... And he seemed to expect his congratulations. He needed to get him out of his apartment so he could call the authorities, but he realized that he was dealing with someone dangerous, unpredictable, and *deranged*. Playing along with him was all that he could think to do.

"Well, you showed them, all right. But why did you bring the poison here?"

In spite of his efforts, he couldn't completely disguise the fear in his eyes, and his approbation rang hollow and forced. When Alan gestured towards the box, Cecil noticed that his hand was shaking. He'd judged him correctly---big talker, but when it came to standing behind his words, he was a coward like all the others.

"I thought you might like to witness how we shall break The Rebirth." Turning his back to Alan, he stood between him and the box, pretending to bend over to look within. Since the other man was not eager to come close, it was easy to slip on a glove and pick up a respirator unseen by him.

"Have a look at this." Slapping the respirator onto his face and taking a capsule in his hand, he swung around, thrust it towards Alan, and crushed it between his fingers, all in one swift movement.

He had no chance to even scream, dying as soon as the liquid came in contact with the air and burst into a million tiny particles, with thousands going into his mouth as he opened it and inhaled in a futile attempt to cry out. The terror on his face remained even after he'd crumpled to the floor in death.

Cecil felt vaguely uneasy about Alan's killing. When he'd voiced his views, Alan had listened and treated him with respect, and they'd had mutual frustrations. He'd almost been a friend, or the closest thing to one that he'd ever had. But Alan had always talked too much, and sooner or later, they would have been at odds, either for that very reason, or for the fact that he had actually come to Cecil's apartment once, unannounced, and might have done so again, in spite of the fact that Cecil had talked about his aversion to having company. Alan had been too social to call himself a true malcontent.

Besides, all of this had turned out rather well for him. The poison obviously wasn't working for him anymore, so it was time to move on. His eyes were still bothering him---only slightly irritated now, but the blurring, especially in his peripheral vision, was disturbing. After tomorrow, though, he wouldn't need to see, and he wouldn't need Alan, either. He had saved one capsule for himself, making this one out of a material that didn't react to Bluemen. He could tuck it into a pouch in his cheek and hold it there indefinitely---this capsule was impervious to saliva. Then when he'd finished his business and his speech, he would finish himself with one quick bite.

He left the body where it had fallen, and laid out his lab supplies on the table, to make it appear as if Alan had been working with the capsules. Then he composed a letter on Alan's messaging screen, and sent it to the broadcasting headquarters. He laid his respirator in one of Alan's hands and folded his fingers around it, to look as if he'd started to put it on, but decided to take his own life, instead.

He went to the door of the apartment and took one last look at the staged suicide. Nicely done. Very nicely done. Walking out the door, he hummed quietly as he closed it behind him.

CHAPTER TWENTY

Hiram came rushing into the waiting room and stopped just outside the double doors, looking for Madelyn. When he spied her, he rushed over, knelt in front of her, took one paw in his hand, and started talking.

"Madelyn, you were right. You were right about everything. They're taking her in for a C-section right now, and I'm going with her, but I wanted to tell you what was happening. They think that with catching the problem this early, she and the baby will be fine. You may well have saved her and the baby's lives. I owe you my life, too, because if anything happened to Gisella or the baby…." His voice began to break, so he stopped, shook his head, and looked back at the dog. "I can never thank you enough, you wonderful, amazing, glorious mutt."

He hugged her, then stood up and turned to go, but came back and kissed the top of her head before rushing back through the double doors. The waiting room was half full, and most of the people occupying the chairs around her had stared openly at the dog and the man during his heartfelt speech. Now the dog purposely locked eyes with each person ogling her, staring back until the human broke eye contact. She stared down each one, and then settled back in her chair to wait for more news.

CHAPTER TWENTY-ONE

A banging on the door, rather than a soft, polite chiming, woke them the next morning. Stumbling out of bed in a rush, Simon grabbed a pair of jeans to step into while he made his way to the door. He flipped the lever for the door screen, to see Joe Bob standing in the hall, bouncing with excitement.

When the door was opened, Joe Bob came rushing in and tossed himself onto the couch, breathless with eagerness to share his news. "Yes, do come in," Simon said, after the fact, and joined him on the opposite couch.

Joe Bob tried to keep his seat, but he was too happy, and jumped to his feet the moment Simon sat down. "I have fantastic news! Late last night, the poisoner sent a message to the broadcasting office confessing everything, and then he poisoned himself. Oh, that sounds terrible of me to be so happy about someone's death, but after all, he did murder two wonderful people, and attempted to kill all of you and the crew of your ship.

"It's just such a wonderful relief, not to worry about who might be killed next. You and your family are safe now---you don't have to feel like prisoners anymore. You're free to come and go without needing an armed guard with you all the time. You don't even need to lock your doors anymore. We can return to living without fear, as we have for as long as I can remember."

Simon felt the same way. Every being had value, but one who took others' lives without mercy or reason was not a great loss to society when he passed. And he hated to admit how afraid he'd been for Bess and Jonas. A huge wave of relief swept over him, and all the tension he'd been bottling up since the first murder suddenly unwound. If he hadn't already been sitting, he'd have needed to.

Elsie had been listening, and now she walked up and sat down in front of Simon, sending, "I need to smell the body."

"What?"

"I need to smell the body. To be sure it's the right one. I have to do it Simon, for everybody's sake. This guy is not going to want me to. He wants it over and done, nice and neat, without anyone questioning the conclusion. But I have to do it."

Simon looked at Joe Bob, who was anxiously watching the mental conversation between the two. "She needs to smell the body of the killer."

"Oh, please, that is completely out of the question. There's no reason for it. We have the poison that they found in his apartment, and we have his confession and his body. How much simpler or more obvious could it get?"

Getting a little testy now, Simon stood up and glared at the Blueman. "You didn't want to let her sniff the bodies of the first victims, either, until your superior ordered you to. This dog has been right about every single thing so far, she saved nine lives last night, and who knows how many of The Seated, by warning them. I don't understand, with that track record, how you could possibly refuse her, or why in the world you would want to."

Raising himself to his full height, he glared back, and in a tone brimming with malice and indignation sent, "I don't believe that any further desecration of the dead with her embarrassing snuffling is warranted. Even a murderer's body should be treated with *some* respect. The case is closed and we needn't speak of it again."

"Fine. I *won't* speak of it again. To *you.* I'll just go downstairs and ask the front desk to find a way for me to speak with one of The Seated about this because you won't cooperate with me. One of The Seated whose life that 'embarrassing snuffling' saved."

He could see Joe Bob trying to control his rage. The Blueman knew that not only would *any* of The Seated immediately grant Elsie's request, but that he would probably be censured for trying to deny it.

"Very well. If it's that important to you, as our *honored guests*, I will allow your *far from reasonable* demand to be catered to."

Simon smiled then, stood up and offered his hand to Joe Bob, who pointedly looked away and refused to offer his own in return. "My family is going downstairs to have breakfast, and when we finish, I'll call you on my little red disc," he said, holding it up and waving it in front of Joe Bob, just to add insult to injury.

Without another sending or gesture of goodbye, Joe Bob stormed out. He was furious, but then he supposed this was just the sort of behavior he should have expected after all the ridiculous pandering to the visitors that had been going on. Where did this human get the nerve to demand that his slobbering beast be allowed in the chamber of the dead? What right did he have?

He'd had second thoughts about telling the human that there were no ships available to take his group home earlier. What a fool the man was, to believe that a society like this would only have a few ships capable of interstellar flight. He was glad he'd lied now. He'd done it then, because he'd thought it was a terrible waste of government money to bring all of these creatures to their planet, only to have them rush home like scared little children before the celebration they'd been brought to honor had even ended. He was glad now, because he couldn't stand the thought of acquiescing to any more of this human's obnoxious demands. He hadn't put a guard on their floor, or security cameras, either. What a waste of money *that* would have been. When he finished this assignment, he hoped to never see a human again.

##

Going into the bedroom, Simon gave Bess the news, and her reaction was much the same as his. She'd been sitting up in bed, holding the sheet in front of her, fearfully waiting to hear what news the pounding at the door heralded. When he told her, she closed her eyes and put one hand on her chest. "Thank God." She fell straight back onto her pillow then, fighting off the impulse to weep out of sheer relief.

He kissed her and sighed loudly. "You can say that again." Then he went to tell their son.

Jonas was still half asleep, but when his dad gave him the news, he took a deep breath and covered his face with his hands for a minute before looking back at him and smiling, shaking his head. "That's the best news I've ever heard. The feeling that we were being stalked---oh man, that preys on your mind. Wow, all of a sudden I feel kind of shaky. That's weird."

"No, it's not. Your mom and I had the same reaction. It's all that tension and fear we've tried not to show. The adrenaline has been keeping us all going, and all of a sudden, we can stop. It's like coming down after being high."

"You've had a lot of experience with that, have you?"

Simon grabbed the other pillow on the bed and trounced him with it. "Get up, and we'll go down to the café for breakfast. I think some food in our bellies might fortify us and get rid of that shaky feeling."

"Sounds good to me."

Ishmael overheard the plan and sent, "Could you just bring me something? I'd like to eat right inside of the balcony door and get an early start on tormenting my would-be assassin. I don't know why I find that so satisfying, but I do."

The creature had been returning every day to watch through the glass door for Ishmael. The two would spend hours sitting almost nose to beak, staring at each other through the glass. The eagle-thing ignored the humans, except to bristle at them in warning if they started to go outside, but when Elsie approached the glass, it would screech and fly away. It always returned though, with the hopes that Ishmael might be caught unawares outside.

Once or twice, the cat had sat on the balcony railing, waiting for the bird to see him, pretending he didn't notice its approach until the last minute, when he'd bound inside and hit the button to close the door, more than once resulting in a stunned creature lying on the balcony, with feathers drifting down from above. Best game ever.

"Okay, we'll bring you something, but don't you think you're limiting yourself a bit by doing this *every* day? You're missing the sights of an exotic, alien city that you'll never have a chance to see again."

"Ah, Simon, you poor humans will never understand the finesse it takes to do what I do. I'm slowly driving this thing insane. What could be more fun? It probably dreams about me when it sleeps. Besides, you know how I feel about cities. No, I'm having a marvelous visit, right here---I was born for this. If only it played chess, my victory could be complete."

"All right. To each his own."

CHAPTER TWENTY-TWO

It was the perfect setting. Cecil adjusted the cameras to focus on the stage, the area in front of the stage, and from the back forwards, so that any action facing the stage could be caught as well. One screen would show a view of what *he* was seeing, from a tiny facial microphone and camera he had temporarily implanted between his eyes. He arranged the others to pick up both sites from different angles, and some to automatically zoom in on faces and action. The cameras were sound and motion activated, so the whole climactic event would be recorded---everything anyone said---even the slightest whisper, and everything that was done, with close-ups to catch facial expressions. He wanted to be sure all the faces were seen, and that his final words were heard by the government and the people. In case they didn't automatically check the cameras, he'd leave a note in his apartment, instructing them to do so.

Deep in the middle of the reserve, in the thickest of the forested area, a large clearing had been made, with an empty space for seating to be placed in front of an earthen stage. The rich brown soil, when packed by machines and flattened on top, had made a very satisfactory platform for performances, and a wooden frame near the back of the stage stood bare and waiting, in case some performers preferred a physical barrier, or a "backstage" area. The park administrators occasionally invited in musicians, or had plays put on by local schools or theatre companies. These performances were always recorded for broadcasting, either on the city screens, or in the schools or theatre group headquarters. Occasionally, they were recorded and simply archived.

When no plays were scheduled, the area was used to lure wildlife in for a recording of the conditions of the different species in the reserve. These recordings were used by the city's biologists, and sometimes shown to the public for educational purposes. Adjusting and operating the cameras for these events fell under the duties of Cecil's job, and he was very good at it. Once the cameras were set, all he need do was to press one remote control button, and everything in the cleared area and on stage would be recorded.

While adjusting the cameras, he suddenly had to fight down a feeling of great melancholy. He didn't really want to die, but after he'd finished his "presentation," there would be no other recourse. Eventually, he would be caught and his mind re-trained. All hostile or negative thoughts would be wiped away, and he would be a happy, simpering, obedient creature for the rest of his days. In other words, *he* would be terminated. What was left of his brain after the adjustment would be someone else. That must never happen---he would never *allow* that to happen. He would go out proud and strong, on his own terms, after explaining and showing the damage that families could do. His own death would also serve as an example of the injury The Seated had brought to bear on the malcontents like him, who were just as important to society as those fools who blithely accepted The Rebirth.

He stopped working for a moment, high up in a tree where he lay on a branch to adjust a camera situated there. He wondered again why he and the others had been unable to accept The Rebirth, while the majority in their society seemed thrilled and fulfilled by it. Was something in their genetics askew? Had something been left out of their make-up? Why could he never respond to people in the same way he saw others do every day? Sometimes, when he looked in their eyes, he thought he could see genuine happiness. Why had he been denied that?

Brushing aside his thoughts about things he had no control over and that were now effectively in the past, he sighed and returned to work. Then he paused again, and thought about his plans.

He didn't think of himself as a cruel person, and yet he knew that some would see him as such, after they'd seen him murder the woman and the boy. No---it would *not* be murder. It would be---an educational exercise. Seeing another in pain was not necessarily enjoyable to him, but he didn't flinch from it, either. No one among The Seated had worried about the pain that The Rebirth would cause for those *like him*.

Sometimes pain was necessary in order to achieve a goal. The goal of abolishing The Rebirth. To change the change. The thought actually made him laugh---laughter was something new that had come with The Rebirth, and he was surprised to hear it coming from his own mouth. It would appear that he, himself, had been contaminated by this travesty. The need to laugh had been bypassed when new Bluemen were being produced in a Development Center. Then in the dormitories, laughter was never heard or experienced. There was no reason for it. Life was set and ordered. There was no irony, nothing unexpected, no humor, no joy. Life was life. It had been clean, simple, and pure.

He turned back to his work once more. The recordings were vital to getting his message out, for once he was gone, the media could interpret his actions simply as those of a sadistic madman, and the citizens would stupidly believe the fodder put before them. But with the whole scene played out for them---with his explanation, and then with his death, they would see that he was actually a hero, a martyr for the minority, a speaker of the truth, giving his life to show them the folly of this new society. *His name would be remembered.*

Besides, how could he be deemed cruel, when he'd been genetically programmed to be who he was? He had never desired or strived to be a malcontent. It was somehow programmed into him and the others like him. And was it not possible that this might be some cosmically ordained difference in him, meant to save their society from slipping back into those dark days of war? Perhaps he was answering some divine call. Beginning to feel better and better about his plan, he could see it playing out in his mind now. It would be beautiful.

CHAPTER TWENTY-THREE

He'd missed his prey again. The big cat, now roaring in anger, had once been king in this forest. Bigger than a lion, he was the largest of his kind in the reserve, with blue stripes on top and white spots on his lower half, and aside from long, retractable claws, he also possessed a very formidable set of teeth and fangs. If it had not been for that one fateful jump over a creek bed, he would be king still.

The chase was on and he'd been closing in on a large antelope-like herbivore. The prey was faster, but the cat had more stamina, and he had been chasing and tracking this same animal for several hours. When it leaped across a stream and seemed to stumble, he'd thought the prey was his, and had jumped across to try and snag a leg with his claws before it could fully recover its feet. But instead, he'd landed in the same hole that had tripped his intended victim, badly injuring his right front foot.

That was three days ago, and he'd caught only a few large rodents since then. He was ravenous, but with his injury, every attempt at catching his usual larger prey had ended in dismal failure. He still forced himself to run on the foot, but couldn't build any speed or maintain a run for very long. Without a decent kill soon, starvation loomed darkly in his future.

Then he'd seen the blue-skinned one. He had eaten one of these many years ago---one who had slipped into his domain in the middle of the night, for reasons unknown and uncared about by the cat. The taste had not been unsavory---not his favorite, but the creature had filled his belly and been sublimely easy to catch and dispatch. Hunger was what drove him now.

Following the blue-skin through the forest, with it seemingly unaware of him, the cat saw the one thing that would stop him---the pain stick. Experience with the pain stick made all of the predators in this wood take pause when they saw one. Then he'd recognized the smell of the blue-skin. This one was in the forest often, always with the pain stick in its hand, and though it had been in the forest for several hours this time, the stick was never out of reach.

For now, the cat would have to content himself with smaller fare, and hope it would sustain him until he healed, or until he found a blue-skin empty handed.

CHAPTER TWENTY-FOUR

The restaurant had a nicely shaded outdoor eating area, and it was a bright, beautiful day. Sven wasn't particularly frightened by the attempted poisonings of last night, for he'd heard on the broadcast this morning that the poisoner had confessed and then killed himself. It was a relief, of course, but since his conversation with Bess last night, he'd been consumed with the idea that maybe it *wasn't* impossible for him to have a family, and nothing else had really penetrated his thoughts.

He ate his breakfast slowly as he looked around the café. Besides being an attractive patio setting on a beautiful morning, and having good food, the café had one other huge attraction for Sven. It was across the street from the Flight Leaders Academy, and many of the students were breakfasting here.

Bess had been right about quite a few things in their conversation last night, and something that had really struck home was the subject of chemistry. Maybe that was another reason for the failure of his past relationships. He'd been attracted to the females he'd tried living with, but when he thought hard about it, none of them had made his heart go "pitty-pat," and he doubted their hearts had been acting up, either.

So he'd decided to breakfast here until he saw a female who affected his cardiac functioning. There were several lovely females in cadet uniforms here, and he sipped his drink while he listened to their conversations, watching them as they moved and interacted with their peers. His heart felt the same though, and the day looked no brighter to him for having seen them.

After almost finishing his second breakfast and getting ready to call it quits for this morning, with plans to return at lunch time, he saw *her*. She was lovely, and she was alone.

He heard her speaking with the counter help, and the sound of her voice intrigued him. It was forceful but polite. More forceful than he would have thought he'd be comfortable with, but he found himself wanting to hear more. He liked the way she moved---very sure of herself, and not the least bit self-conscious. Athletic and strong looking, but then she would have to be both in order to be a cadet in the first place.

She took her food and came out to the patio, sitting down at a table nearby. Knowing he looked foolish and was probably setting himself up for embarrassment and rejection, he still felt compelled to meet her. Standing up, plate and cup in hand, he walked over to her table. When she noticed him standing there, she looked up at him.

He almost dropped his food. She had the most lovely, light-purple irises that he'd ever seen, and something about her ears affected him deeply. He opened his mouth to speak, and when her beautiful pointed ears shifted towards him to catch the sound, he felt---YES---he felt his heart skip a beat! Instantly, everything he'd intended to say vanished from his mind, and he just stood there stupidly, trying to remember. She kept gazing at him politely, until at last, tired of waiting for him to speak, she asked, "Is there something you wanted?"

His immediate thought was, "Well, you of course!" but he had better sense than to blurt that out. He finally managed to stammer out an answer. "It's such a beautiful morning that I thought it would be nice to eat with a beautiful cadet." He couldn't *believe* he'd said such a thing. It sounded ridiculous, but nothing else had come to mind.

He was ready to bow his head in shame and slink away, when she replied, "That's the best approach I've heard so far this week. Have a seat, and we shall see if the man is as charming as his speech."

He was putty in her hands. She spoke of school and her aspirations, asked about his life and how he liked leading a crew, and she responded with an easy laugh to some of his stories, none of which he remembered afterwards. She told him that her human name for the week was "Cleo," short for Cleopatra, the name of an ancient human queen. Sven thought it ever so appropriate. Mesmerized by her voice, and the way she moved her mouth and hands when she spoke, he wanted to beg her to stay when she rose to leave the café.

"Uh, ah, well, um, this was lovely. I love listening to you talk. I mean, the conversation was very nice. You're not married, are you?"

She laughed and tilted her head, looking at him with a touch of pity. "May I help you? I think you're trying to ask to see me again, and since I'd like that very much, why don't I save you the embarrassment of stumbling around, trying to find the right words to woo me, and just give you my communicator number and address?" She whipped out her communicator, pressed in a code, and he held up his to receive it.

"I'm busy with classes for the next two days, but you can call me tonight and we can make a date for a few days from now. Don't disappoint me."

Holding his communicator in his hand, still mute with shock and happiness, he watched her as she walked away. He thought that the light *did* seem a little dimmer after she left. He *did* feel a little breathless. And the strangest thing of all was that he didn't mind her giving him directions. It felt fine when she told him what to do. He was shaky all over for a few seconds, and though he didn't feel a "pitty-pat," he thought he felt a "brr-brr," which was what he'd expect to feel from a heart in his species when that heart was wild with excitement. *Chemistry*. Oh, yes, *chemistry*.

CHAPTER TWENTY-FIVE

Going against his better judgement, Sven called her as soon as she walked into the building across the street, and he couldn't see her anymore. She didn't respond to his first or second call, but on the third, she answered

She scolded him, but he could hear in her voice that she wasn't really annoyed. "I thought I told you to call me tonight."

"Perhaps your beauty affected my hearing."

"Then how can you hear me now?"

"When you walked away and took the sun with you, my hearing returned. Or maybe the sun didn't leave. Perhaps when you left, I was blinded by the longing to hear your voice once more, shutting down my other senses so I could concentrate on every tiny utterance from your mouth." These words could *not* be coming out of *his* mouth. It was like he was *vomiting poetry.*

Now she was laughing---a big, honest, full-throated laugh that thrilled him to the core. "How in the world do you come up with this crap?"

"I have no idea. I don't read poetry or romances, but I think about you and the words just come spewing forth like sea foam on a windy day. See, it happened again. I don't think I'm in full control of my faculties anymore. Not since I first saw you and the vision of amethyst in your eyes. There I go again. Please, make it stop."

"And just how could I do that?"

"See me again. Now."

"I told you I had school, but---"

"Cut class."

"You know a cadet can't cut class."

"I know it but my heart knows no rules that can vanquish love. See? Could you really let me leave here talking like that? I could lose my commission."

"Well, when I got to class---"

"Shall my soul drink of your presence, or shall it thirst unto death? Ugh, did you hear *that*? Come out here before I embarrass *myself* unto death, or people start throwing things at me."

"If you'd just shut up and let me finish, I was going to tell you that when I came into class, the professor told me that the government cancelled classes for the next two days in honor of the celebration."

He gasped and almost shouted, "Does that mean you're coming out to see me, O angel of desire?"

"On one condition."

"Shall I rip out my still beating heart and place it in your hands to prove my---"

"OKAY. ENOUGH. Cut the crap."

"Right. Whatever you say, beloved queen."

"You're pushing it."

"All right. Whatever you desire, my sun kissed flower."

"I'm disconnecting."

"NO, DON'T! I'm sorry. Anything but that."

"My condition, is that you desist with the flowery language. It's one thing to laugh about it over our communicators, but if you embarrass me in public with it, I may have to kill you, and it would certainly be ruled self-defense. In fact, I might even get a commendation for exterminating a public nuisance."

"Ah, but I would die a happy man."

There was no response to this.

"All right. No inspired language. I will do my best to comply, cadet. You do know that I am a Ship Leader and obviously outrank you."

"We're not on a ship, and once I step out this door, you have no authority over me. I don't say 'Sir' unless the law requires it. Get used to the idea."

"Yes, cadet. So you're coming out now, really?"

She switched off her communicator and walked out the door.

He watched her walking across the street towards him and he felt the "brr-brr" again. He *loved* chemistry.

She walked up to him, and he felt something happen to his mouth. His mouth was stretching on both sides. He gasped---was this a smile? He'd heard about them, and seen them on humans, but never on Bluemen. They were supposed to signify happiness, and whatever was happening wasn't painful. In fact, it made him *feel* happy, so maybe it *was* a smile.

"All right. I'm here. So what now?" she asked, and *she* was definitely smiling.

"Do you do that often?"

"What?"

"Smile. It looks stunning when you do it, and that isn't crap."

She laughed then, and her smile got bigger. "Actually, I was watching the broadcast of the human visitors, when I saw the woman smile at her husband, and it just seemed to hold such meaning, and all of it happy, so I decided to try it. It really does feel right---when I'm happy, that is. And when I aim it at someone I want to be with."

There went his heart again. He wondered if it might just come flying out of his mouth any minute. What a glorious way to die. "That means you want to be with me, and that I make you happy?"

"I'm here aren't I? So where are we going? It had better be good, because I don't have many days off."

"I thought we'd walk to the heart of the city for the celebration. There are some friends of mine that I think you'd enjoy meeting, too. We could have dinner later, and then watch the sparklings that they're setting off over the lake."

"That sounds nice. By the way, I'm a big eater, so be prepared for a huge bill. I'm definitely worth it, in case you were wondering."

"I can't think of any way I'd rather go broke." He knew she hadn't recognized him as one of the Bringers of

The Rebirth. He could take her to the most expensive restaurant in the city tonight, and walk out without paying. It must be destiny.

As they started walking towards the city's heart, he debated whether to try something he'd seen Bess and Simon do; something that seemed to carry a special significance, and had radiated such a warmth and caring between them. Well, why not? The worst she could do was humiliate and possibly injure him. He'd risk it.

Very slowly, while pretending to look in a shop window, he reached down and took one of her hands in his. He kept his eyes averted, and he felt a surprised little jerk from her at first, but then her hand relaxed and wrapped around his, and she gave a quick little squeeze. *Oh, Blessed Chemistry!*

CHAPTER TWENTY-SIX

Outside of the building, the noise in the streets was getting louder and louder with the celebration gearing up into full swing. As loathsome and annoying as Cecil found moving through a crowd, with strangers actually touching his shoulders with their own, or having their legs brush against his, the noise and crowds would provide excellent cover for him. No one would remember his face out of the thousands that were out celebrating today.

After watching the visitors for several days, he felt fairly certain they would come to the café downstairs for breakfast, especially now that the threat of poisoning was over. He made sure that he was there much earlier than they usually arrived, and he loitered near the staff entrance until he saw a familiar face getting off the tube and heading his way.

The waiter was one of the malcontents that he knew from their meetings. They had shared a few short conversations and parted on a civil basis. Cecil approached him before he could get near the entrance, and motioned him off to the side. He moved behind a pillar that supported this section of the tube, and his "friend" followed suit.

"Did you see the broadcast?" Cecil asked in a hushed tone, acting shocked.

"Yes, can you believe it? Would you ever have thought anyone could be that crazy? Murder? Like that would accomplish anything. And then suicide? He always seemed pretty calm and rational to me, not the wild-eyed, snorting fire, drooling saliva type at all, like you'd expect."

Keeping himself from striking this worm was becoming more and more difficult for Cecil. He forced himself to nod in agreement, keeping his eyes averted so that his rage wouldn't show through. "I know, it's hard to fathom such rage and violence in a person. Maybe The Rebirth affected him more deeply than the rest of us. But listen, I have a great favor to ask of you. A small blow for the malcontents."

The Blueman took an immediate step back and held his hands up in front of his chest. "Oh, no, not me. I'm not a violent person. I know I complain and whine with the rest of them at the gatherings, but I would never strike anyone. I don't want any trouble."

"Nor do I. But I overheard the human woman and her son talking, and it made my blood boil. She said that the malcontents were no better than animals, and if The Rebirth made them all suicidal, then good riddance."

"She didn't! She actually said that?"

"Yes, and her son agreed with her, adding that the government should just go to one of the meetings, round up all the malcontents and 'get rid of them once and for all.'"

"Those despicable, judgmental, pompous, abominable--- They know *nothing* about what we've been through!"

"Exactly. I was so stunned and horrified by the vicious, ignorant arrogance of the two that I could hardly credit what I'd heard. That's why I felt compelled to strike back for all of us, but only in the mildest way."

"What did you have in mind?"

"When you know what these creatures are like, and then you see them swilling our people's food down like animals, and for free---it's just too much. I thought how fitting it would be if our food fought back. I have these drops---all they induce when ingested is nausea and a very slight stomach ache, and the symptoms subside in an hour or two. They wouldn't be ill enough to need a doctor, or suspect spoiled food. They'll just think that our food isn't suited to their bodies. It would be the simplest thing in the world if you could just put one drop into the glasses of the woman and the boy---a little nausea is not much of a price to pay for their heinous attitude. Only you and I would know, but at least the two of us could find satisfaction in a bit of justice being done. I don't want to make the man ill---he didn't seem to share their sentiments."

The other Blueman put his hands in his pockets and swayed back and forth for a minute, looking at the ground. Finally, he raised his head, and then a look of angry determination transformed his face. "I'll do it. Give me the drops."

Cecil almost shouted with glee. It was all too easy. "Here you go. You can throw the rest away after you put the drops in their drinks. Don't put more than one in for each. We want just a little discomfort, and it needs to start after they've left the table, to avoid suspicion. Do you understand?"

"Yes, yes, now let me go. I don't want to be late for work and draw attention to myself."

He watched as his "friend" hurried to the staff entrance and disappeared inside the door.

CHAPTER TWENTY-SEVEN

Putting on his uniform, "Rupert" was still steaming as he thought about the callousness of that human female. To say such things about the malcontents was simply unconscionable. And to think that he and the other employees at the restaurant had been forced to take assigned human names for the week---what had seemed silly to him before was now repugnant.

His boss yelled for him to speed it up and take orders so that they didn't start the day already behind. He hurried out into the eating area, where he was immediately flagged down from several tables---everyone wanting something different. There were three other waiters on duty, but with the celebration in full swing now, the tables were all full and there was a waiting area full of hungry citizens. He looked around desperately, but didn't see the humans yet. That was a break for him, letting him at least get started on his real job before he had to start his career as a saboteur.

Finally, he saw the humans arrive and take their place in line in the waiting area. When the owner peeked out from the kitchen and spotted the humans, he hurried out and ushered them in to sit at a special table he'd been reserving for them. Embarrassed at the favoritism shown them, Simon tried to insist that they wait their turn like everyone else, but surprisingly, the Bluepeople waiting for seating encouraged them to go ahead, thanking them for helping to bring about The Rebirth. It would've made more of a scene to stand and argue about it, so the four of them, including Elsie, went along with the owner and thanked everyone for their consideration.

For ten minutes or so after being seated, the family was kept busy with well-wishers, and Bluepeople who wanted to take pictures of them. They were gracious about it, and would have continued, had not the owner interjected himself once again, and ordered the celebrity seekers away from their table.

All of the Sayers were uncomfortable at the amount of attention being showered on them, so they decided to order something fast and get out as quickly as possible. The only problem being that the menu was a complete mystery to them. Written in Blueman print, in a language they didn't understand, about dishes they'd never heard of, the menus were as much use to them as a pitchfork with soup.

Bess called over their waiter, "Darryl," and inquired about which dishes were easiest, fast, and palatable, and ordered three of those that he recommended and two bowls of meat for Elsie and Ishmael. Simon was polite to everyone, but Bess and Jonas could see how agitated he was.

"What's wrong, Simon?" Bess asked, and then added, "Wow, that was a really inane question. Murders and attempted murders all around us, and attempted *on* us, and I say 'what's wrong?' Not one of my more intelligent openings."

"I know you're just showing concern---sorry my mood makes that necessary. Never have been too good at hiding my feelings. It's about what you said. This whole thing is so horrible and frightening, and now I find that I have no trust in Joe Bob at all. I think he would've let everything slide, to just be swept under the rug, if I hadn't insisted otherwise. What does that say about who he is, and how trustworthy he is---to let murder go unanswered, and possibly continued? To be willing to let more of his own people die, because it's inconvenient to investigate, or because the investigation wasn't his idea. That kind of attitude is just incomprehensible to me. And our family and friends have been put in his hands.

"I called Elliott yesterday and asked him to check into that power failure in the park, and he said he would, and that he'd leave me a message at the desk. There was nothing there for me last night or this morning. And the fact that he didn't show up at the apartment last night---that just doesn't seem like him. He's always struck me as the kind of guy who would make every appointment five minutes early, and would never miss work, or a work message. I'm worried about him, on top of everything else. What if my request put him in danger? It just doesn't feel right that he hasn't called me.

"Now this thing about Elsie wanting to be sure they have the right Blueman, and the way Joe Bob reacted to that--- He should be so thankful to her, and yes, to me, too, for helping prevent more deaths. Yet all we get is resentment and roadblocks. It just makes me angry and nervous about having all of us here. Our leaving can't be too soon for me."

Elsie nodded, panting nervously. "I smelled fear on him when you talked to him this morning, and anger, too. I'm still working on narrowing this smell down, since I'm pretty new at smelling Bluepeople, but I think I smelled deception, too. I don't like him at all. Since this Blueman who supposedly is the poisoner, died from poison, how do we know that he wasn't just another victim? Any Blueman could send a communication from his apartment."

"That's right, and until Elliott started this investigation, they've never even fingerprinted here, so something like that would have been ridiculously simple to orchestrate. I'm glad you're insisting on this, Elsie. What a great dog you are."

She visibly puffed her chest out, then wagged her tail and settled back down on the floor.

In the kitchen, meanwhile, Rupert was going crazy. He had five tables he was supposed to be handling, plus watching for which food was going out to the humans. And *then*, he was supposed to somehow manage to get just one drop of the liquid into the woman's and boy's drinks. And his friend thought this would be so simple. Let *him* come in here and try it!

Finally, he saw the drinks being prepared to go out to the humans' table. A new problem was how to tell whose drink was whose. He went over to their glasses with a slice of garnish for the drinks, even though they hadn't asked for any, and stood in front of the glasses so that his back was to the rest of the kitchen and obstructing the view of what he was doing. He put a drop into each glass, and then asked their waiter if he could take the glasses to them so that he could thank them for being bringers of The Rebirth. Darryl didn't mind—he was too busy to turn down any offer of help.

Bess looked up and smiled at Rupert when she saw him bringing their drinks. *She looks so pleasant. Hard to believe she's such a vile creature underneath.* He put their drinks down, and made a big show of thanking them for being bringers, making a grand gesture at the end of his performance, which caused him to "accidentally" knock the man's drink off the table.

Some of the drink splashed onto the man, and he got up and brushed it off his clothes, while Rupert apologized profusely. The human told him not to worry about it, no harm done, and sat back down again. Rupert rushed back into the kitchen for an untainted drink, congratulating himself for his cleverness.

After delivering the man's drink, he walked by the backdoor of the kitchen and feigned a cough in order to stick his head outside to "cough" and signal to the other that it was done.

##

It must have been preordained that he complete his efforts and go out victorious. Everything was falling into place. He'd barely even had to plan anything, for at every turn, opportunities seemed to be put into his hands. This was the humans' last day on the planet before their return flight tomorrow, so surely they and their friends would want to go out and see some of the celebrations. Alas, the woman and her whelp would feel too ill to participate, and would encourage the others to go without them. They wouldn't be lonely for long.

CHAPTER TWENTY-EIGHT

When they returned to the apartment, Bess delivered Ishmael his standard "to go" meal by the balcony door, where his eagle-thing sat and stared at him from the other side. Bess shook her head at the sight. "Buddy, I think you're playing with fire."

He dug into his chow and sent back, "But it feels so good!" and kept chewing.

She shook her head again and turned away to plop down on one of the couches, taking her shoes off and putting up her feet. Starting to feel a little queasy, with the bare hint of a stomach ache, she didn't think it important enough to mention until Simon asked her, "Do you want to go to the morgue with us to see the body?"

She groaned and looked at him in disbelief. "Under no circumstances that I can think of, would I *ever* like to see a dead Blueman. Much less now. I think that breakfast didn't agree with me. The cereal stuff was a little slimy for my taste."

Jonas heard her remark and came into the living room. "I feel kinda queasy, too. Just a little bit, and a very mild stomach ache." Saying this, he deposited himself on the other couch with a sigh.

Simon held his hand to Jonas' forehead, and then to Bess' in concern. "Should I see if I can find a doctor for you?"

Both Bess and Jonas immediately shook their heads. She rubbed her hand across her stomach and looked up at him. "If the food had been bad, it would take longer than this for us to have symptoms, I would think. Nah, this is really a mild discomfort. Just feels like I should scratch alien gruel off all my future menus."

Jonas nodded in accord. "Yeah, I feel the same. Like it will probably blow over in an hour or two. We'll be fine, Dad."

"I know it probably seems paranoid, but what with everything that's happened, I don't like leaving you two alone. I sent to Eli, and he and the others want to go with me. They want to see the face of the Blueman who tried to kill them. Except for Barnabas. He sent that he's seen enough death in his lifetime, and wants to go shopping for something to take back to his wife."

Pacing back and forth before, now he sat down on the couch. "I'm calling Joe Bob and telling him we'll go later today, when you both feel like coming. I'm too uneasy with the idea of leaving you alone."

"No!" the two said together. "Simon, I told you, even if I feel fine later, I am *not* going to go look at a corpse. I'm sorry, but I'm just not. And it's not like Jonas is a little boy. He's as tall as I am, with a lot more muscle, and then we have our resident lion over by the balcony."

"Yo!" Ishmael sent, without stopping his meal.

"And you can send to Barnabas to come by here as soon as he finishes his excursion. If he's like most males, his shopping tolerance won't be very long."

"Dad, it's really important for everybody that Elsie establishes this guy as the killer. None of us will ever feel completely at ease until we get her take on it being the right guy, and if it's *not* him, then the authorities need to know so they can keep hunting. We'll be out of here by tomorrow night, but they'll still have a maniac on their hands. You need to get it done ASAP."

Sighing, he slapped his thighs and stood up. "Okay, I guess you're right. Just be sure you lock the door after me and keep your red disc handy to call Joe Bob if there's a problem. Call if you think anything is suspicious. Promise me---don't wait."

"Okay, okay, we promise."

"Now for the divine pleasure of calling Joe Bob, the little bastard."

"Hey!" Ishmael sent, and his head popped up from his dish. "I resent you using my name on that jerk! It sullies the friendly nuance attached to your endearment."

"No, no, Ishie, you're the '*cheeky* little bastard.' He's just the 'little bastard,' with no endearment attached."

"Well, okay then."

Bess gave him "The Look," while jerking her head in the direction of Jonas, and said in a pointed tone, "Simon…"

"All right, all right. Sorry. Jonas, you didn't hear that."

Jonas rolled his eyes. "Like I've never heard that before. Mom, you have no idea, all the stuff I hear at school. It would curl your hair."

"Oh, Jonas, do you think I'm an idiot, deaf, or completely out of touch with reality? I've picked you up from school before. I've heard all the language. What you have there is a bunch of kids trying to sound tough and grown up by using foul language, and what they don't realize, is that it makes them *sound* like a bunch of kids trying to sound tough and grown up.

"I'm not trying to shelter virgin ears. I just don't want that to be language you hear in our home. Yeah, we may lose it sometimes and say things we shouldn't, but it's not a cool thing, nor something to emulate. When we're dead and gone, the last thing I'd want you to recall about us is how we sounded when we were using profanity. We have more class than that. *You* have more class than that. Got it?"

"Yeah, yeah, got it, got it. But I do think Dad's right about Ishie."

"Me too," sent Ishie.

Simon had gone into the other room to make his call, and when he came back in, his face was red. Bess saw his color and looked over at Jonas. "Uh oh."

"Well, our caretaker said there are tickets for the tube waiting for us at the desk, with the name of our stop on it to show to the riding staff, so that they'll be sure and let us off at the right place. Then when we get there, he says we're to put my little red disc on the screen, and we'll be allowed in. The staff there will call him when we arrive, so that he doesn't have to *waste valuable time*. He's sending us by way of mass transit in these crowds. I'll bet it takes us twice as long to go to and from as it would with private transport. The haughty little---jerk."

She mouthed "Thank you" to him.

"Well, I guess I'm off to round up our Elpies. Come on Elsie. Hope you both get to feeling better soon." He leaned over and gave Bess a kiss, then leaned over and planted one on the top of Jonas' head, too fast for him to duck away. Back to his usual form, he said, "Ycch," so his dad came back and punched him hard on the arm. "Ouch! Yeah, that's more like it!"

Men.

The door clicked shut, and they heard the lock engage. Jonas lounged a few more minutes in the living room, and then told Bess he was going into his room and try to sleep it off. Bess thought that an excellent idea, and slid further down on the couch to try and do the same.

CHAPTER TWENTY-NINE

Barnabas enjoyed browsing more than he would have admitted. The colors of the city captured his imagination, and every bright or shiny thing in the shop windows seemed to blend in with the colors of the buildings to make the whole world sparkle. It was all amazing, but he missed home, and he missed his family. His five children were all grown, with families of their own now, but they lived close by. He saw his grandchildren daily, and they made him warm with pride and affection. Most of all, he missed his wife.

He'd always loved his family, and thought about them when he was gone, but with the exception of the time he'd spent helping to care for Simon twenty years ago, he'd never been away from them for more than two or three days. Now their absence was like a physical ache inside, and he was shopping more to ease that ache than because his wife desired any trinket from the Blueman planet. Getting something for her would ease his loneliness for the rest of the trip, because he would have something of hers with him.

He looked at clothes, but tired of that quickly, for Colders didn't wear clothes except in the most extreme weather. He didn't know how long food would last on the ship, so he decided against anything edible. What to choose for someone who had nothing and needed nothing?

He was strolling through a jewelry store, when he saw it---a beautiful bracelet of copper colored metal that framed and backed a mosaic of glittering stones portraying bird-like creatures of wildly varied hues. He could picture it high on her upper arm, the green of her skin setting off the colors of the stones.

He had been told that anything in the city was theirs for the asking on these celebratory days, but he didn't feel right without trading something. The only thing he'd brought with him was his necklace of gold stone cemented together with the fangs of some beast that the Bluemen had left on his planet. He'd found the skeleton, and pried the fangs out of the skull to make his necklace many years ago, and had strung the decoration on a leather thong. That was in the days when he was courting his wife, and he'd thought it made him look strong and fierce.

He chuckled to himself at the thought now. After these many years together, he didn't need his necklace to prove anything to his wife. She *knew* he was strong and fierce, and at just the right times, too.

He approached the counter where the bracelet lay, and looked for Bluepeople staff with devices attached to their heads, for these would be able to understand his sendings and send to him. He'd been standing there awhile, looking for the telltale devices, when he realized that he'd gathered a crowd of Bluepeople behind him, standing a polite distance away, but watching his every move with fascination. He turned around to face them, and sent outwards, asking if anyone could help him. A dozen Bluepeople rushed forward, so he bowed his thanks to them all, and chose a young looking female that he supposed would know about jewelry.

She nodded her head at his sendings, bubbling with enthusiasm at the chance to send with and actually assist a bringer. Not to mention, she thought he was cool looking for an alien. She grabbed the first Blueperson staff member she could lay hands on, who happened to be the owner, as well, and dragged him over to the counter. The Colder had explained to her that he wanted to trade for the bracelet, and she relayed this to the Blueman.

He took out the bracelet that the Colder had indicated, and blanched. Barnabas had chosen one of the most expensive items in the store, and this Blueman and all of the other merchants in the city had specific orders that anything in their stores that the bringers desired during these days of celebration was to be free to them. This represented a substantial loss to his business, but he swallowed and decided that since he had no choice but to follow the edict, he would be dignified and gracious at the loss.

He had the youth explain to Barnabas that the bracelet was a gift to him, with his thanks for bringing them the Rebirth. Instead of taking it from his hand, Barnabas shook his head vehemently, and sent to the Bluegirl that he would not rob the man of his business. He must take his trade, as humble as it may be. To be polite, the Blueman accepted the trade, which he supposed would be some piece of junk, or a knife that he would never need.

Nodding his head in acquiescence, the owner had wrapped the precious piece lovingly in a soft material, and then placed it in a beautifully engraved metal gift box. Barnabas handed him his necklace, bowed his thanks to the owner and to his translator, and left. Looking at the pitiful piece in his hand, and shaking his head, more to himself than anyone else, the owner was suddenly bombarded by the watching crowd, who had surged forward on the departure of the bringer, and began shouting offers to buy the Colder's necklace. Within a few minutes, he had offers of three times what the bracelet would have sold for.

Feeling very happy with his trade, and thinking about how pleased and touched his wife would be with her gift, Barnabas turned and began to make his way back through the crowds to the apartments.

CHAPTER THIRTY

After an hour on the tube with well-meaning Bluepeople who were sending and speaking their thanks and crushing in on them from all sides, making them feel that suffocation must be imminent, the six were finally released at their destination with sendings and shouts of farewell from those still on the tube. The whole group was a little shaky from the experience, and Ruth turned pale and had to sit down on the steps of the building to regain her composure for a few minutes.

For creatures like the Elpies, who lived their whole lives on the plains, in forests, or mountains, where the population was exceedingly sparse, to be crammed into a small space, crushed between other living beings, with little fresh air to breath, was a claustrophobic's worst nightmare. Dulcie, Martha and Eli knelt in front of Ruth solicitously, and Simon searched frantically for anything that looked like a public fountain where he could get her a drink of water.

Seeing nothing outside, he ran to the building in front of them, slammed his red disc onto the screen and hurried in when the door opened. He spied a machine with a picture of a waterfall on it, and cups set to the side of it in a large container. Rushing over, he grabbed a cup, and was gratified to discover that this *was* a water machine, and the controls were simple enough for even an alien human to master. Precious cargo in hand, he ran back outside and handed the cup to Ruth. Eli had given her something from his medicine pouch, which she was chewing slowly, and she accepted the water from Simon with a great sending of thanks.

Another five minutes saw her much steadier, and her color had returned. Simon sent to her, expressing doubts that she should go in to see the body, thinking that it might be too much for her, but her answer to him was emphatic, and *she* led the way into the building.

For a morgue to be solid orange seemed somehow very wrong to Simon, but after all, this was not his planet. The inside was even worse, done in yellow of the brightest hue imaginable, and he could only wonder if this was supposed to cheer up the relatives who came to identify the bodies of their loved ones, if they even did that kind of thing here. Other than the colors, he found everything else very morgue-like---quiet, freezing, and with hardly anyone in the halls. They kept walking until they found someone at a desk. She was polite, and ushered them into a room with some uncomfortable chairs to sit on while they waited for Joe Bob. The Bluewoman who ushered them in went to call him and assured them it would only be a short time until he arrived.

After a wait of about ten minutes, shorter than Simon had expected, Joe Bob entered the room, and without addressing any of them, opened the door to the storage area and motioned for them to come in. One glance told Simon that not many Bluemen died at the same time, and that the government didn't plan on wasting a lot of money on decorations that would never be seen. The room was small, only about as large as the standard two car garage back home, and there was one long table with three bodies on it, covered with cloth. The walls were a bright chartreuse here, and the color and its location made him a little nauseous.

Joe Bob merely walked up to the table and pointed at the first body under the sheet. Simon steeled himself, and pulled the sheet back. He didn't recognize the Blueman, but death was such a sad thing to behold, that he almost felt compelled to pat the hand or the shoulder---to give some kind of sympathy.

The Elpies moved in and took a long look, and then stepped back and let Elsie do her thing. She sniffed the corpse from top to bottom, up one side and down the other, and then sent to Simon, "This is *not* the poisoner. I sniffed every scene where poison was found, and I know all of the scents that were there in the rooms. His wasn't one of them. This guy was probably a victim as well."

She sent the same message to Joe Bob, who just looked at her as if she were some stupid animal without intelligence or meaning in the world. Simon found his voice rising as he asked, "Well, aren't you going to call someone? Let somebody know that they need to keep up the security, and keep looking for this maniac?"

Joe Bob looked at them scornfully. "This is a dog. I'm not taking any more actions on a dog's advice, or yours either, for that matter. We've catered to your little fancies long enough. You'll be leaving the planet tomorrow and needn't concern yourself about it anymore."

"You lazy, arrogant, incompetent, little bastard!" Simon started moving forward, pressing Joe Bob back against a wall. "You'd be willing to let more murders take place in your city, not to mention put my friends and family at risk, just to make it look like you have everything under control? Is that why you're acting like this? Is it? ANSWER ME!" He was shouting now, only inches from the Blueman's face.

"Get away from me!" he screamed. "You're completely ignorant about our planet and our way of conducting business, and yet you come in and start taking over everything, calling The Seated like a child tattling to its mother, whenever you don't get your way. Why they ever invited you in the first place is a mystery to me. I'm sick of you ordering me around at your every whim.

"For your information, we *did* have a ship that could have taken you home earlier, but you had no right to ask for that kind of privilege, so I made you wait, like anyone else would have to. And there have *never* been guards on your floor, *or* security cameras, because you don't deserve them, and didn't need them."

Suddenly Simon's blood ran cold, thinking about Bess and Jonas alone in the apartment. He was beyond furious now. The two guards standing at the door were watching the scene with mounting concern. His voice became quiet and cold, and his eyes narrowed as he spoke into Joe Bob's face.

"My wife and son are alone in an apartment that you failed to protect. Now your petty little trick of bringing us here by public transportation cost us an extra half hour, but you're going to get us a private ride back and do it NOW, so that we can get back to them. So help me, if any harm comes to them or any of my friends, I will see your head stuck on a pole in front of this building."

Taking Simon's cue, the dog and all four Elpies bared their teeth and advanced on the Blueman.

Frightened now, but still angry and affronted as well, Joe Bob cried out, "Guards! Arrest this human and his lizards, and kill this vicious animal! They're threatening *me*, an official representative of The Seated!"

Just then, Watson came barging in, and ignoring everything else that was happening in the room, shouted into Joe Bob's face. "WHERE IS HE?"

Joe Bob shoved him away, and shouted back, "Where's who?"

Simon broke in then, with a feeling of dread even worse than before. "Are you looking for Elliott?"

"Yes. He came in to see *him* yesterday," he answered, jabbing a finger towards Joe Bob, "to request a weapon before he went out looking for clues about a power failure at the reserve, and this fungal rot refused him! And when I tried to locate him last night for the incident with your friends, nobody could find him. He *always, always* answers his calls. Then this morning I called his home, and his wife was frantic, saying he never came home last night and never called. She was hoping he was working late with me and had somehow lost track of time, and maybe had left his communicator somewhere. But I tell you, Simon, Elliott is the consummate family man. He'd *never* cause his wife that kind of worry, and not even call her. *Never.*"

Now he got back up into Joe Bob's face. "Did you set him up? Did you send him somewhere to be killed? If anything has happened to him, I'll have your head, you little---"

"I have first dibbs," Simon interrupted, looking pointedly at Joe Bob.

"He's fine. We did argue yesterday, and this morning he came in and resigned."

Watson gasped. He couldn't believe that Elliott would leave without telling him or his family. "Why didn't he tell me, or clear out his office? Why didn't he call his wife?"

"I don't know his motives, but he was so angry that he slammed my door and caused a picture to fall off and break, so I assume he left to cool off. But he's not my problem anymore. You aren't either when this is over, because I'll see that you're dismissed."

Watson turned on his heels and strode out of the room.

The guards had been listening to everything. They had heard the edict from The Seated about how important to their planet's integrity it was to honor those who had helped to bring about The Rebirth. This Blueman was their superior in title, but he had just admitted to lying and blatantly disobeying The Seated's orders to accommodate the bringers' wishes. He'd purposely hidden a dangerous situation, dishonored their guests, possibly putting them in danger, and disgraced their whole planet with his behavior. And the only reason they could ascertain for all of his shameless actions was conceit, which made it even more reprehensible.

"I order you take these creatures into custody, and do it NOW!" he screamed.

The first guard replied quietly, "It's *you* we should put into custody, not the bringers." Then he turned his back on the hysterical little official and bowed to Simon and the Elpies.

"We are shamed by the actions of this one, and we can only give you our deepest apologies. We know that The Seated have greatly appreciated your help in stopping the poisonings. There's a vehicle at our disposal that will cut your time back in half, and we'd be honored to take you now."

They all filed out of the room, with the exception of Joe Bob, who stood shaking with anger, indignation, and fear next to the dead, who couldn't have cared less.

CHAPTER THIRTY-ONE

Dozing on the couch, Bess had fallen asleep to the sound of her son's even breathing coming through the open door between the rooms. The sounds of her children's breathing while they slept had always comforted her and given her a feeling of peace. To hear those deep, even breaths was to know that those she loved most in the world were safe and untroubled, at least while they slumbered..

A chiming woke her up, and she tried to get to the door quietly, without waking Jonas. She flipped the lever for the door screen, and there was a tall Blueman in a green employee's jacket, holding a small bottle.

"Can I help you?"

"Your husband stopped by the desk on his way out earlier. He said that you and your son were suffering from stomach distress and asked if anything could be sent up to help you. We apologize for the delay---it took us a little while to locate our company physician. He ordered this medication for you and asked that we deliver it to you immediately. The directions are written in human letters on the bottle."

That's so typical of Simon, she thought. With a smile, she began to open the door, and the next moment it came crashing in as the Blueman threw his weight against it, knocking her to the floor. He turned and rammed the door shut and locked it, and as he did, she lunged for the red disc on the counter. He grabbed her arm, jerked the disk out of her hand, and threw it across the room.

Jonas heard the crash and jumped to his feet, running into the room. Bess screamed, "JONAS, RUN! RUN!" and then threw herself at the Blueman. He was larger than any she'd seen, almost eight and a half feet, and too tall for her to reach his face easily, so she jumped and came down with both feet on the top of his right foot, feeling something break when she landed. He screamed in agony, just as Jonas lunged at him. He batted him away with one huge hand across his face and chest, sending him flying across the room, and then grabbed Bess around the waist with his other two and threw her against a wall.

Hitting the corner edge of the wall face first, she felt a crunch as her left cheek and forehead made contact, and then came a blinding pain in her left eye, followed by a burst of wetness down her face. She was still conscious, moaning in pain, when she saw the Blueman's third hand pointing a fire stick at Jonas, who was running at him again with his shoulder down, hoping to knock him off his feet. She grabbed the back of a chair to drag herself up, but not in time to stop the Blueman. He fired the stick and it caught Jonas on the arm, sending him to the floor in a quivering heap as the shock ran through him.

"NO!" she screamed, and threw herself at him once more to try and smash his other foot. Catching her mid-leap, he picked her up and threw her with even greater force, and she screamed as the table caught her on the ribs and abdomen, and she felt ribs splinter and something tear inside.

Barnabas was just walking to the door of the Sayers' apartment when he heard something bang against the wall, and he thought he heard a scream that cut off abruptly. He threw down his package and grabbed for the door handle, but it was locked. Throwing himself back to balance on his tail, he kicked the door in with both feet and bounded into the room. One look at the Blueman holding a semiconscious Bess up by one arm, and he launched himself claws first, at the creature. His claws just raked one of the assailant's arms before the fire stick caught him square in the chest, and sent him writhing to the floor.

Cecil was overcome with rage. This should have been so simple, and now the woman had injured his foot, and the lizard had clawed his arm. *No more interference!*

Grabbing the Colder's arm with one hand, he dragged him across the floor and pressed the button to open the sliding door to the patio. A huge bird squawked and flew away as he lifted the unconscious Colder above his head with two hands and threw him off the balcony, just in time for the woman to come around enough to scream, "BARNABAS, NO!"

He strode back across the room and kicked her once in the head, lightly. He *wanted* to kill her *now*, but wrestled down his fury, telling himself that he could vent his anger soon enough. He need just be patient a little longer to see his plan out to the end.

Ishmael had been watching everything from behind one of the couches. He knew that with the size of this creature, and with it having three arms, an attack would be pointless. A dead cat couldn't improve the odds for Bess and Jonas. He had to get that red disk and go for help.

When Cecil turned his back towards the balcony, Ishmael ran and jumped onto its railing, waving his tail back and forth until he was sure the eagle-thing saw him. As it swooped towards him, he jumped down, ran inside and between Cecil's legs, snagging the disk off the floor with a claw and transferring it to his mouth in one smooth motion. When he ran between the Blueman's feet, Cecil bent low from the waist, lunging down and outwards to swipe at him with one hand, just in time to meet the eagle-thing's strike. Its claws were already swung forward, ready to spear Ishmael, but they hit the Blueman's chest instead.

Cecil screamed as his flesh tore in the beasts' claws, and he reached out, grabbed it around the throat with one huge hand, and slammed its head down on the table, killing it instantly, but not before its beak caught one of his fingers and snapped it off. Screaming in pain and horror at his mutilated hand, he rushed into the bathroom and ran water over it while he searched for something to stop the bleeding. He found a forming bandage, slapped it against his finger stump, and watched as the bandage wrapped around and sealed itself in one automatic action. Then he rinsed the claw marks on his chest and arm, sealing them with more medicine from the complimentary first aid kit in the bathroom.

Finally, he took one of the pain masking vials, snapped the top off, and swallowed every drop of liquid it held. As the pain subsided, he made himself breathe slowly, trying to calm his rage and anxiety.

Ishmael had grabbed the disk and jumped off the balcony into the trees, gone before Cecil was even sure what it was that had run through the room. The Blueman was so furious that he thought about slaughtering the two humans right then. But no, he had to get his emotions under control. This was about the recording and leaving a message to the world, showing them that The Rebirth was all a terrible mistake, and leaving his name to be lauded as a hero and martyr in the years to come. If he killed them here, all that people would know was that two bringers had been murdered in their apartment.

Walking back into the room very slowly, he made himself look at the scene objectively. Aside from a possible fracture of one of the many bones in his long foot, and a slight wound, (for after all, he still had twenty fingers left), nothing had changed, nothing was lost. He didn't have to worry about a wound infection, because he wouldn't live long enough to develop one. And the lizard's interference was actually a gift, since he'd wanted to kill at least one of them anyway. He just hadn't planned to do it in the middle of everything else.

After opening the two huge shoulder carriers he'd brought with him, he stuffed the woman in one and the boy in the other. He looked the woman over as he shoved her into the bag. The left side of her forehead was flattened in one spot above her eye, so he knew she had a skull fracture, and her left eye appeared to have ruptured when it hit the wall. Her left cheek was crushed, and she had blood coming from her nose, mouth and ear, all on the left side.

On her right, several ribs were broken---he could feel the pieces of bone move under his hand, and she'd hit her abdomen, too, which was discoloring and swelling. He hoped she wouldn't spoil everything and die before he got the cameras rolling.

Shucking off his green hotel jacket, he straightened his preserve uniform he'd worn underneath the pilfered garment. Nothing suspicious about a preserve worker hauling bags of equipment back into the gate. And the crowd was so thick and noisy that even if one or both of the humans woke up and started screaming, no one would hear them. He'd thrown the lizard into an area away from the thoroughfare, so he needn't worry about his body being discovered and alerting anyone.

Grabbing his fire stick and throwing a bag over each shoulder, he left the broken door ajar and trudged down the hall to the back elevator.

CHAPTER THIRTY-TWO

Running down the street with the disk in his mouth, Ishmael searched the heads to try and find one with a translating device on it, but the Bluepeople were all so tall that it was hard to see the back of their heads until they were a good distance in front of him. Every time he'd spot one and try to catch up, the crowds would come between him and his goal, and he'd eventually lose sight of the Blueperson he was chasing.

He'd avoided going back into the apartment to seek help at the front desk. For all he knew, the guy might have murdered everyone in the building, or he might have friends down there waiting to stop any attempt at escape.

Now he was zig-zagging down the sidewalk, trying to get the attention of anyone who would look down. He'd already been accidentally kicked multiple times and stepped on as well. The crowds were just so thick, that not many of the Bluepeople could even see below their own knees.

After getting kicked again, he ducked into a doorway to catch his breath. He had to get someone to listen to him soon. If he could find a Blueman who could receive his sendings, the guy could use the disk to call Joe Bob and he could send help. He shuddered when he thought of what that monster had done to Bess. He'd heard her face and ribs crack from behind the couch. And that poor, ruined eye. Jonas was just banged up and zapped and would probably come around soon, but Bess---he wasn't even sure she was still alive.

He thought about going into one of the shops, but with the crowds the way they were, he'd probably get caught in a door, and that would be the end. He'd just have to keep going until he caught up with someone that was prepared to talk to a cat.

CHAPTER THIRTY-THREE

His foot was killing him. Normally, carrying the two humans all the way to the stage in the clearing would be easy for him, but with a bitten off finger, a slash across his chest, a clawed arm, and a bruised or even broken instep, the going was very slow, especially since he had to keep his fire stick ready at all times. He'd had a close call on the way to the gate, though, and his injuries had actually come in handy.

He'd been limping through the crowds, and some good citizen had laid a hand on his arm to stop him. "Are you in need of assistance?" the young Blueman had asked him. "You have blood on you, and wounds that need tending. What happened to you?"

Not that it was any of this one's business. Nobody left anybody alone since The Rebirth. Cecil had to tell himself that this one was trying to be kind, but to have to interact with him, while he was bleeding and nervous and needing to move, was grating. In this crowd, it would be so easy to just shift his fire stick towards him and discharge a quick shock. Nothing lethal—just enough to drop him and get the crowd engaged in helping him. But he couldn't risk drawing attention to himself, and he could possibly get trapped in the crowd if someone panicked.

"Thank you for your concern. Two of the animals from the preserve managed to escape, and I had to catch them quickly before they got into the crowds and hurt someone." He held up his bandaged finger, and gestured to his clawed chest and arm. "Unfortunately, they didn't want to come home," he said, and forced a laugh.

"You certainly have to be brave to handle a job like that! Did you know you have blood dripping from your bag, and it's red." Not surprisingly, Blueman blood was blue.

"Oh yes, some of our wild ones are from off planet, in fact quite a few. We have red bloods and a few green bloods, too, and we have to inoculate them for our atmosphere before setting them loose. These two got into a fight over a piece of meat I was using for bait, and tore each other up worse than they did me. But we have a clinic for the animals on the preserve, so I'll get them fixed up as soon as I get in, and the physician will fix me as well."

"Fascinating! Are you sure you wouldn't like some help carrying them? At least to the gate?"

"Well actually, that would be very kind of you. If you'd like to take the unbloodied bag, so that it doesn't spoil your clothes, that would give me a little break. I can't take you past the gate, but every bit helps."

"I'd be glad to." Cecil took the bag carrying Jonas off of his shoulder and handed it to the other Blueman, who swung it back over his own. "Oh, it's starting to squirm and complain a bit."

Cecil could hear Jonas moaning, but with the crowd noise, he knew the sounds would be indistinguishable from any other animal's. "If it starts fighting or gets too unruly to carry, tell me and you can put the bag down for me to give it another quick stun from my stick to quiet it."

Mr. Helpful carried Jonas all the way to the gate and then handed him over to Cecil.

"Well, it's been a pleasure meeting you. Get those wounds tended soon."

That had been the most enjoyable time he'd ever spent with another in conversation. Knowing that he was helping him to his destination without ever realizing what he was carrying, had almost made Cecil laugh out loud, despite the aching of his wounds and his distaste for laughter. He unlocked the gate, carried the bags in, and locked it behind him. Putting the bags back on his shoulders, and taking the safety off his fire stick, he headed for the staff pathway.

##

The weather outside of the preserve was pleasantly warm today, with a slight breeze, but here on the pathway, the air was still, every breeze blocked off by the masses of vines hanging down from the trees, and what some might have thought a pleasant fragrance from the flowers became a cloying stench as the multitude exuded their aroma all around him. The ground along the pathway was only partially cleared, and rocks and fallen branches were constant hazards he had to guard against to keep his feet, not to mention that every stone or stick he stepped on was torture to his injured foot.

The tiny flying blood suckers were out in mass, and he swatted them and spit them out when they flew into his mouth as he panted with exertion, and the scent of his blood and that of the woman's, was drawing more than just insects. He knew that they were being stalked. He'd expected it, and kept his fire stick within plain sight, so the predators would know he was armed.

Wiping the blood off his arm, he thought about what had happened in the apartment. Why had that winged one attacked him, and what was that black thing that ran through the room? Had it really been carrying a disk in its mouth, or had his imagination been playing tricks on him in all the chaos? No matter. What good was a disk to an animal?

He heard coughing and gagging from the woman's bag, so after leaning the boy's bag up against a rock, he stopped and sat down on a fallen log beside the path, pulled the woman's bag in front of him and opened it. The woman was choking on her blood, and since he needed her alive, he pulled her out of the bag up to her waist, and got her into a sitting position, leaning slightly forwards. "Spit!" he sent to her.

Only half coherent, she looked up at him with her one good eye, then leaned over and vomited the blood that had been running down her throat from her broken teeth and nose and threatening to suffocate her. He reached in his pocket and took out a rag that he'd brought, in case he'd had to gag either of them, and handed it to her silently so she could wipe the blood from her mouth and nose. When she'd made a clumsy attempt at that, he gave her water from a container on the side of her carrier to rinse out with and try to wash her face. He didn't want her looking *too* pitiful, and arousing sympathy when the public saw his recording.

"My son…what did you do….my son…" she murmured. Then she started coughing and moaning and clutching her head from the pain elicited by the coughing.

"Don't worry, *mother*, your son said he wanted to come with you. He's in the other bag."

She turned her head and gasped at the pain caused by that simple movement. When she saw the other bag, and the small twitches coming from within, she called his name and reached for it, but the Blueman grabbed her arm roughly and shoved her back down into the bag. While he was getting her situated again, he failed to notice the constrictor that was slowly encircling Jonas' bag.

He'd just finished tying up the woman's bag, when he heard a strangled cry from the boy, and looked to find the snake fully wrapped around the other bag and starting to squeeze. He sighed and reached out his stick, giving the constrictor a shot that made it quiver and go limp. Pulling it off of the bag, he opened the top to see if the boy was still alive. He was shaking and gasping, and that was good enough. Cecil had forgotten that when he shocked the snake, the shock would go through to the boy, too. Oh well, he only needed them alive for a bit longer.

#

All she could feel was pain, and the sensation of suffocating. She'd managed to staunch some of the bleeding in her mouth with the cloth he'd given her, but her nose was still oozing. She reached up to feel her eye and cried out when she realized that it was destroyed. Then she touched the concavity on her forehead, and understood why the pain in her head was so terrible.

Jonas. Jonas had been there---in the sack. What was happening? Why was it happening? She prayed for deliverance and for her child, asking for both of them, but praying that her child be spared, above all else. If this was her time, then so be it, but she prayed that her son wouldn't die like this—so young, and brutalized and alone on a strange planet, with his mother too wounded to protect him. Then she passed out again, a mercy to shorten the trip to her fate.

Jonas was starting to come around again, and he began gasping for air as soon as he was able to respond to his body's cry for oxygen. His head had been bent forward, cutting off his air, and now every time he took a breath, he had stabbing pains in his left ribs. He tried to regulate his breathing to keep himself from hyperventilating, knowing that would only make his suffering worse.

He couldn't remember hurting himself, and then suddenly, it came back to him. Everything came back to him. The last thing he remembered was a heavy weight drawing itself around him and starting to squeeze until he couldn't breathe, and horrible, building pressure around his ribs until he'd finally felt a crack and terrible pain. Then a sudden pain from another shock, and nothing more until awakening just now.

He had to think. He had to find a way to get his mom and himself away from this maniac. Why was he doing this to them? After being bounced around in the bag some more, he realized that there was nothing he could do until the Blueman stopped and put him down, so he tried to concentrate on his breathing to keep himself from passing out.

#

The big cat was following the blue creature, with its burdens that smelled so tantalizing. His injured foot was getting worse, and hunting was becoming more and more fruitless. Even catching the small rodents that were everywhere had become almost impossible. The smell of fresh blood was overwhelming, but seeing the stick shock the constrictor had reminded him of the pain that the stick could deliver. He could see that the blue thing was tiring though, so he would have his chance. He would keep following, and one way or another, he *would* eat today.

CHAPTER THIRTY-FOUR

The transport pulled up in front of their lodgings, and the group disembarked quickly while Simon turned back to the guard who'd driven them.

"You have my deepest gratitude for the ride and for standing up to your 'superior.' I know that's never an easy thing to do."

The guard bent his head in acknowledgement. "Again, I can only apologize on behalf of our planet, for the treatment you've received at the hands of that despicable one. I'll be reporting all of this to a higher authority, and all of you will probably be asked to give your statements to support my claims."

"Oh, believe me, we would all be more than happy to do that. Now, if you'll excuse me, I need to be sure my family is safe. Thank you again for everything." He shook just the one hand offered out the window of the vehicle, and rushed to join the others.

When they were in the elevator, Elsie suddenly growled, and sent, "He's been here. This scent was at every one of the poison sites, and it's fresh here. *HURRY!*"

Two seconds later, they reached their floor and took out at a run in the direction of the Sayers' apartment. From forty feet away, they could see the open, shattered door. Elsie shot through the opening first, with Simon close behind.

He shouted "Bess! Jonas!" and began running through the apartment, still shouting their names while he frantically searched every room and closet, even checking with dread inside of the huge drawers in the bureaus.

"Simon, in here!" Elsie sent, and began barking.

He ran in and his knees almost buckled when he saw the blood on the wall and the floor below. "It's all Bess' blood."

"No, no," he moaned.

Then he saw the dead eagle-thing on the dining room table and the open patio door. Running to the railing, he looked down and saw the Colder. "Oh, no! Barnabas! Barnabas!" he shouted, but there was no response from the still form of the Colder splayed out on the ground below.

"Here! There's more blood on the floor, but this is his blood---the poisoner's. I can track him---come on, let's go!"

Eli and his wives were already rushing to the balcony, and as they ran past Simon, he caught Eli by both arms and almost shouted in his face. "I'm going with Elsie to track him. After you see if there's anything you can do for Barnabas, catch up with me. If I get close enough to see him, I'll send Elsie back to show you the way."

The Elpies looked down, and seeing Barnabas, instead of going through the building and taking the stairs or elevator, the four jumped off the railing to go to their friend below.

Running down the hall towards the back elevator, a thousand horrible scenarios flashed through Simon's mind. *Why* did he leave them alone? What was he *thinking*? There he was, rushing off to help in some investigation where he wasn't even wanted, while *his own family* was being---no, he wouldn't let himself think that. They couldn't be dead. *They couldn't.*

Elsie sent that he'd taken the elevator back down, so rather than wait for the elevator to return to their floor, the two flew down the stairs and to just in front of the elevator doors, where Elsie caught the scent again. They ran out the back door and along the path leading to the preserve. When they reached the gate of the preserve and found it locked, with the scent leading straight in, Simon threw the top of the fire stick chest open---and stumbled back with a cry when he saw Elliott's body crammed into the chest, congealing blue blood coating his arm and shirt, and still oozing slightly from a hole in his chest.

"Oh, God! Elliott! I'm so sorry. I'm so sorry." He wanted to stop, to do something, but there was no time. He reached to the side of the body, pulled out two fire sticks and jammed them through the opening between the side of the gate and the fence. He leaned on them, and when that didn't work, he tried throwing all his weight against them, but it was no good. He could have climbed the gate, but couldn't have made it up and over carrying Elsie without having to drop her from the top of the gate onto the other side, and he couldn't risk crippling her in a fall and losing his tracker.

He looked around frantically to find something to use as a battering ram. Finally, he saw a log that was tilted against one portion of the fence to brace a repair, and he ran to it, pushing and pulling until it finally came loose. He would never have attempted to lift it under normal circumstances, but his Adrenalin was pumping so hard, and his frenzy for action so great, that the impossible weight of it never crossed his mind. He wrapped both arms around it and let it fall in his arms until it was parallel to the ground, and then, with muscles straining, and veins bulging on his neck and arms, face dark red, he carried the log to within fifteen feet in front of the gate. With a roar, he ran towards the gate and slammed the log against the center of it.

The gate popped open, and Simon dropped the log, sinking to his knees as he waited for his vision to return and his head to stop spinning. He had shards of wood shoved under the skin of his palms, but he barely noticed them, or the pain in his back and arms. Elsie was standing in front of him and barking, and that helped to bring him around. He pushed himself off the ground, grabbed one of the fire sticks he had thrown aside, and began running after the dog as she barreled down the path that the poisoner had taken.

##

After pulling the boy out of the bag, he tied his hands together behind him, and then tied his ankles, but loosely enough for him to stand. The boy was coming around from his second shock, and starting to moan and move his head, but he was still groggy enough to be tied up without a struggle. He dragged him over to the right of the stage, then dragged the bag with the woman in it to the center. He opened the bag, but left the woman inside, to keep the smell of blood in the air less prominent.

#

Jonas had thought that he'd be able to do something once he was out of the bag, but found that he was still too weak from the second shock to have full control of his arms and legs, and he was dizzy when he tried to open his eyes in the daylight.

#

Having positioned his victims, the Blueman set out to check the cameras one more time, and to position the microphones, to be sure they would pick up every detail of his final act.

##

Elsie had stopped barking, understanding that they needed to surprise the Blueman if they were going to get Bess and Jonas away from him without further injury. They followed the tunnel of vines and bushes, and the ancient trees that towered above them, running on and on, leaping over fallen branches and rocks, and ducking low hanging vines. Twice, Simon tripped and fell, but he rolled back to his feet and kept running, mindless of the cuts and scrapes just acquired, and ignoring the searing pain in his back and hands.

At last, they saw the clearing and the Blueman straight ahead, with his back to them, walking towards the steps of the stage. Simon sent to Elsie to stop, and she trotted quietly back to him. He sent to the dog, "Elsie, I need for you to go back and get Eli. Show him the path, and then go to the front desk of the building and send for someone to get help. You're a great dog, Elsie."

Since they'd had to go out the back way to follow the trail, there'd been no time to stop at the front desk and ask for a call to the authorities. His red disk was only programmed to reach Joe Bob, so that was useless. He knew he wouldn't answer.

She began to run back the way she'd come, and Simon crouched, took the safety off his fire stick, and began advancing on the enemy.

CHAPTER THIRTY-FIVE

Hand in hand, Sven and Cleo were watching the celebration as they ambled in the direction of the humans' and Elpies' apartments. A river ran through the middle of town, and a lot of activity was centered on it and along its banks.

Homemade boat races were in progress, and the participants could use no adhesives or ties on their creations, so everything had to be fitted in tight angles in order to make the boats waterproof. Since most Bluepeople were not engineers or boat wrights, most of their vessels weren't watertight, and sank before reaching the finish line. The life guards were very busy, but the water wasn't deep, so there were no casualties, and lots of laughter.

Eating, of course, was a major event, so there were tables full of fruits and sweets, and succulent roasted meats, and the sellers were having a record take. Sven bought them both drinks, and a plate of meat to share between them as they walked.

It was a wonderful day for the children, and all kinds of booths that catered strictly to them had been set up. There were balloons, which looked very similar to Earth balloons, except that they were square in shape, and the material was of sparkling, thin, pliable metal. The important aspect of them was that they floated up into the air, and that's what captured the minds of the little ones. Children laughed and screamed as they played chase, and begged their parents for rides on the amusement machines set up everywhere.

Cleo seemed to be enjoying the sights, but Sven was having difficulty focusing on anything but her. She felt him staring at her, and turned to stare back.

"What?"

"Oh, nothing. Just that I feel like the luckiest man on the planet right now. I can't believe you're here. With me. This will make you think me less strong and virile, but I must tell you that you make me feel bubbly inside. In a strong and virile way, of course."

She laughed and squeezed his hand. "You are truly the strangest man I've ever met. I like that."

"I can be even stranger. Just give me the word."

"Don't forget, this is a national holiday, so technically, all ship leaders and cadets are on duty for emergencies, so you can't get too strange."

"I know, I know. I'm just hoping for no accidents within our area. Let the next leader deal with them."

"That doesn't sound very responsible."

"Oh, I'm very responsible. Do you like responsible?"

"Of course."

"Well, I'm your man. Mr. Responsible. No, no--King of Responsible. Did you remember to bring your medical disk with you?"

"Of course." She drew a grey disk out of her pocket and wiggled it in front of his face.

"Did you?"

"You can seriously ask that of 'King Responsible?' Of course I have it." He pulled a grey disk out of his pocket and wiggled it in *her* face. All pilots and cadets were considered guardians of the public during any national celebration or disaster, and expected to help in keeping the peace, as well as doing medical triage and emergency transport. Upon entering cadet training, each Blueperson was awarded a transport disk for use in teleporting serious injuries to the nearest medical facilities. These disks were to be kept on their persons at all times, and to be caught in public without one would lead to instant dismissal and the ruination of the career of the negligent party.

"Have you ever had to use it?"

"Oh yes. The last time was just before The Rebirth. In fact, you're going to meet the one I used it on, today."

##

Ishmael had just gotten kicked again, and this time he'd landed in a ditch beside the walkway. Exhausted, and unsure how far he'd run, he wasn't even certain of where he was. He'd taken so many turns to avoid getting kicked or stepped on, that the direction he'd come from was now a mystery. And with that last kick, he'd dropped the disk he'd been carrying, and it had been stepped on and crushed within a matter of seconds.

He hurt all over, but knew that nothing was broken. Thirst, however, was maddening for him, and when he saw a container of water that someone had dropped, he could have kissed the careless party responsible. Rushing to the container, he pulled it over with his paws, but no matter how he manipulated it, he found it impossible to open.

Getting hold of the lid with his teeth, he dragged the container up onto the walkway and then leapt out of the way before the next huge foot came down on top of him. He peeked up over the side and watched, and sure enough, someone finally stepped on and broke it, sending it flying back into the ditch. *Am I good, or what?* He went to the torn container, lying open and half full only a few feet from him.

Drinking his fill, he took another few minutes to rest, and then charged out into the melee again, searching for a head that was wearing a device and looking down.

He had almost given up hope, when he heard a sending in his mind.

"Ishmael?"

"Yes! Where are you?"

"Right here." A huge, seven fingered hand reached down and scooped him up. He looked into the face of the Blueman, and sent, "Sven!"

#

The moment he'd finished sending to Sven, the Blueman pulled his communicator out, made a call to send help to the lodgings, and he and Cleo took off running, with Ishmael in his arms.

CHAPTER THIRTY-SIX

Twenty feet from the Blueman, he set his fire stick to maximum and charged. Cecil heard his footsteps at the last second, whirling around just in time to knock Simon's fire stick to the side with his own stick before he could fire it. Simon's stick flew out of his hands and landed on the ground, away from the stage, but he kept charging, getting in underneath the other's stick and hitting him full in the chest with his shoulder.

The Blueman outweighed him by at least two hundred pounds, but the force of Simon's entire weight coming at a dead run threw Cecil backwards onto the stage. His stick went flying up behind him, landing to rest at the edge. Simon's rage propelled him on, and he flung himself upwards from the Blueman's chest to deliver two hard blows to the face before Cecil grabbed his hair and pulled his head back with one hand, then with the other two, lifted him up over his head and threw him off the stage.

As soon as Simon's body left his hands, Cecil rolled and grabbed his fire stick, then jumped to his feet and put the stick to Jonas' head. Jonas had been lying on his side, awake, pretending to be unconscious while he struggled to think of a way to free himself and get to his mom. When his dad had charged the Blueman, he'd had hope for a brief moment, until he saw the thing lift his dad up in the air and toss him away like a doll. Now he could only cringe as the fire stick pressed against his head.

When Simon hit the ground, the wind was knocked out of him for a second, and he felt a grating, catching pain along his right ribs, but he rolled back to his feet, grabbing his fallen fire stick to charge again. The Blueman screamed something in his own tongue, and the sending was clear. "Stop where you are or I'll blow his head to pieces!"

Not even waiting for the demand, Simon tossed his stick away, threw his hands in the air, and shouted, "NO, NO! Wait! You don't have to do that! Look, I'm right here, unarmed. Please don't hurt him!"

Cecil lifted Jonas to his feet by the back of his shirt, and kept the stick next to his head. Simon moaned at the pitiful sight of his son, with the whole right side of his face one massive bruise, and that look of despair on his face. He would have been gratified to see the blue blood oozing from the Blueman's mouth and his left cheek, where his punches had landed, but other than freeing a little blood, they seemed to have had no effect on him.

Looking at Simon, who was standing with his arms held outstretched and palms forward, he began talking in his own tongue, relying on the translating programs on him and in the alien to do their jobs.

"I've worked here for many years, and I've been using a fire stick for just as long. The charge I use when dealing with very large predators can either stun or actually kill them if there's a need to, and will make a rather large hole in your son's head if I choose to pull the trigger. And this particular stick is set to have a hair trigger, so that should you somehow decide to try and hurt me again, you should know that any jarring of my arm will make it go off. Not to mention, I can fire it at a distance, and I'm an excellent shot. In case you doubt my word---"

He suddenly swung the stick around and fired it at a fruit hanging on a branch a good twenty-five feet away, and the succulent orb exploded in a flash of quickly ending flame. In a split second, the stick was back against Jonas' head.

"Where's my wife?"

"Oh, you mean this?" He rubbed his eyes and then reached down into the second bag and lifted Bess out. He pulled her up against him, holding her with one arm, facing her towards Simon, and used his third hand to pull her head back by her hair so that he could see her ruined face.

Simon cried out in shock, and then sobbed at the sight of her. She was unconscious now, hanging limply from the creature's arm. The left side of her face was purple and swollen grotesquely; her eye was flattened in the socket, with congealing liquid still oozing from beneath the lid. The left side of her forehead was partially concave and bloodied, her beautiful black hair matted with gore, nose at an unnatural angle and swollen, with dried blood below it. Fresh drops leaked slowly from her mouth onto her red streaked shirt.

When the full force of the damage seemed to have been absorbed, the Blueman spoke again. "Oh, and let's not forget this." He let her head drop to free a hand, and pulled her shirt up to expose her misshapen rib cage, and the abdomen below it, bruised and bulging oddly.

Simon was openly weeping now, his hand over his mouth, maddened by the thought of what she'd suffered. He stared at her ravaged face, and was paralyzed with anguish. Bess…his Bess…

Then he came back to himself and shouted, "Look, I don't know *why* you're doing this, but they've done *nothing, nothing* to harm anyone. What honor is there in killing a human boy and woman? Let them go, and take me. You can take me anywhere, right now, somewhere they'll never find my body, and do whatever you want to me, *but let them go*. They'll never catch you that way, and you can still have a life. My family won't be able to identify you---all Bluepeople look the same to them. Please, I'm begging you. If you *do* this, if you *kill* them, there will be such an outcry that there'll be no place you can hide."

Cecil actually thought about this for a moment, while he shook his head and rubbed his eyes again with the back of one hand, but then remembered that he'd already turned the cameras on, and everything thus far had been recorded. He hadn't delivered his speech yet, and he wouldn't have his climactic death scene if he stopped now.

At that moment, Eli ran into the clearing, and Simon screamed, "ELI, DON'T MOVE!"

The Elpie looked at Simon, and then up at the stage, and when he saw Bess, his mouth opened in horror. The Blueman looked at him and ordered, "Get over there with your *friend.* It's a shame I didn't have time to finish off at least one of *your* wives, but you know how time constraints can be."

When Eli and his wives had jumped down to help Barnabas, they'd found him with a head injury and a few broken bones. When he'd roused slightly and recognized them, he'd sent for them to leave him and go to help Simon, because it would take all of them to save his family. Seeing that he was stable enough to wait for help, the Elpies had done as he asked.

Now, as Eli walked slowly over to stand beside his friend, Simon saw that the three sisters were down on all fours and crawling towards the Blueman from both sides of the back of the stage. They'd changed their skin color from green to brown, to match the stage floor, and flattened against the ground as they were now, they were almost invisible. Simon hoped the apparent problem Cecil was having with his eyes would keep him from noticing them until the last moment. He felt a glimmer of hope, but sent to the sisters, "Not yet. Movement will make the fire stick go off. Stay down and wait for my signal."

Cecil pulled himself up to his tallest, but had to stop and rub his eyes with the back of one hand to clear them. His peripheral vision was still fuzzy, but after a few more blinks, his central vision cleared, and he addressed the microphone, looking straight out into the center camera, and started his speech.

"For as long as any of us remembers, we were formed and incubated in facilities meant to limit indiscriminate procreation, and produce new citizens who had desirable qualities. We were raised in large dormitories, and taught that our people stood alone. That families are factions of the worst kind, making prisoners of people in the need for love from offspring, spouses, or other relations, even to the point of turning against those outside of the family in order to protect their own. We were happy in our own way, never needing the manipulative ties of *friendships* or having to deal with whining, filthy infants, who imprison their caregivers with their constant needs.

"Then The Rebirth came, and suddenly we were expected to have miraculous changes of attitude and heart. To start thinking of ourselves as completely different beings, longing for companionship, and craving our own families. Obviously, for some, this was not a hard thing. But many in our society have not been able to change the way we feel and think, because we were *made* to scorn these emotions, through genetic manipulation and through the messages we were given from the time that we were infants. We crave the solace of solitude, and to be allowed to do our jobs as before, without having the company of others forced on us at every turn, and without being considered *sick* or *aberrant*. We are what we were made to be, and we *must* and *will* be respected and honored for being true to that making, for that is what society demanded of us.

"These humans have been brought here and honored as Bringers of The Rebirth. These three are a perfect example of the fallacy of family. It has been touted since The Rebirth, that families are a source of strength, but I will expose that lie today.

"Look at this woman. She opened her door to me because I told her that her husband sent me."

Simon sobbed and shook his head.

"When I forced my way in, she might have been able to escape, but her instinct for survival was weakened by her need to protect that one, her son," he said, nodding towards Jonas, who was standing slouched over, head down, with tears dripping from his face to wet the ground below, as he thought, *the warrior, the she-bear.*

"She attacked me, despite the idiocy of that action, and screamed for her son to run. *He* could have run out another door and lived, but he ignored his mother's orders, which is typical of the young, and he *also* attacked me. He was a prisoner of *his* need to protect his mother---his *family*. Even after both were injured, they attacked once more, each trying to protect the other, despite the obvious futility of their actions.

"Prisons! Ties are prisons, and they enslave us! I had planned for these two to forfeit their lives to show this, and to show the terrible effect their loss would have on the husband, the father. Even when family members die, they *still* imprison the other members through grief---shackling, debilitating grief. Families make us slaves *forever*.

"But something unplanned has happened, and the father has appeared. So let us see what a slave he is to his emotions."

"What is your name, Earth man?"

"Simon."

"You may call me 'Cecil,' since you lack the capacity to speak or understand our civilized tongue."

"Tell me, Simon, do you *love* your wife?"

"Very much."

"And do you *love* your son?"

"With my whole heart."

He looked towards the camera again as he spoke. "Love. They talk about how wonderful love is, but love is a trap and it is a killer, as we shall see today."

"You may leave, Simon. Go back to your lodgings. Save your life."

"My life is up there on that stage. I leave with them or not at all."

"Would you die for your family?"

"Yes."

"No hesitation?"

"No."

"You have only one life, so you can only die for one of them. Whom do you choose to save?"

"My son."

"What, no inner turmoil, no whining about your great love for your wife?"

"No."

"And why is that?"

Afraid that any answer he gave might cause this madman to kill his son, he was silent until Cecil shook the fire stick against Jonas' head, and raised his voice.

"I *asked* you *why*?"

He thought of deserting Bess, and his voice broke as he shouted at Cecil, "Because we're parents---and parents protect their children. If I saved her---and let Jonas die---she would die a thousand deaths inside, as would I. I don't *have* to think about it, because she's a mother who loves her children above all else, and this is what she would have me do."

Cecil addressed the cameras again. "Do you see, citizens, why we should return to our old ways? Did you hear what love demands? It demands desertion of one for another. And today it demands death."

"You say you would die for your son?"

"Yes."

"Show me."

Jonas started screaming then, "NO, DAD, DON'T! He's going to kill both of us anyway---he won't keep his word and let me go. Don't do this, Dad, *please don't do this*!"

"Shut your son up or I will."

"Jonas, *please*. If you love me, be quiet. I love you, son, and this is *my* choice, and your mother's. Now be quiet, and look away."

Then Jonas heard his father's voice in his mind as he sent, "You'll be a fine man someday, Jonas. No, that's wrong. You already are."

Cecil held up Bess with one hand and threw a large knife to Simon, then picked up another and held it just below Bess' ribs, pointing upwards to reach her heart. Simon could hardly breathe when he saw that, and held out his hand again.

"Please don't."

"Take off your shirt."

Still wearing the long sleeved shirt over a T-shirt he'd put on against the cold in the morgue, he ripped it open, pulled it off, and threw it on the ground. Eli reached down and picked it up. *As if a shirt will matter to him anymore,* thought Cecil in amusement

"Pick up the knife." Simon bent over, grabbed it by the handle, and stood back up.

"Now I want you to slice open your left arm. Up above the elbow, and very deep. I want to see muscle, and arterial blood. The brachial artery I think."

Jonas was staring and sobbing quietly now, shaking his head at his father. He remembered feeling that strength of will in his mind, and when he looked at his face, he knew he was going to do it. His dad was going to die for him, and by his own hand.

His hand---he thought about how gently that hand had lifted his wrist in the tube, when his arm had been injured saving Dulcie. Those hands feeling for swelling and dislocation, and then moving the bag underneath his arm to try and soothe his pain---moving with such care and gentleness, and those hands gently laid against his own and his mom's face this morning to check for fever. And now those gentle hands would work for his son again, with savagery against himself.

He pleaded with his eyes as he shook his head even harder at his dad, dreading what he would see, but unable to turn away.

"It's all right, Jonas. This is my choice." And without giving himself time to think about it, Simon held his arm out, palm up, pressed the blade down and sliced deeply across his upper arm. For a moment, nothing happened, and then blood started rushing out, in thick, pulsing gushes.

Jonas turned and vomited. Shaking his head and spitting, he reached out then with his mind to touch his dad's pain, and was jolted backwards with the burst of agony that hit him. He jerked his mind away, and looked back at his dad, still standing, with his teeth clenched against the pain. The blood was pumping down his arm in a miniature, scarlet cascade, and he knew he was watching his father's life ebbing away with each little gush.

Eli stared in shock, and automatically reached for Simon's arm, to try and stop the flow, but Cecil screamed, and sent "NO."

Simon shook his head at his friend, holding up the knife and shaking it too. He swayed slightly with the pain and the sudden blood loss, but kept his feet and refused to cry out.

"Excellent! Now the other."

He tried to grasp the knife, but couldn't grip or hold his arm steady with all the blood and the damaged muscle. He held the knife out to his friend and pleaded, "Please help me, Eli."

The Elpie looked at him in horror, shook his head violently, and stamped his foot.

"You're running out of time. My arm is getting tired, and if it jerks, this trigger just might get pulled."

Simon looked at his friend again in desperation. "You have sons, Eli."

Then he held out the knife again. "Do it."

With a horrible noise of grief, Eli grabbed the knife with one hand, and putting the other under Simon's outstretched arm to hold it steady, slashed cleanly nearly to the bone. Simon's head flew back as he gasped, and then he brought it forward with a groan, his mouth wide open to try and take in air through the pain. His legs almost went from under him, but he pulled himself back up and still refused to scream.

Cecil looked back up at the camera. "You see, Citizens? Love is killing this man."

CHAPTER THIRTY-SEVEN

Sven, Cleo, and Ishmael reached the front desk just as Elsie did. Sven sent that he'd already called for help, and told her to lead him to the Sayers. The exhausted dog swung around and headed back to the gate. Jumping down from Sven's arms, Ishmael sent that he was going to see if the Colder was still alive, and ran around to the back of the hotel.

At the gate, Elsie stopped and sent to the two, "I may lag behind, but don't stop. Take the main path. It's faster than the staff entrance. Much easier going. Keep looking to your left, and when you get to a clearing, you'll see the stage---that's where he has them."

Sven nodded once and took off at a run, his long legs eating up ground faster than Elsie would have thought possible. Cleo ran to grab fire sticks from the chest, and jerked back in surprise when she saw Elliott's crumpled body within. Without taking time to see if he was dead or alive, she took out her disk, slapped it on his chest, and when is body disappeared, she grabbed two fire sticks and ran to catch up with Sven.

He looked over his shoulder when he heard her coming, and shouted, "No, go back. It's too dangerous!" She put on a burst of speed and overtook him, tossing him a fire stick as she passed him, and replied over her shoulder, "Then *you* should go back."

He kept running, shook his head, and smiled to himself. *Could she be any more perfect?*

##

Barnabas was lying on his back, in terrible pain, and thinking about how he had failed his friends. He lay at the crest of a small rise just beyond the apartments, with his right side facing them and his left facing the forested area of the reserve. From where he lay, the ground dropped off in a steep slope on his left. He had just missed being thrown down that slope, where he would have come to rest against the fence of the reserve.

He should have thought it out, found a weapon. He knew he would survive, but Bess and Jonas might already be dead. He closed his eyes and shook his head, trying to think how he might have done it differently.

Something shifting in the grass beside him caught his attention, and when he looked up, a huge, turquoise, bear-like creature with implausibly long jaws, was standing on its hind legs, towering over him a mere five feet away, with its great mouth opened in a snarl. Barnabas tried to throw himself upright, but his head made the world go sideways, and he couldn't find his feet, so he threw his arms over his head in what he knew was a futile gesture. Waiting to die, he thought how odd that they should all die on the same day.

Just then something screaming and black sailed over his head to land on the face of the creature. Startled and stung by the attack, it tried to back away, still standing on its hind legs, swiping at the black thing that was tearing at its face, and in the process, lost its balance on the incline and rolled down the hill, away from Barnabas. It hit hard against the fence, and when it found its feet again, Ishmael was in front of it, prancing and bouncing around jerkily on his toes, with his back arched, tail up, and every hair on his body sticking straight out, while he howled, screeched, and spit so loudly that the bear-thing began looking for a way to escape. Abruptly, it turned tail and ran back along the fence until it found the hole it had come out of, and then squeezed itself back through as fast as it could.

Barnabas had seen the whole thing. As Ishmael strolled back up the hill, he tried to appear nonchalant, but failed miserably, since his fur was still puffed out and his tail looked like a bottle brush. He sent to Barnabas and told him that help was on the way, and that if he needed him again before it arrived, he had only to send for him with his mind. Then he trotted to the front desk, so that he could lead the help back to one very surprised Colder.

CHAPTER THIRTY-EIGHT

Bess was coming to, and when he saw this, saw that she really was still alive, Simon sent to her. "Bess, can you hear me?"

"---hear you. Jonas?"

"It's Simon. Bess, he wants me to take my life in exchange for Jonas,' but he won't let me save both of you. I have a plan, but it may not work. I have to do this. I have to save Jonas. I'm so sorry, my love, so sorry. I love you, Bess."

He could tell by the way her mind felt when he sent to her, that her brain wasn't working right. She was having trouble focusing on what he was sending, and he didn't know if she'd understood him. But then she sent, "Whatever you have to—save---son…. love you."

He closed his eyes and prayed for the strength to do what he had to do, and prayed that it worked---that at least his son could walk away from this horror. He was swaying badly now, covered with sweat and blood, chilled to the bone, shaking, short of breath, and thirsty---so thirsty. He clung desperately to consciousness. The pain came and went---one minute excruciating, and then deep moans would escape his lips unbidden, and the next, a sort of numbness would take over. Eli had a hand on his back, trying to steady him. He didn't think he could walk anymore.

He shouted at Cecil, with slurred, halting speech. "Why don't---you end this? Finish it yourself. I can't use---my hands anymore---and he," nodding towards Eli, "won't help me. What's a matter, 'fraid---for me to get close to you? ---'fraid I'll leap up---with these useless arms and take your weapons---away from you? Come on, ---tired of your games. Be a Blueman, Cecil---have the guts to end this yourself."

Cecil bristled at the taunt. "Very well, I will. If I hit the femoral artery, you should finish bleeding out in a few short minutes. Especially if I hit both. Have your *friend* put the knife through your belt loop, and come on up. I'd like for your wife to see this."

"Been studying anatomy, have you?"

"It pays to know the enemy before you go into battle."

"So that's what you call this—battle?"

Fighting to concentrate against the darkness that was threatening at the edge of his vision, he started sending frantically, first to Jonas. "When he puts the knife to me, Jonas, throw yourself backwards. He'll be expecting you---expecting you to fall forwards. DO NOT look back---sisters---sisters coming at him from behind. Your only chance, Jonas. Fall---fall backwards, but not until the knife is going in. Will be the one time his physical focus---on something else. I love you, son."

He could feel Jonas trying to reach him, to tell him not to do it, but he ignored him and reached out for Dulcie, sending for the sisters to each try to take one arm, but not to move until the knives went into him, when all Cecil's concentration would be on the feel of the kill. Then he sent that he loved them, thanked them for being his friends, and saving his son.

Eli couldn't hold him under the arms, so he hooked one arm around him, just below the hips, and carried him up the steps, with every step jarring Simon's wounds and sending piercing waves of agony through him. He tried to stay upright, but felt himself falling forwards, with his chest leaning, and his head hanging down over the Elpie's shoulder, his useless, bloodied arms dangling, one behind Eli's shoulder and one in front. Eli gently put him on his feet in front of the Blueman, and helped him to stand upright. He had forgotten how strong Elpies were.

Jonas could feel how hard his dad was struggling just to stay standing---to stay conscious. He could feel his essence slipping away.

Simon sent to his friend, "It's your call, Eli. Signal---wives when you see him push in the knives. Bess---still alive.---might even make it if---this works. I love you, my brother. Thank you."

Cecil was holding Bess up so that she could look into her husband's face when the knives went in. This was better than Simon had even hoped for. If Cecil wanted her to see him, then he'd have to hold her up with one arm, and if he used two knives, he'd have to take the knife away from her ribs, *and* he'd have to put down the fire stick long enough to use the second knife. *Thank you, God.*

"Look at your husband," he said, and raised her chin up so that her good eye faced Simon. To his annoyance, when their eyes met, they both mouthed the words, "I love you," and then Simon said quietly, "Look away."

"And you, look at your father!" He looked at Jonas menacingly. "I'm going to put down this stick for a few seconds, boy, but you saw how fast I am with it. Make a move and your brains will be on the stage before your head hits."

He pulled the other knife from Simon's belt loop, and cried out to the camera, "See what love, what family does for you?" and plunged both knives into the tops of Simon's legs, twisting the blades as they shoved through his flesh, to tear the arteries asunder.

Everything happened at once. Simon screamed, Eli lunged for Bess and pulled her away, and Jonas threw himself down and cried out when he saw the mortal agony on his father's face as he fell backwards from the force of the knives shoving into him. The sisters leapt in unison, seizing the arms of the Blueman in their powerful jaws, their razor sharp teeth slicing through tissue and imbedding in bone, then throwing their heads back, to tear the limbs from his body. Cecil screamed when the sisters ripped into him, and blue blood gushed out of the wounds for a few seconds, but he was dead before he hit the ground---the poison capsule he was holding in his cheek for the grand finale had been popped ahead of schedule.

Eli threw Simon's shirt to Martha, who ripped off the sleeves with her teeth and tore each one in two, vertically, to use as tourniquets. He flipped the body of the Blueman off of Simon, and then Martha and he began frantically tying tourniquets. Simon was already unconscious, lying in a pool of his own blood, his arms, legs, and most of his T-shirt covered in it, and his skin a deathly, waxy white. Ruth cut the bindings off of Jonas, helped him to his parents, and then rushed to help Eli.

The wounds in Simon's legs were so high up that it was impossible to tie tourniquets above them, and Eli was at a loss as to how to stop the bleeding there, where it was the worst. He finally just wadded up the tourniquet and pressed it hard over the jagged hole on one leg, and had Ruth put pressure on the other.

Holding Bess' head in her lap, Dulcie felt her hand on her arm. When she looked down at Bess, she caught her garbled sending, and nodded her understanding. Sliding her gently over to Simon, Dulcie laid her with her head facing his and her body lying in the opposite direction, to keep her out of the way of all the blood and the efforts to save him. Her face was less than a foot from his, and Dulcie had placed her with her good eye up, so that she could look at him without turning her head or bending her neck. Then the Elpie put her hand under the wounded side of Bess' head, to cushion it from the hard floor as she lay and gazed at Simon's face.

She could see the dark green of the trees rising up behind him, their branches swaying slightly, and one lock of hair that hadn't yet stuck to the sweat on his forehead, waving gently in the breeze. Everything seemed hushed and far away, as if the whole world consisted only of the silent, swaying trees, that lock of hair, and the still, white face of her dying husband. She reached her hand over and stroked his cheek, and then ran a finger over his pale lips. A tear trickled out from the corner of her remaining eye as she half whispered, "Best father---best husband---best man."

Suddenly, there were arms around her, as Jonas enveloped her, sobbing and begging, "*Don't do it* Mom, don't let go, please don't die, please, please, Mom, stay with me! Dad would want you to—Genny and Colder, think about them---they're still little, Mom---stay, please, please."

Eli was tightening the tourniquet on Simon's right arm with one hand, and leaning on his leg with the other, when the gouts of blood that had been pumping out of his arms slowed and then stopped. For a split second, he was relieved, thinking that the strips of shirt had done the trick, and then he realized that the blood had quit pumping out because the pump had stopped. He looked in panic at Simon's chest, and it was motionless, so he laid his head on his chest, listening…. listening….

At last, he sat up and looked at Simon's face, pale and lifeless. Reaching out with one hand, he gently closed his brother's eyes, still partially opened, but forever unseeing now. He placed a hand on his chest, and still looking at his face, made some quiet chittering sounds. He was silent for a moment then, as he began slowly pounding his fist against the stage floor, but as his pounding came faster, he let out a guttural, rasping cry that increased in pitch to a piercing whistle, and then died away.

Jonas saw the blood---the impossible amount of blood---his dad was covered with it, Ruth, Martha, and especially Eli, were covered with it, and it was smeared everywhere around him from the Elpies' frantic efforts to staunch the bleeding. He saw the white, white skin, and the slack expression on that face that had studied his own in such concern in that shop---only yesterday? And he understood. He held onto his mom, and cried softly, "No, Dad, no."

Bess knew he was gone. She could feel it. He had saved them, and now he was gone. She thought how easy it would be to let go herself and just drift away to meet him, but Jonas' shuddering cries made her remember her children, and so she lived on.

Sven and Cleo burst out of the trees then, with Elsie not far behind. His heart sank as he saw Simon's bloodied body and thought, *How many times can we cause this man's death?* When Elsie saw him and smelled his death, she stopped running, sat back on her haunches and stared. Slowly, she gathered herself up, raised her head and howled---a long, eerie cry of utter desolation.

Cleo, two steps ahead of Sven, leapt up onto the stage, grabbed Jonas' arm and shook him, sending, "How long?" Jonas looked at her in shock, and then stumbled out, "Just now. Two, three minutes, maybe, I'm not sure."

She already had her disk out, and she slapped it onto Simon's chest. He disappeared just as the big cat, who'd been watching everything, finally made his move. He'd slunk closer when all the screaming started, and now he launched himself at the boy sitting where the smell of blood was the strongest, and youth promised the sweetest flesh.

Sven had seen the cat when it moved its hindquarters in a wind up for its leap, and with two long strides he leapt onto the stage, kneeling and planting himself and the end of the fire stick between the cat and the humans. Sven fired the stick as it caught the creature in the chest when it came sailing through the air, and used the stick to continue the cat's momentum and hoist it over his head and the heads of those still lying and sitting on the ground. The stunned animal was slung to the stage floor, where it jerked and quivered for a minute, and then was still.

Cleo, who hadn't even flinched when she saw the cat leaping towards them, reached over and put the disk on the chest of the now unconscious Bess, who disappeared instantly, took one look at the boy, bruised and battered, with a look of abject horror and loss on his face, and she put the disk on his chest, too, and he vanished as well. She stood up then, and Sven came over to her. He had one gash on his top right arm where the cat's claw had caught him, but otherwise, he'd come through unscathed.

He looked at her face and said, "You're amazing. You didn't move or stop what you were doing at all when that beast was charging. You didn't even look up."

She examined his wound and replied, "I didn't need to. I knew you were there."

CHAPTER THIRTY-NINE

He awoke lying in a bed, after being treated for two cracked ribs that he attributed to what he thought must have been a snake, some minor burns from the shocks, and deep bruising and abrasions on half his face. Jonas stared at the ceiling, feeling a hollowness in his chest, as if everything inside of him was gone. The room was grey and sterile looking, with a few monitors making quiet, repetitive noises, but there was nothing attached to him. They'd said he was in shock, had given him some IV fluids, an injection, and told him to rest. They'd put him to sleep, and now he didn't know how long he'd been out, didn't know if his mom was dead, or if they'd been able to resuscitate his dad, and he was too afraid to ask.

Tears welled up as he thought of his dad standing there, with both arms laid open in huge, gaping wounds, and hanging limp at his sides---his dad fighting to keep standing, waiting to be killed---*planning* to be killed, and he saw his face when the knives went in, when they were *twisted.* He saw him falling to the ground as his life gushed out of him. He'd let himself be---no, he'd *orchestrated* his own *slaughter* for *him.* To save *him.* He thought about what his dad had said---that his mom would choose to save him over herself, and he knew he'd been right---his mom would have wanted to die if anything had happened to one of her children. He'd always known, deep inside, that either of them would die for their kids, but he never thought they'd have to. Never thought he'd see it…

Letting the numbness of too many tears take over, he lay motionless, feeling dull and empty, until two Blue physicians walked into the room. They stood beside his bed, but waited for him to look at them before they started. He wouldn't make eye contact at first, because he didn't want to hear the words they would send to him---"We're sorry, but---"

Finally, he made himself look at them, and said, "Tell me."

"Your mother is in stasis at this time, but she'll be fine. Her internal injuries were more extensive than we'd thought at first, and of course, she had severe fractures of her ribs that pierced several organs. One of her eyes was destroyed, and she had facial fractures, broken teeth, a skull fracture---"

"I thought you said she'd be *fine.* How can she be *fine* when she's lost an eye, and her *head was bashed in*?" He was sitting up now, fighting hysteria after hearing the list of injuries his mom had sustained.

"She'll be fine, Jonas, because we're growing new internal organs for her, a new eye, new bone mass, and new teeth. She's in stasis while the fresh growth takes place. She had some brain swelling and some minor damage to her brain, but we've been able to make repairs without complications. She'll be back to normal within a week."

Could it be true? He'd have his mom back, whole, healthy and happy, the way she'd always been? But---she'd never be whole again if his dad was gone. Would she even want to live? He was so relieved at the thought of his mom being alive, but he dreaded seeing her face when she heard about his dad. His dad. He could barely bring himself to ask.

"What about my father?"

"Your father's case is more complicated, I'm afraid. To be put into stasis, we have to resuscitate him, and that means that we need to get his heart pumping blood long enough for us to activate the maneuver. But he'd already lost most of his blood."

"So just tell me, *is he alive or not*?"

"Yes. We're delivering oxygen straight to his brain and his other organs, and we're giving him fluids to fill his vascular system, but we can only sustain him like this for a few more hours. Since we've seldom had humans on the planet, we don't keep a supply of human blood. He needs some of yours."

"Oh, man, take it! Take whatever you need, anything! Except, I don't know what blood type he is---we may not have the same---"

"That's not an issue for us. We just need human blood. If we can put human blood into him, even as little as you can safely give, we can make it react with and stimulate the fluids we're giving him to make more, and we can use it to grow more. It's very likely that we'll need to do a total replacement of his organs as well, with the exception of his brain, of course, since a loss of blood this massive can cause organ damage that may not be discernible at first, but would cause failure later. We'll just have to monitor him closely. Are you ready for us to take your blood?"

"Oh, yeah. So you *will* be able to save him, right?"

"We will do our best."

##

They took his blood, then told him to rest, and gave him another painless injection. He drifted off immediately, and when he woke, all of the Elpies were sitting in his room, waiting patiently for him to stir. Just seeing them brought back everything, and he covered his face with his arm, turned his head away from them, and wept.

Eli came to him, put a hand on his head, and sent him a soothing. No words or pictures, but it did calm him some, made him know that he was cared about, and that others shared his pain. His family was in this room, too.

Barnabas was with them. Jonas took down his arm to look at him when he probed his mind gently for permission to intrude. They had mended his bones with their machines, he sent, and watched him for a day to be sure that his brain was healing normally, then had given him some medication and released him. He had come to say he was sorry for failing his family, and not protecting him and his mother as he should have.

That snapped Jonas out of himself, and he reached out to grab Barnabas' hand, squeezing it tightly. "You almost gave your life for us, Barnabas. What more could you give? The guy was like, eight or nine feet tall and had three arms and was super strong. Nobody could have stopped him at that point. I'm just so grateful to you for trying, and thankful that you're okay. You're a hero in my book, man." Then he pulled him closer so he could punch him in the arm, and he felt Barnabas' smile in his mind.

"There's no way I can ever thank all of you for what you did. Ruth, Dulcie, Martha---taking that guy out like you did---we'd all be dead if it hadn't been for you.

"And you, Eli..." He started tearing up again as he saw it in his mind once more, and wiped his face quickly with the heel of his palm, frustrated by his inability to hold it together. "All these years, Dad has talked as if you were his brother, and now *I know* you are. When he asked you to cut him, I could feel that it about killed you to do it. But you did it because you loved him enough to honor what he felt he had to do. To see you standing beside him down there while he was bleeding, holding him up when he was so close to passing out, and---" He had to pause again, the tears unstoppable. "When you carried him up the steps, all I could think of was that if Dad was going to die, at least he had his brother standing beside him at the end."

He covered his face again, then took a deep breath and sat up. "Does anybody know where my clothes are? I'm okay now. There's no reason for me to be lying in bed like I'm sick or something. They healed my ribs, so I'm good to go."

There was a knock on the door, and when Jonas called, "Come in," Sven and Cleo walked into the room. Sven looked slightly surprised at all the others in the room. He nodded to them in greeting, and they nodded back. Looking at Jonas, he seemed unable to send for a moment, looking away and then back again. Finally he sent, "How are you?"

"I'm okay. I had some cracked ribs from a snake that tried to kill me on the way to... But they fixed them with some machine, and I'm okay, now. Whoa, and thank you for taking out that big cat. Man, you were so fast and cool headed. I had no idea anything was going on until I saw that lion or whatever, go sailing over my head. I would've been lunch, no question. And Ms.---"

"This is my friend, Cleo."

"Hey Cleo. Right now, I guess I'm---the spokesperson for my family." He had to stop again to gain control, then took a deep breath and continued. "So I want to thank you for sending all of us here. They told me that my mom will be okay after they---grow her some organs and a new eye. They're not sure about my dad. He---"

"We know. We spoke to the physicians on the way in to see you. They said that your blood will help to get things started for him. They've been working on him nonstop since he was sent in two days ago.

"Jonas," he began, and stopped, then started again. "Jonas, I can't tell you how sorry I am about everything that's happened to your family. We brought you here for a celebration, and you came believing that you'd be sharing joy, and you would be protected and safe, and we have failed you all horribly. It would have been bad enough if it were only your parents, but to think that you, one of their children, was almost killed, and to see the trauma that all of you suffered---there's no apology adequate for that."

Jonas looked down at his hands, saying nothing.

"The government took the recording that 'Cecil' was making, and everything is on it. The cameras were shooting the area from multiple locations---even from a body cam in his forehead, so that all that took place is on record, from the time your father first attacked him, until you were all transported to the hospital. The Seated had it shown on the government broadcast, for the planet to see. And for those who didn't have the translator devices implanted, there were subtitles at the bottom of the screen, so that everyone could understand what was said by you and your parents."

Jonas stared at him in disbelief. His hands were clenched into fists around the sheets, his face turned red with rage, and his voice shook as he struggled not to scream. "You *gave* him his *wish*? So he could be the big star, after what he did? After he *slammed* my mother into the walls until she was *nearly dead,* and then *slaughtered* my father? You *gave* him his own show, just like he wanted? *Why would you do that?"*

Sven was shaking his head and his hands, with palms forward in denial. "No, it's not like that at all. They broadcast it because your family showed our world why we were right to change. Every word that Cecil spouted---what he thought he was proving---he was proving just the opposite. His face has been blurred on the recording, and his name is not given---so that he will never have his moment of fame. No one will know who he was. But your family---nothing has ever moved this planet the way that this broadcast has.

"Our people saw that family ties---yours or ours---are worth dying for. And it showed us how strong the ties of true friendship can be." He gestured towards the Elpies then, with a wave of one hand. "They had no idea what they would be up against when they ran to help you. But they stood with you and went to battle for you with as much passion as they would have for their own families."

Eli held his head up, and sent to Sven that they *were* family. Sven bowed his head low and nodded in acknowledgement.

"You and your mother trying to protect each other; what your father said when 'Cecil' told him he could go free--- And then what your father did to save you---" He looked down and shook his head. "Those actions showed not just courage, but strength, and the power of love to transcend our own individual needs. That madman wanted to show that love is a prison, and that it weakens us. But instead, your family showed that it frees us to do whatever we have to, and gives us the courage to stand and even die, if we must, without regret or second thoughts.

"Jonas---your father picked up a log, which should have been physically impossible for him to carry, and not only did he lift it, but he broke down the gate to the preserve with it to come after you and your mother. The physicians told us that they had to surgically excise huge splinters of wood that had sliced into and embedded in his palms when the log hit that gate, and hefting it tore muscles in his back and arms as well.

"We don't have that on film, but the evidence is clear. That he did the impossible there---that's written at the beginning of the broadcast, too. That's the message that this broadcast sent to everyone who saw it---that there is nothing stronger than love of family, or the friends who become family. Not even death. Our world thanks you for that. Everyone is hoping, and those of faith are praying, that you will all recover."

Jonas had sunk back into his pillow, lying with his eyes open and staring at the ceiling, tears streaming down his face as he listened to the Blueman's words, and heard for the first time, everything that his father had done and suffered just to reach him and his mom. When Sven finished and the room got quiet, it took a minute for him to pull himself together. Then he spoke quietly. "Thank you for telling me. I don't blame you. Every society has its crazies. But I don't think we'll be visiting here again."

"There is good news, too. The investigating officer, 'Elliott,' survived. He was shot with a fire stick by that beast, when he went to the reserve to investigate the loss of power to the force field while all of you were there. He met Cecil, who had on a reserve uniform, and told him that he was there to investigate the same thing. Supposedly, he was taking him to look at the power unit, when he suddenly whirled around and shot him in the chest from just a few inches away. When we arrived at the reserve, Cleo went to get fire sticks for us, discovered him in the storage chest, and sent him to the hospital with her disk before she ran to join me.

"I had already called for an emergency team, but before they arrived, another Blueman on the investigating team, 'Watson,' came with a number of his staff to search for Elliott--- he'd been missing since the day before. When they came into the reserve, they met us as we were coming back out, and when they described Elliott, Cleo told them how she'd found him and what she'd done. He was barely alive---he'd been in that chest for nearly a whole day, but the physicians said that he survived because the blast not only missed all of his vital organs, but also cauterized some of the blood vessels, and that kept him from bleeding to death. He's expected to recover completely, and he sent word with me to tell you how sorry he is about all that happened. He feels that he too, failed your family."

"Oh, man, I didn't know anything about that. He was such a nice guy, and Dad said he and Watson were the only ones that really cared about investigating things. The only ones he felt like were trustworthy. He really respected them. I mean---" He fought back the tears again when he realized he was talking about his dad in the past tense. "I mean, he really respects them.

"If you see him, will you tell him my family thanks him for everything he tried to do, and we're really glad he's going to be okay? He risked his life for us. Tell him what---what my dad had said about him---how highly he thought of them. *Thinks* of them. Dad had been worried about him, too, when he hadn't heard from him, because he thought Elliott was way too conscientious to not get back with him. No way would any of us feel that he failed us. He did his best---tried his best to do what was right."

"I'll make it a point to see him on my way out, and I'll tell him what you said. I'm sure it will mean a great deal to him."

"One more thing. When you leave the hospital---that is---until your mother, and hopefully, your father comes out of here, I'd be honored if you would stay with me in my apartment. I have lots of space, and I know you'd rather not go back to your apartment after everything that's happened."

Barnabas made a chirping sound, and his mane tilted forwards as he sent to Jonas, who smiled at the sending. Nodding towards the Elpies, he answered, "I appreciate it, Sven, but I'll be staying with family."

CHAPTER FORTY

Elsie and Ishmael sat in the apartment together, watching the authorities gathering up their family's belongings to send to the hospital. They'd gone downstairs together earlier, requested their meals, and eaten them in the dining room, since they had no hands to carry them, or to open containers. Bluepeople were crowding around the restaurant windows to try and get a look at them, and a few were holding signs that were a complete mystery to them, until the owner of the restaurant sent to them what the signs were saying: "We love you, Bringers. We're praying for you, Sayers."

They hurried back upstairs as soon as they'd finished, and the two of them decided to stay together in the ruined apartment because they could still smell their family there, and it eased their homesickness a little. When they'd first come back to the rooms, Elsie had found a pretty little metal box in the hallway, and she sent that it had the Colder's smell all over it, so she picked it up in her mouth and took it with her into their apartment. She kept it separate when the Bluepeople emptied their family's rooms.

Watching Ishmael washing himself, Elsie sent, "Barnabas sent to me about what you did out there. He sent that you attacked a bear to save him, and then showed the medical Blues where he was. You're a hero cat, a lion heart. High five, buddy." She held up a paw.

Looking at Elsie in an only slightly condescending manner, Ishmael replied, "Thanks, but cats don't do high fives with dogs. Or anybody. It's too---demeaning. But I do appreciate the sentiment. And you're quite the hero yourself, with that nose of yours, not to mention your pee."

Elsie accepted the compliment and ignored the small insult, just chalking it up to the nature of cats. She'd known this one for twenty years now, and through Simon, she knew that he was a cheeky little bastard, but she thought he must be one of the best.

"Do you think they'll save him?"

She started panting just thinking about seeing him all bloodied and still, with the death smell coming from him. It made her want to howl again. "I don't know. They did before but---he was so white, and there was so much blood. I'm not sure how much they can really fix."

"What if they can't?"

"Then we'll just have to be there and do what we can for Bess and for the kids. They'll need us more than ever. But my heart will never be the same. Sharing his memories and experiences makes him a part of me. To think that only Madelyn and I would share those memories now---it's such a lonely feeling. The *source* of all those memories would be gone. We wouldn't even understand all of them.

"I used to go and ask him about them sometimes, and he'd always sit with me and stroke my head while he explained, like the good father he was---or---is. Now---it's like there's this big empty space out there that should be full. Of him."

Seeing the look on the dog's face, and feeling her devastation, the cat sent no more, but moved to lie against Elsie's stomach, curled up in a ball, and started purring. Elsie looked down at Ishmael, somewhat shocked, and then wrapped herself around the curled up cat and went to sleep.

CHAPTER FORTY-ONE

Three days had gone by. The hospital had officially discharged Jonas, but he couldn't bring himself to leave with both his parents still there, so they had allowed him to stay in the room he was in. The Elpies had been there a lot of that time, only leaving occasionally to go to their rooms and get a few hours of sleep before they returned.

He hadn't been able to see his mom yet, but they'd let him go in with his dad. The doctors said they'd tried to get his heart started to see if it could work right and feed his other organs, but it had stopped four times, so instead of risking it again, they were going to replace everything, like they'd talked about before. They were going to start working on him in an hour or so, and after that, Jonas wouldn't be able to see him for a few more days, if everything went well.

They'd prepared him to see his dad, but it still shook him to see him this way---he was floating about a foot above the surface of a metal table, and he had tubes and wires stuck into him---all over him, like---just everywhere. The doctors said the tiny wires were delivering oxygen to his tissue to keep it from dying. They even had them stuck into his eyelids and his lips. The wires connected to a sort of gel-filled membrane that was floating above him, and the walls of the room were covered with monitors and machines that connected to the membrane and the tubes. Every machine made some kind of soft noise, and they all had dozens of lights in them. The astounding number of lights would have looked festive if he hadn't known why they were there.

He'd thought that they would've had the huge wounds on his arms sewn up by now, or would have made them disappear altogether, but they were still there---just clamped shut with metal things that looked like they should be holding a box together instead of a person. His dad was covered from the waist down, in respect for human modesty, which was more than fine with him. He didn't think he could stand to see the wounds on his legs. The doctors said they were going to replace the muscles and nerves in his arms and legs, as well as the vascular system, because they'd been so messed up by the knives, especially in his legs, where that monster had twisted them to tear the arteries.

To see his dad, this man who had raised him, laughed with him, talked with him, held him when he cried, sat up with him when he was sick, tossed him around and thrown him in the air when he was little----this man who was always such a warm, strong, *physical* presence---to see him like this just didn't make sense. This was the man who'd fought a huge Blueman monster for him, and had even made the thing bleed. How could this really be him? They said he was alive, but he was so still and white, and he just looked so---gone. Absent. Dead.

They sent that he could only touch him where there wasn't a wire or tube, so he found a spot on his right shoulder where he could lay his hand on him and talk to him, which they said would be good for him. But looking at him, he couldn't believe that he could hear or understand anything he might say. He needed to talk to him anyway, though, just for himself.

"Hey Dad, it's Jonas. I don't know if you'll get any of this or not, but I just really needed to see you and---touch you. I think you're like---the bravest man I've ever known. What you did to save me… When Mom was whispering to you when you were both lying on that stage---"

He had to stop talking then, and it was a few minutes before he could resume in a half-normal voice. "Well, I heard what she said, and she was right. Dad, we need you to come home.

"I want to be the kind of man you are, someday, and Colder needs help just to grow *to be* a man, period. We need you there to teach us, Dad. Who's gonna throw the little guys up in the air? Well, Eli can, but it's never the same, because he's not you. We need *you*, Dad. We love *you*, and nobody loves *us* like you and Mom do. And you've gotta stay for Mom.

"Dad---remember when you and Mom were dancing in the kitchen a few months ago, when you thought all of us were asleep? Well, I saw you. I can't believe it's taken all these years for me to understand, but I finally got it---what you really mean to each other. She won't ever be whole again without you. None of us will. So please, Dad, if you can hear me---if you have any control over this, please come back to us. I love you, Dad."

He found a spot on his forehead without wires, just big enough to put his lips on, and he gave him a kiss, like his Dad had always kissed his sons, and then he left the room in tears, wondering if this might be the last time he'd see him alive.

##

His mom was supposed to be waking up tonight, and they wanted him to be there when she did, so she'd know he was alive.

##

Sven asked him if he had Hiram's cell phone number, which he did, and then he sat him down in his room to talk with him. "We need for you to call him for us, so that he can talk to your grandfather. The rest of your family was expecting you back, and we want to let them know what's happened. Hiram would be the most level headed to speak with, so that he can relay the information to the rest of your family. The Seated also want to send the recording to him, so that he can show the adults in your family, and it will have the translation of what 'Cecil' said, as well as what your father did at the gate, in English."

"Oh man, that's a terrible idea! Do you know what that would do to my grandparents, to see my mom like that? It would kill them."

"Not if they know that she's completely repaired. And they need to know so that they're ready to support her in case---in case things with your father don't go as planned. You can't just return to Earth as if nothing has happened. You'll need to talk, and this way, they'll understand what you went through, or at least as well as anyone can.

"The government wants the rest of your family to see what you did, and to know how your actions have impacted our people. We've already sent a ship out so that it will be close enough to earth to send your signal, and to teleport a disk with the recording. But we'll need you to talk with Hiram to be sure the children don't see it, and for him to hear your voice---to know you're okay. Will you do this for your family, and for my people?"

"Are they still thinking they might---lose Dad?"

Sven looked down, then back up at Jonas and answered, "He hasn't responded as well as they'd hoped. They're working on him now, and they're growing everything new to replace all that's been damaged, but sometimes they just can't make the body survive. They're still hopeful, though, so you must have hope, too. Your father is a strong man, and he survived much longer than would be expected while---while he was---"

"Being mutilated? Being slaughtered?" Jonas snarled out angrily.

"Yes. His love for the two of you helped him survive to assure *your* survival---perhaps that same love will give him the strength to return to you. I'm---I'm so sorry for all of this." Sven sighed and put his head down, ashamed to look at this boy that soon might be fatherless by the hands of one of his own kind.

Jonas' anger slipped away as he felt Sven's sorrow and remorse for something that he'd had no part in. He reached over and put a hand on Sven's shoulder. "Don't. Don't blame yourself. I'm sorry to strike out at you. Everything you did was with good intentions, and you saved my life, and maybe, hopefully, the lives of my mom and dad. I know that. I'll make the call."

##

"Hello."

"Hiram?"

"Yes, who's this?"

"It's Jonas. I---"

"Jonas! Hey, traveler of the galaxy! You want to talk to Gisella?"

"No, Hiram, I need to talk to you."

"What's wrong? You sound terrible."

He'd told himself he *would not* cry. But hearing a voice from home brought all the longing to the surface, all the fear that nothing in his family would ever be good or complete like it was before. He wept as quietly as he could, hoping Hiram wouldn't hear, but now his brother-in-law was focused on every sound, every nuance of their conversation.

"Oh Lord, Jonas, talk to me. What's happened?"

And so, in broken sentences, punctuated by quiet sobs and long pauses for control, Jonas relayed to Hiram only a pittance of what had happened. He told him that he was fine now and that his mom was fine, or at least would be by tonight, and that tomorrow she would call them herself, to ease her parents' minds. A disk was going to appear on the desk of his study in a few minutes, that would show him everything, and Jonas told him to watch it alone, first, or maybe with Madelyn, so that he could try and get everyone else prepared before he showed it to them. Then he told him to be sure that Genevieve and Colder weren't anywhere around.

The worst part was telling him that his dad might not make it. He knew it---had known it from the beginning, but to say the words to another family member was just too hard. It made it part of his life back home, instead of just here, in some bizarre, sci-fi place that wasn't a part of his *real* life. By the time he gave the transmitter back to Sven, he was so broken that he had to go and lie down in the dark alone.

##

Gisella watched the disk after Hiram, and when she was able to stop crying, she went to the nursery and held her precious little daughter to her breast and cried some more. The thought that Simon might never see his almost-granddaughter was too horrible to think about, and the pictures of what they had suffered were burned into her brain. Hiram came in and wrapped his arms around her and their baby, and held them both. He could think of nothing else to do.

Gisella called a neighbor and asked if she might invite Colder and Genevieve over to play games or do something with her children for a few hours, without letting them know that she'd requested it, so that she and the McPhinneys could tend to some urgent family business. Then she called Viola and Tom and asked for them to come to the main house in thirty minutes. She waited until she saw the kids leave with the neighbors to go skating, before she and Hiram and the baby went to have the hardest conversation of their lives.

#

Sarah was nearly hysterical *before* watching the disk, and she kept repeating the same questions. "But you're sure she's all right now? You *know* she's okay? There's no question about her being healed?" Angus' eyes first filled with tears, and then went dead, and he started saying, "Just show the damn disk. Just show us the damn thing."

Viola and Tom were horrified, but they said nothing—just sat and waited for the disk to play. During the viewing, Sarah came close to passing out, crying out and screaming once, and Angus wept in silence and cursed constantly. Viola cried quietly, and Tom found himself groaning at times without even realizing it, with one arm around his wife and his other hand holding hers.

Madelyn had watched it first with Hiram, and she had growled and whimpered, and at last, when she'd seen Eli bow his head over Simon's blood covered body, she had howled, and Elsie's howl coming from the TV had blended with hers in a heartbreaking, eerie harmony. Now she remained quiet, but went to Sarah, leaned against her legs, and laid her head in her lap, to give what little comfort she could.

Two hours later, Angus called his oldest grandson.

"Eli, this is your grandfather. Your mom and Jonas are okay, but something has happened. We don't know yet about your dad. You need to come home, son. There's something we have to show you."

By the time Eli made the long drive home, in record time, the kids were back, so Tom and Viola invited them to their house for s'mores and a movie. They knew that *something* was going on, because they could tell people had been crying, and Eli had come back home, but from the look on their grandpa's face, they knew better than to question him now.

After learning what the disk would show him, Eli said he wanted to watch it alone. Sitting quietly in the next room, Giselle, Hiram, and his grandparents heard him cry out his parents' names in horrified denial and grief, and they wept to hear him moaning and sobbing. When it was over, he ran to the bathroom and vomited until there was nothing left to come up. Then he rinsed out his mouth, washed his face, and came back out. Sitting on the couch with his head in his hands, he asked, "How long before we know about Dad?"

Hiram sat down next to him and put a hand on Eli's shoulder as he imparted what he knew. "Jonas said they're working on him now and re-growing his internal organs and muscles. He said that takes a few days."

"Oh, Mom. Poor Mom."

##

"Mom. It's time to wake up, Mom. That's right, you can do it."

Before she opened her eyes, her hand flew up to her face and felt her cheekbone, her nose, settled on her eye and felt the whole orbit, and then felt her forehead where it had been caved in before. Finally, she sighed, and said, "Oh, thank God, Jonas. You wouldn't believe the horrible dream I had. I can't even tell you, it was that---"

Opening her eyes, she saw the Bluemen, and the hospital equipment. She whirled around to look at Jonas, and then sat up and looked around the room for Simon.

Looking back at Jonas' expression, she knew. Her face crumpled and she covered it with both hands, and cried, "Simon! Oh, Simon, no, no!" as she began to weep bitterly.

Devastated by his mom's anguish, Jonas got onto the bed and grabbed her hands away from her face to make her look at him. "Mom, Mom, Dad's alive! He's alive!"

She stopped in mid-sob, looking hopefully at him, and then her expression dissolved into grief again as she said accusingly, "If he were alive, he'd be here!"

"Mom, they're still working on him, growing him new parts, like you said they did back on the Elpies' planet. It's been a lot harder for them to get him back than it was to repair you. He bled to death, and that complicated everything when they tried to resuscitate him. But he's alive. Oh, Mom, I just *really need* to hold you. *Please.*"

He put his arms gently around her and then held her tight, crying quietly on her shoulder, so glad to feel her in his arms, healed of her ghastly wounds. After a second, she returned his embrace with full force. "Oh, honey, I'm so relieved that you're okay. This must have been so awful for you, to have to deal with both of us being 'repaired' at the same time, and you all alone."

"I wasn't alone. I had the Elpies."

She held him back from her then, and searched his face, wanting to look inside of him, to absorb and soothe away some of what he'd been through. Seeing his exhausted, haunted expression, she stroked the hair back from his face the way she had when he was a little boy, kissed his forehead, and then pulled him back into her arms while she prayed for his father.

CHAPTER FORTY-TWO

She had suffered this before---the waiting. But it was so much worse this time. Because *he* was so much more to her now. With their ability to send to each other, she had shared thoughts with him for twenty years. They had raised children, shared dreams and heartaches, supported each other's ambitions, worked together for mutual goals, built a home where there had just been a house. They were companions, lovers, partners, best friends. He was her past, present, and she hoped, her future. The idea of raising her three youngest without his steady, loving presence in their lives and her own---she couldn't even imagine it. She wouldn't let herself.

The last time she'd had to wait, they'd told her that he would be well and whole and better than before. This time they told her they were "doing their best."

They gave her a room at the hospital, like the one they'd given Jonas, because there was no way she would walk out of there without knowing. She tried to focus on Jonas, and what he'd been going through, and to learn what all had happened, for she'd been semiconscious or out completely through so much of the nightmare. Finally, the idea of not knowing everything that her family had gone through was too much for her, and she asked Sven to bring the disk for her to watch.

Not wanting Jonas to have to relive it, she sat in her room alone to watch. Seeing her own ruined face, that distorted rib cage and misshapen, swollen abdomen, almost made her vomit, and she caught herself screaming, "NO, DON'T!" when Simon sliced through his own arm and then begged Eli to destroy the other. She keened his name when she saw the knives go into his legs---at the sheer agony on his face as he fell. By the time she saw his lifeless, blood-covered body at the end, she was reduced to whimpering.

Sitting on a bed, she felt unable to speak or move, so she let the horror, grief, and sorrow take her over. She had locked the door to her room, and now she screamed and cried into a pillow until she had no voice, and was all but blind from the swelling around her eyes, only opening the door, finally, when Jonas threatened to have someone break it down if she didn't let him in. Then, when she saw his face, knowing that he had seen all of this, *lived it*--- she held her arms out to him and held him tightly when he rushed to her. She told him she was sorry, so sorry for what he'd had to face, and for his having to see her like this now. Just one more awful thing to deal with—seeing his mother fall apart.

For those few, terrifying minutes when she wasn't answering, and her door was locked, especially after hearing her crying his dad's name in that seriously eerie sounding voice, Jonas had been afraid that she might have taken her own life. He was so relieved to see her open that door, even though he could hardly recognize her with all the freaky swelling and redness she got when she cried. It was still his mom under all that mess.

She'd already talked to her family at home, but after seeing the recording, and imagining what her parents and Eli must have gone through when they watched it, she called them again to tell them she was fine, she loved them, and was sorry for what they'd seen. All they'd said to her was, "We love you. Come home, baby," and "Come home, Mom."

At last the day arrived for them to wake Simon. It had not gone well at first, and they'd come very close to losing him for good, but after things began turning around, everything improved rapidly. Extremely pleased, at last, with the results of the replacements and his body's response to them, the physicians sent that they were sure everything would be fine, but then sent that they needed to explain some things to the two of them before they saw him.

Jonas sat down with her and they waited for more bad news. Seeing their faces, the Bluemen reassured them that there *was* no more bad news---only instructions and precautions.

"How are you feeling, Bess?"

"I feel great, except for wanting to tear my hair out and being scared out of my mind. I'm sorry that I haven't really thanked you for the amazing job you did on me. My vision is better than it was before, and I can't see any difference between one eye and the other, my head feels fine, and I *love* the beautiful new teeth, not to mention the ribs and organs. And I can't thank you enough, of course, for taking care of Jonas, too. But what about my husband?"

"When he went through this the first time, twenty years ago, he awoke fully healed and strong. It will be very different for him this time."

A feeling of dread swept over her, and her voice cracked as she asked, "How so?"

"He will be extremely weak, and prone to fainting if he stays upright for long. He'll have all the symptoms of someone of your species who suffers from very severe anemia---dizziness, overwhelming fatigue, shortness of breath, headaches and nausea. But rest assured, all of these symptoms are temporary."

"Why can't you heal him completely, like you did us?"

"Massive blood loss such as he suffered—actually bleeding to death---is not as easily overcome as other types of cardiac arrest, and your husband responded very poorly to treatment at first. We've given him some of your son's blood to start the process of making new cells with the fluids we've given him. With the help of your son's blood, your husband's blood cells caused a reaction with the chemicals in the fluid, and the cells within it started changing into the beginnings of new blood, but the process is very slow. We're going to give you pills to give him every eight hours, and make no mistake---if he doesn't finish them, he *will* die, and no human technology will be able to save him. But if you're faithful about giving these to him, in six weeks he'll be back to normal, with all his previous energy and vitality, and no sign of trauma on his body.

"Until then though, you *must* watch him carefully when he walks or stands, because the dizziness and fainting spells can be sudden and quite severe, and the last thing he needs now is head trauma from a fall. If he suffers an injury during this time, contact us---do *not* take him to a hospital. And under *no circumstances* should you allow him to receive a transfusion. The introduction of other blood would cause a reaction with the medication and the forming processes going on, and kill him within a matter of minutes. We would advise you to let him see no one outside the family until he's well, because of the way he looks. If anyone in the medical field saw him, a court order for a transfusion would probably ensue.

"Prepare your family for this, and the fact that he may have trouble concentrating or remembering at first, his emotions will be labile, and he will be *very, very* pale.

"But what you can look forward to, is the fact that if you give him the medication as it's prescribed, see that he drinks plenty of water, and rests when fatigued, you will see improvement every single day.

"Just in case you should lose a pill or two, we're giving you extra, in another container, and a disk that you can call us on if you have any other problems. We'll make sure that a ship is within transmitting distance until the six weeks is up. Any questions?"

After sitting stock still, and trying to memorize every word, she almost had to shake herself to come out of her trance. "No sir. But is there any way you can write all that down? In English?"

"Sure."

##

"Simon, it's me, Bess. Jonas is here, too. We're both fine, honey, and we're waiting for you to come back to us. Wake up, sweetheart."

Bess was holding one of his hands, and Jonas the other, when Simon opened his eyes and looked at them. He looked at his arms, with no sign of trauma, and then, pulling his hand out of hers, reached out for Bess' face, brushing back her hair and running his thumb gently across her forehead, cheek, and finally, her eye that she closed for him to caress. Then he looked at Jonas smiling down at him, and he put his head back and started laughing and crying at the same time, and both of them were doing the same. He reached an arm out to each of them and pulled them to him, raising his head to hold it against theirs as he kissed them.

They were so right, Bess thought. *He looks like death.* He was almost as white as the sheet that covered him, his cheeks were sunken, there were deep circles under his eyes and lines in his face that hadn't been there before. But he was alive and he was Simon.

There had been no way to prepare him before he woke up, for the symptoms to expect, so remembering his repair of twenty years before, he sat up suddenly in bed, ready to get his clothes on and join the living again. But instead, he gasped and clutched his head with pain, falling back down to his pillow, even whiter than before. Fighting back a sob at seeing him in pain again, Bess clutched his shoulder with one hand and put the other on his chest to try and comfort him. He kept his eyes closed until the pain let up enough for him to speak, then opened one eye to look at the physician. "So it's going to take some time to get over this, eh?"

She laughed then, at the sheer joy of hearing his voice again. He sounded tired, but so much stronger than she'd expected from the way he looked. Leaning over, she put her face next to his and whispered how much he meant to her---to all of them.

CHAPTER FORTY-THREE

When Bess called Hiram to tell him about Simon, all the adults were in the room, waiting for the call. He was almost afraid to answer, sure that something else must have gone wrong. Picking up the phone, before he could even say hello, he heard Bess shouting, "He's alive! Simon is back!"

Sarah started weeping, Angus closed his eyes and said, "Thank God," and Eli started shaking so badly that he had to sit on the floor. "Dad's alive," he whispered, and then leaned back against the couch to repeat those words to himself as he reached out for Gisella's hand, covering his face with his other, to let the tears come as they would. Then Bess told them what to expect when they saw Simon, and what he'd be going through for a while. That sobered them all up a little, but couldn't diminish the joy her news had brought.

Knowing how hard this had been on his grandparents, Eli offered to tell Genevieve and Colder about what had happened, but in abbreviated, gentler terms. They needed to be prepared for what they'd see when his dad got home. His offer was gratefully accepted.

He washed his face, then went upstairs and knocked on both their doors. They'd supposedly already been in bed for an hour, but of course, both had been lying with their ears pressed to the floor, trying to hear what was going on. They hated being kept out of things, but everybody had seemed so stressed out, that the two had decided not to pester anyone just yet.

"Hey, munchkins, come on out and go to the loft with me so we can have a talk, and I'll finally tell you what's been going on. I know it's been making you crazy to be kept out of the loop like this, and you've both been really great about it. Come on, let's go in there and sit down."

They followed him in like puppies and sat on the floor in front of him. He hadn't called them his "little turdlings" or his "favorite bean brains," so they knew this had to be serious stuff.

Now that he had their attention, Eli realized he had no idea what he was going to say. How to even start. He needed to go back to his room and prepare some notes first, but it was too late, so he just started talking.

"Well, ah, the first thing you need to know is that Mom and Dad and Jonas are all okay. Or, well, Dad's not, but he will be in six weeks."

"They're not coming back for *six weeks?"*

"No, no, they're coming back in just a few days."

"So what's wrong with Dad?"

"Okay, let me tell you from the beginning. There was this bad guy who was mad at the government, and he was crazy too, and unfortunately, he was a really *big* Blueman. And he hurt mom and Jonas and kidnapped them."

Shocked gasps from both kids, and threatened tears from Genevieve.

"Hey now, remember when I'm talking, about what happened, that everything's okay now. Okay? No need to cry, all right? Huh?" He ruffled the hair on both their heads, and they both slapped away his hands in annoyance, but nodded their "okays."

"Well, anyway, for ransom, instead of money, he wanted Dad to hurt himself."

Colder jumped up in anger. "That's crazy! Why would anybody want that?"

"Because---you nailed it, bud, the guy was crazy."

Genevieve covered her mouth, but said through her hand, "So Dad hurt himself, didn't he?"

"Yeah, he did. He cut himself, pretty bad, but all the time, he had this plan to save Jonas and Mom."

"All Right, Dad!!" the two shouted in unison, and then high fived each other and Eli.

"What was the plan?"

"Well, he knew that if he let---he knew if he let---" And suddenly, without warning, he was crying, not little sniffles, but full blown sobs. The two children leapt into action---Genevieve rushing to bring a box of Kleenex, and Colder charging downstairs to get a glass of water. That's what they *always* did in the movies for *everything*---they'd get a glass of water.

When Colder ran through the den to the kitchen and frantically grabbed a glass from the cabinet, filling it with ice and then water, both Sarah and Angus followed him into the room.

"What's up, Colder?" Angus asked.

"Nothing. Eli's just telling us about Dad, and he's crying, but don't come up---we got it covered." He ran five steps up and then ran back for a straw, and then got two steps up and ran back and rummaged around in the cabinet to get one of those little umbrellas that his Mom put in drinks when she was giving a party. She said the umbrellas made people happy. Perfect!

When he got upstairs, Eli was rubbing his eyes, and wiping his nose with a Kleenex, trying to get himself under control. Genevieve was standing beside him with her head on his shoulder, rubbing his back the way Mom did when one of them was upset, and holding out a box of Kleenex for him. Colder rushed up and shoved the glass of water at him, and when Eli saw the umbrella, he started laughing, and shook his head. "Thanks, dude, and dudette."

"Okay, I got it now. Sorry about that. There's just no good way to say this. But Dad's plan was to let this guy kill him so that Jonas and Mom would be safe."

He heard gasps again, and Genevieve dropped the box of Kleenex.

She was tearing up now, her eyes big as saucers. "He killed him?"

"Yeah, he did---but *remember*, he's gonna be okay, 'cause the Bluemen brought him back, just like before."

"How did they kill him?" Colder asked.

"With knives. The crazy guy cut arteries and he bled to death."

Now both kids were crying. Damn, he'd really blown this. He hadn't meant to get this specific. But they'd asked, so what was he supposed to say?

"But the thing is, the bad guy thought it was his idea, but it was really Dad's idea, 'cause you know how smart Dad is, and how sometimes he can make you think something's your idea, and then you realize that he sort of fooled you into doing what he wanted? Like when he told you, Colder, that battles were fought on open fields, with lots of clean space and you were all into your little plastic soldiers then, so you cleaned your room. But you hadn't even bought the set of enemy soldiers yet. Dad just wanted you to clean your room.

"And remember, Genny, when Dad said broccoli made your hair shiny and carrots made your eyes sparkle, so he wanted all of them for himself at dinner, because he wanted to look nice when he gave a speech at the hospital? And right away, you're starting to get all whiny, because *you* wanted shiny hair and sparkly eyes, so he *shared* the broccoli and carrots with you. Remember that?"

Both kids nodded at each other and then at Eli, with the "Ahhh" expression on their faces.

"So that's what he did with the bad guy. And it worked. The other Eli grabbed Mom out of his hands, and Jonas got away while this guy was using those two hands to---"

"To kill Dad!" Colder filled in happily. "Because he had a plan!"

Eli swallowed hard. "Yeah, that's right! And then the three Elpie sisters jumped the guy from behind and took him out."

"You mean they *killed* him?"

"They probably would have, but when they jumped on him, he accidentally bit down on some poison he had in his mouth and killed himself. So Dad's plan worked out just right!"

"He's the Rad Dad, the Rad Dad!" Colder started the chant, and then Genevieve joined in, chanting the words quietly, facing each other bent over, with their heads down, and arms outstretched towards each other, fingers spread wide. Shaking their hands back and forth, rotating at the wrist, they increased the volume of their chant as they slowly raised their hands higher, finally straightening their bodies until they were standing with arms stretched above them, and their shouted chant turned into happy whooping.

Another primitive munchkin ritual to film for National Geographic.

When they finished their cheer, Colder shook his head, smiling. "You gotta hand it to Dad—who else woulda thought about getting killed to fool this guy?"

Genevieve started giggling, and said, "I'm glad he didn't go that far to get me to eat my broccoli!"

They all started giggling then, and Eli laughed for what seemed like the first time in forever.

"Oh, and remember Sven?" They nodded. "Well, while his girlfriend was busy sending Dad to the hospital, this Blue-tiger---no, it's true---this Blue-tiger jumps out and he's leaping through the air, about to eat your brother, when Sven jumps in the way with a stun pole and just throws the thing over their heads!"

Colder's eyes went wide, and he shouted, "NO WAY!"

Genny's eyes narrowed. "He was just stunned, right? They didn't kill the tiger, did they? I'm sure he didn't mean to hurt anybody. He was just hungry." Then she started giggling again. "And our brother just looked so delicious!" They all laughed again and then Genevieve turned serious.

"Did it hurt Dad a lot when he got killed?"

"Yeah, I'm sure the pain was pretty terrible. You know, I think we have the bravest dad in the world, and he loves us so much that he'd do that for any of us if he had to."

Genevieve got her mad face on then. "Even if it *was* his idea, I just wish people would *quit killing* Dad! We're lucky the Bluemen are always around to zap him, or whatever they do."

"Yeah, hopefully, this will be the last time. You know, Mom was really brave, too, and so was Jonas. When the crazy guy went to their apartment, at the beginning of the whole thing, Mom attacked him and jumped on his foot, to try and protect Jonas, and then Jonas went at him to try and protect Mom. Even after they were both hurt, they still tried to protect each other. Mom would do anything she had to, to protect any of us---and Jonas probably would, too."

"Way to go, Mom and Jonas!" Genevieve yelled.

Then she got serious again and looked at Eli knowingly. "You'd die to protect us, too, wouldn't you, Eli?"

The question surprised him, but the answer was easy. He reached out and squeezed her hand, and his voice broke just a little as he replied, "In a heartbeat, bean butt."

Suddenly, she was in his arms, clinging tightly to him. "I love you, Eli."

Blinking hard to keep the tears at bay now, he held this child, this sister whose faith in her big brother was absolute, and laid his head on hers. "Love you, too, sweetheart."

Genevieve let go after a couple of seconds, and looked at him as she said quietly, "You sounded exactly like Dad when you said that."

Finally, one tear escaped, and he brushed it away quickly before replying, "You know, I couldn't ask for a nicer compliment."

Trying not to notice the tear, Colder declared loudly, "Geez, we're not just the tall family, we're the brave family, too." Then he smiled at Eli and nodded his head in approval.

Eli smiled back and winked. "Oh, and I forgot to tell you. The Colder, who goes by Barnabas now---"

Colder was incensed. “Barnabas? That’s a stupid name!”

“Is not. Jonas really likes it,” Genevieve countered. “He said it was cool because it means, “Son of exultation.”

“All right,” he sighed with resignation, “what does that mean? I know you’re dying to tell me.”

“It means really, really happy and joyful. I looked it up.”

“So why didn’t they just call his dad ‘Happy,’ and make it simple? You could say, ‘Happy, the house is on fire!’ and the firemen would get there in time to save everybody, but by the time you said, ‘Oh, Mr. Exultation---’ the whole house would be burned down. It’s a stupid name.”

“It’s way more cool than ‘Happy.’ ‘Happy’ sounds like a dog’s name.”

“What does a really happy Colder look like, anyway? Colders always look way fierce and mad.”

“I don’t know, but do *you* want to tell the Colder that his new name is stupid?”

“No way.”

Should he tell them? Nah.

“AS I WAS SAYING,” Eli broke in, “the Colder attacked this guy in their apartment, trying to save Mom and Jonas, but this Blueman stunned him with the tiger stunner---”

“Ouch!”

“Yeah, Ouch is right, and he throws him off the balcony!”

“Whoa, *that’s* gotta hurt!”

“So while *he’s* waiting to get rescued, a bear tries to eat him and guess who saved him?”

“Davy Crockett! And I’ll bet he was only three!” They were all giggles now, including Eli.

“Will you little turd toads let me finish?” Ah, this was the Eli they knew and loved.

“Ishmael saved him!”

"The cat? Wow, we thought he only played chess and now we find out he's 'NINJA CAT.'"

"Yep. The Colder, I mean Barnabas, sent that Ishmael came charging out and jumped on the bear's face, and it was so scared, that it rolled down a hill, and---"

Colder and Genevieve smiled at each other and started singing, "The Bear went over the mountain, the bear went over the mountain---"

"Okay, my little banana brains, I can see that story time is over for you. You're way past dealing with. But there's one more thing we have to talk about. Dad is gonna be sick for about six weeks while he's waiting for his blood to grow back. They said he looks really white and awful, and he might pass out if he's up for too long. He's also gotta take these pills every eight hours or he could die."

"*AGAIN?*"

"Well, that's not going to happen because *we* aren't going to let him forget his pills. Everybody in this house is going to set their alarms to the time he has to take them, and with, let's see, one, two---that will be six alarm clocks going off at the same time! That'll be awesome!

"Okay, tooter butts, it's been real, but I'm trashed. And you know what?"

"What?"

"I really do love you little broccoli breaths. You're the absolute best." Grabbing them around their necks, with one arm around each, the way his dad would have done, he kissed both of them on the forehead. He followed this up by going into each of their rooms, and with them both screaming and laughing, tossed them through the air to land on their beds. He left them to go back downstairs then, thinking, *Yeah, they really are.*

CHAPTER FORTY-FOUR

They teleported Simon onto the ship, because he was still too weak to walk that far, even with help. After he arrived, the crew made sure that he looked out the open hatch at the area around the ship, and when he did, to his shock, there were Bluepeople everywhere. The huge crowd that had gathered for their send-off was sprouted with signs and balloons, and when the three humans looked out, a cheer arose. The Elpies stuck their heads out then, and the cheering got even louder, and Bluepeople started waving. They all waved back, then got into their seats for take-off, overwhelmed by all the love they could feel coming from the crowd.

Mona was looking out a window and translating some of the signs for them. "'We love you, Sayers,' and that one says, 'So glad you are restored,' and that one says, 'Thank you, Bringers, we will never forget you!'" Then she looked closer at one sign and started laughing.

"What's so funny?"

"I think I know who wrote that sign. It says, 'It was great, Jonas. Call me.'"

##

Thinking about Colder, Eli, and Genevieve, Simon was getting more and more antsy to see them. It was always like this when he'd been gone. He could be having a great time, and hate leaving to head home, (though not in this particular case), but the moment his mind turned in that direction he would start thinking about his children, and that longing to see them would get worse with every mile closer he got. By the time he was in town, he'd be breaking every speed limit there was to get home, hold them, and toss them up in the air, simply for the pleasure of hearing them laugh, (with the exception of Eli, since he outweighed him now and was two inches taller, and Jonas, who was as big as Bess). He thanked God that he would be *able* to hear their laughter again.

Bess had gotten all the written instructions from the physicians, and was holding Simon's pills next to her in her bag as if his life depended on them, which it did. She was so happy to be going home that she felt like dancing. Her children, her home, *her husband.* She'd come so close to losing everything.

On this ship, the seats were set with five in a row, with five facing them, and there were several sets of the ten. At first, Eli and Simon sat across from each other so that they could send, and they carried on this quiet communion until the strain from being upright started to show in Simon's face, and Bess had him lie down, telling him to sleep.

He needed no encouragement---he was out almost before she finished suggesting it. She knew she shouldn't let it get to her, but---he looked so much like he had back on the Elpies' planet, when he was dying. So exhausted, and barely able to stay conscious for any time at all near the end. The memories ate at her.

Jonas was sitting with Barnabas and Ishmael, getting all the details of exactly what had happened with the two of them that day in the apartment. Like Bess, it irked him to have been partially out of it and to have only fuzzy memories about some things. What he did know, was that the Colder had risked his life to try and save them, that he'd been badly injured, and that he'd delayed his own rescue so that the other Elpies could come to help him and his family. Without that last act of selflessness, they'd probably all have been killed.

Barnabas happily regaled Jonas with his story of Ishmael and the bear-thing. The Colder sent that he owed the cat his life, and Ishmael sent that he had given him back the lives of his family, so he figured Barnabas was still ahead in the owing category. Jonas had never known cats could be gracious, and *especially* not Ishmael.

Elsie had returned Barnabas' bracelet to him, and he was overjoyed at getting it back. That had been his one regret---having lost that gift for his wife. The more he thought about her, the more he realized what she and the rest of his family meant to him. A trinket couldn't relay what he knew she was worth, what she was to him. But *he* could, and he planned to as soon as he got home.

Finally tiring of sending, Jonas leaned back in his chair to doze. He let his mind wander, and as he started thinking about it, he realized something for the first time. *It was crazy---everybody saved somebody. Wow, if that doesn't make us family, I don't know what does.*

#

On the day of the attack, the sisters had spent a large part of the remainder of the day rinsing their mouths. Bluepeople tasted incredibly foul. They'd rinsed and spit and raided the Sayers belongings in search of mouthwash, tooth paste, tooth brushes, and dental floss. Two bottles, two tubes, two brushes, and two packs later, they still had a nasty taste in the backs of their throats. They made a pact, that should they ever have to do battle with a Blueman again, they'd use something other than their teeth.

Once Simon was out of the hospital, Elsie never left his side, except to tend to bodily functions. Seeing Simon dead had traumatized her more than anyone realized. She was normally such an ebullient animal, but now she simply sat and watched him. She'd never seen a living human look so white, and she could smell his frailness now. But she didn't smell death anymore, and she had to keep reminding herself of that.

Eli had reveled in the fact that he could still send with his brother. Knowing he'd failed to save him for the second time had torn his heart out, and seeing Simon alive again, cheerful and positive, restored his spirit. He had already thanked Sven and Cleo, and the physicians at the hospital, multiple times. Though he didn't like the way Simon looked, he, like Elsie, no longer smelled death. He assumed it was part of his calling, but Eli had always had a warning sense when someone was close to death, and Simon didn't trigger that sense anymore, as he had during that terrible day when Eli had stood and watched his brother's life pouring out onto the ground.

##

As his mind drifted over the whole episode, Sven was struck again at how the lives of the Bluemen, Elpies, humans, and animals on this ship had converged and become intertwined, and how one action had led to another. Whom he used to think of as "subjects," he now thought of as close friends.

But mostly, he thought about Cleo. Because of what Bess had told him, because she'd cared, he'd found Cleo, and because he'd found her, she'd been with him to help save the Sayers. Very fitting.

When he entered the passenger section looking for Bess, he saw her sitting across from Simon, watching him intently as he slept. He came over and asked if he could send with her for a while. She smiled and gestured to the seat next to her.

"Bess, I hadn't thought it appropriate until now, but I wanted to tell you that you changed my life."

"What? How?"

"I went to the Academy for Flight Leaders and across the street, there's a café. I ate and drank until I found her."

Bess gasped. "You found somebody? Already? Are you sure you're not rushing into anything?"

"Oh, I would rush into marrying her today, if I could. She's the one---the one who makes my heart do pitty-pats, although they're really more like 'brrr-brrr's.' We have *chemistry!* I just wish—well of course I wish all of this hadn't happened to your family---but I wish circumstances had been different enough that you could have met her. She's wonderful, Bess. The only female I've ever had this kind of feelings for, or who has affected my cardiac functioning."

"Oh, she's the one that sent us all to the hospital! I saw her on---that recording."

Sven reached over and took her hand. "I am so sorry about everything. I would give anything to undo the horror that you've suffered."

She smiled at him and stood up so she could reach to kiss him on the forehead, which shocked him just a little. "I know that. You risked your own life to save my son's, and you've apologized enough already. Let's just be happy about your girl! I wish we could email or something, and keep in touch, so that you could tell me how things work out for the two of you."

"Oh, I think we'll be making contact with you in the future. The Seated have a plan."

Ten minutes later, sitting quietly, and watching Simon sleep, Bess was suddenly overcome by uncontrollable giggles. She was prone to these when under stress, or just exhausted, and something that would be only vaguely amusing to her when she was in her right mind could unexpectedly set them off. She had to leave the room to get herself under control, so that no one got an inadvertent sending about why she was giggling. She'd just realized that Sven was hung up on a space cadet.

#

When he opened his eyes, Bess was sitting across from him, watching him with that haunted look in her eyes that he'd seen so many times. He raised his seat to sit up and looked at her questioningly. "Why aren't you sitting next to me?"

"I needed to be where I could watch you better."

"Why?"

"Because you're not well, yet. I need to watch you."

"Bess, come here. *Please.*" He patted the seat next to him.

She came over and he took her hand in his and turned towards her. "Bess, my heart, you have to let it go."

"Let what go?"

"The past. My poisoning. I look in your eyes now, and I see that fear that I've seen every time I've had a cold, or done anything even slightly risky, for the past twenty years. Every time I've taken off in a plane, or on the highway. I see your fear for me---that you're going to lose me again."

She put her other hand over her eyes and leaned back in her seat, embarrassed to look at him. "Oh, geez, you've seen that for all these years, and never said anything?"

"I didn't know what to say."

"I'm sorry. You must think I'm a nut case."

"No. I think you love me. Bess, I believe that in some ways, my poisoning, this recent horror—well, in some ways, they've been harder on you than they have on me."

"*No*, no, Simon, you can't compare what you suffered to my---neurosis, I guess you'd call it."

"Well, not *physically* harder, but mentally harder. I had a dose of that same medicine when I saw you up on that stage." He turned his head away and swallowed, looked down and then back up at her. "I saw you so broken---*destroyed*---and I thought you were dead, at first. To think that the beautiful light that you are, was gone from the world---and with those horrible injuries---the pain you must have suffered---" He stopped and put his head down, shutting his eyes tight to try and stop the tears. Then he took a deep breath, looked back at her, and continued in a voice shaking with emotion. "To know that someone *did* that to you, *deliberately*---and *I wasn't there* to stop him, to help you. If I hadn't needed to keep it together to try and save Jonas, I don't know what I might have done. When I saw our son, bruised and beaten, with a look of such despair on his face… I should have been there. I should have protected the both of you." Then he put his head down and covered his face with his hands to hide the tears when he couldn't keep from weeping any longer, as his tormented confession unexpectedly boiled to the surface at last.

Jonas had been watching them, and as soon as his father started crying, he rushed over and put his arms around him. Simon kept his face covered, shaking his head, and all they could hear was, "I'm so sorry, so sorry." The Elpies were watching, and Eli wanted so badly to comfort his brother, but he knew this was something the three humans had to work through on their own. Jonas and Bess both had their arms around Simon, trying to talk to him, soothe him, but his quiet weeping had become wrenching sobs.

"Dad, Dad, what's wrong? Talk to me, Dad! What's he saying, Mom?" Jonas was beside himself with anxiety over his dad's breakdown. He'd been so strong---even while he was being killed---to see him like this now was tearing Jonas apart.

Simon took his hands down, and with a look of pure anguish on his face, shook his head, and said again, "I'm so sorry. I *knew* I shouldn't have left you alone, I *knew* it! Why did I? I'm supposed to protect my family, and I left you alone to be attacked and kidnapped, and almost killed. If you had died in that apartment, Bess, there'd have been no Bluemen to transport you in time to resuscitate. If Barnabas hadn't sent the Elpies when he did, you might both be dead. I'm so sorry. I'm so sorry. I failed you both so badly."

He'd been sitting up all this time, and his posture and the torrent of emotion suddenly left him weak, dizzy, and short of breath. Bess saw him break out into a sweat, turn even more pale, and start trembling, so she pushed his chest gently to lean him back into his chair and tilted it to lie him down and get the blood back to his head.

Jonas looked at Bess in confusion. "He's apologizing for leaving us in the apartment? But he tried to get us to go with him and we wouldn't. *We* refused. He wasn't responsible for that!"

Simon was just coming around again, when he heard what Jonas said. "But I'm your father. I should have done *something.* I *knew* there was danger. I could *feel* it, and I *still* walked away and left you. How could I have done that? I almost got you both killed. I'm so sorry."

He'd stopped sobbing, and was trying to get himself under control, and to catch his breath as well. He shut his eyes tightly and pressed his lips together, trying to keep the tears from coming, but they still escaped from the sides of his eyes. The picture kept going through his mind---he saw Bess, with her ruined face, being held up by that monster---unconscious, helpless, so close to death, and his son, with that stick next to his head, afraid for his life, beaten, and mourning his mother---he had left them and given them over to their fate.

Suddenly, his head was jolted to the side by a hard, stinging slap on the face, and he looked up, shocked, into Bess' angry eyes as she stood over him.

"MOM!" Jonas shouted, grabbing for her hands. "*What* are you *doing*?"

Ignoring Jonas, she looked angrily down at Simon, and said in a low, threatening voice, "How *dare* you talk about my husband that way! My husband went to that morgue, in the crush of the crowd, in a stuffy hamster tube, to do his duty---to prevent the possible murders of more people, even though he'd been insulted and almost turned away for trying to get to the truth. He spent a part of his last day looking at a dead body. He took that responsibility on himself because that's what good men do.

"Jonas and I *refused* to go with him. He couldn't drag us. We didn't feel well, and even if I hadn't been ill, I wouldn't have gone because I didn't want to, and I'm a grown woman with my own mind. There are risks in this world, and every day is dangerous. *I* took that risk, not my husband!

"And when he found that we'd been taken, he went after us. He picked up a log that he couldn't possibly have carried, broke down a gate with it, leaving him with torn muscles and huge shards of wood in his hands, which he refused to acknowledge in his determination to find us, and then he ran until he caught the creature who'd taken us. He attacked him, even though the thing was eight or nine feet tall, and outweighed him by a ton. He got thrown maybe twelve feet from a height of oh, probably thirteen or fourteen feet---if you calculate in the height of the stage *and* the Blueman---cracked some ribs, which he also refused to acknowledge in his frenzy to try and save us---and then rolled back to his feet to attack again, only stopping when he saw the fire stick pointing at Jonas' head.

"And *then* my husband offered himself as a sacrifice, in a trade for our lives. He *mutilated* himself, made his best friend help in the mutilation, and then let himself be horribly murdered---just stood there and waited for those knives to rip him apart, to save his son, and maybe his wife, or what was left of her. He *died* for us! Don't you get that? He gave his *all* for us! So don't you *ever* let me hear you criticize him for *anything* he did on that day, or buddy, I will *take you out!*"

Jonas and Simon had just stared at her in shock through her whole speech, though Jonas was thinking, *the warrior, the she bear.* When she finished, she stormed back over to her seat and threw herself into it. Simon pushed the button to raise the back of his chair again, his eyes never leaving her. Jonas looked at his father and said, "Uh, yeah, Dad, that goes double for me," and then punched him on the arm. Twice.

Simon stared at both of them, burst into a surprised laugh, then silently teared up, and put out an arm for each of them. Pulling them to him, he kissed Jonas' forehead and Bess' lips, and whispered, "Thank you."

##

An hour later, after sleeping with Bess' hand in his, Simon broached the previous subject again.

"I'm sorry about that meltdown. That's been preying on my mind since the moment Elsie told me she smelled that creature in the elevator." Bess gave him the bad eye, so he held his hand up, tilting his head down. "But that's done with now.

"What I'd wanted to talk to you about, before I lost it, was that all that time that you spent taking care of me when I was poisoned, wondering each day if that would be the day that I died, worrying about every new symptom---well, it scarred you, sweetheart. After twenty years, you still have dreams about it."

"How did you know?"

"I've heard you moaning, and saying my name in your sleep---and not in passion, either. I'll wake up, thinking you're calling me, and look down to see that you're crying in your sleep, and I just know. Besides the fact that you broadcast to my mind when you're extremely upset."

"Oops. Forgot about that."

"*I'm okay*. I know that the horror you suffered in the apartment isn't going to just leave your mind overnight, but I don't think that's what's eating at you the most. I think it's seeing me dying on that recording. And seeing me the way I am now, when you were expecting a complete healing."

"That's the problem with living with someone who can actually go inside your brain---it's hard to keep secrets." He smiled at that, since they'd both had that experience. "It's just that when I look at you---you're whiter than you were at the very end of your poisoning, when you were dying. You're so weak, and I know you have an awful headache and nausea that you're not mentioning---"

"You got into my mind when I was sleeping, didn't you?"

"Just for a second. I needed to know how you felt, and it was pretty bad."

"But it's different this time, Bess. Yes, I admit, I feel like death warmed over. Bad choice of words---but I don't feel like I'm dying. I'm not getting worse. It's like having the Flu. You feel like dying, but inside, you know you're not, and you know that you *will* be okay if you can just tough it out for a couple of weeks.

"I'm so thankful to see you restored, and Jonas alive and well. Then knowing that our whole family will be together in a few days---it's hard not to be *euphoric* at times. The one thing that was preying on my mind---well, we just went over that, and I've been threatened and warned to never mention it again, so I won't. But aside from that, I feel so positive and---*blessed.* You need to let go of my deaths, instead of reliving them. I'm done with them, and you need to be, too. I'm not dead and won't be for a long time. So let's just live and enjoy our lives. You've got new innards, and I've got new innards, so chances are, we'll both live to a ripe old age."

He pulled her to him and kissed her, and heard from a few seats away, "Hey, get a room!"

They laughed, and he made a few verbal threats, but then Bess became serious again. "I know this sounds awful, but---" Tears threatened again, and she shook her head to try and make them stop. "I've started to wonder if being murdered is your destiny. I just want to protect you so badly."

"Well, they say three's the charm, so I don't intend to go on any more trips with the Bluemen. But there's been something I've wanted to share with you and Jonas." He stopped and looked across the room at his son, who'd been sitting and watching the two of them interact, with a half-smile on his face.

"Could you come back over here for a minute, son? I want to talk to you and your mom together."

Jonas came over and sat across from them with an apprehensive look on his face. "You're okay, aren't you, Dad?"

"Yeah, yeah, I'm fine. I wanted to tell you something that I don't think I'll ever repeat again, because it's starting to fade from my mind. It's as if the purpose for it is over, and it's not something I'm supposed to remember. But I want to share it with you two, so that you can remember, and understand why I feel so positive about things.

"When I died from the poisoning, I only remember waking up healed. But this time, I suppose because the Bluemen took longer to bring me back, I remember dying, and what came after.

"I remember the pain, and then the sensation of my life just flowing out of my body with my blood. I can't begin to describe how cold I felt, and how dark things were getting. But then everything started getting warm, and it was the most wonderful warmth. I hate to sound like a cliché, but this beautiful golden light was ahead of me, beckoning me forward, and I forgot everything in this world. I started seeing three figures in the light, and as I came closer, I recognized my parents, and my sister." He stopped to wipe the tears away, and to swallow a few times, before continuing. He took a deep breath, and leaned his head back on the seat.

"I've dreamed about them a million times since they were killed---some good dreams, some bad, but the thing that I always remember about those dreams, is that I was never able to touch Marian or my parents. When I walked into this light, and saw them standing there, they held out their arms to me and I rushed into them and we embraced. I *felt* them in my arms. I can *still* feel them."

Bess was silent, but tears were running down her face, and she held her hand over her mouth, shaking her head. Jonas was staring in silence, intent on every word.

"They were real and solid, and they looked so healthy and happy. I don't remember if I spoke, or what I said if I did. I just remember holding them. And then they stood back, and my father said, "Well done," and told me he was proud of me, and then my mother did too. My little sister just kept hanging onto me, and then she said that she had so much to tell me. That was always the first thing she said to me when we hadn't seen each other for a while. Then my mother said I had to go back and be the father and husband I was intended to be. My father said I still had a lot to do before I was called home, and a lot of years of work ahead of me.

"I didn't want to leave. There was this amazing sense of serenity that made it impossible to even think about leaving. But then all three of them kissed me, and started saying your names: Genevieve, Colder, Jonas, Eli, Bess---I heard your names over and over, and suddenly I remembered, and all I wanted was to come back to you. And here I am.

"So Bess, I don't believe I'll be leaving you for a long time yet. And Jonas, I'll be bugging you about your room, and homework, and staying out late, and all those other annoying things that dads do to their teenage sons."

Jonas leaned forwards and put a hand on Simon's knee. Looking at the floor, he scrunched his lips together tightly, nodding his head. He was still nodding when he finally raised his head and met his father's eyes, cleared his throat, and answered, "Looking forward to it."

CHAPTER FORTY-FIVE

"No, no way! That's just wrong! You *ruined* the whole thing!" Genevieve cried, shaking her fists furiously at her brother Colder. She was looking in disgust at the banner on the floor that the two of them had been decorating all morning. The banner that she had *trusted him with* when Grandma had called her downstairs for a few minutes.

"What's wrong with it? Eli said Dad was gonna be really, really white. He'll get a laugh out of this, and it'll make him feel special!"

Eli walked in, after hearing Genevieve's cries from down the hall. "Hey, booger butts, what's going on?"

Genevieve pointed angrily to the banner. Eli read it and cracked up, then sobered himself and said, "Colder, that's really not funny, and even if Dad laughed, and he might, Mom would never forgive you. This isn't a funny situation, you know. They've been through some terrible stuff."

The banner read in big black letters, "WELCOME HOME, CASPER AND FRIENDS."

"Fine. We'll be all serious and boring. Dad would have liked it. But you're right. Mom would probably kill me."

"RRRRRR," Genevieve growled, shaking her fists in the air and gritting her teeth. "All that work, and I leave him alone for ten minutes, and he ruins it."

"Well how about I break out another roll of paper, and I'll help you with this one?"

"Great!" they shouted in unison. Everything was more fun when Eli was there, calling them awful names and making them laugh. He went downstairs and came back up in a few minutes with another roll of white paper, and this time he rolled out two long strips down the hallway.

"Why two?" Colder asked.

"One for Mom, Dad, Jonas, Elsie, and Ishmael, and one for the Elpies and Sven for saving all of them."

"Oh yeah, I forgot about that. They did, didn't they?"

Genevieve laughed and pointed downwards in the direction of the kitchen. "Grandma didn't forget. She's been baking macaroons for three days straight. I think she has about a thousand bags full of cookies down there."

"Well," Eli replied, "if I know her macaroons, and I do, then I'll bet the Bluemen are not really coming to bring our family home. I bet they're really coming for the macaroons. And there's so many, that they may have to leave a crew member here just to make room for 'em. Ooh, that'd be great, wouldn't it? Having our own Blueman to play Monopoly with---and oh my gosh, would he be great at Twister, or Bunco? Three hands? We could form Bunco teams for high stakes in Vegas, and just when everybody's thinking, 'Man, we're gonna take these kids for everything they've got,' WHAM---we bring out our three handed ringer! And we *clean them out!* Whoo hoo!" They laughed and gave high fives to each other and the two wished Eli would never go back to college.

Three hours later, the booger butts and their brother had finished their masterpieces, just in time for dinner. The first banner read:

WELCOME HOME, MOM, DAD, JONAS, ELSIE AND ISHMAEL. YOU ARE OUR HEROES.
WE LOVE YOU.

The second banner read:

WELCOME ALWAYS, TO OUR HERO ELPIES AND SVEN, FOR SAVING OUR FAMILY.
YOU ARE FAMILY, TOO
NOW AND FOREVER

They'd had to make a third banner when they'd remembered the other Bluepeople.

P.S. MONA, LUCA, AND MAURICE: YOU'RE FAMILY, TOO

##

Sarah had been feverishly baking for three days when she finally pulled the last batch of macaroons out of the oven. When this batch cooled, she'd have sixty bags of macaroons---thirty for the Elpies and thirty for the Bluemen. She was aware that the family thought she was a little crazy when she went on a baking frenzy, but she knew something they didn't.

When she was seventeen, her parents had rented a cabin by a lake in a remote wooded area, with the plan of staying for two weeks. Sarah was thrilled with the idea. Having always loved baking, she had actually considered going to culinary school and maybe someday opening her own bakery. She loved going to a place like the cabin, where she could be away from every other distraction and just bake. Her idea of a fun evening was experimenting with different recipes, something that her new boyfriend, Angus, was all for. She was a cheap date and he got cookies on top of it. Not to mention, she was a knockout, he was head-over-heels for her, and liked watching her do just about anything.

On their second night in the cabin, her parents were going to a nearby town for a festival, and taking her two brothers with them, but Sarah begged off. She wanted to experiment with an idea she had---double fudge caramel macaroons. After the first batch, she decided they needed more chocolate, and after the second, more caramel. The third batch was perfection.

She immediately made three more batches to try out on her family and on Angus, who was driving out to spend the day with her tomorrow.

Standing at the window, looking out at the lake while she was washing the thousand dishes she'd used in her experimentation, she saw a zigzagging light in the sky. It would stay in one spot, then move at blinding speed to another, and then hover awhile before it moved again. It came closer and closer to where she stood, in this same crazy pattern, until it finally landed by the lake, straight in front of the cabin, about a hundred yards away.

There were no weapons in the cabin, other than her brother's sling shot, and she figured that even if she'd had one, *they'd* have one that was better. Always believing in extraterrestrials, at one point she'd thought it would be fantastic to meet one, until she'd seen a movie about body snatchers, and that had sort of cooled her enthusiasm for interstellar tourism.

Never a shrinking violet, Sarah decided to go on the offensive with the only weapon she had available, and the one she was best at wielding---her macaroons. She threw as many warm ones as she could on a plate, and headed out the door in the direction of the ship.

She walked without a flashlight, because she couldn't carry the plate with that many cookies on it and handle a flashlight at the same time. Ahead of her, something, or *somethings* were exiting the ship and seemed to be coming her way. She was never sure exactly what they looked like because she only saw them in the dark, but they walked on two legs, and appeared to be hairless. Their heads were slightly conical, they had small round eyes, noses, and mouths that had big fleshy lips. No ears that she could see.

When the creatures came to within about thirty feet from her, she waved and shouted, "Hi! Boy, you must have travelled a long way, and I'll just bet you're starving! How about a macaroon? Fresh from the oven!" Then she gulped, took a deep breath and started walking again. There were two of them, and the creature in the lead was holding something that looked like a weapon, which he was pointing at her. The closer she got, the higher he raised it, until his arm was fully extended in her direction. She extended *her* weapon, her macaroons, shut her eyes and kept walking.

When she was only about five feet away, they smelled her macaroons, and the leader lowered his weapon. She kept smiling and moved towards them slowly, with the plate extended. To show them the macaroons were okay, she took a bite of one, rolled her eyes, swayed her body and moaned with pleasure. "Oh, these are the best things I have ever made! Try one!"

There was a standoff of about ten minutes, with the aliens staring at her, deciding whether or not to kill her or abduct her, she thought, and her muscles got so tired of holding the cookies and smiling, that she got a muscle twitch in her face that made her look like she had a split personality, (smile, frown, smile, frown), and spasms in the muscles of her arms that almost made her toss her cookies---literally.

Finally, the leader slowly gave his weapon to the guy behind him, and reached for a cookie, while Sarah prayed that he wasn't allergic to coconut. One bite, and she heard a little moan from him. Suddenly the hand of the other creature shot out and snagged one, resulting in a similar moan from him. She invited them to the cabin with gestures, and they followed her, but refused to come in until she doused the lights. All these years later, she still couldn't understand that. Like what---she was going to ID them in a line-up?

She had turned off the lights, brought them inside, and given them glasses of milk, explaining that milk really set the cookies off. The milk didn't go over well, (and in truth, she'd never thought about what havoc lactose intolerance might wreak on a space ship), but they ate every macaroon she had baked, and waited while she baked another batch so that they could take some with them. She chatted about everything she could think of, and they never made a sound in return, other than the groans of pleasure when they'd bite into a macaroon, but she got the feeling that they understood at least some of what she was saying.

At the end of the cookie fest, they stood up, and one of them put its hand on her shoulder and handed her what looked like a purplish stone, a little smaller than an egg. She didn't know exactly how, but they got the message across to her, that the next time she made macaroons, she was to put the stone in the window, and they just might visit.

Her parents showed up about an hour later, very upset about their car. They'd just paid a fortune in repairs and tune-ups to have it put into good shape for their trip, and suddenly, on the way back to the cabin, everything just shut off. No sound at all from the engine, and no lights---nothing. Her father had tinkered with everything he could think of, to no avail, and then, just as suddenly, everything came back on and they finished their drive home.

The dishes were already washed and put away, the crumbs from the aliens---who were very messy eaters---all swept up. She told her parents that her experiment had been a disaster, so she'd dumped the mess out in the field for the raccoons, who'd eat anything they could get their greedy little paws on.

She'd never told her parents, Angus, or *anyone*, about her experience, because she didn't think they'd believe her, and if they did, they wouldn't approve of her choice of friends. But she begged to go to the cabin every year, and started buying and packing her own supplies, so that her parents wouldn't be upset about her wasting their grocery money. And every year, she would make her macaroons, put her stone in the window, and have polite but messy company for one evening.

That in itself would have been enough to thrill and satisfy her, but the best thing was that apparently she'd gotten something of a reputation, and sometimes when she put out her stone, she'd have different looking ships with different species of aliens showing up for cookies. The aliens all had two things in common. They were all polite, and they all loved macaroons.

After she'd married Angus, she'd cut back on her midnight macaroon meets. He'd had the occasional business trips when she would entertain, and sometimes she and the cookies would be beamed up into a ship for a quick visit. Sometimes they just beamed up the macaroons. But those interludes had remained her secret all these years.

That's why she knew to make massive amounts of macaroons, because she'd never met an alien yet that didn't adore them. This was the least she could do for the beings who had saved the lives of her daughter, son-in-law, and grandson. Now that she knew about everything in Bess' past, she was so relieved to know who to pass the recipe and her special stone to when she died. She'd always thought she would take both to her grave, but not anymore.

CHAPTER FORTY-SIX

They could hardly wait to see the kids. The Bluemen had informed the family that they'd be landing in fifteen minutes. Bess said her parents had called Eli and shown him the disk, and after that, he'd decided to stay, see them home, and spend some time with them before going back to school. So all of their children would be there, and Gisella and Hiram, too.

"Can't wait to see how big Gisella is now. She must be the size of a house," laughed Simon, and Bess reached over and slapped his arm playfully.

She gasped at what she'd done. "Oh, honey, I'm so sorry. Are you okay? What was I thinking? I'm so sorry---"

"Bess, stop it! Good grief, I'm anemic, not glass. I'm not going to break, and you can still slap me when I really deserve it, but don't get carried away. Besides, slapping me earlier didn't seem to bother you."

"That was a medicinal slap."

"Hey Dad, can I punch your arm when you really deserve it?"

"No."

"Well, I don't see how that's fair."

"It's not. So what?"

"Right. That's age discrimination, you know."

"Just wait until six weeks from now, when I can pound your arm to smithereens, and we'll have this discussion again."

"It's a date."

"Count on it."

Men.

When they were getting ready to land, a small argument broke out amongst the happy group. The Bluemen and Bess wanted to teleport Simon into the house, and he would have none of it. The Elpies, the dog, and the cat stayed out of it.

"Listen to me. I've seen what I look like in the mirror. If I appear in a chair in the living room, they'll think I died on the ship and my ghost is just making a farewell appearance. When they see me walking with all of you, they can get used to the sight of me from a distance. You know the doctors were right. I'm a little better every day. I can walk to the house, no sweat."

"Well at least let Eli and Barnabas walk on either side of you so that if you do get faint, you won't fall and crack your head on a rock and spill your brains all over the area."

"Gosh, dear, you have such a sunny outlook, it's no wonder I love you."

"I'm serious! You know if you get hurt, we can't give you any medicine, or take you to the emergency room, because they might accidentally kill you."

"All right, my trusty body guards can escort me." He looked over at them to ask for their assent, and they both nodded. "I'm sure Sarah's baked cookies for everyone anyway."

When the hatch opened a few minutes later, they heard a cheer from the little group waiting for them. Bess rushed out and grabbed her two youngest into her arms, and she could feel her eyes swelling already. Then she grabbed Eli and her parents, and soon they were all crying with happiness and relief at being able to lay hands on each other, to feel that they were all really there, alive and whole. Elsie, Ishmael and Jonas jumped down, and the process was repeated with Jonas, and partly with Elsie and Ishmael, except that the only ones doing any kissing then were Elsie and Madelyn. Hiram and Gisella weren't there, but Viola said they'd gotten tied up with something and would meet them in the house.

Then Simon stepped out of the hatch, and all conversation stopped, though a couple of involuntary gasps were heard. They'd been told, but nothing could have truly prepared them for Simon's appearance. None of them could imagine that anyone living could look that white, drained, and haggard. To those who had watched the disk, it was as though everything horrible that Simon had gone through was still visible in the strain etched on his face.

Then Eli went forward, threw his arms around his dad and began sobbing. Simon was sick to death of crying, but in Eli's arms, hearing his big, almost grown son, who was famous in the family for never crying---hearing him sobbing uncontrollably broke Simon's heart, and he found himself crying and holding the back of Eli's head, pressing it into his shoulder, as Eli said over and over, "I love you so much, Dad. I'm so glad, I'm so glad you made it. I'm so glad you made it."

Then everyone started forward, and Bess told them that they needed to keep moving towards the house, so that Simon wouldn't be standing for long. They started walking back together, with the Elpies on either side of him, but with Colder and Genevieve each holding a hand, when suddenly, his knees buckled. The two Elpies caught him effortlessly, and put their arms around his waist, and his arms around their shoulders, and kept walking. Dazed, he looked at both of them and sent his thanks, then concentrated on putting one foot in front of the other. The second Eli stepped in front of the first and Angus stepped in front of Barnabas, and said, "May we?" as he motioned to Simon. The Elpies understood, and lifted Simon's arms off their shoulders and into the hands of his son and father-in-law, who lifted them onto their own shoulders, saying, "We got you, Dad," and "We got you, son."

When his parents and brother had left on this excursion, and Eli had hugged his dad good- bye, he'd felt warm, solid, and strong. Now he felt so frail and cold in their arms, and he was trembling badly with the tremendous effort that just walking was costing him. When they were about twenty yards from the house, Simon passed out completely, and Eli the first had them lay him down so that he could lift his legs to get blood back to his head. Eli the second pressed the back of his fist to his mouth to try and keep control after feeling his dad go limp in his arms. He was so afraid for him after seeing the way he looked, afraid that he might die on them at any moment.

Sven stepped up and dialed some coordinates into his medical disk and laid it on Simon's chest. He disappeared, and Genevieve and Colder both screamed and started crying, until Bess told them that Sven had just sent him to the living room lounger.

As much as they had been prepared, neither child had ever even seen their dad sick. He'd had the Flu about fifteen years earlier, before either of them were born, and that was the last ailment he'd had that he'd bothered to complain about. He'd spent many a night when they were younger, holding their hands or just watching them when they'd been ill with one thing or another, but he'd never caught anything from them. He seemed invincible to them---even coming back from the dead---twice now. He was the strong one---the only one strong enough to throw them up in the air, even now, as tall as they were. Well, Eli could now, too, since he'd put on muscle. But he never got them as high up as their dad did. To see him unconscious on the ground, helpless and white as death, rattled them to the core. Bess hugged them both while the others went on ahead, and reminded them again that this was temporary, and that if Dad took all his pills, he'd be fine in six weeks. They leaned into her, hugging and loving the feel of having their mom there to hold them again.

Eli the second was still standing with his fist against his mouth and the other arm across his waist, attempting to look as if he was thinking about something instead of trying to control his shaking. Eli the first felt his fear and came up beside him, holding him back while the others walked on. He sent to him that he had seen his father improve each day on the ship, and that he did not sense death on him anymore. Then he sent his namesake a soothing, and his shaking stopped. The human looked at the Elpie, and then put his long arms around him in an embrace, and thanked him for loving his father, for being his brother, and a friend to all of them.

When Simon opened his eyes, he looked out into the living room and saw the banners, and then Hiram and Gisella walked into his line of vision, holding little Viola Marie, whom they had named after both their mothers. Simon started tearing up again, (damn, but he was sick of crying), and held out his arms for the baby.

Gisella made sure that he was situated safely in the lounger before she put little Viola in his arms, just in case he got woozy again. Babies were a wonder to him—always had been. He loved Gisella as a daughter, so he saw this little miracle as his first grandchild, and he was stunned at the emotions that came sweeping over him at the feel of her in his arms. Bess came rushing into the room to be sure Simon was okay, and stopped dead in her tracks when she saw him holding the baby. She gasped and looked at Gisella and Hiram with open mouth and questioning eyes, and they both nodded and smiled.

Screams of delight and oh, God help them, more tears, until they were all exhausted with happiness and completely boggy sinuses. Genevieve made her famous Kleenex run, and Colder brought everybody glasses of water, *with* ice, straws and umbrellas, which took him the better part of the evening.

Sarah passed out her macaroons, and when she informed Sven and his crew, and then the Elpies, that she was sending thirty bags home with each party, they almost drooled with anticipation. The Elpies and Bluemen alike were touched by the banners in their honor, and all sent, (fortunately, since their mouths were crammed full of macaroons), that they *felt* like family. More Kleenex, more water on the way.

The Elpies were anxious to be heading back out, especially Barnabas, who was seriously missing his own family after seeing this one again. So, after many thanks had been sent to the Elpies and Sven for saving their family, and many returned, for the macaroons, Sven used his disk to send Simon to his bed. Dulcie embraced Jonas one last time to thank him again for saving her.

He pulled away to look at her face as he spoke. "Well, Dulcie, since all of you saved me *and* my mom and dad, I actually owe you two more saves." With a smile then, he stepped into her arms again and hugged her back. He wasn't above stealing a good comeback from a cat.

The Elpies and the Bluemen all promised to return in the not too distant future. Sarah, holding her macaroon stone in her pocket, knew that they would.

While Bess walked the group back out to the ship, Eli and Angus went up to check on Simon. He was leaning back on several pillows, and they could see that he was struggling to breathe. When Eli started to panic, Simon grabbed his hand and stayed him, talking between precious breaths.

"Son, it's all right. The doctors told me----this would happen with exertion. I'm just miserably uncomfortable-----I'm not dying. When my-----heartbeat slows down, and-----the oxygen level catches up a little bit---- I'll be okay. I'm getting better every day."

"This is better? Geez, what were you like yesterday?"

"Don't ask."

Angus put his hand on Simon's shoulder. "We saw that disk, Simon. I still can't believe what you did to save your family."

"You don't hate me--- for choosing to save Jonas over Bess?"

"No. Especially after you explained it to that creature. But I would have understood anyway, because Bess is just like her mother in that respect. If I'd had to choose between Sarah and Bess, I would have chosen Bess with the same certainty that you chose Jonas. Mothers die inside when they lose their children. Oh, their bodies keep going, because they don't have a choice, but part of them just withers and dies. I don't know any normal woman who wouldn't rather die than see something happen to one of her kids.

"But what I wanted to say, was---that I'd count it an honor to call you 'son.' If it's okay with you."

Simon looked into Angus' face, at the unshed tears in his eyes. "Oh dammit, Dad, don't make me cry again." They both laughed, and wiped their eyes, and then turned to stare at Eli in shock when they heard his raised voice and angry tone.

"So what's up with you, Dad? Every time you freaking go off planet, you die! Geez, can't take you anywhere!"

They both just looked at him, stunned, and Eli thought, *Oh crap, I've done it now.* Then Simon burst into laughter, which didn't help his breathing at all, and Angus and Eli cracked up, too. Simon laughed until he cried, *of course,* but it felt so wonderful to laugh again, even if he *was* pushing his oxygen deficit. Then Eli told them about Colder's original welcome home sign, and the three of them cracked up again. Simon finally had to force himself to sober up when it became evident that he had to make a choice between laughing and breathing.

He held out his arm to Eli, who came and dropped to one knee, leaning forward so his dad could wrap his arm around his neck and pull him over to kiss his forehead. Bess heard all the laughing, and walked in to ask, "What's so funny?"

"Oh, it's just this oldest son of yours--- telling me in his own manly but really sick and twisted way---'Geez, I love you, Dad.'"

"Yep. That's exactly what I meant."

Men.

EPILOGUE

For six weeks, every alarm in the house was set for seven a.m., three p.m., and eleven p.m., when Simon's pills were due, and for the first week, the whole family stood and watched him take them, until he couldn't stand being stared at anymore, despite all the good intentions, and banished everyone from the bedroom. True to the doctors' words, his family could see him improving on a daily basis, and he was extremely thankful to *feel* the improvement on a daily basis, as well. At the end of six weeks, his color and strength had completely returned, and he and Bess found even more reason to cherish every day.

##

Despite his promise, Simon did *not* put Joe Bob's head on a stick in front of the morgue, although Barnabas had serious thoughts about it and wondered if it would look better by the flower bed or next to the fountain. Occasionally, in extreme anger, which he seldom suffers from, Simon is prone to threatening actions that he would never actually carry out. In all of his fifty-four years, he has never once put someone's head on a stick.

But, at Sven's request, per orders sent from The Seated, after they received a report from the guards at the morgue, Simon dictated a detailed report on all that Joe Bob had done and refused to do, and all that he had sent to Simon, the Elpies, and Elsie. He also included his ordering the guards to shoot Elsie, the dog who was responsible for saving many of their lives.

Since no immediate action had been taken against him, Joe Bob thought he had dodged a bullet. But after their return from the trip to take their visitors home, Sven, Maurice, and Luca Pacioli had a long talk with The Seated, and with their full knowledge and consent, the three picked Joe Bob up at work one day, took him just outside of the city and had a very serious talk with him.

After getting out of the hospital, where he spent several days, due to the seriousness of this discussion, Joe Bob found that his job was no longer in his possession. His new assignment was to be for the duration of his life.

When he found that he was to be the wildlife reserve's veterinary assistant, he was relieved, thinking that it could have been much worse. That is, until he found out that his job was to collect poop from each species, and then rummage through his samples every day, looking for any sign of blood, unhealthy food preferences, or parasites. This included collecting guano from the nests of the eagle-things, necessitating climbing a ladder and then wandering through massive tree branches while wearing a helmet and full body armor.

OSHA was not a factor on the Bluemen's Planet, so he was forced to eat lunch on the job every day. He was not allowed to carry a fire stick, due to the spiteful nature he had demonstrated with the planet's honored visitors, and so at first required armed accompaniment on his various forays into the fascinating world of feces. Eventually this precaution was dropped when staff noticed that animals shied away from Joe Bob, and they realized that his job-related odor made him too foul for even the hungriest predator to consider eating. Even animals have their standards.

##

Elliott recovered completely, and was given Joe Bob's former position, along with a stun gun to carry for use only when his own or someone else's life was at stake. He has yet to use the weapon, and by virtue of his character, probably never will. He has since raised the quality of the Bluemen's police department to an excellence that does his planet proud. He has also opened up investigations into all the previously uninvestigated deaths that Watson had deemed suspicious.

Watson was indeed given a much larger budget, a much larger lab, and has used his knowledge, his budget, and his genius to make huge strides in forensic medicine on his planet. His wife still threatens to kill him on occasion, but since the threats are made only out of love, it is doubtful that he will ever need his own services.

##

The guards at the morgue, who had the courage to stand up for what they knew to be right, received commendations, promotions, and the eternal gratitude of the Sayers family. Sarah sends them each a bag of her Marvelous Macaroons once a year.

##

Following up on his suspicions, Elliott eventually traced the source of Jonas' and Bess' sick stomachs, which had allowed for their isolation and abduction, back to Rupert the waiter. When questioned, Rupert confessed and asserted that he had been duped, which was true, but he had still committed assault through the drops he had slipped into the glasses, an action which had almost led to three people being killed. He did not serve time, but was put on probation and banned from ever working in the food industry again. He was forced to watch the disk of the Sayers' ordeal multiple times, and each time it was impressed upon him that he had made this brutality possible. Since that time, he has written letters of confession and apology to the Sayers at least twice a week. He reads them aloud to himself and then burns them, in the hope that the nightmares will go away.

##

Due to Elliott's new finger printing procedures, he was able to exonerate Alan from having anything to do with Cecil's crimes, and he will go down in history as an innocent victim, rather than a twisted monster.

##

After the Sayers had been transported from the stage to the hospital, Sven and Cleo had examined the big cat, who still lay stunned on the stage. They discovered the broken, infected foot, and his state of near starvation, so Sven used his disk to send the blighted beast to the reserve's veterinarian. Disgusted at the neglect that Cecil had shown the animals he was supposed to be safeguarding, Sven felt no great compulsion to stay and guard his body while waiting for authorities to arrive on the scene. His remains were quickly consumed by his previous charges, who did not share the Elpies' distaste for Bluemeat.

##

Cecil's true Blueman name was ordered to be taken off of all public records, and his face to be blurred on the Rebirth Recording, (as the recording of the Sayers' ordeal was named). These measures were taken so that not only would his name *not* go down in history, but as an individual, he would not be recorded or remembered. His recording served the opposite purpose of what he had in mind, actually glorifying rather than vilifying family.

Had he spoken only of his heartache, and that of the other malcontents, without the insanity of brutality and murder, the now forgotten Blueman might have become an eloquent spokesman for the problems of these troubled souls. As it was, however, his sadistic and barbaric choices destroyed this possibility. Some of his words remained, but had to be separated from the twisted reasoning of his mind, which was too fouled with hate and rage to relay any logical argument. His actions almost destroyed any credibility that the malcontents had established during their official protests of earlier months, which unfortunately, had been made to Joe Bob.

The Seated, after careful consideration, began to see that the sudden changes recommended during the Rebirth might have been impossible for some to embrace, due to the way these individuals had been made and indoctrinated, through no fault of their own.

They broadcast an impassioned plea to all those who considered themselves among the malcontents, to come to the Council's headquarters and register. There were no electrodes or lobotomies in store for these Bluepeople, but group therapy sessions were set up instead, and studies launched to find the best way to acclimate these individuals to the society they now lived in.

After seeing the Rebirth Recording, most of the malcontents were so appalled that someone of their persuasion had perpetrated such a horror, that they willingly went to register for help, if for no other reason than to prove that *they* did not share an attraction to violence. Years after the therapy sessions were started, many of the malcontents were married, some with families, and most of the others were at least more comfortable with interactions on a day to day basis in their lives.

##

The stage and the area around it, where the Sayers' had suffered and Simon was murdered, were turned into a monument, of sorts. When visitors come to pay their respects, the Rebirth Recording may be viewed on a screen at the kiosk. Since humans were involved, a human custom is followed, and flowers are often left at the site, in honor of the Sayers, the Elpies, Sven, and Cleo.

##

The small area below the balcony, where Barnabas was thrown, and where Ishmael fought the bear-thing, was also set aside, with a plaque in remembrance of the bravery of both parties.

##

Standing prominently in front of the Hall of The Council of The Seated, is a life-sized statue of Elsie, with a plaque proclaiming her role in preventing the poisoning of most of The Seated, along with the rest of her extraordinary actions during her days on the planet. She has ever been a great dog.

##

Sven and Cleo were destined to become soul-mates. They were married very shortly after their meeting, and eventually had two children who are exceptionally bright, affectionate, and disciplined, and who mean everything to them. Sven still wonders to himself if Cleo could be any more perfect. Cleo still thinks he's strange, still loves that about him, and would still put her life in his hands with complete confidence, any day, anytime.

##

Barnabas' wife adored her bracelet, and it truly did look stunning against her lovely green skin. The other females thought it a perfect way to show affection and appreciation to a wife, and the other males got the picture quick-like and started scrambling to make bracelets for their own wives or sweethearts, using pretty stones, woods, or whatever struck their fancy and could be made to fit an Elpie arm. The giving of the "love bracelet" finally reached the point of becoming a traditional Elpie wedding gift from the husband to his bride, making Barnabas and his wife very proud.

##

When Sven gave his last bag of macaroons to The Seated on that fateful day, he had no idea what he was unleashing. The Seated shared the cookies, and became immediately mesmerized by the amazing flavor and mastication experience. Not wanting to withhold such ecstasy from their people, The Seated arranged for Sven and his crew to make periodic stops at the Sayers,' and advanced warning is always given to be sure that Sarah is present. They have offered her a permanent position, with riches beyond her wildest imaginings, as the macaroon matron of the planet, but of course, she would never leave her family.

In honor of the Sayers and the Elpies, The Seated allow the fuel expenditure twice every human year, (while of course, making a macaroon run), for the Elpies to be picked up for a visit with the Sayers. They have all become closer, if that were possible, with this wonderful gift. Simon and Eli will forever be brothers, Bess has her sisters, Gisella, her Elpie moms, and little Viola Marie has *all* of them wrapped around her finger.

Sarah has given the Bluemen the macaroon recipe, without the customary leaving out of one ingredient, as many chefs do to make sure that their own rendition of their recipe is always the best. The Bluemen claim, however, that no one can make a macaroon like Sarah, so they return, year after year. She is always lavishly reimbursed for her supplies and her time, with cash beamed up unbeknownst from various nefarious individuals. The beaming up of cash remains a source of great amusement and occasionally is employed as a game to ease boredom on excessively long trips in space. Mona puts Sarah's payments into a special account set up by her, which, she assured her, will never be audited.

Sarah felt it only right to finally inform Angus of her interplanetary macaroon dynasty that had spanned the whole of their life together. She feared the worst, but he simply said, "If a cat can play chess, I guess you can make cookies for aliens," and gave her a little kiss. He has mellowed a great deal since seeing the disk.

##

Bess and Jonas both had some difficulties with PTSD, not surprisingly. Fortunately for them, since ordinary therapy was impossible, they happened to live with the best therapy dog on the planet.

Elsie may have suffered the worst case of all, though she sent of it to no one except Ishmael, who was amazingly sympathetic, for a cat. She saw Simon's bloodied body lying lifeless on that stage whenever she closed her eyes, for many months after the incident, and relived that feeling that half of her was gone. At first, she clung to Simon like glue, never wanting to be more than a few feet from him, and watching him when he slept, to be sure he was breathing, until finally, claustrophobia compelled Simon to gently but firmly tell her to back off and give him some space, never knowing the constant anxiety she was experiencing.

As soon as Madelyn was satisfied that little Viola Marie was not having any problems in her sleep, she conferred with Elsie and they agreed to trade duties, with Elsie sleeping in the nursery every night and following the baby through the day, and Madelyn staying at the main house, splitting her time between Jonas and Bess, comforting and healing them without their ever understanding why it was that they were losing their nightmares and periods of anxiety. Madelyn's gift comes not from her training, so much, as from her soul.

Elsie's healing came with the new life she chose to guard and nurture. Life and death cannot be kept in the forefront of the mind forever. Sooner or later, one or the other will take precedence, and when Elsie looked at Viola Marie, life won, hands down.

##

Ishmael had no such problems. Everything came out okay in the end, as far as he was concerned, and he got to be a hero twice—once by finding and retrieving Sven's help, and once by saving Barnabas. He'd always known he was hero material, and it was gratifying that others had finally become aware of the same. He is still the grand champion of the Beat the Cat Chess Web, and yes, still a cheeky little bastard, and proud of it.

##

Simon had surprisingly few emotional difficulties after being so brutally murdered, perhaps due to the fact that his murder was his *intentional* sacrifice for the love of his family, but also perhaps because of the experience of seeing his parents and sister again. He was right in believing that he was meant to forget the experience. A week after he shared it with Bess and Jonas, it was completely gone from his memory, but what he retained was a new sense of peace and purpose in his life. Bess and Jonas remember and sometimes discuss it between themselves, but never with Simon, for they know he would never believe that he could have forgotten such a thing.

Bess and Simon had always shared the deepest of bonds, but they added one more strengthening experience when they each agreed to die for their child. It was something they did together, as husband and wife, and parents of the first order.

##

Eli the second had indeed found "The One," and after his marriage, his sweet Babette became privy to all of the Sayers' family secrets. The whole family, Bluemen and Elpies included, loved her from the beginning, and she has learned to make the Marvelous Macaroons.

##

Jonas told his brother Eli about the things he had seen when he'd looked into the souls of their parents. He was desperate for another sibling to know, lest he forget something over the years, and the brothers never again saw their parents in the same light as they had before the trip.

Whenever Jonas looks at his mom, he feels that incredible warmth and welcoming softness, but he is always aware now of the warrior, the she-bear, who lies beneath. When he looks at his dad, he sees courage and strength, and the great love that can call on these at will.

Since seeing his father bloodied and lifeless on that stage, he has never again avoided his neck-hugs and forehead kisses, but instead has come to treasure them and savor the feel of his father's warmth as the proof of his loving and living in this world once again. And sometimes, when he sees his dad performing some small act of kindness, he would swear he can see him shining, just a little.

Eli never misses a chance to tell either parent that he loves them, for he has seen how uncertain life is, and knows that the chance to say what is important may not come again tomorrow. After seeing the disk, he has come to understand that the vulnerability and the nobility of his parents are intertwined and woven around the love for their family and friends.

And Jonas---his *kid* brother, is now the brother who had risked his life to save a friend, fought for his family, been through Hell and back, and served as the guardian and representative of his parents when they were both too wounded or shattered to take responsibility. The experience left him irrevocably changed: he became a man during those trials, and one who was gracious and loving like his father. After this man, who had left as a boy, came home and shared his experiences with him, Eli found a new respect and a deeper love for this brother, whom he could never call "kid" again.

##

The trip to the Bluemen's planet was an incredible, illuminating adventure turned traumatic, brutal, and bloody beyond anything the Sayers could have ever imagined. But humans, Elpies, and Bluemen alike, came away at the end, convinced of one great truth: that there is nothing in the universe that compels the spirit, nothing that enables us to rise above what we are and do the impossible, more than love. (And sometimes, macaroons.)

#####

L. M. Nisgow was born and still resides in San Antonio, Texas, with her husband and their dog. The gold one at the bottom of the picture. The black one in her lap is just a publicity hound.

L.M. Nisgow

Made in the USA
Middletown, DE
25 August 2021